OFF

Married with fou[...] author of *A Few Little Lies*, *Just Desserts* and many erotic novels. Born on the edge of the Fens, she is perfectly placed to write about the vagaries of life in East Anglia. She was the runner-up in the *Mail on Sunday* novel competition in 1995, and winner of the Wyrd Short Story prize in the same year. She is also a scriptwriter and her comedy 'Write Back Home' was part of the 1999 Channel 4 Sitcom Festival. *Off the Record* is her third mainstream novel.

SUE WELFARE

Off the Record

HarperCollins*Publishers*

HarperCollins*Publishers*
77–85 Fulham Palace Road,
Hammersmith, London w6 8jb

www.fireandwater.com

A Paperback Original 1999
5 7 9 8 6 4

Copyright © Sue Welfare 1999

The Author asserts the moral right to
be identified as the author of this work

A catalogue record for this book
is available from the British Library

ISBN 0 00 651349 2

Set in Sabon by
Rowland Phototypesetting Ltd,
Bury St Edmunds, Suffolk

Printed and bound in Great Britain by
Omnia Books Limited

To my family and friends – you know who you are

'Of course I lie to people. But I lie altruistically – for our mutual good. The lie is the basic building block of good manners. That may seem mildly shocking to a moralist – but then what isn't?'

QUENTIN CRISP, *Manners From Heaven* (1984).

Chapter One

Spread out across the hearth rug, Liz Chapman's wedding album – antique cream leather with hearts and ribbons embossed on the front cover – had been stripped down to its component parts and was waiting to be re-assembled.

It had had a thorough and, in Liz's opinion, very appropriate going-over. Here a goatee, there an eye patch, on an enlargement of the main wedding party, Mike, her ex-husband, had had his pompous, 'master of all I survey' pose enhanced by the addition of a rather fetching wooden leg, an incontinent parrot and a lot of facial hair; an improvement which would be obvious to anyone who knew him well.

Liz helped herself to another glass of wine, sat back on her heels and surveyed the fruits of her labour. Earlier in the evening collage had been a possibility, lots of hats, extra limbs, animals and spare heads snipped from magazine pages, but Liz hadn't been able to lay her hands on a decent pair of scissors and the Pritt stick was all dried up, so she'd settled for the simple pleasures of indelible black marker and a bottle of Tipp-Ex instead.

At the sound of the wine being poured Winston, the family's resident tabby, periscoped up from amongst a nest of cushions on the sofa. He opened one jaundiced yellow eye just long enough to precis what was going on. Apparently there was nothing to concern him unduly, so duty done, he settled back down again.

Liz picked up another photo and tipped it so that it caught the light. The bride and groom looked terribly tense, wedged cheek by jowl, smiling nervously from amongst an over-indulgence of cream lace and orange blossom. It was hard now to believe that she had ever been that bemused joyful girl, so obviously lacking in natural cynicism or any sense of self-preservation; the lens was smeared with something to soften the focus in an effort to add an extra touch of romance. Liz took a mouthful of wine; bittersweet.

While the photographer's assistant had been orchestrating their expressions, fluffling her veil and hair before retiring to the wings, Mike had been moaning under his breath about the shaving foam 'best wishes' scrawled all over his classic Rover, which would, without a shadow of a doubt, completely ruin the paint work. Liz seemed to remember that she had apologised, even though it was really nothing to do with her, which had set the tone of their relationship for the next fifteen years.

It would have saved everyone a lot of trouble if she'd followed her natural instincts, punched the arrogant little bastard in the eye and made off with the best man. Or was that just the clarity of hindsight? Whatever, the photographic evidence was a lot more palatable now that Liz had coloured in the groom's front teeth.

'So, here's to you, Mike Gull, you selfish miserable lying little git,' she said aloud, raising her glass in a toast. 'I hope you choke.'

He had rung earlier in the evening, just after six, half an hour before he had arranged to come over and collect their sons, Joe and Tom, for the weekend.

Something had come up, and to be honest there was just no way he could make it, Mike had said, managing to sound both offhand – as if collecting the boys was of no real importance – and breathlessly busy. No, unfortunately he really didn't have the time to explain it to the boys, well, not now and Liz would be able to do it *so* much better. Make sure they understood. She knew how it was,

Mike added casually. Oh, Liz knew how it was all right. But he would definitely be there next weekend. Six-thirty on the dot. Definitely. Promise. Absolutely. Really. But he'd have to go now, an important call had just come in on the other line.

Liz pulled the top off the felt-tip pen with her teeth and added two pointy little horns and a Hitler moustache. There now, wasn't that better.

Joe was nearly eleven, Tom was coming up to thirteen, and their father had promised them too many things far too many times. It had been a very long and moody evening.

Somewhere on the periphery of her hearing Liz caught the sound of the telephone ringing and then the machine as it cut in.

'Pick the bloody thing up. I know you're there,' snapped a female voice over the crackle of Liz's recorded apologies. 'I'm just on my way in to town to pick up a curry. Stick a couple of plates in the oven. I should be there in about – er – what time is it now? – about half an hour. I've got a little proposition for you.'

Stiffly, Liz clambered to her feet and started to clear away the remnants of the arts and crafts session, the pens, the wine. Winston, nap over, stretched and dropped noise-lessly onto the carpet beside her.

Husbands might come and go but good friends, the best sort of friends, like Claire and come to that, Winston, seemed to hang on in spite of everything. They bullied, fed, fetched and carried, gossiped, partied, giggled, teased, sympathised, stroked and listened with the kind of intuitive fuzzy logic that only women and cats ever seemed to get a real handle on.

An hour or so later Claire was hunched over Liz's kitchen table, talking through a mouthful of vegetable biriyani, while mopping up the remnants of the chickpea dahl with

3

a great fold of naan, and waving away Liz's protests.

'Oh c'mon, Liz, you used to do this kind of thing week in week out when we worked at the *Advertiser*. And you said you'd be interested in doing some freelance work if it came up. So here it is, on a plate, for God's sake. It's not rocket science. You could do it blindfolded. It's all set up.

'The newspaper want me to cover the Princess Royal opening a new hospital ward. I can't be in two places at once, and this guy, Jack Sandfi, can't see me any other day, or so his bloody agent says. All you've got to do is turn up at the Flag Hotel in Norwich and do the interview. 12.30. What could be simpler?' Claire looked at her appealingly. 'Please, just say you'll do it, Liz. Jack Sandfi's promoting his new exhibition – you're not exactly going to have to drag an interview out of him. Half an hour, half a page feature. We've already got the photos from the exhibition catalogue. The newspaper will pick up your expenses and you get paid the standard rate. C'mon, Lizzie, just say you'll do it.' Claire paused. 'Please? My editor is going to kill me if I don't get this while Sandfi is doing the rounds.' She grinned. 'And if it works out well, you could maybe offer the review round a few of the glossies too. This guy's work used to be the bee's balls. Everyone but everyone is interested in his comeback.'

Liz held up her hands in surrender. Claire was dressed in a no-nonsense don't-screw-with-me trouser suit, real working clothes. Liz glanced down at her own leggings and tee shirt, and as she did she thought about her wedding album, now safely tucked back in the bookcase. Mike always referred to her career on the local newspaper as 'the little job Liz had until I made an honest woman of her'.

'Friday?' Liz asked, ripping the heart out of another naan.

Claire nodded. 'Uh-huh, week today. 12.30. At the Flag

4

in Norwich. It's right near the railway station.' She indicated Liz's plate. 'Have you finished with that onion bhaji?'
Liz grinned and picked up her fork. 'No.'

Chapter Two

On Friday morning Liz found herself staring into the mirror and then down at the magazine open on the dressing table. It was tough trying to perfect a whole new look in the brief outbreak of calm between the boys finishing breakfast and the last minute rush to find all the things they'd forgotten.

Winston observed from a warm rift valley in the duvet while she tugged at the lapels of her favourite jacket. The magazine assured her that softer lines were in. Maybe taking the shoulder pads out had been a big mistake. The whole thing now said refugee a whole lot louder than it said sexy newshound. But it would be okay, just add a big scarf, something slightly bohemian and arty. Liz wrestled open the top drawer of the dressing table, one hand spread out over the contents so they couldn't make a break for it.

Plan Friday had taken its first gasping breaths around six when the alarm aggravated her out from unconsciousness. But so far it had all gone remarkably well: up early, feed the cat, shower before waking the boys, stay in dressing gown until after breakfast to avoid milk, tea, marmalade and any backwash from chocolate cereals, and then let the boys watch cartoons while Liz painlessly transformed from ugly duckling into – she glanced up into the mirror and took a long hard look at her reflection – Polish refugee. Would it be too mumsy if she wore a cardigan and a mac?

Liz turned her attention back to the tangle of scarves, tights, belts, bracelets and beads crammed inside the dressing table drawer. There was just no way she would have been this nervous when she worked at the *Advertiser* and *Post* full time, when jobs like this and days like this were ten-a-penny. The trouble was that seemed like a lifetime ago.

Catching hold of a familiar tail, Liz chased an Indonesian batik wrap out from amongst the pack, while earrings and stray beads, bright decoys, sprung out onto the thick cream carpet, staging suicidal diversions as she got closer to her prize. They'd be easy to find later when she'd got bare feet.

Liz shook the wrap clear and then pressed it to her face; not too creased and it smelt okay. Joe, who had wandered by the bedroom door cradling his trainers and got mesmerised, groaned in consternation. 'You're not going to wear that one are you? God, I used to wear that with my Batman costume.'

Liz looped the superhero's cape around her shoulders and then secured it with a big open knot. 'In that case it'll be absolutely perfect,' she said with a grin, scooping up her notebook and Claire's spare tape recorder. 'And I promise I'll take care of it.'

Joe grinned. 'I think I've still got the mask and the glow in the dark bat-ring somewhere if you want to borrow them.'

Liz pulled a sarky face and Joe's grin widened out a notch or two.

'It's time you two left for school. I've got a train to catch.' As she spoke, Liz scooted all the rest of her things – make-up, hairbrush, perfume, cheque book and purse – across the top of the dressing table into the big business-like shoulder bag that had been in her collection since the boys were in nappies. She glanced at the clock; another twenty minutes to get them off to school and catch the train to Ely. After that it would be okay to relax, let the

7

train take the strain, change at Ely for Norwich, bus from the station up into the city centre, look round the Sandfi exhibition and then scuttle back down to the Flag for the interview.

Plan Friday involved arriving early at the hotel, find a nice table, get settled, order coffee. She ran a finger down her mental check list one more time to make sure that it all still hung together and then hurried downstairs with Joe on her heels.

'Change at Ely,' the ticket collector said, as he snipped a big bite out of Liz's ticket, as if there was any chance she might forget. She'd caught the train with seconds to spare and settled herself down in a window seat.

Pulling Jack Sandfi's press release from her bag, Liz lay it alongside the catalogue for the exhibition and set about reading them through once more, with feeling. Sandfi, it said, was a contemporary sculptor, a complex and reclusive man seldom seen in public. This was his first major public exhibition in over ten years. Liz grinned; maybe a mac and a nice mumsy cardigan wouldn't have been such a bad idea after all.

'Please could you tell me which platform the Norwich train leaves from?' Liz asked when she arrived at Ely. Behind her there seemed to be an awful lot of people milling about and mumbling in a low edgy way for a mid-morning train.

The uniformed man sniffed and squared his shoulders. 'Today,' he said, pausing for dramatic emphasis, 'the train t' Norwich is – a bus.'

'A bus? Are you sure?' As if there might be some doubt. As if he might be making it up.

He gave her the look she deserved. Liz's stomach tightened with a mixture of frustration, disbelief and resignation. Above them the TV screen that normally announced arrivals and departures flickered and then rolled, its one gammy eye struggling to focus on the company logo

'A bus?'

He nodded. ''S right.'

Liz glanced down at her watch. 'And what time does the bus leave?'

''Xactly the same time as the train – 'bout five minutes from out the front of the station,' he said, in a soft sing-song Fenland voice. 'That's a blue bus. Can't miss it. Says Ely to Norwich train on a bit of cardboard in the winder. We've hed a lot of trouble with the connection this week so we've hed the bus on standby. Reckon the driver'll soon be able t'do that route blindfold.'

Perhaps all was not lost. 'And what time does the bus get into Norwich?'

''Bout an hour later than the train.'

Liz heard the first fissure open up in Plan Friday. There was a serious queue for the only phone box on the station. Above the platform the clock steadily ticked away the minutes to the bus's departure. The crack opened a fraction wider.

Liz took another look at her watch, measuring off the quarters. There had been just enough time to get to Norwich, skate around Sandfi's exhibition, do the interview and then hare back home to meet Joe and Tom from school. Now, if she was lucky, she might just make the interview. Just and might; not very auspicious words to re-launch a career left to rot under a pile of domestic bliss.

Liz thanked the man in the uniform and headed out of the station to find the blue bus.

* * *

9

Over in Norwich, in a small sunlit flat above the delica-
tessen in Kingsmead Terrace, Nick Hastings glanced into
the mirror that hung above his mantelpiece and practised
his best smile. The silvering was pitted in places, although
the frame was still very handsome. After a few seconds the
fixed rigor assumed a slightly manic aspect and after half
a minute Nick looked like an escaped axe murderer.

How many years was it since he had had an interview?
Undoing his tie, he dragged it out from under the collar
and twisted the top button undone. The soft cotton shirt
sighed with relief; Nick too.

The interview was arranged for one o'clock, but it was
too early to leave yet. He pulled off his jacket, dropped it
over the hard shoulders of the kitchen chair and switched
the kettle on. Another coffee, a quick look through the
papers, that would kill a half-hour.

'I like these sort of meetings to be informal initially.
Perhaps we could talk over lunch –' Jeanna O'Hanlon had
said on the phone.

Nick sincerely hoped she planned to pick up the bill.
After all, he reasoned, she had invited him. It was something he should have cleared up before accepting but he'd
been too busy trying to sound urbane, creative and confident to think about it.

They'd never met before, which made it all the more
difficult.

And did she really mean a full lunch? Aperitifs and start-
ers, and crisp newly baked rolls, entrées, linen napkins,
vegetarian alternatives and all that stuff, and if she did,
how, realistically, could he sit through the whole performance, knowing full well that if they ran his credit card
through the machine it would sing out his insolvency loud
and clear. He needed this job.

Nick picked up the tie and shuffled it between his fingertips like the beads of a rosary, wondering whether it was

too late to cry off – except that he knew he wouldn't. Jeanna's firm was looking for a projects manager, all he needed to do was convince her that they were looking for him.

And O'Hanlon Furniture were really gaining credibility, particularly since that big feature about them in the *Sunday Times*. Nestled comfortably under Jeanna's wing Nick would be able to find everything he needed: a good job, one of the cottages on the company's estate, the time and the space to develop some ideas of his own – a way back out from the wilderness. But then again, it didn't do to look too desperate.

Nick picked up his jacket. Jeanna said she was planning to catch Jack Sandfi's new exhibition up at the Review Gallery while she was in town, and then come on to meet him. Maybe he'd have coffee down at the Flag Hotel instead. Settle in to his surroundings. Relax. Nick rolled up the newspaper and tucked it under his arm.

From the flat, the hotel next to the railway station was downhill all the way, which made Nick's smile broaden. The day was bright and sunny and he had a good feeling.

Once he arrived at the Flag, Nick told the girl on the reception who he was waiting for – just in case Jeanna couldn't find him – took a table in a window seat over-looking the river and ordered coffee from a passing waiter. He was very early.

Across from his table, in a shadowed alcove, was a party of drunks. So early in the day their intoxication seemed raw and colourful and wildly inappropriate. They were, at once, both incredibly embarrassing and great fun to watch. Like sparrows, the drunks plumped and preened, five men and a middle-aged woman, handing round a bottle of Glen-fiddich to fortify the cups of coffee that circulated in the opposite direction to the malt. The whole thing was remarkably well choreographed and took Nick's mind off

Jeanna O'Hanlon's arrival. It wasn't market day and they weren't farmers, it was quite fascinating.

*   *   *

'What I'm saying is that *we* can leave. I'm not at someone else's beck and call. *I* can go, really, I do not have to stay here –' protested the man dressed in a toffee-coloured linen jacket. Although well-worn the jacket was expensive, Nick could tell. The drunks seemed louder since his coffee arrived or perhaps it was just that his ear had tuned into their pitch. It was like a soap opera and he was slowly drawn in, trying to collect clues to their identity and what exactly was going on.

So far it appeared that they were all friends of Linen-jacket and it was because of him that they were all gathered there – and were all drunk. Some of them had already been somewhere else, which had been thoroughly ghastly, but then again what could one expect given who had been organising it? Gales of laughter. And they, or possibly just Linen-jacket, were there to meet someone else or possibly more than one someone else – who had been early – or possibly late. It was hard to tell, but Nick was confident he'd be able to work it all out if he was given just a little more time.

The woman, a well preserved blonde with capacious breasts and buck teeth, was called Hermione. She kept catching hold of Linen-jacket's arm and whispering things to him, things that by turns amused and then enraged him.

'For fuck's sake, Arturo, just go and get me a cab, will you?' Linen-jacket growled, waving towards one of the group. 'Do it now, please, for pity's sake, while I can still crawl out under my own steam and this bitch hasn't sucked every last ounce of charity out of me. I've had enough – please, go. Go now.'

12

The woman grabbed his arm again. This time Linen-jacket made no attempt to shake her off. Instead, as her fingers tightened, he kept his eye fixed on his compatriot who was rising very slowly to his feet.

'You're a good man, Arturo, the best –' Linen-jacket shook his head to clear it. 'Fuck, I really can't handle this sort of thing any more. It's old age, you know, old-fucking-age . . .'

The colourful language careered around the genteel confines of the hotel foyer like a flight of trapped starlings, crashing into the windows and studiously ignored by the other guests.

Nick hoped that Arturo, now making his way unsteadily towards the desk, would get side-tracked, called back or perhaps even pass out before he could arrange for the taxi to take all or some of them away, but the receptionist already had the phone in her hand.

In the alcove Linen-jacket clambered to his feet, folded a scarf into the neck of his jacket, and – by arranging his battered fedora, and patting his pockets – quickly re-assembled his dignity from amongst the debris on the table. And then he was gone. Without him the pack rapidly fragmented and dissolved. After much airkissing Hermione and Arturo hurried away too, arm in arm, and then quite suddenly they were all gone.

There was a huge silence in the aftermath of their departure. Their table, strewn with side plates, cups, spoons, coffee jugs, glasses and crumpled napkins, looked bereft, and dirty. Nick, pretending he wanted to go to the loo, sidled past, hoping that by casting an eye over the remains he might be able to fathom out exactly what had been going on. There were lots of clues. And on one of the leather benches lay a copy of the catalogue for Jack Sandfi's exhibition.

A gift from the gods. Somewhere up in the city, Jeanna

O'Hanlon was busy browsing her way round the Review Gallery. Side-tracked from detection Nick leant over, casually retrieved the book, tucked it into his jacket pocket and headed for the gents.

By the time he returned, Linen-jacket's table had been cleared, wiped and reset, and Nick had read the commentary on Sandfi's first public exhibition for ten years.

As he settled back at his table, a waiter approached bearing matching silver coffee pots. 'Coffee, sir? Black? white?'

Nick feigned non-comprehension, working out how much he had left in his pockets.

'Bottomless pot eleven to two, you can have as many refills as you like, sir,' the man pressed.

'White please,' Nick said, sliding the Sandfi catalogue across the table out of harm's way.

The waiter nodded in the direction of the now empty alcove, sensing a sympathetic audience. 'See them, did you? Not a brass farthing between the lot of them. And the mess they left. Not so much as a tip, nor a word of thanks, nor kiss my arse, nor nothing. No better than pigs some people.' He paused and pointed towards the catalogue. 'Not waiting to meet him, were you? Not wanting autographs or anything like that?'

Nick shook his head, and then looked up in astonishment as the ill-assorted pieces fell into place. 'That was Jack Sandfi? The one in the linen jacket? That was him, wasn't it?'

The waiter nodded. 'That's right. The arrogant little bastard.'

'I've arranged to meet someone here for lunch. Jeanna O'Hanlon? She was going to see his exhibition this morning.'

The uniformed man topped up Nick's coffee cup. 'Waste of time if you ask me, sir. You're better off down here.

Save yourself the shoe leather. Derivative all of it. The man's got nothing left to say, no soul, no vigour, no balls. No one in their right mind would give the new stuff shed room. It was different back in the seventies, of course.' The waiter paused as if catching hold of a very specific image and then continued, 'You know he has students staying over at that place he bought out near Swaffham, do you? They reckon he lifts their bloody ideas, sketch books, working drawings, the whole kit and caboodle. Even the photos of him in the new catalogue are donkey's years old.'

Nick could only stare. The waiter hurried on his way, bearing the coffee pots before him, sprinkling indiscretions like confetti as he moved gracefully from table to table.

Nick picked up Sandfi's catalogue. It would certainly give him something to talk to Jeanna about.

* * *

On the bus, on the outskirts of Norwich, Liz collected together the ring fence of things she'd arranged to ensure no one sat next to her, and took another look at her watch.

The man at Ely said they had to drive from station to station: Shippea Hill, Lakenheath, Brandon, Thetford, Attleborough, Wymondham and now, at last Norwich – crow-straight by rail, it was a journey around the dark side of the moon by road.

Liz had spent so long staring at her watch, willing time to stand still, that it almost surprised her that there were numbers left on the face to read. Her stomach had plaited itself into a macramé fruit basket with a sheep shank and two half hitches.

Tick-tick-tick. Liz glanced out of the window. Surely it wasn't that much longer now? She couldn't quite bring herself to embrace the state of powerless resignation that would ease the tension.

On the seat opposite a man in very clean overalls, cradling a mobile phone, was calling waymarkers into the receiver; he had phoned home the moment everyone clambered aboard and had kept up a running commentary ever since.

'That's right. We're on Newmarket Road now, yeh, and that's ever so busy too. Got the road up – gas I think or that might be cable TV.'

Liz took another look at her watch.

The bus driver, a hunched and bitter soul, who steered the bus as if he was stirring a cauldron, caught her eye in the rear-view mirror before announcing, 'Once we arrive at the station you can pick up your compensation claim forms from the ticket office.'

When Liz broke reflected eye contact she realised she could finally see their destination at the bottom of the hill. It was twelve twenty two. Her stomach started to unpick the tangled knot. Unless something catastrophic happened in the next half mile they'd arrive with a few minutes to spare; Jack Sandfi wouldn't be kept waiting long after all. She sighed. Plan Friday was still just about on track.

'Mr Sandfi –' for one last time in a quiet part of her mind Liz practised their introduction, '– so wonderful to meet you at long last.' She would extend a hand as she spoke.

Jack Sandfi would get to his feet, doff his soft felt hat and indicate she should sit alongside him. Their hands would touch and he would press her fingertips to his lips before beginning to strangle vowels with his heady foreign accent.

In the long reach of her imagination artists were all dark-eyed, brooding Europeans – mostly French, sometimes Spanish, very occasionally Hungarian, once in a blue moon disaffected Cockneys – but all of them had droopy, well-used beagley faces. Faces that recorded youthful excess and bore witness to a gradual but hard won ascent towards serenity and wisdom.

In the photographs in the back of the catalogue, taken in black and white when Jack Sandfi was a student, he looked a little nondescript and grainy for her tastes.

'So, Meess Chapman, what deed you theenk of miii exhibition?' whispered the imaginary Sandfi, finally relinquishing her hand.

Liz accepted the glass of mataro he had poured for her and smiled. 'Breathtaking, Jack, really, quite breathtaking. I've always followed your career with interest; it's such a privilege to find myself here to witness your renaissance. Your use of light is as astonishing as ever, that and the stunning combination of line and form –'

Across the aisle of the bus a woman slipped a hand inside her shell suit top and hoisted her large breasts up a notch or two, before gathering together a vast collection of nylon holdalls and carrier bags. The bus was slowing down and most of the passengers were already up on their feet. The woman was wearing flip-flops.

Liz fought the compulsion to join them; why was it that they couldn't wait until the damned bus stopped? Struggling to get loaded up and then standing, feet braced, swaying precariously from side to side while the bus rolled down over those final hundred yards or so, was complete madness.

Perhaps, she thought, it harked back to some archetypal childhood fear that if they weren't ready to get off the very instant the bus, the train, the plane or the taxi drew to a halt, helpless, voiceless and powerless to resist, they would be whisked away to some unknown, ungodly destination. All except Mr Mobile-Phone that is, who was even now saying, 'Yes, well we're just pulling into the station at this

17

very minute. Yes, oh very busy. They've got the road up –'

The swaying helped the woman with the holdalls shift a wet belch; the driver reminded them about the claim form.

Liz clambered unsteadily from the bus. The form would have to wait until the trip home. Tugging the scarf into submission, Liz scurried across the car park towards the Flag, her head down, meaning business. If she was really quick there was still time to go to the loo and touch up her make-up before going in to meet the infamous Jack Sandfi.

It was twelve thirty-six when, with her head up and shoulders back, Liz Chapman glided elegantly into the hotel foyer, an apology on her lips along with a fresh coat of lipstick. She aimed for the reception desk intending to ask where the Sandfi interviews were being held – there were no signs – but no more than half a dozen strides across the lobby, she spotted a man sitting at a table by the window. Everything about him, his body language, his expression, told her that he was waiting for someone. He was in his mid-forties maybe, dressed in a soft tweedy jacket, white button down shirt. Nice looking.

And as she passed in front of him he looked up, his eyes not quite focused. He was cradling a cup of coffee, but on the table in front of him, prominently displayed, was a very dog-eared copy of the exhibition catalogue. Their gaze met, he smiled and then smiled again, this time using the expression reserved for interesting strangers who you are expecting but have never met.

Liz shivered. Behind him diffused sunlight coming through the net curtains back-lit his hair. It was shot through with veins of gold and white, like marble. No longer grainy or nondescript the real-life Jack Sandfi was absolutely gorgeous. Though not quite as raddled and lined as the artist in Liz's imagination his face most definitely had a lived-in quality. She stopped mid-stride, turned and made her way back towards him.

'Hello, I wondered how we would recognise each other,' she said with a smile, producing the catalogue's twin from her handbag. 'I'm really sorry that I'm a little bit late.'

Jack Sandfi was already on his feet. 'I'm glad you could make it,' he said, extending a hand. His touch was warm and worn smooth like weathered stone. 'Please, do have a seat. I'll order some more coffee; what did you think of the exhibition?'

Liz liked the diffident tone of his voice. His words held a genuine question, as if her opinion, her thoughts on his work might truly count. There was a lack of surety, an uncertain edge to the way he spoke that she found incredibly endearing. This was a man who obviously cared about the way people responded to his art. No wonder he exhibited so infrequently. Liz wished now that she had had the time to go and see his work before meeting him.

He waved the waiter over. 'Would you like some coffee before we eat?'

Liz glanced up in time to follow the gesture. Beyond heavy glazed doors at the end of the foyer the restaurant was already filling up with lunch time customers. Brass and dark wood glittered from behind the heavy plate glass.

Claire hadn't mentioned the possibility that they might be eating, and there wasn't time even though Liz was famished. Right on cue her stomach rumbled noisily. She pulled a notebook out of her bag.

'Thank you, that's very kind. I'd like to, but actually I've got a train to catch – you know how these things – I didn't realise you'd – I hadn't planned to . . .' Liz knew she was waffling and made a conscientious effort to stop, while the waiter stood by and watched her performance. She took a deep breath to stem the flow. 'I'd just like a coffee, please.'

'You get a few fancy biscuits and we do do sandwiches,' said the waiter, 'if you fancy a bite to eat, that is, Miss.'

'No, really, coffee will be just fine. Thank you.'

Sandfi and the waiter nodded in unison.

'Anyway, as I was saying I'm so sorry I'm late, my train was a bus –'

But Sandfi waved her words away. 'It's not a problem. Anyway I'm certain that we said one o'clock.'

How gallant.

Like riding a bike, Claire had said. Liz glanced down at the questions she had composed. They looked even more boring than she remembered. Maybe things would get better once they got started.

'Unfortunately I'm a bit pressed for time; what with the train and everything. You wouldn't mind if we cracked on, would you?' Liz asked. Casually she slid the tape recorder out and stood it alongside her bag.

'Not at all,' said Sandfi, shaking his head. 'Where would you like me to start?'

'Can you tell me why you've waited so long to stage this comeback?' Liz said, settling herself opposite him. Sandfi pulled a face and reddened furiously. Liz felt a little nip of unease, wondering if perhaps her choice of language had already upset him. Sensitive and reclusive it said in the press release, but it was too late to claw the words back now.

'It's taken me a few years to get my act together if that's what you mean,' he said uncomfortably. 'And well –' He grinned; it took years off him. 'I've got to be honest, I've never been that good at promoting myself or my work. I've always had a lot of good solid creative ideas, but totally lousy business sense, though I do think the past few years freelancing with the design team at Newlens has really helped to sort me out in that area. It's just that I feel it's time to move on now.'

Liz stared at him. It wasn't quite the sort of answer she had expected. 'Newlens?' she began. The name meant absolutely nothing to her.

Sandfi held up his hands as if in defence, his colour deepening. 'Okay, okay so I know they are crassly commercial but I've learnt so much working alongside the team there. And it's been a real trial by fire, lots of pressure, lots of very demanding situations. But, well, what can I say? I've come through it older and wiser and having learnt a lot about how this business really works.' He smiled disarmingly. 'And I've got some really great references should you want to see them.'

Liz laughed nervously. 'I really don't think that will be necessary.'

Sandfi looked relieved.

She took another quick look at her notes. 'I'm interested in where you go for your inspiration; there seems to be a tremendously naturalistic feel to your work.'

Liz had carefully culled phrases from the press release. She could sense Sandfi beginning to relax. He smiled, took a deep breath and was about to answer when the waiter, who was delivering the coffee, caught his eye.

'Excuse me, Miss. Message at the desk for you, sir,' he said.

Liz's companion got to his feet. 'If you'll excuse me for just a second –' Liz nodded gratefully; it would give her time to re-think the way she had structured the interview and maybe come up with something a bit more interesting to ask him.

Chapter Three

Nick headed off towards the reception area. As the door to the main restaurant opened, the rich perfume of onions and gravy wafted out on a warm savoury cloud. Nick's mouth watered.

The tension that had been haunting him all morning was gradually easing. Jeanna O'Hanlon seemed genuinely nice, certainly nothing like the woman he had expected, for one thing she was younger – younger, and a lot less aggressive than she had sounded on the phone. He had also pictured someone a good deal hungrier, and Nick regretted now that she had been so quick to dismiss the suggestion of lunch. It would be nice to know more about her before they got down to the nitty-gritty of qualifications and the formal interview process. He grinned; maybe things were looking up after all. It would be great to wake up in the morning knowing that they would be working together. And she had the most exquisite, expressive hands. And those big smoky grey eyes.

'The waiter said you had a message for me. Nick Hastings?'

The receptionist smiled up at him. 'Mr Hastings? Oh yes, that's right.' She picked up a little notepad. 'Here we are: A Miss O'Hanlon rang a few minutes ago to say that she was most terribly sorry but she won't be able to meet with you today after all. She sends her apologies and says she'll ring you asap to reschedule. Flu, she said, and she did sound really awful.'

Nick was about to protest and then glanced back down

into the foyer. His mysterious guest had already got her coffee and was now sorting through a tray of fancy biscuits provided by the waiter. She was smiling and chatting to the uniformed man who, to show his appreciation, offered her a few more choice morsels from a tin on the trolley.

For the second time since arriving at the Flag, Nick made his way to the relative privacy of the toilets, this time to consider exactly what he ought to do next.

Whoever it was she had come to meet Nick wasn't it. He would have to say something. Simple. It shouldn't be that difficult. After all it was just a mistake. She was looking for someone, he had been waiting for someone else. Easy.

'I'm so sorry about that,' Nick said, when he returned. 'I didn't quite catch your name.' He kept his tone warm and confident.

'Liz Chapman.' Her expression revealed an unexpected flurry of uncertainty. 'I'm standing in for Claire Morton from the *Bishopston News and Advertiser*. The editor was meant to have rung your agent to let you know that I'd be coming instead. I'm freelance.'

A reporter. Nick nodded, although she didn't strike him as some hardened hack. He could hear her seeking his approval. She clearly thought he was someone of importance, someone worth interviewing. She flipped to a clean page of a spiral bound notebook that was balanced on the edge of the table and looked up at him expectantly. 'Okay, so let's get back to business, shall we?'

Nick reached around for some sort of opening, aware that the longer he left it the harder it would be to begin. All he had to do was take a deep breath and explain that they'd both made a mistake – an easy mistake but a mistake nonetheless.

Liz Chapman would probably feel embarrassed when

23

she found out and possibly blush, most definitely laugh – he had already seen the good humour in her eyes – and then they could talk about how ridiculous it was. How silly. And he would insist on paying for her coffee, it was the very least he could do.

But she was already ahead of him. 'I'm really quite nervous about this, so would you mind if we pressed on?' Before he could reply she had taken the split second necessary to compose herself. 'The name Jack Sandfi conjures up a certain image in the popular imagination –'

Nick felt the breath being sucked out of his lungs. Jack Sandfi? His mouth dropped open in complete astonishment.

But Ms Chapman was busy finding her form. 'In the biographical notes in the front of the catalogue it says –'

Nick held up a hand to stop her. 'Liz, look, before we go any further there is something I really have to tell you.' Why was it so hard to find the right words? Maybe if he changed tack, found another way to break through into the conversation he really wanted to have with her. 'Do you do a lot of this sort of thing?'

She was smiling again, and to his surprise as their eyes met her expression ignited a tiny white hot spark somewhere deep inside him. He fought to suppress a groan.

'Between you and me this is the first interview I've done in years.' Her eyes twinkled, revealing the delicate tracery of laughter lines. And then there was that glowing spark again. Damn. 'Like you, I'm staging a comeback after a lot of long hard lessons. You are part one of my fresh start.'

Nick's stomach contracted sharply; there was just no way he could tell her that he wasn't Jack Sandfi.

'Why don't we have a sandwich?' he said, waving the waiter over. 'My treat.'

* * *

Liz could hardly wait to get home to replay the tape. God, what a day, what an interview, what a man. She hurried back up to Joe's school from the station, arriving in time to join the parents who congregated inside the gates. The new security fences meant that the playground looked like the exercise yard of a particularly liberal open prison, but nothing could spoil her sense of euphoria.

Like grazing herbivores some of the mothers glanced up nervously at her arrival, alerted by the squeak of the galvanised iron gate. Others, the more aggressive look-outs, leant with their backs against the faded golden brick walls, shoulders bracketed by targets painted in white emulsion, and gave her the once over, before resuming chewing the cud with their neighbours.

Uncertain what it was they were looking for but equally certain that she didn't have it and was a great disappointment to all of them, Liz fixed her attention on the heavy arched door that led into the classrooms.

Joe was funnelled out around half past three, shirt buttons undone, hair awry, scanning the faces for hers, bag dragging along behind him. He grinned when he spotted her and nosed his way through the pack. She stroked the mop of dark brown hair back off his face, relishing his puppy-ish smell. Here and there the sun had bleached a few strands to gold. It was his last summer at junior school and she kept catching glimpses of the man he would eventually become. It made something inside her hurt.

'Good day?' she asked, as he shouldered his sports kit and fell into step beside her. He nodded and caught hold of the long batik scarf. It came away without a whisper of protest and he swept it over his shoulders, cape again.

'Do you think it brought you good luck?'

Liz thought about Jack Sandfi and the way he had looked at her. 'Uh–huh. Most definitely.'

Joe's grin widened. She pulled a packet of crisps and a

carton of drink out of her bag. 'I got you these at the station.'

'Great, did you get Tom some? Only I'm starving. I could eat his too, he'd never know. By the time he gets home they'd be long gone.'

Playfully Liz clipped him round the ear. 'No. You really are a complete pig.'

Joe ducked out of her reach.

Together in the companionable space that exists between mothers and their sons, Liz and Joe made their way back home to Balmoral Terrace.

*   *   *

In Norwich, Nick Hastings, who had spent most of the afternoon wandering aimlessly around the Review Gallery staring at Sandfi's soulless sculpture, unlocked the street door to his first floor walk-up, still clutching the exhibition catalogue like a holy relic.

What a bloody fiasco. The encounter with Liz Chapman stuck up in his mind like a splinter against which every other thought brushed, though perhaps, against the odds, he might just have found a way to retreat out of the mess.

It was a flash of inspiration that struck when he saw Liz switching off the tape recorder. He hadn't noticed the little machine before, standing there beside her bag – and of course by then he knew that Liz Chapman was in earnest. The Sandfi interview was really important to her.

It was too late then for the truth; the truth was far too messy. An intense sense of panic surfaced and it occurred to him that she hadn't mentioned the tape earlier – perhaps he had found a way to back-track.

Wasn't she supposed to tell him that their conversation was being recorded? She'd reddened furiously when he'd pointed it out; she'd been taking notes too, that was the whole idea of an interview, she said, but Nick insisted it wasn't the same thing at all. No, not at all.

He smiled, trying to appeal to her better nature. Surely she must have realised that some of the things he'd told her really weren't intended for public consumption? She nodded, embarrassed to be caught up in his candour. And so, against all the odds, before Liz left the Flag, Nick had managed to persuade her to send him a draft copy of the interview.

His current plan was that once she sent him the article for his approval he would simply refuse to let the newspaper publish it. It was so simple, the more he thought about it the better it got. Nick could almost feel the weight of guilt lifting from his shoulders. Everyone would put it down to artistic temperament. Tales of Jack Sandfi's bad behaviour were legion. It wasn't much of a plan but under the circumstances it was the best he had. Of course there was always the possibility that she wouldn't send him the story either.

It was such a pity though. Liz Chapman was really good to be with, funny, clever, with a laugh that made him feel warm and relaxed. What a crying shame that she wasn't Jeanna O'Hanlon and he wasn't Jack Sandfi.

*　　*　　*

'So, come on then, how did it go?' asked Claire, as she made her way through into Liz's kitchen carrying a white cake box.

'Hang on. I'll be there in just a minute –' Liz was busy ferrying two beakers of orange juice out through the French windows into the little courtyard garden at the back of the terraced cottage. The two boys were taking their supper alfresco, shaded by two old sheets slung between the linen line and the fence. They were being watched over by Winston, who had found a sweater in the shade to pummel into perfection. It was the most beautiful still early summer evening.

Liz slid the tray onto the picnic table alongside their plates.

'Is that dad?' asked Joe with his mouth full.

'No, not yet, love. It's Claire.' She stood back to survey their efforts. 'You know, it looks really good out here. And don't worry, there's loads of time for him to show up yet.' The roof of the makeshift tent flapped in the breeze, a pink flannelette Bedouin tent resplendent under a blue hazy sky. Strewn with cushions and old blankets it looked cool and oddly inviting.

'Dad said that he'd take us down to Hunstanton swimming tomorrow. If he doesn't come, can we sleep here instead? I could bring the sun bed out,' Joe continued.

'Who says I want to sleep out here?' said Tom, from behind his magazine.

'Don't talk with your mouth full, Joe. I'll put your trunks in your bag.'

'And what about sleeping outdoors?' pressed Joe.

'We'll see.' Plans and contingencies were rapidly becoming the story of her life. Liz headed back into the cool darkness of the kitchen.

'Sorry about that.'

Claire was busy peeling the tape from the cake box. 'Not a problem.' She resembled a Celtic warrior woman, tall and very upright, with a cheerful understated strength and dependability that was both admirable and slightly intimidating. Although they had never talked about it Liz knew that Claire would have been everyone's first choice at school when it came to picking teams.

'Mike is supposed to be coming over to pick the boys up at half past six. I like to make sure they've eaten before he gets here. He forgets –' She glanced up at the kitchen clock. 'He shouldn't be long now.'

Claire's face contorted into a grimace. 'If you say so.' She slid the box of iced doughnuts across the kitchen table and lowered her voice, 'I thought I'd bring dessert. It'll help ease the disappointment when Mike rings to say something really important has come up.'

'And so how was the Princess Royal's visit?' Liz growled.

Claire took a big bite from a lavishly sugared puck, launching gouts of thin red jam down her chin. 'You should have been there; the whole thing was a master class in toadying. Let's face it when you've seen one ribbon cut, you've seen 'em all, but the way the great and the good reacted you'd think she'd just split the atom. Anyway she annoys me, she always wears such bloody sensible shoes.' Claire wiped away the bleed of jam and glanced around the interior of the tiny kitchen-cum-dining room. 'You're really turning this place round. And I adore this –' she ran an approving finger over the newly emulsioned warm golden-yellow walls. 'Come on then, no more delaying tactics. How did it go with the mad-bad-highly-dangerous Jack Sandfi?'

Liz grinned. 'Brilliant. It was just a shame I didn't have more time with him. But I've already been through the tape once; it's pure magic. He was a little bit guarded to begin with and a lot more vulnerable than I had imagined he would be, he's got greying hair, great big brown eyes, a nice lived-in face. Quite angular. Completely different to how I had expected. Funny, interesting. And we got on like a house on fire. He asked me to have lunch with him. And I would have done if it hadn't been for the bloody trains.'

Claire lifted an eyebrow. 'Sweet Jesus, he must have mellowed. Jack Sandfi's classic response to nosy reporters involved dragging them outside and giving them a good kicking.'

'Maybe he just took pity on me.'

29

Something about Liz's tone made Claire look up. As their eyes met, Claire snorted, 'Oh for Christ's sake, Lizzie Chapman, you fancied him, didn't you? Tell the truth and shame the devil.'

Liz shrugged and without a word took the teapot off the stove and poured them both a mug of tea. Claire had always had the instincts of a blood hound.

'Okay, okay,' said Claire, waving the silence away. 'So maybe I'm wrong, I take it back, maybe you didn't fancy him at all, and even if you did it's none of my business. Just sit down, have one of these doughnuts before I eat them all myself and tell me what happened. What did he say?'

Liz grinned triumphantly. 'What didn't he say? I'll play you the tape in a minute if you like. It was amazing. We got on so well. I felt completely at ease, as if I'd known him for years –' She paused, aware that her enthusiasm had flattened out a little. 'The only thing is he's asked to see a copy of the interview before it goes to press. He was a bit upset when we finished because I hadn't mentioned the tape recorder.'

Claire's face contorted. 'Oh my God. Don't tell me you hid it?'

'Give me a break, Claire, I know better than that. It was in plain sight, on the table, all the time. It's just that I don't think he noticed it was there until we got to the very end and then, well, he wasn't exactly angry but he wasn't very happy about it either. He said, he said –' her voice faded as she caught sight of Claire's expression.

'You told him you'll send a copy for his approval, didn't you?'

Liz nodded. It had been far too late to work out what was on the record and what not, what was for her private consumption and what was for Joe Public. As it was she had had to run to catch the train home.

Claire winced. 'What a bastard. You know that isn't how it works, babe. He was playing you up. He's busy doing the rounds at the moment, being interviewed by the world and his wife. He knew the tape recorder was there all the time. It's no wonder he was so bloody forthcoming. It was a trick – give you what you want and then claw it all back. What a pig. Well, two can play at that game.'

Liz reddened. 'I'm not with you –'

Claire took a long pull on her tea. 'The *Bishopston News and Advertiser* is only expecting a half-page, with the photos, non-controversial stuff: how nice, how tasteful, how come it's taken him so long to get around to exhibiting again. You can get all that from the press release. Send your Mr Sandfi a copy of that. Then, if this tape is anywhere near as good as you reckon it is, do something else with the rest of it – another article – something with real pzazz for one of the big Sundays.' Claire's expression hardened a little. 'I'm absolutely serious, Liz. I've got a few contacts that you could try. And they'll adore it. I told you that Sandfi's stuff is hotter than hell at the moment and he's got a reputation as a complete and utter git. Double-page feature with your by-line, and a nice fat cheque, baby? What do you reckon?'

Liz kept her own counsel. She found it hard to believe that the man she'd met at the Flag was as devious as Claire suggested. But then again, Liz thought, she'd been fooled by men before, perhaps it was just that she had never developed a nose for bullshit.

Liz took a bite of a doughnut. 'I'll think about it. Promise.'

Claire snorted and pulled the notebook on the kitchen table closer. 'I'd do more than think if I were you.'

* * *

It was after ten when Liz went upstairs to her bedroom. She pulled the door to, switched on the tape recorder and the WP, and after a few minutes when the screen had cleared, began to type. The tape would loop on and on until she had had enough.

Winston crouched beside her on the cramped desk, curled into the in-tray, happy to supply company and a mute audience. It didn't take very long to compose a basic, 'who, what, why, where, when,' piece for the *Bishopston News and Advertiser*. With the sound of the sculptor's voice still working its way through the tape machine, Liz printed off one copy for the newspaper and then another for Jack Sandfi.

She fed the sheets of paper through the fax machine; the story would drop onto Claire's desk, and be there, all ready and waiting for her regular what's-on page.

Liz carefully folded the second copy in half and slipped it inside a brown envelope with Jack Sandfi's name and address printed on the front. There was just one problem – after listening to the interview over and again she was beginning to believe that Claire was right; Jack Sandfi really had been toying with her.

As the interview unwound there were times when she could hear a peculiar quality in his voice, something cautious, a circumspect tone that didn't ring true. He had talked a lot but told her virtually nothing and there were several places when Sandfi had most definitely shifted the thrust of the conversation.

Liz picked up Winston, pressed rewind on the cassette player, and then settled back to listen one more time to the complete interview. With her eyes half closed, gently working a flat palm along the cat's sinuous spine, this time she was certain. Behind the laughter and the sharp asides she knew, without a shadow of a doubt that Jack Sandfi had been lying to her. That flirtatious bonhomie hid some nebulous unknown something that he was deliberately steering her away from. Claire had been right about Sandfi after all. The realisation made Liz feel sick. What a complete and utter bastard.

She opened her eyes and stared at the computer screen and then, before the sense of indignation and hurt left her, gently set Winston down on the floor and began a fresh page:

'The popular image of sculptor, Jack Sandfi, as a hedonistic bon viveur, a hard-drinking, womanising bad boy of the art world, is blown apart in this revealing exclusive interview with Liz Chapman, as the artist discusses his work, his fears and his dreams of finding a good woman and settling down once and for all . . .'

It took Liz a while to re-fashion the contents of the tape into the exact shape she wanted. What slowed the work was the unpleasant taste the whole thing left in her mouth, but she forced herself to concentrate on the job, the construction, the way the words hung together, and not on the good-looking man who had sat beside her in the Flag, the man who had flirted and laughed and persuaded her that he really was one of the good guys.

It was late when Liz finally printed the article off. The only word she wasn't happy with was 'exclusive'. Chances were, in the event of Jack Sandfi having truly changed his spots, he had already spilt his guts to every other reporter covering his new exhibition, but if that was the case she would find out soon enough.

Pinned to the notice board above the desk were the names and numbers Claire had left her; the first one was for the features editor on the *Sunday News*. Liz would ring in the morning and if they were interested in her Jack Sandfi exclusive she could fax it straight through. If not there was always the next one on the list.

Liz leant back in the swivel chair and pushed the heels

of her hands up in to her eye sockets to try to relieve a growing sense of weariness. Claire was right, a decent cheque would be really nice; a little bit of mad money to compensate for a bad feeling. Winston was still on duty, lying sentinel in the middle of the bedroom rug, with one eye closed, as if he was struggling to keep conscious until the end of his watch.

Closing the computer down Liz glanced at the neatly typed pile of pages. Jack Sandfi's flawed truths spilled down over the crisp white A4 pages, cradled and enhanced by her carefully considered prose. Like good lighting they subtly revealed the true nature of the edifice whilst still dignifying it with a certain bleak beauty, brick by brick, crack by crack.

It had a kind of melancholic honesty that Liz sensed would cut Sandfi to the quick. She had pruned away the nervous jokey good humour, and instead painted him with icy precision as a poor lost soul, a lonely man, reduced to playing mind games with an unknown female reporter in a hotel foyer, afloat on an ocean of uncertainty, isolated by his talent and his reputation.

Around the main thread she had woven descriptions of the work from his new exhibition, the light and the dark. It was good, it was very good. Vintage Chapman, she thought with a thin humourless smile, and then got up from her desk and stretched.

There were still no proper curtains up at the bedroom window. The pole and rings were propped against the wall, the puzzle of fixings and screws set out in a row along the windowsill. The window was open, cutting a wedge into the velvet dark.

Inside the lampshade a handful of moths had flown in to add a fractal rhythm to her typing, and from the yard below the scent of honeysuckle and roses drifted in on an almost imperceivable breeze. Balmoral Terrace with its tiny handkerchief gardens overlooked an old chapel; there was no real need for curtains at the back of the cottage but it would say something about her life if they were hung. It would say that after nearly two years on their own that she and the boys and the cat were home at last rather than just camping out inside a new life. Without them, without that fall of soft floor-length cotton and the rattle of rings as the curtains were pulled open and closed, the sense of transience lingered.

A subversive voice surfaced inside her head, an echo of her ex-husband, Mike's voice. 'Oh, for God's sake stop going on about it, Liz. Don't worry I've already told you I'll do that for you, haven't I? No, not now, for God's sake. You really are getting to be such a nag. I need the right tools. Have you seen the chuck key? It was here. I put it down on this table and now it's gone. Did you move it? Look, if you're that bloody desperate to get the curtains up why don't you just do it yourself? I'll do them tomorrow, or maybe one day over the weekend. Okay? Promise.' Echoes from the recent past that could still make her shiver with a mixture of fury and frustration.

Across the landing Tom and Joe were sound asleep. In the stillness she could just make out the rise and fall of their breath, the sound as comforting and calming as an ocean tide. Mike hadn't come to collect them; another in a long line of promises broken.

Without looking back she turned off the bedroom lights, finally setting the moths free. The curtains could wait another day.

Behind her in the gloom the cat unfolded, turned half circle and tracked after her. Out on the landing Liz hesitated. Amongst the soft summer scents there was a hint of something less attractive, a dark counterpoint to the heady perfumes of evening – pungent and familiar.

Winston, tail up, flounced down the stairs totally out-

35

raged that she could even consider the possibility that the smell had anything to do with him. Liz grinned as she pulled the door to; perhaps she was finally learning to detect bullshit after all.

Chapter Four

'And the traffic, God, you just would not believe the traffic. Hours it took us, hours. And parking –' the real Jack Sandfi rolled his eyes heavenwards even though Morwenna, his partner, was not looking at him and had not looked at him since he had stepped down into their kitchen.

They had never married. If they had, Jack suspected that they would have divorced and gone their separate ways long ago, carrying exaggerated stories of cruelty and mutual abuse on to amuse and edify other people in other places. Instead, their relationship, undefined by the mores of social convention, was like some great virulent climbing weed, binding them together without a shred of compassion. No sooner had one of them hacked away and destroyed one knotted green tendril than another sprouted to trip and entangle them more completely than the last.

Still Morwenna did not turn.

The kitchen of the old rectory they shared seemed very dark, despite the clinical glow from fluorescent tubes hanging down amongst gothic beams. On the dresser a large black cat opened one mustard yellow eye and peered at Jack for a few seconds before uncurling itself from the breadboard and plopping down onto the rug beside him. Tail up, it sauntered out into the hall, leaving him to face Morwenna alone.

Jack wasn't altogether certain exactly how long it was that he had been away from home – it could be a few hours, a day, two, a week; everything looked very much as he remembered it. Summer flowers in a bowl on the table. Roasting tins soaking on the windowsill, the cat, Morwenna. He dragged out a chair from under the refectory table. The sound of it scouring across the flagstones made him wince. The expression was overdone, comedic and the effort of sustaining it was enough to ricochet Jack's thoughts away from the fictitious state of the roads in Norwich.

'Oh and Tilly Morrison asked after you, said she'd call in to see you in the week. I saw her outside Jarrolds with that new man of hers. Big blonde chap, can't quite remember his . . .' Still Morwenna did not turn.

Sandfi's gaze was now fixed on the animated expanse of creamy flesh between her shoulder blades. She had bright auburn hair and her skin had that interesting translucent quality peculiar to redheads. She was working at the sink and was dressed in a navy and white striped apron and a pair of very yellow rubber gloves; he could smell bleach.

She appeared to be wearing a sequinned evening dress under the apron and Jack thought that she might be humming although he wasn't altogether sure. There were a lot of noises in his head and he was having considerable difficulty working out which sounds were internal and which were not.

Jack chose not to sit down, instead he leant heavily over the end of the table, holding fast to the edge in an attempt to maintain his equilibrium.

'Anyway I've asked Arturo and Philip to come back for a little nip; a wee dram as it were. Roger and Hermione said they had other plans. I didn't think you'd mind. I said I thought you'd quite like to see Pip, he's been over in the States you know, New York and . . . So, how's it been with you, anyway?' The last words tumbled out in an ungainly rush. Tension, like a ligature, finally strangled the voice from him and he waited for his sentence to be meted out.

Morwenna turned a fraction so that he could just see

her profile. 'Fine, Jack,' she said in the softest of tones over one creamy white shoulder. 'Just fine.'

Jack winced and doubled up as if she had punched him in the solar plexus. 'Fine' was a dart thrust into the bull's shoulder by the picador. Harmless at first sight, 'fine' well might be bedecked with bright ribbons, but was cruelly barbed so that it could pierce his flesh and work ever deeper. Though 'fine' alone could not rupture a vital organ it would help wear him down and distract him from his purpose, allowing other words in to do their more deadly work.

'So, where are they, all these friends of yours? Philip, Arturo and the others? I take it that it isn't just Pip, it sounded more like a coach party.'

'They're over in the summer house. I didn't think you'd want them in the house. Not all of them.'

Morwenna nodded.

'That's a very nice dress,' Jack said, moving a little closer and knowing he'd made a terrible mistake the very instant the words were out.

She rounded on him, one great crystal tear clinging to the sooty mascaraed lashes that framed her bambi-sized eyes, while another, as if choreographed, rolled down her cheek. Once upon a time it would have melted Jack's heart, now it just made him flinch.

In the unforgiving light of the kitchen he could see every line on her tiny heart-shaped face, and pick out the unblended edges of her make-up; she reminded him of a cadaver on a slab made up by an over-enthusiastic mortician.

'Freddie and Ellis thought it was lovely too,' she said in a tight, high-pitched breathy voice.

Jack looked away, all the better to hear the emotionally charged in-breath that preceded the next sentence.

'You told me you'd be home last night, Jack. You

promised me faithfully – though I suppose, after all these years, I really ought to know better than to believe anything you say. I made my special celebration menu with sour cream and a whole salmon. All ruined now of course, completely ruined.'

Despite the rubber gloves Morwenna picked up a cigarette from a saucer full of butts wedged between the taps and took a long drag.

Jack had absolutely no idea what she was talking about but it didn't disturb him unduly. Life with Morwenna was often like that.

He could really use a drink.

Jack once used to argue that alcohol was the socially acceptable anaesthetic that softened the harsher edges of his existence, a tool that blunted the more intense perceptions. Without it his thoughts were too difficult, too intense to live with, at least that was what he told anyone who would listen. Other than the odd joint he had never dabbled with drugs. The last thing he needed was to unchain his raging mind. Alcohol had begun as a liquid leash, an analgesic, or so he said.

Now, standing in the kitchen Jack had a moment of divine revelation. He had a vision. When he wasn't looking, his consciousness had managed to slip away from its keeper, escaped, dug its way out, and was now apparently imbuing random objects with a kind of messianic brilliance, a corona, a halo. He wondered fleetingly if this was one of the mystical states pursued by gurus, a state of being where time and space ceased to exist and all thoughts were one.

It was unfortunate that Jack could never remember this much or know this much or understand this much when he was sober.

Even though his field of concentration was narrow it was total, and so now, as Morwenna spoke, all Jack could see – to the exclusion of almost everything else in the kitchen – was the little flotilla of lines that corrugated the pastry coloured flesh above her beautifully painted top lip.

'Why do you always do this to me, Jack?' she sobbed. 'Can you just tell me why? I've given you everything. What in the name of heaven have I ever done to you to deserve being treated like this?'

Sadly, it was not one of the things that Jack Sandfi, guru and lesser god, knew, and closing his eyes for an instant to shut out the sheer radiance of Morwenna's glistening flesh, he stepped into the darkness and allowed it to swallow him whole.

It was a relief. A great relief. The darkness that opened up was cool and still, and the only sound Jack heard before the black absorbed him totally was his skull hitting the edge of the oak table, but even that seemed like an abstract and distant echo.

*   *   *

First thing on Monday morning Nick Hastings scooped up his post from the door mat, including a plain brown A5 envelope addressed to 'J. Sandfi c/o 34b Kingsmead Terrace, Norwich'. Liz's address was printed on a little label stuck neatly across the flap. His stomach tightened up a notch. He would have to do something now. Once the envelope was opened.

In his head Nick had composed a letter to the editor of the *Bishopston News and Advertiser*. Actually he had composed several letters. He would begin by being kind and extremely courteous, pointing out that under the circumstances there was no way they could publish Liz's interview. He would withdraw his permission, refuse to co-operate – something like that – it was just a matter of finding the right form of words.

Or might it be better to ring them? There was probably less chance of the original deception being uncovered that way, but then again considerably less chance of the editor taking Nick seriously. Perhaps he ought to threaten to sue them, or maybe just pretend to be incredibly angry? Didn't the real Jack Sandfi have a reputation for being difficult and totally unpredictable?

Nick tucked Liz's letter behind the others and jogged back upstairs.

At this time of the morning sun-light flooded in through the first floor kitchen window adding a diffused golden glow to the stripped pine floor. Under the window stood a classic scrub-top Canadian pine table, flanked by two very finely turned ladder-back chairs – copies of the Shaker work Nick had made when he was a student; between them stood an elegant screw-thread stool. Even dust could look good in the right light.

On the centre of the table was a sea-grass basket of oranges, a jug of coffee, an enormous breakfast cup and an ice blue side plate bearing a single croissant. In a spot-light of citrus yellow sun-light the whole thing looked like an impressionist painting. Perfection.

Nick settled himself in the chair that gave the best view down onto the terrace and sorted the rest of the post. Amongst the advertising circulars and bills was a card from Jeanna O'Hanlon, thanking him most warmly for the bouquet of flowers he had sent her as a get-well gift.

How thoughtful, it said. The card, with a little hand-written note tucked inside, was a pen and ink of one of the company's estate cottages. She apologised profusely for cancelling their lunch date at such short notice.

Perhaps, Jeanna suggested, as soon as she was feeling a little better, Nick would like to drive over and have lunch with her? It might be a week or two as the doctor had advised her to have a complete rest, but she knew some wonderful country pubs close to the estate. And she'd be happy to show him around the workshops; they'd have a chance to talk about what Nick might be able to offer O'Hanlons. And thanks once again for the flowers. So sweet, so considerate. She was really touched.

Nick reddened furiously as if caught out in a blatant lie. The flowers hadn't really been meant for Jeanna at all, at least not in the way she imagined. They had been a desperate offering to the gods, a fragrant supplication to whichever deity he had offended at the Flag Hotel.

But even so, buoyed up by the card, he poured himself another coffee, opened Liz's letter, turned back the printed compliment slip and began to read their interview. Might as well get it over and done with.

He scanned the first line, and the second and then the third. It was not anything like Nick had imagined. The whole article was flat, dead, completely and utterly bland. To his surprise his first reaction was not relief but acute disappointment.

He had been expecting to see something so much better than this. Nick read to the bottom of the page to see if there was any improvement and found none. It really disturbed him. Had he made so little impression on Liz Chapman that she felt the need to churn out – almost word for word – exactly what was written about Jack Sandfi in the exhibition catalogue?

And then the penny dropped; Christ. Of course, that was exactly what she had done. Nick thought about it for a second or two and knew he was right; after his reaction to the tape recorder Liz had decided to play it safe. The real Jack Sandfi would probably have sued or demanded a retraction or compensation, something dramatic that would have made a huge furore. Perhaps Liz's editor had suggested they avoid potential trouble by paraphrasing the catalogue. It certainly made sense under the circumstances.

Nick smiled, broke the croissant into pieces and made a start on his coffee, tension easing; the girl was a genius.

Thanks to Liz's quick thinking there was no need for a letter, no frantic phone calls demanding that they stop the presses, no empty threats of legal action. No outrage by proxy. However rusty, Liz Chapman was obviously a complete professional, and because of her he wouldn't have to do anything at all. Nothing. The last remnants of the guilt quietly melted away.

Nick tucked the copy of the interview back into its envelope and glanced at the little address label on the flap. Liz Chapman's phone number was on it and despite everything he was tempted to ring her up and thank her for being such a hero.

But he didn't. Maybe he could get away with sending her flowers too. Nick picked up the coffee and what remained of the impressionist croissant, and headed for the spare bedroom which doubled as his studio.

Clipped to the drawing board were the latest sketches for one of Newlens' projects; a baroque and tartan interior for some ageing ex-jockey with considerably more money than taste. As Nick had told Liz Chapman when he thought she was Jeanna O'Hanlon, they were crassly commercial, but at least they paid the rent.

*   *   *

'I was just out this way pricing a job up and thought I'd just drop in on the off-chance. See you, see the boys, see that everything is all right at the old homestead, you know –' Liz's ex-husband Mike lifted his hands, palms up, trying to encompass some enormous imaginary act of philanthropy, whilst at the same time very obviously trying to sound casual. 'So, how are you then?'

Liz didn't speak. After the interview on Friday – a little

44

flash of excitement – the new week had unfolded like count-less others, with no great surprises, just a very strange sense of anticlimax. It was late Wednesday afternoon and Mike was the last person on earth Liz had expected or wanted to see.

'You know that I'm teaching tonight,' she said flatly. 'You're very lucky to catch me in.'

'Right, I couldn't remember which nights you were out and I was just driving by, in the neighbourhood, you know.'

Mike had shaved very recently and smelt of something deep and meaningful by Paco Rabanne. He was doing his level best to look sexy and was wearing a soft cotton shirt just like the one Liz had bought him the last Christmas they were together. The colour really suited him. Dark hair curled in the open neck and he had a light tan. Liz realised she was salivating and stamped out the little flurry of erotic images that passed unbidden through her mind before they had any chance to flare and catch light.

Mike grinned and she wondered if he'd been able to read her mind. If so it would be a first.

'You know, you're looking good, Liz. Really good. Single life obviously suits you,' he said.

Liz folded her arms defensively across her chest. 'Right. I'm afraid the boys aren't here at the moment, they're stay-ing over at my parents' tonight. Mum and dad picked them up from school, they've all gone swimming.' Liz was tempted to add, 'because you didn't take them, even though you promised', but didn't.

It was intended to head him off, diffuse whatever little plans Mike had in mind, although even as she spoke Liz wished she hadn't said anything. Now he knew she was alone. Would he see it as an invitation, a desperate plea? With Mike almost anything was possible.

Until he disturbed her Liz had been sitting out on the

terrace, barefoot, savouring what seemed like the first truly free time she'd had for weeks. The welcome sensation of not having to be anywhere, not responsible, of not having to be the only resident grown-up washed over Liz like warm oil. The tension in her shoulders had eased. It felt wonderful, eating a chicken salad, drinking a glass of wine, reading the paper, taking the time to tip her face towards the old-gold glow of the afternoon sun and relax. God, it was almost as good as the simple things in life get.

Liz stretched. There was just one last toffee yoghurt hidden away in the back of the fridge, safe under a bag of salad. There was a pot of tea brewing, after which Liz had promised herself a leisurely shower before leaving for work. And there were a few little treats planned for after work too. She'd hired a video, something sexy and highly strung with Gene Hackman and Mel Gibson, and bought a large bar of Cadbury's Dairy Milk which was busy cooling off in the chiller box even as she stretched. Bliss, pure and simple.

And then the door bell had rung. At first Liz had been very tempted to ignore it, except that her unexpected visitor had applied a thumb and carried on pressing until she couldn't stand the raw edgy threat of the bell any longer.

Mike had been standing out on the pavement carrying a new and expensive looking leather jacket hooked on one finger over his shoulder. He shifted his weight nervously from one foot to the other and glanced up the road, avoiding her eye.

She looked very pointedly at her watch, underlining the fact that something or someone else was waiting. 'So, what exactly *did* you want, Mike? Only I've got to get myself organised for work.'

'Actually, it wasn't the boys I came over to see at all. I met Claire in town the other day. She said you were doing really well. A busy lady these days –' he grinned sheepishly and leant against the door frame, all his weight rested on his forearm, in a pose that only men ever strike. Something about his stance implied dominance and a flirtatious sexual edge that made Liz wince. Mike really must be desperate to try to pull that one out of the hat.

'So, how are things going then?'

'Are you going to tell me what is it that you want, Mike? Only, to be perfectly honest, I haven't got either the time or the inclination to play twenty questions with you.'

Liz saw him considering one more round of flirtation, a little more flattery, one last gargantuan lie and then Mike shrugged and switched the glamour off. The game was up. It had always been too hard for him to sustain, too much. Liz looked her ex-husband up and down and tried to fathom out what mysterious alchemy had kept them together for so long. He was utterly transparent.

'The thing is, Liz, life is a bit complicated at the moment. You know how it is. I was wondering if you could just help me fill this in. It shouldn't take very long, it's all pretty straight forward,' he pulled a thick fold of printed paper out of his inside pocket. 'It's a little short-term loan to help sort out my cash-flow situation. Nothing for you to worry about though. Just a business loan. You know how these things go.'

Behind her Liz heard the phone ring and for an instant Mike stopped speaking. Caught in a no-man's land of possibilities Liz knew she hadn't got time to get rid of Mike before the caller rang off and also knew that she hadn't bothered to switch the answer machine on.

On the other hand, if she went in to answer the phone Mike would follow her inside, because – despite several very sound reasons – Liz couldn't quite bring herself to shut the door in his face. Not yet.

'Could you just wait there?' she asked politely, indicating the doorstep.

'You really ought to put some net curtains up at those front windows, Liz, people can't help but look in, you know. It's human nature. And you should get a security chain for the front door,' Mike said, trailing behind her into the kitchen.

Liz picked up the phone.

'Hi, this is the features editor for the *Sunday News* here. May I speak to Liz Chapman, please?' asked the female caller. Once Liz had introduced herself and the basic niceties had been exchanged, the woman continued, 'I just wanted you to know that we all *really* loved the Sandfi piece. Personally, I'm totally amazed, it's extraordinary. I met Sandfi in New York a couple of years back, and to get stuff like this out of him, to be perfectly honest, it's unbelievable. Anyway, the bottom line is that we'd really like to go with your interview. I just need to run a few things by you. Oh, and we'll probably have to edit it down a little bit for the space we've got available. Is that okay? We'll try and liaise on any changes we make.'

Liz murmured thanks, delight and agreement as the woman pressed on.

Across the kitchen, Mike was picking over the remains of her supper and had helped himself to a glass of wine. As Liz took a notepad and a pen off the table, he switched on the little portable television that stood on the dresser. She glared at him but he was completely oblivious. He pulled out a chair and, leaning across in front of her, turned up the sound.

'We wondered if you'd got any more recent photographs?' continued the woman at the far end of the line. 'All we seem to be able to get our hands on at the moment are all those moody monochromes from Sandfi's tortoiseshell specs era. You know, the ones that are in his new catalogue? Nice stylistically though. Did you take a photographer with you?'

'Er, no,' Liz said, waving at Mike who'd found a noisy dayglo orange children's game show on three. 'Excuse me for just a second would you?' Liz pressed the secrecy button on the handset.

'Do you mind?' she snapped furiously at Mike's back.

He looked round wide-eyed with genuine surprise. 'Sorry, is it private? I'm not bugging you, am I? Do you want me to go in the other room?'

Picking up the remote control Liz switched the television set off and then returned to her call. It didn't take long. The *Sunday News* were offering a very good fee, and said that if she had anything else, they'd be really interested to see it. They liked her work.

Liz looked out into the garden, struggling to contain her delight and smother a triumphant smile. She really didn't want to share the good news with Mike, who, when she turned back, had shifted his attention to the contents of her fridge.

'Something really stinks in there,' he said, closing the door as Liz finally dropped the phone back in its cradle. 'Using your maiden name again, I see?' He picked up a copy of the *Sunday News* article from the dresser. 'Liz Chapman, now there's a name that brings back a lot of memories.'

Liz plucked the sheet of paper out from between his fingers and forced her expression into neutral. 'It *is* mine.'

Mike aped offence. 'Oh but, Bizzie-Lizzie, I gave you mine.'

She slid past him. 'And I gave it back, Mike, if you remember. Just in case any of the others might want to use it. Now, was there anything else you came for, only I've got a lot to do before I leave.'

Mike unfolded the bundle of papers he had left on the kitchen table and smoothed them open with a flat hand. 'I thought that once you've got them done, maybe we could go out for a drink or something? Just like old times.'

Heaven forbid. Liz took a deep breath, keeping it all as light and polite as she could manage. 'Thanks for the offer, but I'm not filling the forms in for you and I've already told you I'm teaching at the tech' tonight.'

He stepped closer. 'Oh yeh, that's right, you said. The thing is it's all fairly simple; name, age, date of birth, address, previous employers, the boys' details, and yours – only I really wanted to get them in by the end of this week, you know how these things are. I could leave them here if you like and you could fill them in when you've got a few minutes to spare.'

Liz straightened up, losing the struggle to keep her tone neutral. 'You still don't listen, do you, Mike? I am not doing them. It's not my job, not now, not ever. Nothing to do with me any more. Just exactly how much clearer do you need this to be?'

Mike shrugged. 'If it's because you're pushed for time, Liz, don't worry. I could nip back a bit later, get us both a take-away or something for when you get home from work if you like. Have you got any more wine anywhere?'

Liz picked up the bundle of forms and handed them back to him.

Mike frowned. His voice dropped to a childish whine. 'Oh come on, Liz. I didn't think you'd mind, just have a quick look through them for me. I hate filling forms in, you know that. I really need help.'

She waved him towards the front door. 'Probably, but not from me, not any more. It was nice of you to come by to see how we all were. Any chance that you'll be picking the boys up next weekend?'

Mike groaned and aped pain. 'Why did you have to bring that up? I knew you'd have to say something; you never let anything rest, do you? Pick, pick, pick. I've already told you that it really wasn't my fault, Liz. Something came up. Tell you what, I'll ring you later in the week. Promise.'

Although Mike had taken the forms he hadn't put them away and as they reached the hall he held them out towards her like a bouquet, as if there might still be some likelihood Liz would change her mind.

Liz sighed. 'Why don't you get whatever-her-name-is to do them for you, the latest one?'

Mike shook his head as if in desperation. 'You don't change, do you, Liz? I know I can always depend on you to turn it around. You have to take a pop at me, don't you? How many times do I have to tell you –'

Liz, who was already edging Mike back towards the street door, held up a hand to silence him. 'You don't have to tell me anything any more.'

'But I thought . . .' he began.

They were at the door now. She pulled it open and gently but firmly guided him back onto the pavement.

'Look, maybe we could arrange to barter. I could come over some time and fix the safety chain, put up the nets, that sort of thing. And what about your curtains upstairs –' As all the possibilities finally slipped away, his tone became increasingly frantic and Mike waved the papers at her again. 'C'mon, Liz, I really begrudge paying that bastard accountant, when I know that you can do them for . . .'

The words dried mid-sentence and then Mike reddened furiously, well aware that he had just revealed his whole hand. Trying to claw back lost ground he smiled flirtatiously, struggling once again to look boyish and vulnerable. 'Once upon a time I seem to remember you were really keen on bartering.'

For the first time since Mike arrived, Liz laughed out loud. 'Nice try, Mike, the thing is that these days you just haven't got anything I want.'

Before he could think up a reply she shut the front door

on him. He stood on the step for a few seconds and then headed back towards the car. She watched through the bull's-eye glass set in the top of the door panel. The glass distorted Mike like a carnival mirror until finally, as he reached the kerb, he appeared to flip upside down. It seemed strangely fitting.

Now that the coast was clear – Mike had always loathed cats – Winston jumped out from under the hall stand and sashayed down the corridor, adding a little extra oomph to emphasise his outrage. Liz grinned and pushed thoughts of Mike aside. Much better to concentrate instead on how wonderful it was that the *Sunday News* wanted to run the Jack Sandfi article.

She really ought to ring Claire and let her know before leaving for work. Liz paused mid-stride and then laughed again as a random thought flittered through her mind; it was a real shame that she couldn't ring Jack Sandfi and tell him the good news as well.

Chapter Five

'Open the door will you. You should see what I've got. Ta-tara. Cue fanfare –' Claire banged the back door with one hip and, after Liz had scrambled to unfasten it, half-circled her way into the kitchen. Laid out across her arms like freshly laundered sheets was an enormous pile of newspapers, copies of the *Sunday News*, its pristine pages lagged with layer after layer of financial supplements, colour magazines and TV guides.

'Bloody hell, when you said you'd pick up the papers you weren't joking, were you?'

It was half past nine on Sunday morning, the sun was pooling like spilt syrup all over the kitchen floor, Winston was asleep on the windowsill, and Liz had a pot of coffee plopping fragrantly on the stove.

'I hope that it's in there. Did you buy all of them?' Liz asked, pulling out a chair so that Claire could make her way unhindered over to the table.

Claire aped offence. 'Picky, picky. I just bought one for you, one for me, one for your mum and dad, one each for the boys, one for Mike –' she glanced up and caught Liz frowning. 'Okay, okay, so maybe not one for Mike. But there were plenty left for other people. Anyway this is a special occasion. Your return to the world of ink, stink and deadlines. Here, take a look. You're going to be so chuffed when you see what they've done with your article.' Claire eased the pile down alongside the celebration fresh cream sponge Liz had taken out to defrost, and grabbed a copy of the magazine from inside one of the papers.

'Cover story in the review section, take a butcher's, page 10. You made the lead article, baby.' Claire passed it across. 'So what do you think? Good or what?'

Liz stared down at the cover for a few seconds, feeling a peculiar combination of lightness and tension. 'Oh, my God,' she murmured. 'Will you just take a look at that.'

On the front was an exquisite, moody shot of a young Jack Sandfi caught in three-quarter profile, lighting a cigarette. His hands were cupped around the flame as he challenged the breeze that was ruffling his Beatle cut, to try to snuff it out.

It was hard to believe it was the same man. Time had been very kind to Jack Sandfi, mellowing and redefining his features while eroding the anger and rebellion – the years had somehow brought him into tighter, more benign focus.

'Back from the wilderness. Jack Sandfi, sculpture's original bad boy talks exclusively to the *Sunday News*,' read the banner headline. Liz felt dizzy and grinned inanely. 'Wow, will you just take a look at that,' she repeated in a whisper.

'Big potatoes,' said Claire with approval, riffling through the pages of another copy. 'Ah, and here we are –' she folded the magazine back on itself and began to read, ' "The popular image of sculptor, Jack Sandfi as a hedonistic bon viveur, a hard-drinking, womanising bad boy of the art world is blown apart in this exclusive revealing interview with Liz Chapman, as the artist discusses his work, his fears and his dreams of finding a good woman and settling down once and for all . . ." '

Liz's grin widened a notch. 'My God, I wrote that.'

Claire laughed and helped herself to a slice of almost defrosted cake. 'Well, what a surprise. It's just such a shame that your Mike wasn't a celebrity – you always write so much better when you're really pissed off.' She swiped a gobbet of crystallised cream off the table with one perfectly manicured finger and popped it into her mouth. 'May I safely assume from the fact that the cake is still in one piece that the man in question finally dropped by to pick up the fruit of his loins for the weekend?'

Liz shook the magazine into submission. 'Only after I rang twice to remind him. He swore blind that it couldn't possibly be his weekend to have them, and then, when he realised he'd forgotten about not having them last week, he back pedalled so hard that I thought he was going to choke. Oh, and *then* he told me he has a problem with the days of the week – it's a syndrome apparently, said he'd seen a programme about it on BBC2.' Liz paused and added a little topspin to her tone. 'So it has to be true.' She gave the paper another spiteful flick. 'And I'd rather you didn't mention loins if you don't mind. I've got the most terrible ache for wild uncomplicated passion at the moment. Something earth stopping, life changing –'

Claire stared at her. 'Not with Mike surely?'

'Good God no. Even I'm not that desperate, it's just that I'm so fed up of being on my own. I want a real relationship.'

'Have you got anyone in mind?'

Liz shook her head; she couldn't quite bring herself to tell Claire that images of Jack Sandfi filled her rogue imagination. She sniffed and turned her attention back to the magazine. 'Nice cover.'

Claire grinned. 'Bloody hormones. Okay, so all mention of loins is right out. What shall we do? Do you fancy going out for a drive? What time did the Boy Wonder say he was bringing Tom and Joe back? We could drive over to Norwich if you like and take one last look at the Sandfi's before they get all boxed up and barrowed off to the Smoke? What d'you reckon?'

Liz grimaced. Scanning down through the article had

sparked off all kinds of thoughts. A picture of Jack Sandfi's face filled her mind in crisp sunlit close-up. She had had no idea just how much detail she had absorbed from their meeting at the Flag: those dark glittering eyes, his softly lined sun-tanned face, and the head of thick, neatly trimmed old-gold hair, shot through with white that he habitually pushed back from his forehead with long fingers. Liz shivered. The picture was so vivid that she could almost smell his aftershave and was so intense that it made the breath catch in her throat. She had been dreaming about him too.

Whatever had happened afterwards, whatever it was Liz had thought or discovered when she got back home from the Flag, Jack Sandfi had made a really good first impression. Even if what he had told her had been – as it now appeared – a pure fabrication, which she still found very hard to believe, the way he had treated her when they had been together, the good manners, the good humour and gentle flirtation had unexpectedly stirred up a lot of forgotten things. Things like desire and attraction and need, all that pleasant warm emotional and sexual curiosity that she was convinced her marriage to Mike had killed stone dead.

But, inspite of that, meeting Jack Sandfi was also still a raw thing; how could her instincts have been so out of kilter that she hadn't realised he was lying to her? Jack Sandfi had made her feel incredibly good, more desirable and more sexy than she had felt for years, which made the game he had been playing all the crueller. Had he done it knowingly?

Had it really all been a lie – a horrible, dark, nasty, manipulative lie – and if so, why? Had he hoped to seduce her? Have a good laugh at her naiveté. Or was picking up lonely women the way he got his kicks. The thought made her horribly uneasy and angry too. She certainly didn't see herself as anyone's victim. But whatever it was that Jack Sandfi had been playing, Liz really wanted him to pay for it.

The ways Liz looked at the meeting with Jack made for a very volatile mix. She closed the magazine, hurt and indignation rising up in her belly like the head of a coiled viper. She avoided Claire's gaze and slid a piece of cake out from the pack. It instantly collapsed into a froth of light sponge and goo that trickled between her fingers.

'So, what do you think then?' said Claire. 'Shall we go over to Norwich?'

'Only if I can take my felt-tips along for the ride.'

Claire frowned. 'I'm not with you. Is that a yes or a no?'

Liz waved Claire's look of puzzlement away. 'Don't mind me. I'm just feeling very cynical and cruelly betrayed.'

'So, what's new? Do you want to go? We could grab some lunch on the way, if you like.'

Liz hesitated; it would be interesting to see Jack Sandfi's work. She might be able to catch a glimpse of whatever it was that drove the man. The whole idea was tempting and torturous and, although she wouldn't admit it to Claire, there was some tiny part of her that hoped Jack might be there to supervise the dismantling. Finally, Liz nodded. 'Why not?'

*   *   *

At around the same time, in Norwich, Nick Hastings was calling a halt to his ritual Sunday morning lie in. He stretched, pressed the heels of his hands up into his eye sockets and then slid the novel he'd been reading back onto the bedside cabinet, finally compelled by a full bladder to get up and take a long hard look at whatever the new morning had to offer. From under the bedroom window came the familiar and oddly comforting whine, hum, and rattle of a milk float heading home, back to the dairy after finishing its rounds.

Nick rolled slowly out of bed and stretched again, achiev-

57

ing one of those wonderful, even, emotionally satisfying stretches that makes every bone and every joint click gently back into place like the teeth of an expensive zip.

Across the hall, the bathroom floor was icy cold under his feet.

Whilst wandering through the broad expanses of sleep he'd bumped into the reporter from the Flag – Liz Chapman, that was her name. And set adrift inside a surreal Norwich dreamscape he'd been really pleased to meet up with her again, and vice versa. She looked just as good as he remembered and, as one often does in dreams, he'd invited her up to his flat for coffee. He'd been delighted when she had accepted, smiling, warm – something inside had fluttered as he reached out to take her hand. It had been really good to see her again. Nice to see the waiter too; he'd been there as well, serving their coffee, handing out indiscretions along with the tray of biscuits and copies of Jack Sandfi's catalogue.

As details of the dream floated back Nick realised how relieved he was that the whole Sandfi interview thing had blown over so quickly, and with practically no effort on his part, turning out, against all the odds, to be no more than a storm in a teacup.

It was a shame that he hadn't been able to meet up with Liz again; they'd got on really well and he knew she had felt that compelling little arc of desire crackle between them, the same one that had tracked an icy finger up his spine when their hands touched.

It had to have been nearly two weeks since he and Liz met for the interview – and she had loomed large in his thoughts and imagination for quite a lot of that time – which prompted Nick to remember that he really ought to ring Jeanna O'Hanlon to see if she was well enough to reschedule their meeting.

Once back in the bedroom, Nick opened the sash

window and let the morning breeze billow out the long white nets like full sails on a clipper. Pulling on jogging bottoms, an old pair of trainers and a crumpled tee-shirt he headed in to the kitchen, filled and plugged in the kettle, and then headed downstairs.

Beyond the street door, out in the sunlight, a straggle of other Sunday morning folk were already on their way down to collect the papers from the newsagents on the corner of Bellmost Alley: a small elderly woman with a large hairy dog, two children, a boy and girl, and a thick set man in a muscle vest and jeans, who was already on his way back home, his mission complete, a rolled red-top tucked tight under one armpit and cigarette clamped between what few teeth he had left.

Nick and the thick set man had cheerfully not really known each other for years – since Nick had moved into the flat in fact, just after he and his wife had split up when life felt dark and strange and ragged round the edges. Their entire acquaintance was neatly bracketed inside the slight inclination of the head that they exchanged most mornings on their way to or from the paper shop.

Nick sniffed before stepping out into the street, drawing in a little fresh air seasoned with the miasma of cigarette smoke and the scent of yesterday's coffee from the deli. If he timed it right and the newsagents weren't too busy he could be there and back in about the same time as it took for the kettle to boil.

In one of the wire-fronted hoardings hanging outside the shop – a flyer for the *Sunday News* – someone had written in thick black marker, 'Local bad boy sculptor reveals all. Jack Sandfi exclusive inside.'

Nick acknowledged the coincidence as the words caught his eye and then tucked them away into a distant corner of his mind. It seemed as if Jack Sandfi had managed to give some lucky soul an interview after all. Linen-jacket's drunken indiscretion had caught up with him at last – there was a sense of natural justice about it.

Inside the little shop Nick picked up a *Mail on Sunday* from the pile, and then dallied over what else to buy, the *Telegraph* maybe? Did he need some milk? Or a packet of chocolate-chip cookies?

As Nick was about to pay, the small elderly woman, who had been tying the hairy dog to a downpipe outside, stooped to pick up the *Sunday News* and as she did the magazine sections slithered out, spilling special offers, TV pages, book club flyers and coupons all over the battle-scarred lino. She grumbled, bending to retrieve them, assisted by Nick, who, as he picked up the magazine, caught a fleeting glimpse of Jack Sandfi's face on the front cover, his profile framed by cupped hands.

It made Nick stop, frozen uncomfortably between crouching and standing, and look again. The picture was an enlarged detail from something he had seen in the catalogue. It was beautifully reproduced, re-touched by an expensive state-of-the-art computer graphics programme no doubt. Nick stood up slowly, knees cracking in complaint as he stared down at the elegantly arty image. It was beautifully done.

For an instant something stirred low in his belly, a sensation that later he would dismiss as hunger. But at that moment Nick Hastings instinctively recognised it as something else, something less benign, a physical manifestation of the sure and certain knowledge that fate planned to make him pay for deceiving Liz Chapman – and pay in spades. The bouquet for Jeanna O'Hanlon hadn't been anywhere near recompense enough.

The old woman thanked Nick for his help, a subtle hint that she wanted the rest of her newspaper back, which was enough to break into Nick's chain of thought, but not enough to stop him flicking through the first few pages of the magazine. It might be interesting to see what they had written about Sandfi, after all, for a few brief moments, he and Nick had shared a life.

With his mind on scan, Nick absorbed the double-page spread, the catalogue photos of a couple of the sculptures, the neatly spaced columns and odd words from the feed-in line: '. . . popular image, Jack Sandfi, bon viveur, bad boy, blown apart, exclusive interview by Liz Chapman.' *Liz Chapman?*

The words settled like dust on his consciousness. For the briefest of instants the name on the by-line seemed vaguely familiar and then it lit up like a phosphorus flare, setting light to the blue touch-paper inside his head.

'Oh, for Christ's sake – sweet Jesus,' he gasped in complete horror. Liz Chapman, Liz Chapman. Maybe there were two of them, maybe Liz had discovered that he had lied and gone off and tracked down the real Sandfi after all, maybe – *Liz Chapman?* He began to read the introduction and groaned.

The elderly woman, who had been discreetly trying to retrieve her newspaper took a step back and glared at him.

'Mad bugger,' she muttered, bending to pick up another copy of the *Sunday News* from the pile. But Nick was oblivious now, his whole consciousness caught in the headlight of Liz Chapman's article.

'You gonna buy that, mate?' asked the man behind the counter. Nick nodded dumbly, dropping a handful of coins onto the counter.

'You wanna bag for them, do ya?' The man indicated the milk, the *Mail* and packet of chocolate-chip cookies that Nick had squashed under his arm.

But it was too late, Nick Hastings had already turned on his heel and was heading for home.

* * *

Meanwhile, near Swaffham, in the Rectory kitchen, Jack Sandfi instinctively dived for cover, narrowly avoiding a Royal Doulton side plate as it exploded like a mortar shell against the dresser six inches above his head. One razor-edged shard curled a nick out of his cheek, whilst another unseated a small yellow china bear full of coppers that had been on the shelf near his shoulder.

For what seemed like forever the little bear wobbled backwards and forwards on the very edge, although there was a certain morbid inevitability about the outcome, and then at last it fell, face forwards onto the flagstones, where it exploded with an enormous and totally disproportionate bang. Pennies and tuppences scattered and scuttled and rolled across the dusty floor like alms for the poor. There was a brief lull in hostilities during the weighty silence that followed.

Jack knew it was pointless asking what it was he was supposed to have done. He was meant to know.

Across the kitchen, Morwenna drew in another great red-raw gasping sob, refilling lungs decimated by intense emotion. It was the signal to end the brief time-out.

Crouched like a hundred metres runner, up on his toes and fingertips, Jack glanced around with gimlet-sharp eyes, surveying the kitchen table, the plate rack and the big wooden draining board, weighing up what might be used next as ammunition and what might be spared, all the time well aware that Morwenna could easily have something held in reserve, hidden in the sink.

Surreptitiously he looked towards the back door wondering whether he was still nimble enough to make it across the three or four yards to freedom without sustaining serious injury, or whether it might not be better to feint right as if heading for the back door and then double back through into the hall.

The atmosphere in the kitchen had almost reached critical mass, Morwenna was crouched a little lower now, right arm winding up like a West Indian bowler out for the kill. Jack sensed that he had left his exit a split-second too late and was about to close his eyes when Lily Howard, their daily help, stepped down into the kitchen bearing a tray and humming something that appeared to have no tune.

She glanced left and right, and then very daintily – despite her considerable bulk – picked her way through the bubbling magma of smashed crockery and glass and soap suds.

'So what did he say then?' she asked Morwenna, as if nothing untoward was happening and the kitchen did not resemble the aftermath of an air-raid. Morwenna wiped her face with the back of a hand, scouring away a damp tendril of red hair that hung down across her eyes and was undoubtedly spoiling her aim. She looked pale and hot and waxy in the most unhealthy of ways.

'Nothing,' she said unsteadily. 'Nothing at all, the bastard. What could he say? That he's sorry? That it was all a terrible mistake. What *could* he say?'

Lily nodded and then turned her attention to Jack. 'Well, what *have* you got to say for yourself?' She indicated the Sunday newspapers, which lay open on the kitchen table.

Jack – who had spent the night sleeping off an excess of merlot and a rather good brandy in the summer house and had only come indoors to find something very wet to drink – arranged his face into an unknowing, uncomprehending, non-confrontational expression which Lily wiped away with a curt gesture.

'And don't you go trying that sort of thing with me, it don't cut no ice,' she snapped. 'You should be totally ashamed of yourself, all the trouble you've caused. Poor Mrs Sandfi is really very upset about all this.'

Jack blinked; not only was it the same tone of voice that Lily had used to scold the cat when it ate the smoked haddock, but she spoke as if Morwenna was laid waste with weeping, inconsolable up in her bedroom, sniffing smelling salts, her heart breaking with pain and torment, not crouched on the far side of the kitchen table like a rabid dog, a Waterford Crystal vase cupped in one hand like a grenade with the pin out.

Jack took a breath; both women still had their eyes firmly fixed on him.

'Well,' he began, lifting his hands in surrender. Was it only in his imagination that Morwenna and Lily both craned forward in eager anticipation of his explanation. It crossed his mind that it would be far simpler to apologise now, promise something wild and rash and expensive and then take whatever terrible punishment the two had in store for him.

Seconds passed, the silence hanging in the air like the smell of cordite. Under pressure Jack's mind finally emptied like a cracked cistern.

'Well, you see, the thing is, Morwenna, I ... What you must understand, is that, that I'm, I'm sorry, most terribly, terribly sorry ...' His voice faded away. What else was he, other than floundering horribly? Adrift in an open boat on an unfriendly ocean, circled by sharks, he reached out for some kind of explanation and found nothing. He would just have to drown now.

Morwenna took a step towards the long narrow table that divided them – Jack's first instinct was to flinch – and then she set the crystal vase down amongst a crackle of glass shards.

She pointed at the open newspaper on the table and began, it appeared to Jack, to recite rather than read what was written on the page: ' "All I've ever really wanted from life is the same kind of thing that everyone else wants; it's no great secret; someone who loves me, children, a family, a real home ..." you bastard.' Morwenna glanced up in his direction. 'Your interview, Jack, timed perfectly, I suppose, for the opening of the exhibition next week in London. You should be very pleased with yourself – a glossy double-page feature article in the review section – very nice.' She lifted the magazine to reveal the front cover. '*Sunday News*? Liz Chapman? Does it ring any bells, Jack?'

Morwenna fixed him in her sights, and then dragged in a huge breath.

Jack braced himself for whatever was to follow.

She leant towards him, elbows bent like a prize fighter, all her weight resting on her knuckles.

'You really don't care at all, do you, Jack? Not about me or anyone else come to that. Did you honestly think I wouldn't find out about all this?' She slapped the page with the back of her hand. 'Did you think that I wouldn't see this little confession? Or is it that you think I'm so trampled so, so, crushed by the weight of your total indifference, that I don't care what you say about me any more? God, in some ways I only wish that were true, I really do. It would make life so much easier if I couldn't feel the pain anymore. But, you're wrong, so wrong, Jack.' She added a nice and rather compelling little vibrato to the end of the last sentence to ensure that it lingered in the mind.

'I suppose it was that little bastard Arturo who set this up, wasn't it?' she continued after a few seconds' pause which added a little more dramatic weight to her words. 'I've always thought that he would make a much better pimp than he does an agent. What was she like then, Jack? Tall, blonde, buxom? I presume you did sleep with her?'

Jack wondered if he was expected to say anything. Morwenna seemed to be doing wonderfully well all on her own. Although he had felt no instant gleam of recognition, nor any sense of old sins coming home to roost as she had read the article, Jack was still well aware that a bottomless pit of guilt, accusation, retribution, recrimination, tears and torment had just opened up in front of him.

There was another brief pause. Morwenna was still waiting for his reaction and almost at once he realised that some part of his brain had begun to speak, a part that apparently was totally without shame.

'What can I say? What do you want me to say? There has to have been some kind of mistake, darling, they've totally mis-quoted me. Really. I never said anything like that, well, I wouldn't, would I? And it's all been taken completely out of context. I think I really ought to go and ring my solicitor, don't you? What do you think? I mean, I have to say something about this, don't I?' There was even a hint of righteous indignation in the voice.

This Liz Chapman must have been something very special for him to do his brooding moody, 'Just give me a good woman and a few good acres', speech. And thank God she had had the good sense to paraphrase him, Jack thought, or he would never be able to use it to pull again. He just wished he could remember exactly who she was and whether or not she had succumbed to his charm.

Morwenna looked up at him, eyes bright with pain and the closest thing to genuine tears that Jack had seen there in a very long time. Who exactly was this Liz Chapman? The name rang no bells at all, which in an odd way struck him as strangely exciting.

'You really are the most complete and utter bastard,' Morwenna hissed between those perfect, pearly-white capped teeth. She had a very slight underbite which was always more apparent when she was angry. Jack struggled hard to keep his attention on what she was saying rather than on the apparatus.

'I don't think you have any idea what I do for you; all the things I've given up to be with you, all the things I've put up with, year after year. Stuck out here in the arse-end of nowhere so you can play lord of all you survey. You really are so selfish, Jack, so terribly, terribly self-centred. No one knows why I stay with you, you know, my family, my friends – even your friends Jack, they all think you treat me like dirt. I could have been someone, you know, everyone says so. My first exhibition, Cambridge, summer, 1976 – the art critic from the *Sunday Times* said that in my work he saw the authoritative new voice of British water-colour – the new voice, Jack.'

Jack frowned. It was very hard to retain any real interest when the words and phrases were so very well worn, many so well-used that they were almost shiny from the constant buffing.

The sound of the Waterford vase exploding on the floor next to him snapped Jack's attention back.

'A real home? Children? What the hell is all that about? Are you listening to me, you bastard?'

Jack blinked to tighten his focus. 'What?' he said.

'That's what you told this Liz Chapman woman. Don't try and deny it, I know you, Jack, it's all in here in black and white: "All I have had in my life for the last few years are a series of friendships, good friendships I suppose, but nothing that has meant very much, no one great passion, except of course my work, in some ways my work is my mistress, driving me relentlessly on."' Morwenna curled her lip. 'So was Liz Chapman a real blonde?'

Jack took a step away from the table; the red flush of fury was rising fast in Morwenna's eyes. But before she could pick up another missile he darted right, feigned left, circumnavigating Lily Howard as he did and then dashed out through the back door into the morning sunshine.

The sharp, fresh morning air hit Jack like a body blow but he knew better than to slow the pace of his escape. Despite the crackling snapping pain in his skull and the fester of last night's booze rising in his gut, he sprinted across the dewy grass, shoulders hunched forward, elbows tucked tight in like an American quarterback.

Behind him Jack heard a banshee shriek of rage and an instant later a cauliflower exploded like a wet fart on the unkempt grass beside him. Before the artillery could get a positive fix, Jack swerved left and then right, dodging under cover of the trees before nipping smartly behind a row of flowering currant bushes. From there he hurried across the expanse of lawn towards the safety of the summer house.

Inside the summer house, under cover of the dark silken shadows, Arturo, Jack's agent lay curled up under a blanket, snuffling softly, an unlit cigarette nipped in the junction of his pale outstretched fingers. The little room smelt like a hamster cage and was littered with empty bottles and full ashtrays and the congealed remains of Cantonese dinner A for four persons. There was still a crush of prawn crackers under foot. Jack looked around for somewhere to take cover in case this was the moment when Morwenna finally crossed the great divide. Until now the summer house had always been his holy of holies, a sacred space, sanctuary, but there was always a first time for everything.

As the door swung shut behind Jack, Arturo opened one crusty reptilian eye and licked his lips. 'Trouble at t'mill, lad?'

'Christ, I thought you were asleep. You frightened the bloody life out of me,' gasped Jack, clutching at his chest.

With some difficulty, Arturo hauled himself up onto one elbow. 'One of the students came in a little while ago and said that you and your good lady were having a little altercation.' He sucked thoughtfully at the interior of his mouth, grimaced and swallowed with some reluctance. 'That little blonde buxom one. I told her to be a dear, and run along and put the kettle on in the studio, whip us up a pot of tea.'

Jack, who was still keeping an eye out for any possible enemy activity through the smeary windows, nodded distractedly. 'Sounds like a damned good idea to me. What did she say?'

While Arturo began to frame a reply, Jack clambered over the piles of well-established debris and lifted a rusty bike out from behind a battered armchair.

'What the fuck are you up to?' murmured Arturo.

'Do you have any idea who Liz Chapman is?'

Arturo shrugged and lit the cigarette. 'Dunno. It's not that blonde student, is it?' Jack shook his head, so Arturo continued. 'Or what about a sculptor? Artist? I don't know, what? Who is she?'

'My problem exactly,' said Jack. 'I'm just going to nip down to the post office and pick up the Sunday papers.'

Arturo's face contorted like a side-show mirror. 'On a bike? Are you completely mad? Are you going to tell me what this is about, Jack? You're not having some sort of a break-down are you?'

At that moment the summer house door swung open; Jack ducked instinctively.

A small blonde girl with disproportionately large breasts stood outside under the veranda, her silhouette framed by a backcloth of unused sunlight. She was carrying a tray. Arturo grinned.

'Wonderful, thanks. Look, sweetheart, while you're here, would you mind awfully taking the bike down to the village and getting us the Sunday papers?'

He fumbled about under the blanket and pulled out a handful of change.

The girl frowned. 'You've got a bleedin' cheek. I'm not your bloody slave, you know, and anyway I'm busy.'

Arturo feigned hurt. 'Oh come on. Pretty please –'

The girl snorted. 'You really are a pair of sad old farts. What do you want me to get you?'

Arturo nodded towards Jack, in the assumption he would supply the answer.

'A couple of copies of the *Sunday News*?'

'And if you're going that way, maybe you could drop into the offie on the way back?' continued Arturo.

The girl pulled a face.

When she had gone Arturo settled himself back under the blanket, cradling a mug of tea in one exposed hand and a cigarette in the other. 'Australian, isn't she?'

'Who?' asked Jack, with one eye still fixed on the window. 'Liz Chapman?'

Arturo shook his head. 'No, no, you silly bugger, the little blonde creature.'

Chapter Six

Nick Hastings had spread the whole of the *Sunday News* out in front of him, with the review section open at Liz Chapman's article. Not that he was reading any of it, or even really seeing it. Nick's gaze was fixed in the middle distance while his mind was busy chasing its own tail.

It was completely ridiculous. How the hell had this story with this by-line ended up here in the Sunday papers? To begin with Nick had thought that Liz had found out the truth by accident, but he knew he was kidding himself. The quotes in the article were all things he had said, and some phrases he recognised must have been lifted straight from the tape. Although somehow Liz had managed to soften and alter the way that they were originally meant. Nick sighed and ran his fingers through his hair, wondering what the hell there was that he could do about it.

The first thing that occurred to him was to look for some way to set things right and make amends. Apologise, own up. But make amends to whom exactly? The milk was already well and truly spilt, wasn't it? There was no going back now, oh no.

The voice sounded uncannily like his ex-wife's – Nick could never see anyone else's point of view. Insensitive, that was what she had said he was. Insensitive.

Nick could feel a large gristly lump of guilt lodged somewhere high up in his throat, though given a little time he knew the acute sensation would fade. Maybe it would be a better idea to forget the whole episode and chalk it up to folly?

He shifted his focus back to the evidence; the review section of the *Sunday News*. Jack Sandfi's expression in the photographs appeared to be one of haughty disinterest. Nick sighed. And what the hell did all this matter in the great scheme of things? One insignificant article, tucked away in the review pages of a national newspaper hardly constituted the Hitler diaries. No one would ever really know what had happened at the Flag. And perhaps more to the point, who really cared?

Jack Sandfi? Nick doubted very much that the sculptor would be able to remember anything about the long noisy drinking session he'd had in the hotel lobby. Besides, Jack Sandfi was famous, probably used to being mis-represented and mis-quoted; probably happened to him all the time.

And the *Sunday News*? One newspaper's inability to recognise a flagrant lie would hardly constitute an earth-shattering revelation to anybody, and there was a part of him that truly believed neither Sandfi nor the newspaper really deserved any kind of apology. About then, just as Nick had almost convinced himself that this really was a case of least said soonest mended, the ruminations came full circle and settled on Liz Chapman, which was more or less exactly where they had started an hour earlier when he arrived back from the newsagents.

Liz Chapman; the name seemed to roll very easily off his tongue. With hardly any effort at all Nick could imagine her sitting next to him, smiling, leaning forward to catch tight hold of what he was saying and record it for posterity.

Shit. The guilt shifted again, scratching its way down into his gullet. That was where any amends really ought to be made. It didn't matter how much Nick tried to sweeten the pill, he had lied to Liz Chapman and managed against the odds to take her in completely. And said like that, straight out loud, just those bold bare-faced facts, it sounded incredibly cold blooded and spiteful rather than the act of philanthropy that it had seemed at the time. However stupid it seemed now, Nick knew that he had been trying to spare Liz, not hurt her – Christ, he had lied with all the best of intentions – where the bonfire burnt all the brighter.

He and Liz hadn't spent that much time together, but once they had moved away from sculpture and the exhibition she had been amazingly easy to be with. She had seemed genuinely interested in him. No, not him, Nick reminded himself ruefully, Sandfi, Jack Sandfi, that rude drunken bastard – that was who Liz Chapman thought she was talking to, though there had been moments when Nick had almost forgotten that he was supposed to be someone else.

He winced and struggled to bring his mind back to the newsprint, but the mental images of Liz Chapman sitting in the Flag Hotel refused to fade. Far from it, Liz was laughing now, long fingers wrapped around a coffee cup, long legs tucked under her chair, watching his face. Shit, shit shit.

What Nick really wanted was the opportunity to start all over again, and as that was impossible he would try for the next best thing – find some way to reach across the void and make things right, although there was nothing that would make it an invisible mend.

Even so, there was a sense of relief now that he had come to the decision to do *something*. A resolution, no matter how painful, had to be better than this awful dragging sense of guilt. Alongside the *Sunday News* was the compliment slip that Liz had sent. Maybe he could talk to her. He picked up the phone.

Although on the other hand, if the story did get out would it scupper Liz Chapman's fledgling career? Ruin her credibility? Even if he told her the truth, what on earth would it do for her confidence? Whichever way Nick looked at it, it was bloody messy.

Nick had read the article in the *Sunday News* so many times that he practically knew it off by heart. He scanned it one more time, phone in hand, line by line. It was really good. The poignant rather reflective tone drew him in. It was beautifully crafted, wonderfully written; Liz Chapman needn't have worried about losing her touch, she'd got a real gift, and somehow, in the little time they spent together, she had managed to catch hold of a lot of things Nick had spent years trying to hide.

In amongst the words he found a sense of desolation that unnerved him. Had he really appeared so terribly lost and needy? Why had she written about him in such an intimate personal way? It was almost as if Liz Chapman had been looking over his shoulder into the bathroom mirror as he faced down all the demons that haunted him. And if he was honest, wasn't that the real reason why he wanted to see Liz again?

Nick closed the magazine and with his eyes shut slipped it back between the pages of the newspaper; a magician hiding a card in the deck, putting Jack Sandfi's face back where it belonged. There was something dark and horribly unnerving about reading your life neatly reduced to a couple of dozen, clean crisp paragraphs, it felt uncomfortably like an obituary.

The dialling tone got tired of waiting and the phone began to buzz like a disgruntled bee.

It made a lot more sense to leave things as they were.

But was there some way they could find something out on the far side of angry? Nick knew that he was interested and attracted enough by Liz Chapman to want to try; which was crazy, just plain crazy.

Before his courage finally failed him, Nick found the dialling tone and tapped in Liz's number. He coughed to clear his throat and relieve the tension in his stomach. Christ, what a mess. What if she wouldn't speak to him? What if she hung up as soon as she heard his voice, or worse still what if she had no idea who he was?

The phone rang once, twice; silently Nick ran through his opening lines. He hoped Liz *did* recognise his voice, because he certainly had no intention of giving a name. So, no name then, just straight in with the introduction:

'Hi, Liz. How are you? I just thought I'd give you a quick call. I read the article in the *Sunday News* this morning and I wondered if we could maybe get together, have lunch or something, and talk about –'

And then he heard the phone being picked up and was just about to speak when a recorded Liz, who sounded as if she was smiling, said, 'Hi there. Whatever it is, can you please leave it after the long tone? Talk to you soon –'

And then, long before Nick really had time to consider the consequences of what he was doing, the tone cut in and he left a message – those first carefully rehearsed words together with his telephone number.

It was done now, no going back, no reverse. He sighed with relief. It was just a case of being patient, and waiting for Liz to call back; she would ring surely? Or maybe she wouldn't, and then he could convince himself that the attraction was fleeting after all, a case of mistaken desire as well as identity; perhaps he ought to ring up and arrange to send her flowers now. Did Interflora do olive branches?

Just as he was starting to feel better and a warm sense of anticlimax began to seep through into his bones, the phone rang. Nick's heart rate went through the sound barrier as he snatched up the receiver. Liz Chapman ringing back, it had to be. God that was quick, maybe it wasn't going to be as hard as he had imagined.

'Hello?' His voice sounded cracked and uneven, but

anything else he planned to say was whipped away by a great gust of female laughter.

'Well, hello yourself. How are you?' said an unfamiliar voice. 'Thanks for your call. I've been meaning to get in touch. I hope you don't mind my calling you on a Sunday, day of rest and all that, but I've got a window in my schedule first thing tomorrow morning, and I wondered if we could possibly get together then? I know it's terribly short notice, but you seemed very keen to come over here and have a look round, although I'll quite understand if you can't make it. Lunch, I thought? Are you free? Would you like to check your diary and get back to me? I'll be in for the rest of the day.'

Nick stared down at the phone. It was most certainly a female voice, but in his present state of mind it took him longer than normal to realise that it wasn't Liz Chapman who was speaking but the furniture designer, Jeanna O'Hanlon.

He sucked in a long patchy breath and then, after a second or two, managed to drag up a reply along with his composure. 'Good morning, Jeanna, how very nice of you to call. Are you feeling better now?'

His tone was a shade or two too bright and had an element of false heartiness, but Nick was certain, by the time he had arranged to meet Jeanna at the workshops and hung up, that she was totally unaware that she had nearly precipitated a coronary.

* * *

No more than half a mile away from Kingsmead Terrace as the crow flies, Liz Chapman was trailing around the Review Gallery behind Claire, feeling leaden and miserable but uncertain quite why.

'So, what do you reckon this one is called, then? Number

76

34?' asked Claire, peering at a tiny printed number stuck to the floor beside a plinth. 'I knew I ought to have brought my glasses.'

They had finally found the Sandfi's. Claire had folded the catalogue back on itself and was running a finger down over columns of text. 'Number 23, 24, 28 – it's got to be in here somewhere. Have you found it?'

Liz shook her head and took a long hard look around.

They had been in the gallery for fifteen maybe twenty minutes. It was housed in part of an old department store, a big bright space with beech-block floors and a few expensive and incredibly healthy looking plants in terribly chic, plain terracotta pots. Everything was laid out over three floors, a mezzanine garden, with a water feature and lots of different half-levels. There were perhaps a dozen other visitors slowly making their way round the exhibits, all of them trapped under the perpetual dawn of designer lighting.

On the floor in the main ground-floor exhibition area was a simple spiralling labyrinth of tumbled river stones that was very very beautiful and had reached out and rung a little bell in Liz's heart; it hadn't been created by Jack Sandfi.

Liz was ready to leave well before they found the Sandfi's.

Number 34, on the first floor, was a sinuous yet contorted wooden form, liquid, elongated, feminine and yet not quite. It could have been a wave or a Flamenco dancer or perhaps a slice through a rising storm wind.

Set under very soft downlighters with gold filters, the grain of the different woods had been planed and sanded and polished until it looked as smooth and as inviting as spun silk. The shine seemed to go right through to the very heart of the wood and the whole thing cried out to be stroked; a flat palm run from one end to the other in a long slow unbroken gesture of approval.

Liz shoved her hands deep down into her jacket pockets, fighting the temptation. To touch it might suggest that she had forgiven Jack Sandfi.

Beside her, Claire pulled a face. 'Okay, just take a long hard look at that and tell me, in your honest opinion does it look like "Bardswell Bay One" to you? That can't be right, can it? What do you think?'

Artfully the lighting managed to imply that the sculptures were sunlit. Number 34 was the largest of the pieces in the group, which were all arranged around a great curving alcove. Similar pieces, subtle echoes of Number 34, were set in different planes, some standing horizontally, some apparently crouched in waiting on rough-hewn black stone plinths. It was all very slick and very lovely and damagingly tasteful.

Yet inspite of that Liz could feel no sense of the journey that had brought the artist this way. There was no echo of the history, no depth, no sense of the inner progressions and explorations that had brought Sandfi to this creative place. Instead they gave off an air of being exquisitely manufactured. They were very graceful but completely soulless – beautiful but without any sort of emotional challenge. She wondered if she had just discovered the truth about Jack Sandfi.

Momentarily off guard, without thinking, Liz reached out to see if she could feel some part of Sandfi still caught inside them. As her fingertips brushed a shoulder, or perhaps it was a rising crest, or a tumbling breath she was shocked by how cold and dead they felt – so wonderfully smooth and yet completely and utterly empty.

Liz snatched her hand away as if the sculpture had burnt her, and fixed her attention back on the catalogue instead, aware that something inside her was hurting hard and deeply disappointed. Claire had lost interest and was already moving on to the next piece.

'They do just cry out to be touched, don't they?' murmured a middle-aged woman standing a little to their left. Liz looked around to check that the woman was speaking to her.

The woman smiled. She was quite portly, dressed from head to foot in expensively crumpled taupe linen and had a slight American burr overlaying a cultured accent. Liz had already noticed her once or twice out of the corner of her eye. The woman, who was also holding a catalogue but closed and in a far more casual way than Claire, had extremely shiny blonde hair cut into a severe jaw-length bob, buck teeth, and was wearing very red lipstick.

'Please, go ahead, help yourself, don't mind me,' she said.

Liz looked at her in surprise.

The woman appeared to lift a hand in invitation and then curled it around, as if drawing in the whole collection. 'Glorious isn't it? We've been very pleased by the response that Jack's new work has generated. Several major pieces have been sold already. The one you were admiring is reserved. When the exhibition transfers to London I'm certain we'll be looking at a total sell-out.'

Liz couldn't have phrased it better herself. From close by she heard Claire's stomach rumbling. Another time Liz would have wanted to know who the woman was, what she did and how she knew Jack so well, but today her curiosity was comatose. She couldn't have cared less.

'It's all very nice. But I'm afraid we're in a hurry,' she said, hiding the lingering sense of disappointment behind a smile. 'Thank you.' And slipping her arm through Claire's guided her back out into the daylight. Claire did nothing to resist. Outside the sunshine looked uncannily like the lighting rack in the gallery.

'Oh, come on. Let me back in. We didn't even get to see

the bronzes,' teased Claire as they hit the main street blinking like torched rabbits.

Liz snorted. 'Or the matching table mats, mugs or the toning throw rugs. I'm absolutely famished. There's a really good vegetarian place up here on the left somewhere although I'm not sure that they're open on a Sunday. Worth a look though. I think it's just round the back of that church.'

'Can I gather from that, that you didn't think very much of our Mr Sandfi's little show, then?' said Claire, lifting an eyebrow to emphasise the question.

Liz was about to reply when she caught a whiff of something wonderfully hot and spicy and very oniony on the wind.

'Do you really want me to tell you, or shall we just cut our losses and have a decent lunch?'

'All a bit too oily, wasn't it? Slick, clever and completely and utterly heartless.'

Liz laughed without much humour. 'Not unlike the man himself, I thought.'

*   *   *

'Well,' said Arturo, popping the ring-pull on another can of Pilsner. 'It seems to me that you made quite an impression on this Ms Chapman.' He took a long hard look at Jack before scanning the review section of the *Sunday News* one more time. 'What was she like, exactly?'

Arturo and Jack Sandfi were sitting side by side on the sofa of a battered red moquette three-piece that took up an awful lot of the summer house, feet resting on upturned milk crates. From where they were sitting, now that the double doors were fully open, the two men could see into the courtyard of the stable block that Jack had had converted to studios and across to the main house. Jack considered the sofa a place of great strategic importance.

The low run of outbuildings were built from a mongrel mix of local carstone and old red hand-made bricks. In one corner a great phalanx of Russian vine coursed up over the pantiled roofs from very meagre beginnings amongst a sea of yellow, orange and scarlet nasturtiums. Nature had seemed very rowdy until Jack had had the first couple of cans of lager and caught up with it.

From amongst the froth and roar of the greenery, still alight with a corona of sunshine, the blonde girl – now stripped down to a turquoise blue bikini top, khaki shorts and combat boots – was crouched amongst the component parts of an enormous metal sculpture. For one so small she seemed to be making a tremendous amount of noise.

Both men were studiously trying to ignore her but despite their best efforts their attention was drawn again and again to the sound of the hammer falling and the sight of her pert breasts struggling to escape from captivity.

'Very impassioned stuff all this you know, the unrequited lust fairly sings out at the reader,' said Arturo, tapping the magazine pages.

Jack grunted and then turned away from the sweating blonde artisan and grinned. 'Do you really think so?'

Arturo nodded sagely. 'Oh yes, most definitely. So, aren't you going to tell me what she was like then, this Liz Chapman. Freelance, I presume? The name still doesn't ring any bells with me. You'll have to fill me in on all the sordid details.'

Jack, who still had no recollection whatsoever of his encounter with Ms Chapman, looked down, avoiding his agent's inquisitive eyes by wiping away a tidemark of foam that clung to the stubble on his chin.

'Oh come on, Jack,' protested Arturo, 'don't hold back; we're friends, aren't we? There's really no need to be so coy, you old dog. No wonder the lovely Morwenna is so bloody angry with you this morning.' Arturo paused as a few ideas shuffled themselves into a thinkable sequence. 'I suppose this little spat means that Sunday lunch is out the window.'

Jack burped, rolled over onto his side and then giggled. 'Quite possibly in a very literal sense, dear boy. But anyway so what, so fucking what? All this has given the bloody woman something to think about. To her I'm just plain old Jack, day in day out Jack, doormat Jack, same old face, same old habits. You know what they say about familiarity, don't you? Well trust me it's true, every bloody word of it. It seems to me that you've either got that little magic something or you haven't. It doesn't do women any harm at all to be reminded once in a while that they aren't the only ones with an eye for, an eye for . . .' Jack had hesitated an instant too long over the idea and felt the thread slip through his fingers to be lost amongst a thousand others.

Arturo was leaning forward waiting to catch his latest gem of wisdom.

Jack hiccuped and waved him away. 'Anyway, whatever. It isn't important. How about if we take a slow stroll down to the Old Grey Hound for a quick pint before lunch?'

Arturo blinked. 'Excellent idea. Lunch is definitely still on then?'

Jack nodded. He got up, and retrieving his jacket from the back of the nearest chair, stepped fearlessly out into the sunlight.

Arturo clambered a little unsteadily to his feet and pointed towards the stableyard. 'Shall we invite the little blonde one to join us for a swift half? She looks like she could do with one.'

Jack glanced back towards the main house. Across the lawn, crouched amongst the tangle of shrubs and horse chestnuts and copper beech the old rectory eyed him thoughtfully like a feral cat concealed amongst long grass.

It felt uncomfortably like he was being stalked. Jack shivered.

'No, I don't think so, we'll bring her something back – crisps or nuts or something – and besides she already told us that she was busy,' Jack said, patting his pockets and tidying himself in an effort to exorcise the red-headed ghost that perpetually haunted him.

Chapter Seven

'I wondered whether the article in the *Sunday News* might bring Jack Sandfi back out of the woodwork,' said Liz to no one in particular, as Nick Hastings' message came to an abrupt end on her answer machine. His message was followed, a few seconds later, by one from her ex-husband, Mike. By contrast Mike sounded off-hand and annoyed. Something had come up and he wouldn't be able to bring Joe and Tom home until late evening. But there was no need to worry, no problem.

It was mid-afternoon on Sunday, and after an enormous lunch and the drive back from Norwich it was very tempting to just curl up on the sofa in front of a video and go to sleep. Neither Claire, Liz, nor Winston, who had sashayed in through the cat flap as soon as they arrived back at Balmoral Terrace, planned to fight the temptation for very long.

'So, are you going to ring him back, then?' asked Claire, prising open the biscuit tin while Liz made them both a pot of tea.

'Mike? No, there's no point.' Liz picked up the tea tray and then nodded towards the sitting room. 'So what are we going to watch then? There's a thriller I recorded last week or we could go for a trip down memory lane, and watch something in black and white from the pen of Daphne du Maurier.'

Claire stared at her and after a second or two Liz's impassive expression melted a little, and she shook her head.

'All right, I do know that you meant Jack Sandfi. But what can I say to him? Two can play at whatever game it was he's playing? That I can lie really well too? I don't think I ought to ring him back. What would be the point? You said yourself that he was messing me around. You want me to stick my head in the mangler and let him do it again?'

Although it had been good to hear his voice. And he had sounded warm and eager to speak to her, which made Liz remember the way he had leaned across the table towards her, and how for the briefest and most fleeting of seconds she'd wondered if Jack Sandfi was going to kiss her, and then he had refilled her coffee cup and she realised part of her was really disappointed. How come she had forgotten that? And then Jack had grinned and she had been sucked right in by the way the lines wrinkled up around his eyes to emphasise his smile. Oh, Jack Sandfi was very good at what he did.

'Are you serious?' said Claire, breaking unceremoniously into Liz's thoughts. 'Are you trying to tell me now that you *didn't* fancy him?'

Liz snorted indignantly. 'No.' She reddened under the weight of the word. 'And I don't know why you're getting so excited about it, it was you who said that he was a lying bastard. And anyway I didn't say that I fancied him in the first place, did I?' She paused. 'God, I really wish that there was another way of saying that.'

Claire's expression was both amused and expectant.

'Okay,' snapped Liz, setting the tea tray down on the hearth rug. 'So maybe I *did* fancy Jack Sandfi. Maybe I was hoping something else might come of it, maybe he was gorgeous. I shouldn't have to explain it to you of all people, Claire. You know what it's like being on your own. I get so lonely sometimes, trying to be everything for everybody, always doing everything, the boys, the shopping, the bills.

Sorting it all out. I just want something to look forward to sometimes. It isn't that much to ask, surely? And it would be good to have someone to share things with once in a while.'

Claire lifted her eyebrows. 'And you're telling me that you wanted to share things with Jack Sandfi?'

Liz blushed. 'The thought had crossed my mind, somewhere down the line. He seemed so nice. I don't know, my kind of man, a possibility, what can I tell you? It all sounds so ridiculous when you say it out loud. But then there was all that business with the bloody tape recorder, and then the exhibition was so slick and flat and dead. And we both know he was hiding something during the interview. You said yourself that Jack Sandfi has a terrible reputation. He was lying through his eye-teeth, stringing me along. Maybe that's how he gets his kicks. What sort of start would that be to anything?'

Claire snorted. 'Compared to what? The last guy who tried to pick me up offered to show me his gorilla impression, for God's sake. And he was a science graduate. Compared to that, what's a little white lie or two? At the very least we know the man's a dab hand with an industrial sander. That wood in Norwich looked wonderful. I wonder if he'd do my dining table?' Claire paused for a few seconds, waiting to see if Liz would laugh and when she didn't continued, 'You really ought to ring him. He sounded nice. Maybe he was just having a rough day when you interviewed him. Do you want me to ring him for you?'

'No!' Liz snapped defensively.

Claire, smiling still, backed off, palms held up in surrender. She paused for a moment. 'Okay. One thing though, I keep meaning to tell you. Mike asked me out for a drink when I saw him in town last week.'

Liz looked up in complete surprise. 'Mike? My ex-Mike?

Are you serious? What did you say? Did you go out with him?'

Claire shook her head and then settled down on the floor by the fireplace, on the rug, with her back resting up against the sofa. She arranged Winston on her lap and set about unpicking a new packet of chocolate digestives. It seemed like an eternity before she spoke again.

'No, I just smiled and then made a joke out of it – all very noncommittal, you know. Jokey but in a nice way, not a put-down. I wanted to know how you felt first, before I did anything.'

'Anything?' Liz stared at Claire, trying to marshal her thoughts. 'And are you saying that this has got something to do with me ringing Jack Sandfi back?'

Claire shrugged. 'Maybe. Maybe not. Something and nothing. Oh, I don't know. I just wanted to know how you felt, that's all.'

Liz nodded. 'Okay. So what you're saying is that Mike asked you out?'

'Oh come on, Liz,' Claire bristled, 'don't make it sound like I'm Quasimodo or something. I am entitled to a social life too you know.'

Liz waved the remark away. 'That isn't what I meant at all and you know it. It just seems really weird. Mike and you? Why?' The words were out before she thought about how they might hurt, and she instantly regretted them.

Claire beaded her, a glittering flash of something raw and unguarded and wounded passing across her face. 'You're not the only one who gets lonely. And Tim *died* –' She paused and slipped half a broken biscuit into her mouth; a diversionary tactic if there ever was one. 'They don't pop back to aggravate you and take the kids out for the weekend once they've been cremated, you know,' she said through an angry hailstorm of crumbs. 'I've been on my own for twelve years!'

87

Liz felt an unnerving little flare of survivor's guilt, that and a there-but-for-the-grace-of-god feel, and a how-dare-she. And all those intense, outrageous feelings that walk hand in hand with death and life and love and friendship.

'I know, I'm sorry. You know that I'm not trying to be spiteful. It just seems a bit odd, that's all. What I meant to say is, are you telling me that you fancy Mike?'

It was Claire's turn to redden a little. 'No, not really; what I'm trying to say is that I didn't actively fancy Mike until he asked me out, if that makes any kind of sense. You put things like that on hold, don't you? Your best friend's husband is strictly out of bounds, unless you're a complete bitch. Up until recently he felt as if he was technically yours, but yes, okay, maybe I do fancy him – a little bit. I sort of weighed it up when he asked me and thought, yes, maybe I would like to.'

Liz grinned. 'Well, in that case go for it, just don't let him try and convince you he can do impressions of anything.' She paused for a few seconds, the implications beginning to sink in like cold water. 'And don't let him mangle you up, Claire, please, he's always been really good at that.' Liz felt a peculiar surge of raw emotion that took her completely unawares and did something odd to her voice.

Claire looked up in surprise. 'I don't have to go out with Mike, you know – and it was only for a drink. Shit, I wish I hadn't said anything about it now.'

Liz was stunned to find she had tears in her eyes. 'Don't mind me,' she said and waved Claire's concern away. 'So what shall we watch?'

'*Aliens*?'

'Sigourney Weaver and the gorgeous Hicks?'

Claire nodded. 'I think so.'

'Right-o, you pour the tea. I'll put the tape in. Oh, and don't think just because you're going to date my ex-husband that you get to eat all my biscuits as well.'

Claire, mouth still full of digestives, giggled, spraying crumbs everywhere. 'Who me? God, I wouldn't dream of it. So, tell me, are you going to ring Jack Sandfi back now or not?'

On her lap Winston lifted an eyebrow. He wasn't keen on playing with his food unless it had fur and could give you a run for your money.

*   *   *

Meanwhile, over at the Old Rectory, Jack, Arturo, and the handful of students who were staying there for the summer, filed into the kitchen and sat down around the long refectory table. The news that Sunday lunch was finally ready had spread by bush telegraph out from the house, down through the studio as far as the public bar of the Old Grey Hound in the village. Everyone was hungry.

It was well after three o'clock and the babble of conversation that had accompanied everyone's arrival rapidly dried to a tense expectant silence.

While Lily Howard drained the vegetables and then handed out plates, Morwenna held court by the range, hunched over, with her back towards the table as she carved the joint. The whine of the electric carving knife fighting its way through the meat silenced the last peals of nervous laughter.

Arranged down the centre of the table were two large glass jugs full of ice cold water, with tumblers stacked alongside. While the table itself was immaculately set with cruets and matching cutlery, napkins and side plates, the rest of the kitchen looked as if it had been burgled. But no one said a thing, apparently completely oblivious to the fact that the flagstone floor was strewn with broken crockery, cutlery, shards of glass and a fortune in small change.

Finally, Morwenna turned and with some difficulty carried an oval meat dish over to the table. She had a cigarette clenched tight between her teeth. As she set the charger down, the silence of the diners intensified.

A whole joint of what appeared to be pork had been carved into great uneven ragged slices. The outside ones were carbonised to shiny charcoal, seared black, flesh curling away from the glistening white fat, while most of the inside still appeared to be frozen solid. Between the two extremes lay a charnel house. Here and there the electric carving knife had caught the bone and peeled back fingernail-sized chips of translucent white membrane to reveal the moist baby-pink marrow beneath.

In the tureens that Lily Howard now arranged around the meat dish were leathery roast potatoes, boiled white cabbage, soft pale carrots, a great pitcher of gravy and a large dish of black saucer-shaped objects that Jack guessed were probably once Yorkshire puddings.

Arturo, eager to break the terrible stranglehold of silence that had engulfed the diners, said, with a ghastly false cheeriness, 'Well, my dear Morwenna, this looks really wonderful. I don't know about everyone else but I'm absolutely famished.' As he spoke he leant over and speared a great sliver of raw pork.

It was a very gallant effort.

Morwenna lifted one perfectly plucked eyebrow. It was as if Arturo hadn't spoken.

'If you will excuse me,' she said in a murderous undertone. 'I think I can feel a migraine coming on. Please, *do* help yourself, won't you? I've asked Lily to serve. Bon appetit.' She turned and headed at a funereal pace towards the hall.

The silence lingered for a few moments after the kitchen door finally closed, until everyone was quite certain that Morwenna had actually left and then by some unspoken signal the assembled company let out a collective sigh of relief.

One of the oriental students was the first to speak. 'Perhaps if we could just put the meat back into the oven for a little bit longer?' she suggested tentatively in a reedy voice. It was the most anyone had heard her say since she'd arrived at the rectory.

But the blonde Australian was already on her feet, expression mutinous. 'Jesus - H - Christ. What the fuck are we supposed to do with that, bury it? I sure as hell ain't going to eat it. It's supposed to be all inclusive, Jack, that's the deal – three squares a day plus a vegetarian alternative. That's what it says in that smart little brochure you peddle. Basic but wholesome – that's what I paid for.' All eyes turned towards Jack.

The corpse on the oval platter had started to ooze blood now, its vulnerability and raw nakedness emphasised by the delicate trail of cigarette ash that lay along one long crisp blackened flank.

Jack could feel the gorge rising along with the lager in his stomach.

'Pizza,' he said after a second or two of mental callisthenics. 'We'll all go back to the studio and you can ring out for pizzas.'

The diners got to their feet as a single body.

Now only Lily Howard stood between them and freedom, defiant, hands on hips, a slotted spoon clenched in one meaty fist.

Jack smiled benignly. 'Kids these days, eh?' he said, with as much bon homie as he could muster, 'they're all the same, they just don't know what's good for them. Anyway, you take as much as you like home for the family, Lily, as much as you like.'

An hour later Jack and the others sat around on the three-piece in the summer house eating sandwiches and crisps washed down with the cans of diet Coke that Arturo had brought back from the garage. Bob's Big Bonanza Pizzeria was, apparently, closed all day on Sundays.

While they were at the garage the oriental student had bought several copies of the *Sunday News* and shyly asked Jack if he would mind autographing them so that she could send them home for her family. He was only too happy to oblige.

'This woman, she thinks you are very good, a very special man,' said the girl cheerfully.

Jack smiled and nodded, pen busy. The way she looked up at him from under those long dark lashes, ivory skin blushing delicately, made him feel warm and strong, a real hero. He really ought to find out what Liz Chapman was like. It was such a terrible shame he couldn't remember her. But then again how hard could it be to find a reporter?

* * *

By the time Mike arrived back at Liz's house it was nearly ten o'clock. Claire was long gone and the boys, Joe and Tom, bumbled straight up to bed, noisy but exhausted, leaving a trail of discarded clothes, trainers and bags in their wake.

'You can shower in the morning –' she called to their retreating backs.

As Liz tidied up behind them she got a real sense of comfort from the sound of their voices and their presence, it made the house feel whole and alive in a way that nothing else did.

'Sorry about being so late back,' said Mike, without a shred of sincerity. He and Liz met up in the kitchen. 'Bit of a problem, but nothing for you to worry about. I don't suppose anyone rang here for me, did they?'

'No, should they have?' Liz said with surprise, 'surely they wouldn't ring here unless you've given someone the phone number. Have you?'

'Have I what?'

'Given someone my phone number.'

Mike looked at her as if she was losing her mind.

'What's so tricky about that? Have you given someone my phone number or not?'

He shrugged, dismissing her anxiety.

Liz took a deep breath.

While she'd been upstairs quietening the boys down, Mike had settled himself in the kitchen in front of the portable TV and was rocking back on one of the chairs. It disturbed her that when he was in the house he hung around, making himself at home, as if he still held some unspent currency in her life. At a baser level, way below the strained outward pretence of civility and decency, Liz knew that Mike deeply resented paying for the upkeep of something that he didn't have the use of.

She pushed the linen basket under the washing machine and started to load the boys' dirty clothes into it. Who had he given her number to?

'I've put the kettle on,' Mike said, speaking to her over his shoulder without bothering to turn. 'And I got the kids burger and fries on the way home. It was a really great weekend. We went over to that new go-kart place near Norwich, and then we went swimming –' He paused for a few seconds inviting her to say something and when she didn't, asked, 'So how about you? What did you and Claire get up to while I was busy minding the fort? Something important, was it?'

Mike couldn't quite keep the derision out of the question. He always managed to imply that what he did was far too weighty to be put on hold for his family. Since they had separated, everything about the way Mike behaved suggested he only had the boys at weekends as a personal favour to Liz, rather than as a way of continuing his relationship as their father.

Liz handed him a mug of coffee, knowing he preferred tea. There were so many things she could've said to Mike but she knew it made more sense to wait until all the other simpler things had been said and he began to relax, letting his guard down.

It was the same game they had played for most of their married life and even now, out on the far side, she knew that nothing of any significance had really changed between them.

No conversation was ever exactly what it appeared. Every word, every phrase was emotionally weighted or set about with some historical precedent. It was always best to move slowly. Dotted across their landscape were a whole host of places where, over the years, Liz had found it increasingly hard to work out whether what she thought or felt was right or wrong, true or false, up or down. And out on the tidal reaches were all kinds of apparently stagnant pools and backwaters that concealed trick tides and sink holes that could easily trap the unwary.

'I saw that thing you wrote about the artist guy in the *Sunday News*. It was good, very good; looks like you haven't lost your touch,' Mike said, stirring sugar into his coffee. There was a tiny heavyweight pause into which the whole of creation could have dropped unnoticed. 'So, how well do you know him then, this Sandfi bloke?'

Liz winced. Even now, even though they were divorced, the dog was still crouched growling in the manger.

'You make me sick; what exactly has it got to do with you?'

He pulled his face into something that was part smile, part sneer. 'Touchy subject?'

'I don't know him at all, Mike. The newspapers set the

94

interviews up with his agent. Claire was going to do it but she couldn't, so she asked me to do it as a favour.' Liz struggled to keep a rein on her emotions.

Mike sniffed. 'Right. So how many times have you met him since you did the interview?'

Liz felt a red hot flare of fury. She was so very tired of walking over the minefields of Mike's innuendo and suspicion. 'Why do you do this to me? Your bloody paranoia drove me crazy for years. Just go home, will you? I don't have to listen to the dark side of your mind working overtime anymore.'

Mike didn't move, instead he stared at her, expression blank.

Liz felt her pulse rising. 'You were the one with the string of bloody women, Mike. So, no, I haven't slept with Jack if that's what you're trying to insinuate.'

Mike lifted his hands up in surrender, his face a mask of outraged innocence. 'Did I say that, Liz? Tell me, did I say that? I just wondered where you'd met him, that's all. It sounds like the two of you got on really well together, and I'm glad. Truly.'

Liz glared across the table. 'But that *is* what you meant, isn't it?'

Mike made a dismissive noise, blowing air through slack lips as if she had just proved his point. 'But that isn't what I said, Liz, now is it? I just wondered if you had thought about what you're doing, another relationship, you know, the boys, your situation here –' Before she could find a reply amongst the shards of outrage, he continued, 'So are you planning to go back to writing full time, then? Freelance? It's got to be better paid than that little teaching job you've got now, surely . . .'

Liz snapped the washing machine door shut and closed her eyes. She refused to let him goad her into a fight.

'Only if you were planning to do more of that kind of

thing, maybe it's time we started to rethink the way the financial arrangements are set up. A review –'

Liz tacked on a smile as she looked up, trying very hard not to sound confrontational. 'All of what you give me goes on the boys. I already pay for –'

'Oh, right, here we go again,' Mike snorted, looking heavenwards. 'As if I didn't know. What *you* pay for, what *you* have to do. How much *you* had to put up with. How *you* cope on your own. You seem to forget Liz, that you were the one who decided to leave –' the words snapped back so hard and so fast that they made her flinch. 'I was just pointing out that if you earn more then we will have to re-consider the financial position. That's hardly unreasonable, is it?'

For a few seconds the air in the kitchen crackled like the charged stillness that precedes a lightning strike.

Liz sucked in a breath, struggling with the temptation to point out again all the reasons why she had left Mike and how many years she stayed on, desperately trying to make what they had into something good, even though every molecule of her body longed to be free of him.

Mike couldn't see it then, God alone knows, he certainly wouldn't be able to see it now. To be truly free of him she would have to let it all go and move on and, even now, Liz knew she hadn't quite shaken him off.

'Please, I don't want to start this – not tonight. Maybe you're right, maybe we should look at the finances . . .' she said in her most neutral tone.

'Oh, I know that I'm right,' Mike said and picked up his coffee mug as if to establish a sense of residency.

Liz was very careful not to catch his gaze. The anger she felt towards him was old and cold and fierce and covered in barnacles and seaweed. It was a leviathan that perhaps was better left undisturbed. Liz had no intention of hitting the ball back. Before the divorce their rows had been long and hard and ripped right down to her soul. Sometimes she had thought that the venom and the anger would kill her.

Face to face with Mike the scars of betrayal and fury and vulnerability still ached. Because of the boys. They had kept up a pretence of normality and argued at night, when they were in bed, in strained suppressed voices on the edge of hysteria.

Mike sipped his coffee. Liz felt something tighten in her gut. It was high time Mike went. She could see that he had settled a little and angrily watched the tension ease out of his shoulders.

It seemed almost a shame to begin again, but there was something she really needed to know.

'Claire told me that you asked her out.' The tone was as casual, as neutral as Liz could make it.

Mike smiled lazily. 'And what exactly has that got to do with you, Liz? Eh? I've always thought that Claire was a good looking woman. And I've always had a bit of soft spot for her, you must have known that. So what is it? Afraid we'll talk about you behind your back?' He pulled a face meant to infer that he was incredulous.

'I thought you were going out with a girl from the pub?'

Mike shrugged. 'I was, but she was just a kid, really. No depth. And things got a bit tricky there, you know how these things go.' To Liz's surprise Mike sounded defensive and dismissive and ill at ease but it didn't last. 'It was no more than a casual fling really, wild oats. Nothing serious. Why? You're not jealous of Claire, are you?'

Liz felt a great flare of frustration lifting in her belly, and at the same time, to her complete fury, tears prickled up behind her eyes. 'Couldn't you have picked on someone else? I wouldn't have thought Claire was your type at all,' she said, holding onto the rush of emotion so that the words sounded clipped and icy.

Mike's smile didn't falter. 'And what exactly is my type, Liz?'

'She's older than I am.' Liz winced. That wasn't what she meant to say at all. The words were coming out all wrong.

Mike pulled a face. 'Ouch. What's this then? Not the little green eyed monster, is it? I'm really surprised at you, Liz, or is it that you've finally realised what you're missing? This Sandfi bloke not up to scratch, or did he turn you down?'

He spoke with such venom that Liz shook her head in disbelief.

'Don't be ridiculous, Mike, this has got nothing to do with Jack Sandfi. I care about what happens to Claire, she's my best friend. She has had a really rough time, losing Tim and everything, bringing the kids up on her own. She deserves someone really special.'

Mike's urbane mask finally slipped. 'Oh right, and I'm not special enough, is that what you're saying?'

Liz could feel the quick sand sucking around her feet.

'It's time that you went home,' she said unsteadily, immeasurably relieved that she would never have to climb the stairs or share a bed with Mike again.

Chapter Eight

All night long Liz dreamt that she was being chased by something nameless and grumpy, something big and dark that disapproved of her bright shiny new life and was very keen to snatch back all the things she had become. It wasn't quite frightening enough to wake Liz up, and so instead of being dragged back to consciousness, shaking, wide awake and drenched in a cold sweat, she ran and ran, on through the dark night, hunted, dodging back and forth, desperately trying to find some way to shake off her tormentor.

And then, just as Liz was beginning to panic, Jack Sandfi appeared from behind a convenient bush. It would have been nice to think he had come to rescue her, but some cynical part of her subconscious couldn't quite keep a straight face long enough to accept the fairy tale. So, instead of sweeping her up onto his white charger, Jack invited her to join him for lunch at the Flag instead. Between courses Jack announced that he was planning to elope with Claire. He hoped that she didn't mind, although she must have realised that Jack had always had a soft spot for her.

Liz was delighted when the alarm went off, even though she woke up feeling almost as tired as when she went to bed.

Seven o'clock Monday morning, and with the prospect of getting ready for work, feeding Winston, finding the boys' school uniform, walking Joe to school and then catching the train to work, a sense of normality slowly began to return. It was a relief.

Just over two hours later Liz Chapman pushed open the door of her classroom. She always had a strong sense of the small room being an extension of her personal space, although at the moment it smelt stale and biscuity, after being closed up for the weekend.

Pinned to the display boards that lined the classroom were pages from magazines and bright collages of the class's collective British experience. Fast food menus, a lot of blue stripe food labels, bus tickets, programmes from theatre visits and heritage days and catalogues from museum trips. It gave an odd magpie snapshot of British life.

Although it was shirtsleeve weather outside, someone in maintenance and material resources seemed to think that being foreign the students needed the heating full on. It was hot. The students all had a slightly glossy florid appearance.

'Good morning, everyone,' Liz said as she set the text-books down on the front desk.

'Good morning, Mees Chapman,' they warbled back.

Three mornings and one evening a week, Liz Chapman took the train into Bishopston to teach English as a foreign language, EFL, at the local tech'.

For all non-British nationals, EFL was compulsory, expensive and taught by a group of well-educated, articulate non-graduates who had taken the college's own in-house course, Liz amongst them.

She indicated the windows and spoke in a gentle teasing tone. 'Who would like some fresh air? Isn't anyone else too hot?'

Two of the boys at the back grinned and shuffled to their feet as comprehension dawned.

'Very good.' She turned to address the rest of the class. 'Okay, so, what are they doing?'

A girl in the first row giggled and then screwed up her nose to help shepherd the words out. 'They are doing the windows.'

'Opening,' said one of the boys. 'Not doing. It is too hot, we need more air.'

Liz nodded. 'That's very good.' She turned back to the girl. 'Opening the windows.' Sometimes she felt like a parrot denied any of the bright plumage.

The girl repeated the phrase.

The job at the college fitted in with Joe and Tom, and was reasonably well paid. The EFL department encouraged everyone to teach at least one evening a week so that the college faculty could offer evening classes for the local non-English speaking population after they had finished work.

The college was busily seeking university status, so it was important to be seen as multi-cultural, socially aware and reaching out to embrace the wider community and address their on-going educational needs. It said so in the college prospectus.

'I thought we would look at travel. It will soon be the summer holidays. I'm sure a lot of you have trips planned.' There was a murmur of assent.

'I am going home,' said one of the older boys.

The pupils – mostly mature students from eastern Europe, Asia and some of the poorer regions of the Mediterranean – were polite and well behaved, certainly a very different kettle of fish from the student body over on the main campus.

Liz found the section she wanted and flattened the pages down with her palm.

'Okay, so who would like to tell me about what they've got planned for the summer. If you'd like to open your books we'll be using pages 65 and 66.'

Tuesdays and Wednesday mornings were more earnest,

broken down into tutorials with individual students or very small groups who were taking the same course.

Liz unbuttoned her jacket and, while one of the girls in the second row struggled through a very convoluted account of her planned journey home, reconsidered the wisdom of opening the windows. The mobile appeared to be on a direct flight path from the canteen and the air always seemed to smell of pies, cabbage and frying. Today there was a distinct whiff of bolognaise sauce in the wind.

The travelogue came to an end.

'That was very good. Now we're going to take a look at some of the words and phrases we might need if we are staying and travelling in Britain for the summer. You might like to take notes.'

Liz glanced around and then handed the board rubber to one of the lean young engineers in the front row. Still sitting he snapped stiffly to attention, grinning with delight at having been chosen.

'And how are you today, Mees Chapman?'

Liz nodded an acknowledgement. 'I'm very well. How about you?'

His smile widened to reveal a great henge of pearly teeth. 'I em very hunky-dory.' Everyone tittered at his bravado. Liz's smile broadened with genuine amusement; she certainly didn't intend to correct him.

'Wonderful. Please will you wipe the board for me?'

Whilst he wiped one of the girls on the front row held up her hand. As soon as she had caught Liz's eye she got to her feet and began to speak, 'I see you. Yesterday, I see you.'

Liz nodded her encouragement. 'I saw you, I saw you yesterday,' she corrected and then continued in surprise, 'You saw me? Where did you see me?'

The girl smiled. 'Oh yes. I see you in, in . . .' she pulled a face, apparently hoping that the wild facial contortions might help give birth to the missing word.

Beside her, another of the young men offered, 'She sees you down in the town, in the pub. She is always in the pub. She sees many things.' There was a hoot of good tempered laughter. The girl smacked her accuser in a mildly flirtatious way and then dived into her handbag. 'No, it was not in the pub. Look, I saw you, here. This is you, Mees Liz Chapman?'

The girl was unfolding a very dog-eared copy of the *Sunday News* review pages.

'I have seen this men's work at Norwich. Our design teacher, Mr Jones, he took us on the coach last week. I buyed many postcards. You have met this very famous man Jack Sandfi? Mees Chapman? He is very handsome, yes? You must be a very good writer.'

Liz felt a little glow of something pleasant; she certainly wasn't going to disabuse the girl of her notion that Jack Sandfi was a great man. She gave them a moment or two to let the ideas and words sink in.

'Me – I em a very great writer too,' said the young engineer who had just finished cleaning the board. He posed manfully, turning his huge soulful brown eyes on Liz and then the class generally. 'Many many love poems I have written. My love it is very passionate, very wild. Animal.' He turned his attention back to Liz. 'So how do you get them into book? I would very much like to know how to do this.'

Liz hid her amusement and looked away from his glorious undisguised, unfocused lust and tapped the textbook in front of her. 'Today, I had planned to start with buying a train ticket, but maybe we can talk about writing at the end of the session if there is any time left, okay?'

*   *   *

Out in the studio, behind the Rectory, the telephone rang once, twice, although Jack Sandfi made no attempt to answer it. He was nicely settled on a battered chaise longue, arms folded behind his head, eyes closed, feet up, a news-paper spread over his face to cut out the excess light. He certainly had no intention of moving.

'It's for you,' said a voice from somewhere above him. It was the blonde girl, he would have recognised that anti-podean twang anywhere. She was standing so close that Jack could smell the not unattractive odour of her per-spiration.

No one answered her. 'I said it's for you. Get up, y'lazy bastard.'

Something rattled furiously at his paper teepee.

Jack grunted. 'What, me? For me, are you sure? Who is it?'

'Oh for Christ's sake, get up. It's some bloke, sounds like that mate of yours, Arturo,' snapped the blonde girl.

Jack sighed and then extended a hand out from under the broadsheet.

'Jack, is that you?' asked a disembodied voice. It echoed unnaturally but that was probably the effect of speaking undercover.

'No, Arturo. It's my bloody answering service. This really had better be good. It's barely lunch time.'

There was the slightest pause at the far end of the line and then Arturo said, 'Please, don't remind me. The vision of our recent repast at the Rectory will be seared on my retina for some time to come. However, on an altogether more promising tack, when I finally got home last night there were several calls on the answer machine about your cheery little kiss-and-tell story in yesterday's papers. We've had a very good offer from *Ciao* magazine –'

'*Ciao*? Do we know them?'

'Oh come on, Jack, even you must have seen it, it's a

magazine. Great big glossy thing. Life styles of the rich and outrageous, royals, rock-stars, footballers, and apparently they are terribly keen to do a feature on you.'

'Really? And where exactly do I fit into this pantheon of worthies?'

Arturo coughed. 'Well, my own personal interpretation is that you are the token bohemian, a little turd of culture floating in an otherwise uninterrupted cesspool of puerile nonsense, but please, don't be influenced by my interpretation. However, if you should choose to sell your soul and a few arty stills of the Rectory fluffed up by a camp stylist called Julian, then Maria Ludlow, *Ciao*'s very own queen bee has promised faithfully to press several thousand guineas into your warm pudgy little fist.'

Up until that instant Jack had pretty well made up his mind to decline, but now he could feel his interest surfacing and heading busily towards full consciousness. 'Several thousand. Did you say several thousand?'

'Indeed, and that isn't the best of it. We also had a phone call from Delia Hargreaves, that pushy little woman over at Anglia.'

'The TV people?'

'The very same. I'm sure that we met her at some function for the rejuvenation of arts in rural East Anglia. I seem to recall it was in a marquee . . .' The air between them went dead and echoey as Arturo hunted around for names, dates and the place. But Jack was eager now to get his agent back on track.

'And?'

Arturo sniffed and dropped whatever thread he had caught hold of. 'And they have said that they'd like to do a feature on you for some regional thing called Art-Around. Wednesday nights apparently. Probably seen it, have you?'

Jack hesitated for a few seconds. 'I'm not altogether certain that we still have a television. But the *Ciao* thing sounds very promising. Several thousand you say? When would we get it exactly?'

'I've got absolutely no idea, post publication presumably. I'm sure that I could find out, if you're certain that you want to sell your soul to mammon.'

Jack laughed, 'Who else would buy it?' As he spoke he rolled out from under the layers of newspaper and very carefully sat up. The first thing that caught Jack's eye was a copy of Liz Chapman's article pinned to the notice board. It seemed he owed Ms Chapman a debt of thanks. He screwed up his eyes to focus more clearly. Some wag had added a little pair of horns and a tail to his photograph. Very droll.

The chaise was by the desk, and the desk under the windowsill, on which the phone was balanced. The desk, a great grey ugly metal affair, was strewn with dirty cups, a battered kettle, cartons of milk, half a bag of damp sugar, newspapers, a sketch book, pen and brushes. It all looked too bright to be sorted through by Jack's aching brain.

The blonde girl was making herself a coffee. He didn't mean to stare but something about her drew his attention, and there his mind settled, in an abstracted unfocused way until she winked at him and wiggled her not insubstantial arse.

Jack winced and looked away. 'And what about these TV people, what do they pay?'

'They don't pay at all, old man, not a bean. But it will raise your profile no end, trust me.'

Jack's interest was a fickle thing and now it was flagging fast. While Arturo carried on speaking Jack re-read the headlines above the *Sunday News* article. They made him sound important and generous. He would really have to find a decent copy for his files. One without graffiti. Arturo was still rambling on about the TV and coverage.

'Fuck the state of my profile, Arturo, I'm far more concerned about the balance of payments at the moment.'

Arturo coughed. 'But they'll be publicising your work, Jack, it will be a great boost for the London exhibition. That's an awful lot of free advertising, and apparently the reporter they've got now is terribly sweet. Who knows what might come of it? Commissions? More interviews; almost anything. You know how these things are.'

'No, Arturo, I don't know how these things are, that is why I pay you your pound of flesh –' Jack paused and then laughed dryly. 'Or not, as the case may be. Now how about this Liz Chapman woman. Have you managed to track her down yet?'

'Should I have?'

Jack straightened his shoulders. 'I've been giving it some thought, and I really feel that I ought to meet her again. Soon. The thing is, in some ways, I feel that she is the first person, certainly the first reporter, who has ever caught the true dichotomy of being at the mercy of one's muse, that inner tension, the man and artist in conflict . . .'

There was a peculiar squeaky little noise at the far end of the line.

'So I'd like you to contact her for me,' continued Jack, undeterred.

'You can't remember whether you shagged her or not can you, Jack?' said Arturo.

Jack paused for an instant so that the flawed old clerk who sorted through the records and filed away the memories could do one last circumnavigation of his brain. 'No,' he said crisply after a second or two. 'No, I can't remember.' He tried very hard to keep the slightly miffed tone out of his voice.

'I'll see what I can do. Meanwhile what do you want me to tell them at *Ciao*?'

'Several thousand?'

'That's what they said.'

'I have always felt that we have a moral obligation – a spiritual crusade even – to bring art to the masses.'

'Couldn't agree with you more. And what about the TV thing?'

'Profile raising? Is it really worth the effort?'

Jack could hear Arturo sucking his teeth. 'I'll see what I can do. They'll make a fuss of you and you know how much you always enjoy that. And the woman at Anglia did say that they might be able to stump up a crate of half decent wine. A good Chablis? Something like that.'

'And what about a nice lunch? So that we can plan, plot, discuss our vision, whatever it is they want to call it.'

'Leave it with me.'

'And you won't forget about Liz Chapman, will you?'

Arturo snorted.

When he put the phone down Jack felt ready for anything. Rejuvenated. Fine, up and rolling, on the case, on the ball. King of the road.

The little blonde handed him a mug of coffee.

'You look like shit,' she said, loping off towards the courtyard.

Jack sniffed.

Outside, caught in a great shaft of summer sunlight her sculpture crouched amongst the nasturtiums like a great malevolent crow. She dropped onto her hands and knees in front of it, in what looked an obscene supplication to some ancient deity.

Chapter Nine

Even in her shiny black high heels Jeanna O'Hanlon barely reached Nick Hastings' shoulders, but in all other ways she was a very big woman and she made him feel extremely nervous. It was late Monday morning and while Liz Chapman was wrestling with the mysteries of EFL Nick and Jeanna were standing in front of the O'Hanlon family furniture workshops, ready for the first part of his guided tour.

Jeanna's jaw length blonde hair hung down in a thick curtain towards her broad padded shoulders. Her business suit, with its narrow grey pinstripe and short tailored skirt, was expensive and beautifully cut. In the neat V formed by the elegant lapels, lay a wisp of silky black lace, nestling against creamy white flesh that suggested all manner of warm, womanly and mysterious things hidden beneath.

It was difficult not to be mesmerised by the gentle, almost tidal, sway of her breasts. Hastily Nick looked away but not before Jeanna had caught his glance and smiled knowingly.

Behind them, in the morning sunshine, ornamental doves strutted across an expanse of carefully manicured lawn. The grass was surrounded by a pea-gravel drive, and around the outside of the square was a whole run of brick-built workshops. Sunlight reflected in the old arched windows. There were hanging baskets, a paved walkway, antique gas lamps and areas set with cobbles. Away to their right was an ornate archway. It was topped off with a wrought iron weather-vane on which was set the hunched silhouette of a carpenter planing timber. The archway, with its heavy timber gates led back into the estate proper.

The day was warm. Virginia creeper softened the crisp geometric line of the courtyard, and from somewhere close by rooks were calling the odds. The whole place was awash with a sense of uncontrived timeless beauty. Nick's chest tightened with the pure joy of it.

'. . . And over here is our specialist storage area, custom built, timber in, timber out. Besides the raw materials for our own needs we sell an awful lot on . . .' Jeanna was saying, as she waved an arm to encompass the great expanses of wood cradled in the racks. The warehouse was rich with the scents of the different woods, pungent resins and the soft all-pervading perfume of turpentine and beeswax. To Nick it smelt like the very shores of heaven.

'Kiln-dried to our own specification,' Jeanna continued, running carmine fingertips over the end grain of what looked like a balk of oak. 'Why don't you slip your jacket off? I really don't mind, you know. You must be absolutely sweltering in this heat.'

Nick had been at the estate for no more than fifteen minutes and already knew that he wanted to work there; the only blot on the landscape was Jeanna O'Hanlon herself.

She moved closer, brushing an imaginary speck of dust off his shoulder. The gesture was uncomfortably intimate and Nick blushed.

'Oh come on, relax, you've already made a good first impression,' Jeanna purred and then smiled as if she had caught him out and turned her attention back to the wood. 'A lot of the pieces we turn out here are still based on my father's and grandfather's original drawings. The refectory table, the three cupboard dresser –'

Jeanna was still standing far too close for comfort. He tried to shift the focus of interest casually onto something else and take the opportunity to move away, but she continued to speak, eyes fixed on his. 'O'Hanlon expertise and our personal service has spread by word-of-mouth over the years, which of course is the best recommendation of all. Last year we panelled and furnished an entire baronial castle for a pop star in Ireland, and personal recommendation means no middle man raking off his percentage. This way –' Finally she moved aside so that he could step into the next workshop.

Inside an elderly man was joining two pieces of timber together with pegs and a mallet. Nick's heart sang as the mallet tapped the wood home. The man nodded to acknowledge their presence, although walking alongside Nick, Jeanna was still speaking.

'When I joined the family firm fourteen years ago I very soon realised that if we were going to carry on for the next hundred years, the whole operation needed radically streamlining. We needed to look at how we trained our work force, develop new designs, and investigate the new technologies available to us. Some of the old guard were initially very resistant to my suggestions but I persuaded most of them by sheer persistence. My approach gets results.'

'And what about those who couldn't be persuaded?' Nick asked, although he had already guessed the answer.

Jeanna smiled. 'Don't worry. I gave them all superb references. Here at O'Hanlons, Nick, you're either with me or against me, there are no half measures. One boss. This is not a democracy, although I do give credit where it's due and am always open to suggestions – but I make the decisions. It was my grandfather's philosophy too. It's one of the few aspects of the company that I've left completely unchanged.' Jeanna was still smiling and, as if to emphasise her dominance, took Nick by the elbow, guiding him away from the carpenter and into the next building. Her fingertips felt hot and invasive but he didn't feel able to resist as she slipped her arm through his.

'I've practically had to drag O'Hanlons into the twentieth century single handed. I was the one who set up the contemporary and manufacturing sections, which, to be frank, is really where I see you coming into your own.' Her tone dropped to an intimate purr. 'I really do need you here, Nick. New blood, someone from the mainstream, from the real world used to responding to the demands of the market place. Someone with a proven track record and new ideas who wants to develop his own voice. Someone to help me steer the ship.' Her grip tightened. 'I think you and I were made for each other. Don't you?'

Nick coughed and attempted an easy nonchalant smile. They were very slowly making their way down through the range of converted outbuildings that had once been a dairy, stables, tack room and barns for the main house. Above them the roof trusses and the complex baskets of timber work were eloquent prayers to the carpenters' and builders' art, and, below the twisted time-stained timbers, like echoes from a grand past, the different woodworking bays were a hive of quiet industry.

There was another elderly man, dressed in a brown linen apron and flat cap – the very epitome of the master carpenter – turning table legs on a lathe, while behind him another grey haired veteran planed timber in a vice with an action as smooth as silk.

Nick would have liked the chance to talk to the two men but Jeanna moved him on relentlessly. Finally they stood in the oldest part of the factory where, Jeanna announced, Sean O'Hanlon, her great-grandfather had first begun to make his world famous tables. Here, amongst the bright curls of wood shavings were the work-worn benches, a treadle lathe, the vices and clamps, and on the back walls in custom-made stands racks of chisels graded by size, oiled, razor sharp ready for use.

The whole place was so lovely, and in a strange way, so familiar that Nick could feel a warm glow rising from somewhere deep inside him. This was as close to perfection as Nick had ever been; it was the workshop of his imagination. The image was so compelling that he was almost oblivious to Jeanna standing there beside him. Hanging around the shop on pegs on the backboard were planes and rasps, hammers, saws, surforms and hand drills, a mitre block, and permeating everything was the same rich perfume of raw timber, mixed with tantalising undertones of wood glue, polish and varnish. It made Nick's mouth water.

On the worn flagstone floor in the old workshop where Jeanna's great-grandfather had plied his trade were ringlets of blond shavings from the hand planes, and a gilding of sawdust over every flat surface. Up in the eaves, the sawdust clung in the cobwebs.

It was in this room here, Nick seemed to remember from an article he had read in the Sunday papers, that two of Jeanna's best men had recreated the exquisite decorative panels from a medieval pulpit of a cathedral lost in a fire. To Nick the old workshop was like Lourdes. Respectfully he touched the top of the bench that was closest to him, feeling as humble as any pilgrim confronted by the sacred relics of his faith. His fingers glided over the wood. It felt warm and worn and ready for him.

Jeanna's voice broke into his thoughts. 'Of course this place is not much more than a living museum these days, we don't manufacture in here. Health and safety would have a real field day – no extractors, no safety equipment, not to mention the fire risk – but it is part of the tour. And it makes the perfect back-drop for advertising material, photo opportunities –'

Nick turned in total surprise. 'The tour?'

Jeanna nodded and then glanced down at her watch. 'Yes, in fact they should be here any minute now. It's part of the strategy to make the estate more cost effective and to put O'Hanlons on the map. Coach tours. We're expecting two-a-day minimum during the summer months. And we've opened up part of the main house as well, added a nice little tea room over in the walled garden, gift shop, herbs. Then of course there is the organic small-holding. Very important that not all O'Hanlons' eggs are in the same basket.'

Nick stared at her in horror.

'So, shall we take your car or mine over to the factory?'

'I'm sorry?' he stuttered.

Jeanna indicated the door. 'The factory?' She smiled indulgently. 'You didn't think we still made the whole range over here, did you? We've got a wonderfully equipped unit out on the new industrial estate just off the bypass. It's not very far. And once we've finished there I thought I'd take you to one of my favourite places for lunch. The Halcyon Pub, do you know it?'

Nick looked back out into the sunshine, out beyond the cobble stones, the bright floral tubs and the swoop of the broad pantiled roofs. In the distance he could just make out the cupola of the main house, screened from the old furniture factory by an impressive stand of oaks and hornbeam. Reluctantly he followed Jeanna out into the car park. Right alongside the horse trough the first coach of the day had just pulled up.

* * *

The factory unit was everything Nick expected and feared: anonymous, crouched under a pale green corrugated roof, surrounded by roads that led nowhere and which held the

114

promise that more of the same little blue-grey buildings would very soon seed and take root. Here were all the very things that he worked with at Newlens and longed to escape: MDF, cut and faced with ash veneer, bulk orders of machine-turned chair legs, kitchen cabinet carcasses made from chipboard coated with plastic. It was not that these things were badly made, in fact their barefaced practicality was probably the very thing that Nick loathed most about them.

For weeks he had imagined that O'Hanlons would be his nirvana, a place to create and collaborate on exquisite designs, the marriage of form and function, with soft glowing lines that cried out to be caressed. Antiques of the future. Nick shivered.

Christ, he had even imagined the conversations with the old man in the flat cap and brown overalls. 'What about if we use that nice piece of burr maple for the inlays on the cabinet, Harry?'

And in his mind's eye, Harry would smile and nod. 'You must be able to read minds. I'd been thinking along much the same lines myself. I reckon that'd look just lovely, young master Nick, just lovely.'

At Nick's elbow, her perfume so strong now that he could taste it, Jeanna was pointing towards a metallic blue and orange machine, caged safely behind a great glittering perspex hood. At one end a boy in blue overalls was tweaking something on the control panel that was flashing amber. The machine greeted them with a petulant whine.

'And this is my latest baby. It's one of a series of machines we've leased from the Germans. It's quite superb. It can reproduce anything we set in its sights, reading the surfaces and then recreating the image inside the onboard computer.'

She handed him a hand-carved, stylised Dog rose, as

large as a tea plate, that had once graced the end of a pew. The patina of centuries, the oil from a thousand willing hands, supplicants to a great vengeful Old Testament God, had rubbed over its surface and left a glow that seemed to rise from within. As Nick cradled it, it was impossible not to stroke the timber and as he did he could feel the marks of the chisel, an intensely moving link with the original carpenter who had carved it.

Jeanna O'Hanlon's expression was triumphant. Nick closed his eyes, he knew exactly what was coming next.

'That was one of the test pieces I took over to the factory before we signed up to the lease,' said Jeanna. 'We've always been particularly noted for our architectural and heritage work.'

From a metal cabinet beside the machine she pulled out the rose's evil twin, carved, cut, chiselled away by whatever demon possessed the German computer, an exact unholy graven image of its older brother.

Nick nodded and murmured, 'Wonderful' without a shred of enthusiasm.

Jeanna didn't appear to have noticed. 'Recently we've been working with a local sculptor to reproduce some of his work using this system. It's not unlike casting in some respects, he designs the whatever and then we get the lads to hand finish the pieces.'

Nick struggled to suppress the welter of Luddite emotions that were threatening to surface. Under normal circumstances he had no problem at all with technology but some part of him had hoped that O'Hanlons' factory would be different. Everything he had seen at the old workshops on the estate had convinced him he was right. Now he felt that Jeanna had tricked him. He had been brought to O'Hanlons under false pretences.

In another bay, a teenage boy with very angry skin was stapling upholstery fabric onto a plywood chair carcass. It encapsulated everything Nick had hoped to forget about furniture making.

And then there was a warble. Nick's eyes snapped open in surprise and for the first time since they had arrived at the estate, Jeanna's smile faded to leave behind a grimace. 'If you'll just excuse me for a few moments, Nick?' She pulled a mobile phone out of her jacket pocket.

Nick nodded, delighted to be set free at last. Jeanna quickly moved off to pick up a better signal and at last he felt himself relax, surprised at just how tense he had been.

'Scary, i'n't she?' said a voice from close by, a voice that appeared to have just read Nick's mind.

Nick looked around. Standing behind a half finished kitchen dresser by an open fire exit was a wrinkled little troll of a man, chugging hard on a roll-up.

'Last bloke who she took on didn't even last the trial period, you know,' the old man continued, as if speaking to himself, 'three weeks he managed and then he was off like a shot, couldn't get outta here fast enough. He was a shadow of his former self. By mutual agreement she said. But I reckon she just scared the living shit out of the poor little bugger. Either that or he didn't live up to her expectations, if you get my drift. Ever read *Lady Chatterley*, have yer?'

For the first time the old man looked directly at Nick and then tapped the side of his pock-marked nose with one nicotine stained finger. 'She takes a very active interest in the hired help, does our Miss Jeanna.'

Nick peered at him, feeling his colour rise. 'You mean –'

The old man grinned salaciously. 'Now, now don't choke on it, lad, 'at's only nature after all. Strong willed, healthy red-blooded woman like Jeanna O'Hanlon has her needs, just like the rest of us. And to be honest she's always liked a bit of rough. I've known her since she was a gal and she was like it then, right from the start. And there's nothing wrong with that if everyone knows the score. But I always say to the lads that work here, whatever you do don't take your shirt off, no matter how bloody hot it gets. Christ, she'll be all over ya like a rat on a rubbish tip.'

Nick laughed nervously. Every work place had its teller of tall tales, its joker. Chances were the old man was winding Nick up, except that everything the godless little troll said rang warning bells deep in Nick's psyche.

And any sense of freedom was short lived, too.

'Ah, I see that you've met Eric,' said a familiar voice, now ripe with more than a hint of pique. 'He's quite a character. Eric, this is Nick Hastings.' The introduction was so brief that Nick had a sense of being labelled rather than invited to make any sort of emotional connection.

'Eric's been with us for years, worked for my father too. I don't know what he's told you but you mustn't believe a single word,' she continued from behind an icy smile. 'Now where were we –'

The old man grinned at Jeanna. 'I was just telling Nick here, how you like all your managerial staff to be hands-on.'

Jeanna made a noise that sounded uncannily like a growl before turning her attention back to Nick. 'How about we adjourn for lunch now?'

Nick nodded. He had seen as much as he ever wanted to see at the factory.

*   *   *

Jack pulled open the desk drawer, took out a bottle of scotch, poured a healthy slug into the coffee, and was about to settle himself back on the chaise, when the phone rang again. This time he felt obligated to answer it.

'Hello, I'm trying to contact a Mr Jack Sandfi.' The caller was male, and sounded educated, crisp, and businesslike.

Jack squared his shoulders. It was probably a journalist, someone from one of the broadsheets.

'Speaking.'

The man seemed a little taken aback and hastily took a deep breath to compose himself.

'So, who are you? To whom am I speaking, and how may I help you?' Jack continued pleasantly.

'It's a little delicate. It's about my wife. She interviewed you recently.'

Jack felt an interesting little flutter low down in his stomach. 'Your wife?' he said more guardedly.

'That's right. Liz Chapman? You met her in Norwich.'

'Your wife?' Jack repeated. He found it very hard not to smile. So he really had made an indelible impression after all. Had she talked of nothing else but her encounter with the great Jack Sandfi? Had she screamed out his name at the very moment of orgasm; this really was becoming more and more interesting.

'I had no idea that Liz was married,' Jack said. It was true.

'All right,' said the caller, a little too quickly, 'we're not exactly married, not now, but I still care about what happens to her. I just wanted to let you know that you're on very dodgy ground. And I don't want you messing with her. Do you follow me?'

Jack's pulse quickened. 'I messed with her?'

The caller's voice dropped to a low growl. 'You know perfectly well what I mean. Liz might be naive enough to fall for all that tortured soul-searching artist bullshit but you don't fool me for an instant, you self-serving little bastard . . .'

Jack's smile broadened out a degree or two. A jealous husband in the picture as well. This little diversion was getting more and more to his liking.

'. . . I know exactly what you're after. As far as I'm

concerned it came through loud and bloody clear in that article she wrote about you.'

The burning question in Jack's mind was did he get it?

'Why exactly are you ringing? To threaten me? To warn me off?' asked Jack. 'After all, Liz is a grown woman. She knows her own mind. Surely whatever went on between us is –'

The caller grunted, cutting him short. 'I don't want to know what went on between you. Don't get too bloody cocky that's all, and don't bugger Liz about. Do you understand what I'm saying?'

'Oh absolutely. What did you say your name was again?'

The man coughed. 'Mike, Mike Gull, Liz is using her maiden name now.'

'Well, goodbye, Mr Gull, and thank you so much for your concern,' Jack said, but by the time he got halfway through the sentence Liz Chapman's ex-husband had slammed the phone down. Jack grinned and took a long pull on his coffee, the whisky finally igniting the warm glow in his stomach.

*　　*　　*

The telephone extension over in the Rectory kitchen was a hands-off model that someone had bought Jack for Christmas, a little thing to make life easier when he was working. For some reason it had never made it as far as the studio. All Morwenna had to do to answer a call was to press a button and the call would be broadcast through a small white plastic speaker. She had guessed that Jack was sleeping it off out in the studio, which was why when the phone rang she had waited for a second or two until someone picked up the receiver and then pressed the speaker button. Twice.

So when Lily, the cleaning lady opened the kitchen door,

Morwenna swung round, a single finger pressed to her lips. Lily frowned and then stood stock still, listening in until Jack wished the caller good-bye. Morwenna grinned, although the expression suggested neither warmth nor humour.

She picked up the receiver which lay alongside the speaker and tapped in a number; there was a very good chance that Mike Gull had left his home number courtesy of BT's 1471 who-rang-last service, and if not, then there was always Directory Enquiries.

It would take Arturo days to get his act together but Morwenna was quite certain it wouldn't take her more than a few phone calls to track down Liz Chapman, wherever she was.

*　　　*　　　*

'Can I tempt you with a little more wine, Nick?'

So far Jeanna had plied him with carrot and coriander soup, freshly baked granary rolls, boeuf en croute, mixed green salad, and new potatoes sautéed in butter with shallots and garlic. And, despite the fact that they had barely finished the main course, Jeanna was already eyeing the sweet trolley with considerable interest from their vantage point in the crowded dining room of the Halcyon.

She leant forward cradling the bottle, revealing an expanse of black lace and a great crease of creamy white cleavage. 'Just a little more for you then, Nick?'

Before she could pour it Nick slapped a hand down over the rim of his glass, while still attempting to hold fast to the smile that he'd painted on.

'Driving,' he said hastily, in reply to her raised eyebrows. 'Maybe I could have another mineral water instead?'

'Of course. You know I'm really impressed by a man with so much self-control; I'm looking for someone who can hold back when the situation demands.' Jeanna laughed, the sound bubbling up from somewhere low and venal and then she examined the bottle. 'Ah well, in that case I'll just have to finish it off myself then, won't I? It seems such a shame to waste it. Although, I really ought to warn you that I'm a little tipsy already. It's just as well that you're here to keep an eye on me.'

She beaded him with liquid brown eyes and an instant later he felt her hand drop on his knee. Nick was so surprised he just gasped and said nothing. Jeanna licked her lips, picking up a few stray crumbs of flaky pastry en route. It seemed Nick's silence was all the encouragement that she needed.

'You know, what I really want is a man to take care of me – an old-fashioned man who understands that inside every strong, successful woman is a frightened little girl desperately trying to get out, a woman who wants someone in her life to lean on, a helping hand, a warm passionate equal.'

Nick felt her fingers tighten around his knee. Her speech was slightly slurred, although Nick wasn't certain whether it was really the drink or just pretence. Jeanna leant forward a little further until her breasts were practically resting on his plate.

'You know, I think we could work very well together, Nick. You and I. And there is this really super little cottage on the estate that I just know you'll adore. Right out of the way, set back amongst the trees.' Her eyes had narrowed down to glacial slits. 'Very discreet. It used to be the old gamekeeper's cottage.'

Since Jeanna had grabbed hold of Nick's leg he had been holding his breath. It felt as if he was being sucked into the dragon's maw. Gasping, he pulled back from the very edge of the abyss, struggling to find something to hold onto, some talisman, some magic that would make Jeanna unhand him. And then, just as Nick thought he was truly lost, in the very instant when he felt Jeanna's hand moving up his thigh, he found the answer.

'It sounds really wonderful. I'm sure Liz will absolutely love it. She works from home.'

Jeanna froze and stared at him, eyes now as hard as napped flint.

'Liz?' she said very, very slowly. 'On your application form you said you were divorced.'

Nick gulped in a great uneven breath, opening his mouth before he truly knew what he was going to say, desperately aware whatever happened he daren't let Jeanna O'Hanlon take control of the conversation again.

'That's right I am, but she's my new partner. Actually we haven't been together very long.' He hesitated for an instant, hoping to imply that the relationship was still in the first all-engulfing throes of white hot passion.

Jeanna glared at him, but Nick knew now exactly where he was going and continued on fearlessly.

'Her name is Liz, Liz Chapman, she's a freelance journalist, but maybe you've already heard of her? She's quite well known. She had a big article about Jack Sandfi in the *Sunday News* yesterday.'

Jeanna O'Hanlon appeared to be frozen in time, completely flabbergasted by what he had said, and now the words were spoken and out in the open, so was Nick.

Chapter Ten

In Bishopston Liz finished off her morning's class with a brief résumé of how to get love poetry published. In the Halcyon Pub, no more than a mile or so from the O'Hanlon Estate Nick counted his blessings for having a nimble mind and over at the Rectory Morwenna was busy getting the main course ready for dinner.

The smell of Russian fish pie permeated the entire house. The warm pungent odour of poached cod and a very small number of prawns stirred into a thick creamy white sauce, baked under a crust of mashed potatoes hung in the warm air like ocean fog. It was one of Morwenna's favourite recipes. While it was cooking she and the cat sat side by side in the kitchen sharing the prawns that had not made it as far as the pie.

With great care Morwenna pulled off the heads of the crustaceans, and then nipped off their tails, before unpeeling the glistening platelets of armour from those plump, succulent pink bodies and dropping the unwanted pieces onto a side plate, where they lay, wet and glistening, alongside the tarry yellow spoor of her cigarette.

The fat black cat, at full stretch, up on tip-toe, leant forward and, overcoming his revulsion of the acrid smoke and the curls of volcanic ash, picked out the discards with all the dexterity of a bomb disposal expert.

While she had been waiting for the pie to cook, Morwenna had noted down Mike Gull's and Liz Chapman's home numbers in the back of her phone book. It hadn't taken any time at all to track the pair of them to ground. She had found out, courtesy of his receptionist, that Mr Michael Gull was in civil engineering, a sub-contractor working mostly on steel framed structures. He had, apparently, supplied steel erectors for some of the biggest contracts in Europe although Morwenna declined the receptionist's kind offer to have Mr Gull contact her when he got back to the office.

Two further phone calls to the *Sunday News*, one pretending to be Jack's agent's secretary and another as a dippy muddled PA for *Ciao* magazine had secured Liz Chapman's home number. Morwenna picked out a stray platelet of prawn shell from her teeth; she ought to have been recruited straight out of college by MI6 or maybe they thought a straight woman artist was too risky an option.

Morwenna transferred the numbers to the book in her tiny, sloping, very precise hand. She was hunched over, arm wrapped around so that no one could see what she was doing, although the letters and numbers were so small that even if he looked, Jack wouldn't be able to read them.

The phone rang in the kitchen and Morwenna froze for a few seconds to allow for the possibility that someone in the studio would pick it up. It always seemed far more satisfying to eavesdrop. The bell rang on, the sound as unsettling as glass breaking. Eventually Morwenna had no choice but to answer it herself.

'Hi there, this is Maria Ludlow,' said the voice through the tinny little speaker. 'I'm the editor of *Ciao* magazine? I was wondering if I might speak to Jack Sandfi please?' The woman had the most irritating accent, a peculiar uneven mixture of plummy Home Counties vowels overlaid with wide-boy estuary English.

'I'm afraid Mr Sandfi isn't available at the moment,' said Morwenna, not adding that she had no intention of going to find him. 'I could take a message if you like. I'm his, his . . .' Morwenna paused for an instant; it would be very useful to know exactly what it was that Ms Ludlow and *Ciao* had on offer. I'm Jack's PA. Can I help you?'

'Oh well, that's great,' the woman said, 'I was hoping to speak to him personally, but maybe you're the person I really need. What I want to do is to arrange a date for this interview asap, and set it up for the photographer and the stylist to come down and see the house as well. Obviously, in an ideal world, we'd like to try and tie all this in with the London exhibition, if at all possible, so that really tightens the screws, time-wise.' Ms Ludlow laughed. 'This job can be a total logistic nightmare some times. Oh and while I'm on the line, I don't suppose that you've got Liz Chapman's phone number there by any chance?'

Morwenna suppressed a gasp of horror; somehow she had been found out. She felt her colour draining, but before she could drag up a reply Ms Ludlow continued. 'I saw that piece in this weekend's Sunday papers. Great stuff. So, when Jack's agent, Arturo – isn't he just the sweetest guy? – suggested that it might be a good idea to get Liz to do the interview, well, to be honest, I thought it was a real master stroke. They obviously get on really well together. I felt there was a great sense of connection in the article, and *Ciao* readers love all that sort of thing. So, if you've got a contact number for her it would save me having to track it down.'

Morwenna stiffened. 'I'm most terribly sorry,' she said, slipping the address book down onto her lap in case Ms Ludlow might somehow be able to spot it, 'but I'm afraid I can't help you there.'

*   *   *

Later on Monday afternoon, safely back at his flat after the long lunch with Jeanna, Nick Hastings stared down into the street below the kitchen window. The daylight was just beginning to fade and had taken on the soft old-gold light that heralded the start of a long hot summer evening. At the far end of Kingsmead Terrace the houses and shops stepped back to make way for a small plaza that knotted three other narrow streets together. In the centre was a single city-bound tree flourishing despite being rooted in decorative brick paving, and alongside it stood a reproduction Victorian street lamp with a circular bench wrapped around its base. People were out there, sitting in the sunlight enjoying the remains of the day.

Early evening customers were gathering outside the bistro, drinking house red at the stylish wooden tables set up on the pavement, imagining they were really in Provence. Through the open window Nick could pick out snatches of their conversation and the rattle of cutlery, glasses and china, but the noise almost went unnoticed, no more than a sound track to other more pressing thoughts.

The gods of chance and luck and lies and careless mischief were terrible paymasters. He knew instinctively that he would have to make a very classy act of atonement if he ever wanted to get his life back on track.

The meeting with Jeanna O'Hanlon had to have been part of his punishment. The woman was a siren straight out of the pages of Greek mythology. Nick closed his eyes and tried to blot out the image of her bright red lips, guppying across the dining table, that and the sight of her breasts heading towards him, a great creamy bow wave bearing down on his hapless body while she ran a warm sweaty palm up the inside of his thigh.

Nick swallowed hard, shaken by the sheer intensity of the memory. His mind had already reduced the whole morning, and lunch at the Halcyon in particular, to a cruel parody of the truth in which he was most definitely the fall guy.

Although the barricade of lies about his relationship with Liz Chapman had checked Jeanna's relentless lust for a few minutes, there had been barely enough time for him to muster his self respect behind the battle-scarred ramparts.

Jeanna had been a little shaken by the notion that his fictional Liz worked from home, which was another lie he would undoubtedly have to pay for. And quite why he had chosen Liz Chapman's name when he could have plucked anything out of the ether was quite beyond him – although he had been thinking about her an awful lot. Liz's name and her face and little snatches of the conversation they had had and the way she laughed, kept surfacing unbidden in his mind. Now, thanks to Jeanna O'Hanlon he owed Liz Chapman twice over.

Jeanna's libido seemed to cool over dessert. For a few blessed minutes her attention had wavered, she'd taken her hand off his leg, and eyed him thoughtfully over a bitter-sweet concoction of blackcurrant mousse, fresh cream and crumbled meringues and then, just when Nick had begun to feel it was safe to relax, she had surged forward again. This time running a foot – bare except for sheer black tights, her long prehensile toes squashed together like a packet of chipolatas – up into his undefended groin.

By the time the coffee was served Jeanna had appeared to be quite drunk, and Nick realised then that there was no way she could lose. If he rejected her advances then she could quite reasonably blame the booze for her forwardness. And if he didn't . . . Nick shuddered. It was all too horrible to think about.

Against all the odds, over coffee and liqueurs he had managed to peel himself away from her, easing her foot back onto the carpet, holding up mutual respect and the need to maintain a good working relationship before him like a fiery sword. His one concession had been to imply that perhaps the next time they got together he might be a little more forthcoming; a little more relaxed.

When Nick finally dropped her off, back at the O'Hanlon Estate, Jeanna had grabbed hold of him, pressing her face close for a great wet kiss, catching Nick unawares and managing to ram her tongue halfway down his throat before he could extricate himself from her clutches.

All in all what he had expected to be an informal interview had been a terrifying farce. As a parting shot Ms O'Hanlon had promised that she would ring him about the position when she'd had a little time to consider all the available options. Those final few sentences had oozed with every possible innuendo and double entendre. Back in the safety of his flat, the whole thing sounded so absurd that Nick couldn't help but laugh, even though the laughter had had all the humour wrung out of it.

Nick took a mouthful of water and washed down two paracetamol. His head ached and his stomach felt bloated, not just from the enormous lunch but from drinking gallons of fizzy designer water in an effort to ensure that Jeanna didn't try to ply him with any more booze. It really had been a very difficult day.

Arranged in front of him on the kitchen table, like the bullet and revolver from a hand of Russian roulette, was a copy of the letter that he had originally written asking Jeanna O'Hanlon for more details about the management position at the estate – the irony was not lost on him; he had practically begged Jeanna to consider him, hunger and desperation writ loud and clear between every line – and sitting alongside that were Liz Chapman's newspaper clippings.

On the long drive home Nick had weighed all sorts of things up in his mind, turning them over one last time to see how they caught the light, to see if there was anything he had missed, any facet that had escaped him, perhaps a new route, a new thought, another way out. But by the time he had reached the end of each trail Nick came to the same conclusion. And confession probably was good for the soul.

With a sense of resignation he lifted the phone and tapped in Liz's number again. It was a pity that she hadn't phoned him back after his first call but then again when you screwed around with fate you really couldn't expect a lot of slack.

It rang, once, twice and a voice inside his head reminded Nick that this was how it had gone first time. He would probably get the answer machine again – wasn't that the way these things worked? Another dead end. And what was he going to say if it wasn't the machine? Would he apologise, explain, confess? Or just tell Liz the bare unvarnished truth, which was that despite everything else, lies and all, he hadn't been able to get her out of his mind since they met at the Flag.

'Hello,' said a female voice

Nick hesitated for a split second; it was Liz Chapman.

'Hello?' she repeated. 'Can I help you?'

Nick coughed. 'Hello. How are you? Remember me? I rang yesterday and I just thought that I'd –'

'Oh yes,' said Liz, cutting him short. 'I remember you. Thank you for the flowers you sent. They were lovely, and totally unexpected. So, how are you?'

Nick grinned. There was a delightful mixture of pique and sharp good humour in her voice. It was both defensive and flirtatious and gave him a peculiar sense of delight.

'You're very welcome, I'm glad that you liked them – and I'm fine, thanks. I read the article in the *Sunday News* yesterday and I thought I'd just give you a ring. Keep in touch.' The air between them was taut and uneasy. Nick felt his scalp tingle, God this was wonderful.

Liz laughed, although Nick could detect the slightest

edge of nervousness. 'What did you think of the article, then?' she asked.

'Good, really good – but hadn't we agreed that you were going to let me see it before it was published.'

'I was.' Liz paused and sucked in a deep breath. 'I did. The second one was something else entirely – different.' Nick sensed the little prickle of tension in her voice. 'What I'm trying to say is that I know you lied to me.' Liz said each word with a certain crispness. 'Everyone was completely amazed by just how candid you had been during the interview, but that was part of your little game, wasn't it? Pretending that you hadn't seen the tape recorder.'

Nick winced. 'I really am sorry about that,' he began, 'it was the only thing I could think of to stop you publishing what I'd told you, although it seems that it didn't quite work, did it?'

Liz continued, 'No, you're right. It didn't. But then again I didn't meet the real Jack Sandfi at all, did I? Or are you just ringing up to try and spin me another one of your little con tricks? You didn't have to lie to me.' She stopped as if gathering her thoughts. 'I thought we were getting on, making some sort of real connection.'

Nick felt something dark and heavy slithering off his shoulders. Was it possible that Liz Chapman had discovered the truth after all? That she knew. Someone had to have tipped her off, or maybe she had had to meet or phone the real Jack Sandfi again? God, no wonder that she hadn't returned his phone call. And sending that card with the flowers, the one that had said just 'Jack' because he had no idea what else to put, that had quite obviously been a mistake too. What on earth must Liz think he'd been playing at? The tension in his stomach was easing. Against all the odds Liz Chapman knew the truth and more than that she hadn't hung up on him, at least not yet.

'You're right,' he said slowly, gathering the words

together so that he could find the best ones to explain himself, 'but what I want you to understand, Liz, is that I didn't mean to hurt you or set out to lie to you or make a fool of you. I could see that the interview was really important. You said so yourself. I wanted to tell you the truth but before I got a handle on what was happening the lie kind of ran away with me.' Nick laughed nervously. 'So, no, you're right, I'm not the man you thought I was. And that was what I rang to tell you. That and I'm very sorry.' He paused, trying to gauge how Liz was taking his confession and then sensing that it was okay, pressed ahead with the rest of the things he wanted to ask. 'I wondered if there was any chance that we could meet up? I would really like to see you again. Maybe we could have lunch together after all?'

*   *   *

Liz Chapman had felt her pulse quicken and her stomach flutter the instant she recognised Jack Sandfi's voice. The flowers that had been waiting for her by the back door when she got home from college had been a surprise too – a huge bunch of exquisite cream blooms, velvet soft roses and lisianthus, surrounded by soft tendrils of fern and a card signed just 'Jack'.

Taking a deep breath Liz sat down heavily on the edge of the kitchen table. Sod's law being what it was half a mug of tea performed a perfect back flip all over the students' notes. Damn. With one hand she palmed the warm liquid straight onto the floor, trying to ignore the dripping of the run-off and instead cling to the sound of Jack's voice.

Hadn't there been part of her that hoped Sandfi would ring again? Along with his message, the call on the answer machine had left the ball firmly in her court, but despite the spark of attraction, Liz couldn't quite bring herself to phone him back.

'So, what do you say then?' he concluded. He had the sexiest voice.

Liz guessed that he was grinning. 'Are you serious? About lunch I mean.'

'Oh, absolutely. What about tomorrow, the next day, any day. I suppose that it's too late to do it today?'

Liz laughed. There was this great sense of openness in his voice, and something else that managed to convey a real sense of relief. She shivered. Whatever it was that Jack Sandfi had been hiding it had been no lightweight thing. He seemed almost glad that she had caught him out. Would he tell her now what the mystery was?

'Lunch?' she asked.

'Uh-huh, most definitely. My treat. Or we could do dinner if you'd prefer, or the theatre, the cinema, anything, I'd just like to see you again, soon, get to know you better. All the clichés. All that stuff.' He laughed again. He sounded light headed, and it was infectious. 'God, it's really hard not to sound like something out of a Sunday afternoon film, but what I wanted to say is that I'm really sorry about what happened at the Flag. What do you think? Would you like to start all over again?'

Liz could feel her colour rising while her tongue busily twisted itself into a knotted furry bath towel. She took another deep breath, playing for time to get the thoughts straight inside her head.

'That would be nice, yes, I'd really like that.' There was a deep not unpleasant silence at the far end of the line, so Liz continued. 'And, while we're making confessions, I have to tell you that I went to see your exhibition in Norwich yesterday. I wanted to take a look before they transferred it down to London. It was the first time I'd been. I hadn't seen it the day we met in Norwich, there just wasn't time with the train and the bus and everything. I just wanted you to know that.'

Jack Sandfi coughed nervously, and almost instantly she could hear the shutters closing down again.

'What's the matter?' Liz said, the words out before she could help it.

'Exhibition?' he murmured unevenly. 'You went to see the exhibition?'

'That's right. I and my friend Claire went yesterday and took a quick look around. I hadn't realised what a big place the Review Gallery was. Your sculpture wasn't how I imagined –' she paused, remembering the sense of coolness and the lack of passion, 'although it was very beautiful. I wish I'd managed to see it before we met.'

There had been something missing; she didn't know whether it was heart, or sensitivity, but after meeting him it really wasn't what she had expected at all. Perhaps even in his art Jack Sandfi had found a way to protect the vulnerable inner man.

'My sculpture?' The sound of his voice cut across Liz's thoughts like the buzz of a circular saw, and in those few seconds, in those two words, she heard all the anxiety, all the tension come flooding back. Jack was obviously incredibly sensitive about something. The change in his manner was so unexpected that it made Liz shudder. Something had just shifted and she had absolutely no idea what it was.

'I'm sorry. I just thought you said that you understood what had happened,' he said unsteadily, 'I thought that you knew, God, look, the thing is, Liz, that that stuff at the Review isn't my work, that's what I've been trying to tell you. That's what I thought you knew. I'm not Jack.'

Liz suddenly felt a great surge of apprehension in her belly.

Maybe meeting up with him wasn't such a good idea

after all. Everyone said Sandfi had a reputation of being extremely difficult, but did they really mean that he was unstable? Crazy? If this was a joke he was taking it way too far.

'What would you like me to call you instead?' she snapped, perturbed by the turn of events. 'Or is this all some kind of metaphorical artistic game of words that you play with bumbling reporters?'

'No,' Jack protested. 'No, it's not like that at all.'

Liz thought she could detect a slight edge of hysteria in his voice now. 'Liz, it's really important that we get this cleared up. If we met, face to face, I could explain everything to you, a step at a time. What about if we meet up at the Flag again? What do you think? Please say that you'll come.'

Liz hesitated. She was stunned to realise that even now there was still some part of her tempted to accept his invitation, but the remnants of apprehension hauled Liz back from the edge. After all, she really didn't know anything about him, he might very well be barking mad for all she knew, and certainly his reputation would suggest that the benign flirtatious face she had seen at the Flag was nothing like the real Jack Sandfi.

Liz decided to follow her instincts. 'I'm really sorry. No, I don't think so. My life is complicated enough as it is.'

And before he could say anything else Liz hung up. It was only when the receiver was back on the hook that she realised that her hands were shaking furiously. But, before she had had the time to gather her thoughts, the phone rang again and she wondered if Sandfi had pressed last-number-redial.

Liz was much more abrupt this time. 'Hello?' she snapped.

'Christ,' said her ex-husband, Mike, 'what the hell's the

matter with you? You're not still sulking about me bringing the boys home late, are you?'

Completely wrong footed, Liz mumbled an apology, unnerved that quite a large part of her was convinced that he had been Jack Sandfi ringing back and that, in spite of everything, the same part of her would have been delighted.

Mike was quick to take advantage of the rapid climb down. He always saw any retreat as a weakness to be exploited and now was no exception.

'Had a rough day?' he said in a tone that from anyone else might have been interpreted as concern.

Liz stayed very quiet, anxious not to rush out onto a limb; too many times in her married life the sound that had alerted her to some major crisis in their relationship was the sound of Mike sawing the branch off behind her.

'So, how are things going with you?' he pressed. 'All right, are you?'

'Fine. Thanks.' Liz felt cold now.

From the sitting room she could hear the sound of the TV, Tom and Joe were watching cartoons. On the windowsill beside her Winston was curled up on a pile of clean tea towels, purring softly. Up until five minutes ago it had seemed like a really ordinary Monday afternoon.

'Good, that's good,' said Mike cheerily. 'Just thought I'd give you a quick ring to see how things are.'

Liz already knew that there was something up and longed for him to get to the point.

'And how are the boys doing today?'

'You only saw them last night, Mike. You weren't this concerned when you saw them every day. What the hell is the matter with you?'

He laughed. 'You know you're getting really hard, Liz, bitter. You're beginning to sound just like your mother.'

Liz refused to bite. It was a real uphill struggle. 'What is it exactly that you want?'

'Nothing much. I was wondering if you could see your way clear to doing me a little favour.'

'I haven't got the time or the patience to drag this out of you one word at a time, Mike. Just tell me the bottom line. I'm right in the middle of getting the boys their tea.'

'Okay. Well, the thing is I was wondering if I could come and stay with you for a day or two, a week at the most.'

There was a small silence as Liz replayed the words over in her head to make sure she had heard him correctly.

'Stay here? Can I ask why? What's wrong with the flat? Why didn't you say something about this yesterday?'

'There's no major problem, not really. Certainly not anything for you to worry about.'

Liz shook her head, forcing herself to sound calm and her voice even. 'I gave up worrying about you a long time ago, Mike. But I'm really not keen on the idea of you coming here at all. Why can't you go and stay with the latest blonde – or what about your mum, surely it would make more sense for you to go there?'

She could sense the anger building up even before Mike spoke. 'You know, Liz, you can really be a complete and utter cow sometimes. All I'm asking is to stay round there for two or three days. It hardly seems very much to ask under the circumstances. If it's your virtue you're worried about, don't be. I'm not after your body. I can kip on the sofa.'

Liz took a deep breath. 'Look, I'm really sorry, Mike –' she began.

But he was there a long way before her. 'You always were bloody selfish. Don't forget I helped you buy that bloody house,' Mike snapped. 'Or don't you remember now? You make me sick, you and that smart arsed solicitor, you think you're so clever, so fucking –'

Liz slammed the phone down as if it had bitten her fingers. It seemed that it had turned into a day for dramatic gestures. She took a deep breath trying to quell the great wave of nausea that threatened to engulf her. Bastard, bastard bastard.

*   *   *

Meanwhile, in Norwich, Nick Hastings had pressed redial, got the engaged tone and then pressed five so that it would call him back when Liz's line was free, always assuming of course that she hadn't decided to leave the phone off the hook, and who would blame her if she did?

Nick ran his fingers through his hair; for a few glorious moments he believed that by some twist of fate Liz had discovered the truth. He felt as if he had come this close to making everything all right. All he had to do now was hang on a little longer and persuade Liz to meet him. Beside him the phone burbled to let him know the line was open and ringing.

Liz answered it on the second ring.

'So who exactly would you like me to be?' Nick asked, almost before she had had time to say hello.

'Oh for God's sake, I don't know. As I said, my life really is quite complicated enough without getting involved with someone who doesn't know who they are. Be whoever the hell you like, just clear off and leave me alone, will you?' To his surprise she sounded tired and oppressed, very different from the woman he had spoken to moments earlier.

'Okay,' he said, treading more warily. 'Why don't we start from the beginning again? There is this really good pub I know called the Cat and Fiddle, we could have supper there if you like. How about later this week?'

'Do you have any recollection of what you say to people? Five minutes ago you were asking me out to lunch.'

Nick laughed. 'You're right, I know. Just say you'll come out with me. I'll explain everything then.'

Liz sighed heavily. 'No, I don't think so, not at the moment.' She paused. 'Okay, the bottom line is that I really would like to see you again, but every sensible, mature, responsible sane molecule in my body tells me that it would be a huge mistake, an enormous mistake. Every instinct tells me that you're either stringing me along or barking mad. I don't know an honest good thing about you, although I know damned well that you are a liar and that there are an awful lot of things you aren't telling me.' The words tumbled out in a rapid burst of crossfire.

'Okay, so what about if we had lunch instead then?' he said.

Liz laughed. 'I'll give you ten out of ten for persistence. Maybe soon, but not at the moment, not now.'

'Can I ring you again?' Nick felt the moment, the connection, all the possibilities he had imagined trickling through his fingers like dry sand.

'Why not. I'll look forward to hearing from you,' Liz said and then hung up. Nick stared down at the phone; he would have had to have skin like a rhino not to have noticed the sarcasm.

Chapter Eleven

Liz dreamt a lot about Jack Sandfi on Monday night as well. Her subconscious appeared to have cast him in the star role of the main feature, which struck her as a worrying development. This time Jack turned up on her doorstep wearing a straight-jacket, a spotted bow tie, and carrying an enormous bouquet of red roses tucked up under one arm. Could she go with him to the ball after all? He had ordered up a pumpkin coach but there seemed to be some sort of a delay on the six white mice.

Liz grinned and invited him to step inside. Jack looked even better than he had the night before and seemed really pleased to see her again. Once inside the kitchen he leant forward and kissed her, very gently, a kiss that was more of a polite inquiry than the cutting edge of wild passion. Even so the sensation of Jack's lips brushing against hers made Liz's spine tingle and her stomach tighten with expectation.

It was wonderful to be so close to him, certainly well worth another shot. Although Liz was aware, despite being sound asleep, how sad it was that the whole of her romantic life had been reduced to a fantasy seduction deep inside a dream. Nevertheless Liz was quite disappointed when she woke up to find that Jack Sandfi really was just a figment of her imagination. It would be so wonderful to roll over and find him still there, feel the warm curve of his body pressed up against her, and . . . Liz rubbed her eyes; this really was getting beyond a joke.

Still muzzy from sleep Liz stared across into the vast

expanse of creamy white duvet, unruffled and pristine except for where it was stapled down by the weight of Winston's body. Her current life style struck her as being a terrible waste of a good woman. Perhaps she had been a little too hasty turning down Jack's invitation after all. Or was she clutching at straws, when had a lying madman been any kind of prospect?

Liz rolled over and stared at the alarm clock on the bedside cabinet. Twenty-five more minutes until the bell went off. Twenty-five minutes was a grey area, hardly long enough to risk dozing, but just a little too early to get up. Across the bed, Winston woken by the weight of her attention, looked up, stretched and then oozed across the bed towards her, head out like a furry arrow. Gently he rubbed up against her, warm and soft and desperate for attention. Liz grinned; if only all men were this shameless and uncomplicated.

The cat made another sinuous, fluid circumnavigation of her sleepy body to emphasise the point. Would she be so good as to stroke him if she had nothing better to do. It had been a long night. As Liz ran her hand back over his head, Winston broke into a self-congratulatory purr. She settled back amongst the tangle of pillows, and he pulled himself up alongside her, pouring his spine into the curve of her body, his soft purrs echoing through her like vibrations of his joy. Just as Liz drifted back into the warm hinterland that preceded sleep the alarm went off, only now instead of feeling refreshed Liz felt as if she had been ripped back into consciousness.

'Mum?' From across the hall Joe's voice joined the bell in a seamless conjunction. 'We've got food science first lesson. We've got to take stuff in today. I've got the list in my bag.'

Liz rolled off the bed. Had Joe been laying awake waiting for the alarm to go off or woken with the thought firmly fixed in his head. Whichever it was Winston had already gone. He hated complications.

'Okay, just get washed and dressed and bring it downstairs, love. I'll see what we can do.' There were lots of days when Liz eased slowly into the new morning without too many ripples, getting warmed up before finding her stride, but today apparently wasn't going to be one of them.

'And I think we've got tennis. Have you washed my kit?' asked Tom.

Liz groaned. 'Can the pair of you just give me five minutes to let the blood reach my brain.'

So, later that morning, during her Tuesday tutorial sessions, when Liz caught sight of Mike skulking around outside her classroom she wasn't altogether surprised. It was just going to be one of those mornings. The tint on the windows meant that he couldn't see that she was watching him. After Monday's bright sunshine the day had turned out to be dull and overcast with a light drizzle that clung to everything, turning summer's soft dust into a fine grey mud. Mike was getting wet, his dark hair already flattened down against his skull.

He was hovering around under the stand of mature trees that bordered the annex driveway. As Liz watched, he pulled out a cigarette packet, lit up and then paced out a long slow arc between two big horsechestnuts, one hand in his jacket pocket, keeping to the shadows, occasionally glancing down at his watch. He was unshaven and casually dressed in jeans and a navy blue bomber jacket. He had a peculiar feral look about him. Everything about Mike's stance, the way he moved, the way he looked, dark eyes scrunched up against the incessant rain and the curling of cigarette smoke, looked suspicious and shifty. Liz realised that he looked an awful lot like Winston. Someone on the campus was bound to call security and have him picked up.

With some difficulty Liz turned her attention back to the classroom and the tutorial, although it was hard to concentrate on Louis and his on-going problems with the universal language of welding and agricultural engineering with Mike prowling around outside.

'. . . must be checked at weekly intervals. It is most important that . . .' Louis coughed and wrinkled up his nose. 'It is most important that . . .'

And anyway when security turned up, Mike was bound to tell them he was looking for Liz, so maybe it would be better if she sorted it out before the situation escalated into an incident.

'. . . that the level is maintained as shown on diagram 6a.' Louis came from one of the new emerged post-Soviet nations, he was a very long thin boy with lank hair and a grubby trainee moustache, and was presently completely absorbed in the ordeal of reading aloud from his course notes. As he paused to draw breath Liz leaned forward and touched him gently on the shoulder. Louis looked up with surprise and then relief. English was proving to be a real struggle.

'That was very good,' Liz said with a warm smile. 'But before we move on to the next section, I'd like you to read through that last piece again and see if there is anything you don't understand. I just have to go outside,' she indicated the window, 'to see a friend. It will only take two or three minutes.' She re-enforced the idea with sign language. Louis' smile broadened and he nodded. Liz pulled on her jacket and headed out into the slow misty drizzle.

Mike looked up as the classroom door closed and then lifted his hand in a gesture that appeared to be a combination of welcome and surrender. Liz hurried across the damp grass towards the cover of the trees.

'You can't hang around out here, you'll get soaked if you don't get yourself arrested first. What do you want?' The words sounded more brusque than she intended.

Mike turned, caught in the no-man's land between snapping back at her and smiling; he was obviously very desperate.

'Nothing much. I just wanted to see you, that's all. Just for a few minutes. Nothing very important, really.'

Liz glanced back towards the classroom. Louis would be hunched over his textbook, mouthing the words as he ran a finger under each one in turn, making his way very slowly down to the bottom of the page. Unless of course he had been overcome with boredom and had his nose pressed up against the tinted glass to see what was going on. That would certainly have been her choice.

Liz decided to take Mike's lie at face value. 'Well, in that case, I'm really sorry but I'm working at the moment. I should be finished here at around twelve. Why don't you come back then? If it's nothing important –' she left the word hanging between them, an invitation for Mike to tell her the real reason for his visit.

He sniffed and let his gaze drift off into the middle distance just above her shoulder. 'Couldn't we just have a few minutes now? This won't take very long at all really.'

Liz shook her head firmly. 'No, sorry. Tuesdays are my tutorial sessions and the students don't get very long with me as it is. Why don't you go back over to the main college and have a coffee or something.' She looked down at her watch. 'I'll be done in about half an hour. I could meet you in the canteen if you like.'

Still he hesitated, holding back, reluctant to move. Liz sighed, pulled a handful of change out of her jacket pocket and pressed it into his hand. 'I'll see you at around twelve. Okay?'

Mike nodded and loped off down the drive.

When Liz got back into the mobile Louis was still reading.

Mike was waiting for her at an empty table by the vending machines. By the time Liz arrived the canteen had just started to fill up with the lunch time crowd and the noise level was rising in great ragged waves.

'I had a sandwich,' Mike said by way of an opening remark. 'Chunky chicken and garlic mayonnaise, not bad, not bad at all for the price. And that soup smells really nice.'

Mike looked pale and heavy eyed as if he hadn't slept, although it could just be that he was hung over.

'It's not like you to come to college,' she said in a low even voice, stirring a spoon through the froth on a beaker of hot chocolate. 'And you look awful, are you going to tell me what the problem is or just carry on playing these stupid bloody games?'

Mike grinned defensively. 'You have got such a suspicious nature, Liz, what's happened to that sweet little girl I used to know, eh? I was just in the area pricing up a job. Working hard, couple of new contracts, you know how it is. I've got two new sites up and running, I'm here, there and everywhere, same old, same old.' He paused; the grin flickered once and then faded.

Liz stared at him, trying to push past all the wide-boy defences, past the tattered, time-worn camouflage.

'Actually it's a job to know where to start,' he said, picking at the empty sandwich wrapper.

'Just try the beginning, Mike, and make it quick. I've finished for the day and what I really want to do is to get out of here and go home.' As soon as she finished the sentence Liz knew it had been totally the wrong thing to say.

Mike visibly brightened. 'Why didn't you say so before?

I could've saved myself a quid and had a sandwich at your place. My car's parked round by the plumbing workshop. I can give you a lift home. We can talk on the way.'

Liz took a deep breath. 'That's very kind, Mike, but actually I'm meeting someone for lunch,' she lied, scrambling around for the rest of the story to shore up the deception.

His expression hardened a little. 'Oh right. So I suppose you'll want to be off then.'

'Yes. What did you want, Mike?' her tone was bright and hard.

But he had no intention of letting her off that lightly. 'So, who is it you're meeting for lunch then? Anyone I should know about?'

Liz shook her head. 'No, I don't think so. It's the guy I did the article on. Jack Sandfi? He rang up last night and asked me if I'd like to meet him for lunch. I thought I might take him to that nice little place in Town Street. The Greek café. What do you think?' She tried to sound confident. And it wasn't really a lie, not all of it, there was no need to tell Mike that she had turned Jack down flat, eventually.

Mike's expression hardened, his mouth narrowing down to a nasty little reptilian slit. 'You ought to be more careful, you know. He sounded like a complete and utter arsehole to me. All that artistic temperament crap. They're all the same these artists. I'd watch him if I were you.'

'And you're basing that on what exactly?' Liz said, fighting the inclination to reach across the table and slap him hard.

Mike shrugged as if it really ought to be self evident. 'My natural instincts, your article said it all. It ought to be obvious to everyone exactly what sort of man he is – just after what he can get.'

Liz fixed her gaze firmly on her ex-husband's face, dragging his attention back from whatever dark fetid little alley it had just scuttled down.

'Well Mike, thanks, it was really nice to see you. We must do it again sometime between now and when hell finally freezes over, although I would appreciate a little more notice next time. Now, if you'll excuse me, I've got to be going.' Liz got to her feet, pushed the chair away, tired of the game.

As she turned to leave, Mike made a peculiar little noise and then spread his hands on the table, palms down, fingers spread wide and sucked in a long whistling breath over his teeth. 'Okay, if you must know, I'm being stalked.'

Liz laughed out loud. She couldn't help it. In fact the laughter was out and spilt all over the table long before she had any time to consider the consequences.

'Oh, Mike, come off it. You have got to be joking. Stalked? You? By who? Are you serious?'

He pulled back from the table as if she had spat at him and squared his shoulders, bristling with pure white-hot indignation. 'I can assure you that it is not funny.'

'No, no of course not,' Liz said, struggling to keep her face fixed. 'So who is stalking you, then?' Her voice crackled from the pressure of laughter bubbling up under it. Mike chose to ignore her insensitivity.

'That crazy fucking little blonde from the Red Bull. Tania, Tania Kent. The girl is totally out of her crust, barking. You probably don't know her. I always thought she was such a nice girl. Christ, I only went out with her a couple of times, half a dozen at the most.' He slumped forwards as if crushed by the weight of it all. 'I had no idea what I was dealing with. She is a complete and utter psycho, wacko, a real bunny boiler. She rings me up all the time, night and day, at home, at work; hangs about outside the flat and the yard and on-site.

Leaves me notes, sends me flowers. Look at this.' He opened his jacket and pulled it off his shoulders. Underneath he was wearing an arctic blue Marks and Spencer's cotton shirt. The sleeves appeared to have had been ripped out along the seams.

Liz stared at him as he re-adjusted his clothes. 'My God, are they all like that?' she said, wondering whether she ought to have taken the story a little more seriously.

'No, just the ones I asked her to wash for me, but that's hardly the point is it? I daren't go home now. I know she'll be there, waiting for me.'

'Which was why you rang me last night?'

'I didn't think you'd mind me staying for a few days. It didn't seem such an unreasonable thing to ask under the circumstances. I thought if I could just break the pattern, you know, stay away until the novelty wore off, that she might give up and go home.'

Liz took another pull on her hot chocolate. 'So, did you find somewhere else to go? What about your mum, wouldn't she have put you up for a few days?'

'Me and the boys stayed there over the weekend. She was really pleased to see them. I told her we both thought it was important that Tom and Joe saw more of her. Made her feel good, you know, kill two birds with one stone and all that.' He looked hot and uncomfortable.

Liz nodded; that would certainly explain why the boys had been so clean and well fed when they arrived home.

'So did you go back to the flat after you rang me last night?'

Mike reddened a shade or two more. 'No, no actually I went over to Claire's place. I just gave her a quick bell on the off-chance that she might be able to suggest somewhere and she said I could come over. But there's no need to worry,' he added hastily. 'I slept on the sofa.'

Liz chose not to comment on his ongoing concern over

sleeping arrangements. 'And so you told Claire that some crazy blonde barmaid was stalking you?'

Mike looked indignant. 'Good God no, of course not. No, I didn't want to worry her. I told her I'd got rats in the flat and the council had sent some bloke round to exterminate them.'

Liz sighed. 'Right, and that was a better explanation?' She drained the last of the hot chocolate from the polystyrene cup and picked up her handbag. The canteen was packed now, filled to brimming with noise, students jostling for a position at the servery and the vending machines that lined the back wall. Outside, sitting on the low wall a gauntlet of smokers signalled that classes were over for the morning.

Liz lifted a hand in farewell. 'I've really got to go.'

Mike looked up at her in total astonishment.

'What do you want me to say?' Liz snapped before Mike could say anything. 'That I'm sorry, that I'm not surprised. What? I don't know what to say to you, Mike, and whatever it is it's got nothing to do with me anymore. It's your problem.'

He leant across the table, his voice dropping to a conspiratorial whisper. 'Oh come on, don't be so bloody hard faced, Lizzie, we're still friends aren't we? You've got to help me out here. I don't know what to do. I came over to ask your advice. I mean, you can't just leave me in this mess. Haven't you got any ideas?'

Liz made a real effort to keep her reply to a tiny almost insignificant shrug.

He looked confused. 'I don't understand what the problem is with you. Aren't you going to say something?'

'What's to say?'

Mike's colour deepened a shade more. 'Oh, right, so you're off to meet some bloody arty-farty pouf and that's as far as your sphere of reference stretches these days, is it? Don't worry about me, the father of your children. I ought to have bloody known. I thought I could count on you, Liz, I thought you were my friend.' The words were a distillation of pure emotional blackmail.

With her heart beating like a drum in her chest, Liz turned around and faced him across the table. 'Well, it seems that you were wrong then, weren't you, Mike,' Liz said in a small icy voice and headed off towards the phones. She didn't dare look back.

Maybe Claire was in her office, maybe they could meet up for lunch. Maybe by the time she had walked up into town she would have stopped shaking.

*　　*　　*

Over at the Rectory the soft drizzle had finally turned to rain. Great generous gobbets of water exploded onto the pantiled roof of the studio buildings and ran down over the broad leaves of the nasturtiums.

Inside Jack Sandfi picked up the phone. Arturo sounded very excited, frantic even. Jack had just wandered in from the summer house to do or find something extremely important, although whatever it was it now eluded him. He had only answered the phone because for some reason it was shut inside the same drawer as the remains of his bottle of scotch.

It was wonderful coincidence though, Jack thought, him needing a drink like that and the phone ringing at the very same time. It almost verged on the mystical, a starry conjunction. He looked down at the bottle and tried hard to focus on the glistening amber contents. Someone had been drinking it, he was quite certain of that. There had been at least – well, a lot more, last time he'd looked.

Jack tried to open the bottle with one hand, tucking the

phone between his ear and his shoulder and, nipping the bottle up under his armpit, but just couldn't get the purchase necessary, so he wedged it between his knees, at which point his concentration faltered and the phone slipped off his shoulder and clattered onto the concrete floor. Thank God it hadn't been the scotch.

'For Christ's sake, what the hell are you playing at, Jack? Are you still there?' wailed Arturo, his voice ricocheting out of the handset at the far end of the dangling, twisting flex.

'Can you hang on a minute,' called Jack. With both hands free it took no more than a matter of seconds to wring the top off the bottle. He looked around; there really ought to be a glass or a mug, or a cup somewhere, surely. It was terribly uncouth to have to drink out of the bottle and you just couldn't get enough in the cap.

Jack huffed and puffed and finally tipped the pencils and pens out of a white plastic beaker on the desk and ignoring the smear of sticky blue ink in the bottom, poured a healthy slug of scotch into it and then wound Arturo back in.

'So how are you, my dear chap?' he asked, settling back on the chaise longue. The scotch was already turning a delicate shade of bluey-green.

It seemed that Arturo had no stomach for any more of a preamble. 'The producer of the Art-Around programme contacted me this morning. They would like to do a short segment with you, to broadcast during this Wednesday evening's programme. That's tomorrow, Jack. They've said they'll send a car over to pick you up. It's only a two or three minute piece, that's all, and pre-recorded. You really shouldn't have any problem with that and it'll tie in wonderfully with the London opening next week. They were supposed to have some action painter on from Bolivia or something, but he's had to cancel at the last minute; some

151

problem with his papers and then the drug squad raided his exhibition and seized six of his canvases. Anyway, it's an ill wind. Delia Hargreaves said that if we can help them out with this then she'll try and organise a nice little feature segment later in the season. Maybe a whole show around you and the new work.'

Jack took a mouthful of scotch to clear his palate and his mind. 'And this is the profile raising woman, yes?'

'Uh-huh,' said Arturo guardedly.

'Have you managed to track Liz Chapman down yet?'

Arturo coughed. 'Not directly, but the editor at *Ciao* said that she would try and contact her. I suggested that Liz would be perfect to do the interview for them. And I'm sure Ms Ludlow won't have any problem, after all they're in the same business.'

Jack straightened his cravat. 'Splendid idea. And so do you know what Liz said to *Ciao*'s offer?'

'No idea yet, but I'll let you know as soon as I do. What do you want me to say to the television people.'

Jack sniffed. 'Did they agree to stand us lunch?'

'Dinner. Table for four at the carvery at the Tower once you've finished doing the recording.'

Jack grinned. 'Good show, and what did they say about the wine?'

'A case of something very moderate unfortunately, but I will try and squeeze them a little harder.'

'And they are going to send a car for me?'

'Tomorrow afternoon.'

'What sort of car are they going to send?'

Arturo groaned.

*　　*　　*

In the little restaurant in Town Street Liz poured Claire a glass of house red. It was busy; Tuesday was market day. Five minutes' walk away from the town centre, in an arty little side street, the dining room was tastefully bare. The tables were covered with brightly coloured oil cloth. They had the most uncomfortable fold-up chairs in the universe, none of the crockery or cutlery matched but the food was absolutely wonderful.

'So you're saying that Mike's problem is a crazy blonde?' said Claire. 'Not rats. I don't know why on earth he didn't tell me himself. Christ, I work on a newspaper for God's sake. Sex, drugs and crimes of passion are my bread and butter.'

Liz swallowed another great big mouthful of wine, relishing the sensation of the alcohol hitting her bloodstream. 'Uh-huh, that and the Princess Royal opening hospitals, planning permission and the current price of washed carrots.'

Across the table Claire pulled a face.

Liz grinned. 'Okay, the thing is I already know you're broad minded and a real soft touch, but Mike probably thought that it would put you off if his life looked too complicated. I'm surprised though, he normally likes to project an air of being hard done by. Nothing is ever his fault, poor hapless little bunny.' Liz sighed. 'I've really got to try and wean him off this sort of stunt. It's time we all moved on.'

Claire pulled a breadstick from the jug in the middle of the table. 'And so to help iron out the wrinkles, you told him that you were having lunch with Jack Sandfi?'

'I had to say something. I didn't want him driving me home.'

'Maybe that wasn't such a good move. He was telling me all about Jack Sandfi last night. He thinks you're sleeping with him. He told me he rang him you know, to warn Sandfi off.'

Liz's jaw dropped. 'He did what?'

'That's what he told me. I don't know how true it is –'

Before Liz could say anything else, Claire continued. 'By the way I showed my editor your piece in the Sundays, and he said he'd like to see any other ideas you've got, features, travel, anything you fancy really. He's going to keep your details on file so you'll be first out of the bran tub for any stuff we can't cover ourselves.' Claire flicked a great wave of red-blonde hair back over her shoulder. 'So, it seems to me that the bitch is back.'

Liz grinned. 'Great, but please don't tell Mike. He's got a bee in his bonnet about money amongst other things; I find it hard to believe that he rang Jack. Did he say what Jack said?'

Claire picked up the menu. 'Mike was far keener on telling me what *he* said. Lots of macho don't-mess-with-my-woman stuff. Cold hard cash and Jack Sandfi. You know, for a couple who've split up you've still got an awful lot of things going on between you. Are you really going to have lunch with Sandfi some time or was that just wishful thinking?'

'A bit of both. I think there's a real possibility that Mike and I have both stumbled across a couple of loonies. Jack Sandfi is out of his tree on something. Drugs, booze, ego, God knows what. You're in the newspaper business, you tell me.'

Claire waved the waiter over. 'What and spoil all your fun. I've got to order, I've got an appointment at half past two. Have you decided what you want?'

Liz peered up at the black board with the day's specials. 'I think I'll settle for world peace and a long and uneventful life.'

Claire took a big bite out of the end of the breadstick. 'Too late for that, I'm afraid, m'dear. How about the spicy vegetable lasagne instead?'

* * *

By the time Liz collected Joe from school on her way back from the train, the glass of wine had worked its way out of her system. She picked up a few groceries on the way, and as the two of them turned out of the high street they met Tom ambling along too. It felt good to all drift home together.

The answer machine was blinking as Liz dropped her bags in the hall and the two lads thundered past her up the stairs. She was almost reluctant to press play.

'Hi, Liz, we haven't met,' said a plummy voice, 'this is Maria Ludlow I'm from *Ciao* magazine. I'm really very anxious to set up an interview with Jack Sandfi and we'd like you to do it if at all possible. I've already spoken to Jack's agent, and he is really keen to use you, in fact he was the one who suggested you might be interested in doing it. I'd like to point out that our fees are very, very competitive. Perhaps you could get back to me? My number is –'

Liz stared down at the handset. *Ciao* magazine? *The Ciao* magazine?

'Mum?'

Liz looked up. Tom was standing above her on the stairs. 'Winston is under my bed, he's got a dead bird or something, there are feathers and stuff everywhere.'

'Okay. Just go and get changed. I'll be up there to sort it out in a minute.'

Joe pushed his head under Tom's outstretched arm and pulled a face. 'He's being sick now, all over the carpet and I don't think that the bird is dead.'

Liz nodded, it seemed that big bucks and journalistic fame and fortune would just have to wait for a little while longer.

Chapter Twelve

'That way, that way,' shrieked Joe, jumping up and down on his bed, excitement fuelled by a heady mixture of fear and delight, 'it's gone back under the wardrobe now. There, look. There, there, quick, mum, quick. Grab it!'

Liz scrambled around the boys' bedroom floor on her knees clutching a tea towel in an attempt to catch a remarkably lively pigeon who, by the amount of feathers and fluff and other assorted bits and pieces it had already lost, really ought to be bald and dead and gutless. They had all been engaged in playing catch the pigeon for the best part of twenty minutes and everyone had had just about enough.

Tom, who was still in his school uniform, had a shrimping net, Joe was wearing a pair of shin pads and a policeman's helmet but any element of it being a game had more or less faded. Liz was getting hot and cross. The one glass of wine at lunch time had returned to fuel a killer headache. Why couldn't Mike show up now when he would be useful, she thought ruefully, making another fruitless lunge at the bird.

Outside, on the roof of the extension, framed by a great rolling phalanx of storm clouds Winston lay at full stretch, watching the proceedings through narrowed eyes with an air of quiet indignation, after all, it had been his bird.

'There. It's gone over there now,' yelled Tom. 'Get it, quick, mum, grab it.'

'Sssh, you'll frighten the bloody thing to death if you keep shouting like that,' snapped Liz, feeling her patience finally slip through greasy fingers. She would have suggested that they all went downstairs and left the windows open if it hadn't been for Winston lying in wait.

Joe sniffed, bottom lip trembling slightly despite some very manly attempts to keep it under control. 'I hate birds. I am not going to sleep in here tonight. It's going to die, isn't it? Winston bit it, there's blood everywhere, and Tom keeps making noises. It's going to die. It's going to bleed all over everything and then it's going to die under the wardrobe where we won't be able to get it out.'

The pigeon, propelled by the icy draught from death's door, let out a terrifying screech and made another break for freedom. This time, as Liz launched the tea towel it dived into the Lego-strewn spaces between Joe's toy boxes with one last great flurry of beak, wings and claws.

'Oh for God's sake,' Liz hissed at the bird, and then turned to Joe. 'Does it really look as if it's about to die?' she sighed wearily. 'I think if we can catch it it will be just fine, love. Honestly. And then after we've caught it we'll stick it in a box, take it round to the playing field and let the damned thing go. There are lots of trees and bushes over there.'

'Phone,' said Tom helpfully as the burble echoed up the stairs. He was still up on the dressing table, crouched like a wicket keeper, with the shrimping net in one hand.

Liz, who was on her hands and knees, leaning forward on her elbows, bum stuck up in the air, six inches away from grabbing the bloody pigeon, waved him away. 'Can you go and get it, love? Just take a message and tell whoever it is that I'll ring back in a little while. And Joe, why don't you go down with him as well, have a few minutes' break, get yourself a drink out of the fridge and a biscuit.'

It would give everyone a chance to calm down, not least the pigeon.

But the boys were way too slow to catch the phone. The machine had clicked in before they were even halfway across the landing. Liz recognised the caller's voice straight away and froze mid pounce. It was Jack Sandfi. From its refuge behind Action Man's up-turned jeep, the pigeon met her thoughtful gaze with knowing, rheumy eyes.

'Hello, how are you?' said the disembodied voice. 'I hate these machines, but you did say you wouldn't mind if I rang again. I just want to tell you I've had a really good offer today, just now in fact. I wondered whether you'd like to come and help me celebrate or maybe under the circumstances that should be commiserate. I don't know, I really thought this job was everything I wanted,' Jack Sandfi paused. 'But I'm not so sure now.' He sounded wistful and in need of a friend. 'Anyhow, maybe you'd like to take me up on my invitation to lunch, or dinner, or whatever, the world's our oyster. It would be good to talk to you. Put things to rights . . .'

Discarding the tea towel, Liz sprung to her feet and hurried out on to the landing; there were twelve steps down into the hall and maybe another three, four at the very most to reach the phone on the hall stand and if he would just keep on talking for a second or two longer she'd be able to make it, snatch up the receiver, talk to him.

As Liz swung around the boys and newel post and broke into a rapid downhill descent, slaloming left and right past the p.e. kit, a pile of clean washing and two sports bags, he was saying, 'Okay. Well, I don't expect you to ring back, but I just wanted to tell you anyway. Talk to you soon –' And as she reached out to grab hold of the receiver, he said, 'Bye.'

Bugger. For a few seconds Liz seriously thought about ringing back. After all what would it take? Last number recall and the merest smidgen of courage? Trouble was that she suppressed the impulse just long enough for it to go off the boil and then, without warning, reason bobbed to the surface.

Sandfi was, without a shadow of a doubt, trouble. Complex, duplicitous, maybe even just a teeny-weeny bit mad. It might feel like a good game now, great to flirt and be chased a little, but this was about real people with real feelings, not some sort of abstract imaginary truth that Sandfi could construct around his lies. Better to leave well alone.

Liz patted the phone for luck, and then made her way into the kitchen. Joe and Tom were busy staging a ram raid on the fridge. Liz plugged in the kettle and congratulated herself on being able to resist temptation. Someone had stuffed the local free paper through the back door, maybe it was time to hit the personal ads. Dark thought. Liz rinsed a mug under the hot tap; there was always the gate man at the college if she got really desperate. He winked at her every morning. Liz grimaced.

It took everyone a few minutes to feel restored and ready to do battle with the pigeon. The boys headed back to the fray ahead of Liz.

As she was about to mount the stairs the phone rang again. Liz grinned. Maybe Jack had decided to give it another shot. Or maybe he wanted to add a codicil to his first message. Liz took a couple of deep calming breaths; okay so he was a bad bet but it was still fun to play.

'Hello,' she said, in a voice pitched a point or two above seductive but which was still well inside the warm and familiar range. 'Hello?'

At the far end of the line was a great unfathomable well of silence that seemed to swallow her voice whole. 'Hello,' she said, this time with the slightest edge. 'Who is this please?' Then, just as Liz realised that it most definitely wasn't Jack Sandfi, or anyone else she knew, up from the depths of the pit came a single gulped breath, a surprised nervous breath and an instant later the line went dead.

Liz stared down at the handset. The hairs on her neck, backcombed by fear stood on end.

Upstairs, cracking the silence with a hammer blow, Joe leapt out onto the landing and yelled, 'Mum, mum, come quick. Tom's caught the bird, quickly. Quick!'

Even though she jumped at the sound of Joe's voice, a big part of Liz's mind was still caught in another place. Who exactly was that on the phone? Liz pressed 1471. Apparently the last caller had withheld their number.

'Quick, quick, please, mum!' Joe implored.

Liz forced a smile. 'Coming, love,' and as she hurried up the stairs Liz wondered if Mike's blonde psycho had any idea that he had been married and had a couple of kids tucked away in Balmoral Terrace. Perhaps she ought to ring Mike to find out exactly how much his ex-girl friend knew about his family life. And who it was he might have given her number to and why they might be using it now.

Liz shivered, pushing the thought down hard and stepped back in through the bedroom door. The room was in total chaos, much as they had left it. There were toy boxes and clothes and bed linen pulled out and piled up everywhere, and in the middle of the muddle stood Tom.

He had snagged the pigeon in the tea towel and was holding it at arms' length, eyes tight closed, while the bird wrestled and fought and flapped and made all sorts of peculiar unearthly noises of fear and fury. Another second or two and it would wriggle itself free. As it slipped one wing out from between Tom's closed fists, Liz lunged forward and snatched the pigeon away from him.

Holding it fast, with wings now pinned flat against its body Liz could feel the bird's tiny heart banging away like a ticker tape machine, its fear an echo of her own, and felt herself completely overcome by an unexpected surge of compassion.

'Come on,' she murmured to both boys and bird, still

trying to keep a grip on the flurry of anxiety that lingered in her belly, 'it'll be all right now. Let's go back downstairs.' Liz kept her voice calm and steady, knowing that the act of mothering would be the thing that finally earthed her fear out; after all she was supposed to be the grown-up here.

In procession they headed towards the kitchen and with extreme care Liz eased the pigeon into Winston's travelling basket. The very instant the mesh door was fastened the bird did an enormous explosive poo all over the soft blue witney blanket inside.

'Fear,' said Tom to his younger brother knowledgeably.

'Revenge,' thought Liz, as she switched the kettle on again and glanced out of the kitchen window. She didn't like the feeling that the phone call had left her with.

* * *

With some sense of satisfaction Morwenna stood the phone back on its shelf and tucked the little telephone book into her pocket. Surreptitiously she glanced out of the window just in case someone had been spying on her. The kitchen garden appeared to be empty. Tendrils of honeysuckle tapped at the glass as they rode the edge of the storm wind, their pale green and scarlet fingers framing the view out over the vegetables and the raspberry canes. The climbing roses had already sent out an explosion of runners; she would have to prune them later.

Morwenna pressed the life out of her cigarette and then, still pre-occupied by the phone call and a complicated mass of other thoughts, wafted a very generous handful of grated mature cheddar over the trays of lasagne and the two fresh cream raspberry flans that stood side by side on the kitchen table.

The quality of light in the kitchen was rapidly changing

as the storm moved closer. Everything appeared to have a harder edge, the rolling sun-cracked greyness draining the colour out of the day. The change in light and air pressure made Morwenna shiver with expectation; both helped enhance the thoughts that were already brewing.

Liz Chapman had sounded an awful lot more balanced than Morwenna had anticipated – warmer and not so wounded – and with a country accent, educated but nevertheless of staunch rural stock. All this from a handful of words, but even so Morwenna knew that she was right. It was a dangerous combination. Morwenna scratched her nose with the back of her hand. It was always a good thing to understand the strengths and weakness of one's enemy, and of course, their appeal.

This nonsense with Jack had to be nipped in the bud before it went any further. He had always been so easily led. He needed protecting from himself. Since Morwenna had first known him, Jack had nurtured the fantasy that rural England was littered with great buxom wenches, all only too eager to join him in wild uninhibited earthy couplings. It was, she knew now, one of the main reasons for his buying the old rectory in the first place.

For Jack it seemed that all women divided neatly into those lumbering heavy breasted dray horses who one could enjoy in the most physical and base of ways and those others with whom one had social rather than sexual intercourse. Thoroughbreds, women like herself. But what if in Liz Chapman, Jack had finally found a woman who could cross the great divide.

In Morwenna's mind the fantasy Ms Chapman had been very slowly taking shape, built on layer after layer of her own self doubts and innermost fears, but it was the sound of the other woman's voice on the phone that had finally galvanised the monster into life.

Although Ms Chapman was evidently no thoroughbred,

she did have a veneer of sophistication which promised more earthy pleasure beneath, a combination that made her all the more dangerous.

And of course, Arturo's suggestion that Ms Chapman should interview Jack for *Ciao* had probably cheered her up no end, lifted her spirits. Given her hope. And now the stupid woman would assume that this meant Jack's interest in her was far more than just another of his casual, heartless couplings.

Morwenna shivered again, trying to smother the unthinkable possibility that maybe Ms Chapman could be right. As she considered the impossible Morwenna dredged the top of the lasagne with a heavy snowfall of icing sugar. The situation called for some drastic action.

She already had Liz Chapman's telephone number and the code, and had now heard her voice. What she needed to complete the intelligence operations was the woman's address. If Morwenna could get hold of a Bishopston and District phone book she'd be able to look through the listings. It shouldn't be that hard. If not she'd ring the operator and throw herself on their mercy. Or perhaps press the Sunday papers again.

Morwenna opened the oven doors and let the heat disperse a little before sliding the trays of lasagne onto the top shelf of the range. She would find Ms Chapman and then – she took a long deep breath, drawing in the rich perfume of burning souls – it was probably better to leave her options open until she knew exactly what she was up against.

Once the oven doors were closed, Morwenna felt a little better. Lily Howard would be arriving soon to help clean up the kitchen, lay the table, wash the salad, sort out the dishwasher. Morwenna lit another cigarette and then untied her apron. The woman was a treasure.

Although she occasionally found it difficult to work out

whether Lily truly was a compatriot or a fifth columnist. A part of Morwenna considered that all country women were formed in the same mould. In her mind, Liz Chapman was just a younger version of the bleached-blonde woman who cleaned her house, a plain utilitarian moth drawn helplessly towards the candle flame of celebrity and notoriety as an antidote to her own bucolic monotony.

Occasionally Morwenna thought she saw a look of disapproval flit across Lily Howard's great red face. Morwenna sniffed. It was because of Lily's parochial outlook. Good God, the woman lived in a council house at the back of the playing field, what else could she expect? Lily had no experience of life beyond the village, certainly no exposure to the bohemian intelligentsia amongst whom Morwenna had been raised.

Lily biked everywhere; she came from good country stock with big hips. Salt of the earth. If the old rectory had still been used by the church, Lily would have cheerfully cooked and cleaned for the incumbent, but what a poor existence that would have been by comparison.

Morwenna considered that she had single-handedly broadened Lily's horizons, expanded her vision of what a truly full life could be like. In a way, working at the old rectory had brought Lily out of herself.

Morwenna took a long pull on her cigarette. Lily Howard was all the richer for knowing them. And that was quite obviously one of the reasons why Jack Sandfi would appeal to someone like Liz Chapman. In their brief meaningless encounter the woman had glimpsed the very things lacking in her own dull life.

Outside there was the first great crack of thunder and an instant later the kitchen was floodlit by its electric counterpart.

Morwenna brushed her narrow bony shoulders with a flat hand, smoothing away the little drifts of icing sugar;

there was still plenty of time for her to bathe and change before supper.

By the time Morwenna reappeared Lily Howard would have beaten the chaos into submission; washed, cleared, put away. On the table top, the ghosts of the lasagne dishes were outlined in grated cheese and ridges of icing sugar.

As she reached the hall, Morwenna heard the other woman's key turning in the back door but didn't break her stride. There would be time enough for them to talk later and besides she couldn't quite forgive the country sisterhood for trying to steal her Jack away, not after all she had done to improve their lot.

The thunder rolled again.

*   *   *

Lily Howard sighed as she closed the kitchen door behind her and pulled off her jacket. It had been a real race to get up to the Rectory ahead of the storm. Her heart was still thumping in her chest from pedalling so hard, she was as breathless as if she'd been chased. Rain drops had exploded like mortar shells behind her, but she hadn't looked back. She'd scuttled up the path and under the porch, and now she had won, got inside with not so much as a flesh wound, not one rain drop on her nice dusty pink jacket or her hair. Lily smiled triumphantly.

For a few seconds Lily held onto the sense of triumph and relief and then she turned to look at the kitchen and felt the pleasure ebb away.

The kitchen sink and the draining boards were stacked high with used crockery, bowls, a rolling pin and baking trays. Amongst a tangle of vases and milk bottles and half used jars, something off-white was soaking in a washing-up bowl on the windowsill. The long narrow refectory table was strewn with fox holes of flour and onion skins, forks and knives, and a tablespoon around which was puddled a great corona of golden syrup. On a chopping board half a red pepper and a fanfare of its seeds sat amongst egg shells and icing sugar, and in the centre of the table the cat was busy eating the remains of the butter.

Lily sighed, pushed a strand of bleached blonde hair back off her face, and then took a nice clean blue Bri-Nylon overall out of her shopping bag. It was a job to know quite where to make a start. Lily dragged the swing bin closer to the table and began to sweep things into it and as she worked she mumbled under her breath, part mantra, part curse. 'For Christ's sake has that bloody woman never heard of washing up as she goes along, it's amazing the whole lot of them don't die of food poisoning; three-fifty an hour, I'll give her three-fifty a bloody hour. Daylight robbery that's what that is, slave labour.'

Outside the thunder was tuning up for the overture, Lily took a swipe at the cat with a dish cloth. He growled, seized the furry, chewed remains of the butter and headed for cover.

Amongst all Morwenna's convoluted ruminations and imaginings about country women, it had never occurred to her that their life at the Rectory, their stories, and all her and Jack's idiosyncrasies found their way down into the village post office courtesy of Lily's sharp and highly critical tongue.

*   *   *

Meanwhile, outside in the studio, up under the roof of the old apple store, where the pantiles and the roof trusses formed a tent with the bare wooden boards, the little blonde Australian sculptress rolled over onto her back and stifled a yawn. The stormy early evening air was oppressive.

She picked up her watch from the floor alongside the

mattress and peered at the face. 'What time did you say we were supposed to be eating today? Only I'm bloody starving.'

The light in the loft was grey and gold. The sheets on the mattress were grubby and smelt of sweat and the sweet biscuity perfume of stale sleep and unwashed bodies. One muscular sun-tanned arm was tucked casually behind the girl's head, revealing glorious pert grapefruit-sized breasts and a glistening nest of dark coarse hair in her armpit.

'No idea,' grunted Jack miserably. 'When it's cooked.'

'You really are a complete waster, Jack,' the girl said with a wry grin shuffling herself up into a sitting position. There was a little pause.

He handed her the bottle of wine. 'How very nice of you to say so. Sorry that we couldn't – you know.' He nodded down towards the folds of sheet that covered his groin. 'A little too much booze, booze and hard work, and worry, that's what I think. Maybe we could try a bit later, if you want to, that is?'

The girl took a long pull on the joint that she'd settled between them in an upturned tin lid. 'No worries,' she said after a few more seconds, pulling in a breath to replace the one that had lingered for so long in her lungs. 'I'm not real fussed whether I get laid or not to be honest. The whole thing is a bit over-rated if you ask me. Sometimes it's just kind'a nice to get your kit off and relax with some-one half decent, share a bottle, a smoke, whatever. Trouble is that young guys just get so hung up on the whole per-formance thing. All that full-on macho crap.'

'Right, well my sentiments exactly,' said Jack with grati-tude. How refreshingly earthy and honest this new genera-tion of girls was. A real breath of fresh air.

'And anyway, I'm supposed to be going down the pub with Robbie tonight. You know, the guy with the long hair

168

and the nose ring who's doing photography? So, in a way it's better that we didn't do it. He wasn't very keen on me coming up here with you in the first place. Although he said it was okay. I mean, like it's my life and everything. I told him straight, I sleep with who I want, no need to get so fucking toey about it.' The blonde paused and took another swig of wine, completely oblivious to the stunned expression on Jack's face.

'I told him he could come up and join in if he wanted. I didn't think you'd mind. I told him that you'd been through the sixties, free love and all that, you know. I said maybe he could even take a few photos; it's a really great place you've got up here and the light's so good. I love the way the ivy curls down through the little window, the white painted bricks behind the bed and all that. It's just so cool up here.'

Jack stared at her in complete amazement. 'Cool?'

She nodded. 'Yeh. But Robbie said he'd rather not, said he had no great desire to record your wrinkly old arse for posterity. So it's all worked out okay, really; I'll just tell him that you couldn't get it up . . .'

Jack reddened horribly and then rolled back amongst the tangle of sheets and pillows, wondering what evil magic had delivered him into the clutches of this cheerful little succuba, and whether or not Robbie and his camera were still likely to put in an appearance.

A shaft of storm-bright sunlight, a great wedge that had forced its way between the rain clouds and down through the skylight, picked out the dark roots in the girl's cropped greasy hair. Her breasts were warm and heavy, an ornate silver ring glittering through one rose-pink nipple.

As she wriggled back down under the sheets Jack could pick out the soft perfume of sunshine and wind and sweat and something dark and wild that made his mouth water. He felt something stirring in his groin but chose, against all the odds and almost every instinct he possessed, to try to ignore it.

He concentrated his attention instead on the newly framed, pristine copy of Liz Chapman's article, which hung in pride of place on the wall in the gable end of the apple store. It was in good company. There were other reviews, photographs and articles, many, maybe too many, were yellowed now with age. Liz's hung centre stage and naturally drew the eye.

He had finished mounting it up just before climbing the stairs with the little blonde. The official hanging had been his excuse for bringing her up there. He smiled at his handiwork. The corners he had mitred up for the frame were perfect, well almost perfect, and any little discrepancies could soon be filled by a smear of plastic wood.

Outside the thunder rolled over like a playful dog and lightning split the late afternoon sky.

Chapter Thirteen

The storm decided to hang around for a while, buffeted backwards and forwards by ridges of pressure like a ball in a bagatelle. All night long an improvised new age symphony of thunder and lightning played itself senseless all over Norfolk. Amongst the roll of the timpani and the crash of symbols, the night seemed to be endless and hot and humid, and curled up all alone in his bed, Nick Hastings drifted fitfully in and out of sleep.

He was being chased by his conscience, a great dollop of gloriously detailed erotic fantasy – in his imagination at least the relationship with Liz Chapman had taken a very sharp turn for the better – and a terrifying nightmare strand that seemed to surface again and again in amongst all the other images, in which he found himself crouched under a work bench, hiding in amongst piles of woodshavings and sawdust, while Jeanna O'Hanlon, a vengeful wraith in black leather four inch heels and scary red lipstick tried very hard to track him down.

This part of the dream cycle was far more vivid than any of the others and was the thing that finally woke him. And as Nick sat bolt upright in bed, breathing hard, feeling pursued and wide awake, despite being tired beyond all measure, he knew that to break the enchantment he would have to drive over and make things right with Liz Chapman; and if he wanted to get his life back it would have to be soon.

* * *

Morwenna had always adored the drama of really stormy weather, a remnant of a military childhood spent out in the tropical heat of Singapore. Her nurse would open the shutters so that she could see the storm break over the palm trees, great electrical forks that ripped the sky like sword thrusts. She had never forgotten the sense of excitement, and went to bed early so that she could enjoy the sense of high tension, the light and the sound, viewing the show from the comfort of her four-poster bed.

It promised to be one of nature's virtuoso performances. The great mullioned windows in the Rectory's gothic tower gave her an uninterrupted view out over farm land to the village beyond. As the stony grey clouds boiled up like the list of credits over the horizon, Morwenna settled herself down amongst the pillows to watch the main performance of the evening. It was worth waiting for.

Dressed in a long white shroud of a night-dress, her slim frame covered by a single linen sheet, safe under the embroidered canopy, Morwenna finally drifted off into sleep. While she slept she dreamt of crows circling above a stubble field. The huge birds spiralled around and around like great cogs turning on invisible pinions, spreading their glittering black wings out against a cornflower blue sky. But no matter how hard she tried Morwenna couldn't quite shift her focus down into the field to find out who or what the birds were flying over, although in some dark still corner of her mind she had a strange feeling that it might be a tray of burnt lasagne.

* * *

Once it was dark, Jack Sandfi finally abandoned the little blonde demon to the ministrations of her photographer friend and headed homewards across the sodden lawn.

His progress was illuminated by great forked tongues of

172

lightning that, along with the rest of the evening's events, rather emphasised the futility of his own feeble existence. He paused to take stock; cold, hungry, soaked to the skin, impotent, just how many blessings could one man handle.

By the time Jack reached the kitchen door he was deep in the pit; the lights were off, the house closed up for the night. He felt unwelcome and unloved, set adrift in the storm. With some difficulty Jack found the back door key under a flower pot and let himself into the kitchen.

Another great flash of sheet lightning helped him to circumnavigate the table and then he gave up, engulfed by a great tidal wave of self-pity and self-absorption that left no room for anything else. There just had to be some booze left somewhere. And there was.

While Jack finished off the last of the decent cognac and half a bottle of cooking sherry he found in the back of the pantry, the storm partied on. And when the drink was all gone and he decided that the stairs were quite impossible, even on his hands and knees, Jack settled for a dilapidated sunlounger out in the conservatory. Where, although he had a ringside seat for the most impassioned performance of the entire storm – and there were some truly spectacular other-worldly forks and flares and flashes – Jack slept through the entire performance anaesthetised against his greatest triumphs and his worst fears.

*   *   *

By contrast, Liz Chapman's youngest son Joe was up and down for most of the night, which meant that Liz was too. Tom slept through all the excitement and the noise, curled up under his duvet, snoring softly and occasionally murmuring a few incoherent words of complaint or possibly encouragement.

While Joe was busy chasing imaginary pigeons, looking

for blood and feathers and cats and other far less obvious things and the thunder roared and the lightning flashed, Liz had been looking for a way to bring his temperature down, make him stop rambling and go to sleep. Please.

And then at just after half past three Joe was violently sick and the storm finally seemed to have thrashed itself into exhaustion. By four Liz had fetched fresh pyjamas, remade the bed, snuggled Joe down and put the sheets in the washing machine. When all that had been done, Liz found herself curled up on the bottom of the stairs with Winston in her lap, cradling a mug of hot chocolate in one hand and rubbing her eyes with the other.

It had been a very long night; there was no way that tired would cover it. Liz felt as if she'd been under siege, and although Joe was sound asleep now, she wasn't certain whether he would stay that way or whether he had some sort of bug or just too much excitement. And of course now that he was asleep, time would drop down a gear and accelerate away, so that it would seem like no more than half an hour before the alarm rang to drag her kicking and screaming out of bed and into the new day.

As Liz felt the heavy magnetic pull of sleep, Winston arched up a long serpentine neck to have his head scratched. His feline presence was as warm and comforting as any embrace. Outside, through the bull's eye glass in the front door, Liz could see the first tendrils of early morning light already subverting the darkness.

She groaned and pressed her forehead against the banisters. 'If I go back to bed now what do you think the chances are of me hearing the alarm? Hey? What do you think, cat?'

Winston purred, trying very hard to nudge her into submission.

She sighed, 'All right, I know, I know,' and rubbed a thumb back over his warm wedge-shaped skull. 'You know

174

very well that Wednesday is the longest day of the week. Morning tutorials, and then the shopping, back out again for my evening class. What do you think you're playing at? I always knew I should have bought a dog. Couldn't you have at least waited until the weekend to fill the bedrooms up with wildlife? Mike's mother won't look after Joe if there is the slightest chance he's going to throw up again, my mum and dad always get the short straw. What do you have to say to that?'

The cat looked up at her through glittering narrowed eyes, his whole body trembling with pure physical pleasure. She smiled at his arrogance and complete indifference to her situation and ran a hand along his sinuous spine. He rewarded her by flexing and pressing up against the curve of her palm.

'You really are a bastard, Winston,' she said, draining her mug and then getting very slowly to her feet.

He wasn't in the least offended and cheerfully followed her up to bed.

*   *   *

Liz woke again an instant before the alarm went off and rolled out of bed quickly, just in case the sense of smugness dragged her back over the edge into the warm sea of unconsciousness. She sat very still and very upright, waiting for her circulation to catch up and tried to blink away the eyesockets-full-of-sand feeling. It didn't seem like more than ten minutes since she had slipped gratefully under the duvet. While Liz worked on rationality and taking a few experimental breaths to see if she would live, her toes scurried around the bedside rug telepathically trying to hunt down her slippers.

After a few more minutes she stood up and peered out into the new morning. In the back yard the night storm had ripped the boys' makeshift tent down in a fit of temper and stamped all over it, leaving great big peevish muddy footprints to mark its course, before finally skewering the whole thing to the back wall amongst a tangle of rambling rose and honeysuckle. Leaves and rubbish and other assorted oddments that didn't seem to belong to them had been washed up along the margins of the little garden, like a tide mark of devilment and dark mischief.

From amongst a corrugation of warm bed clothes Winston stretched to test the possibility of waking and then thought better of it.

Liz yawned, sorting the events of the night into their rightful pigeon holes; maybe that was a bad choice of words.

There would be no point ringing Mike's mother. It would only take two minutes to explain to her parents that Joe was poorly and needed someone to look after him while she was out at work, and at least fifteen minutes and a lot of false joviality and unnatural gratitude to get anywhere near that far with Mike's mother, once she had recovered from the shock of being called so early. Unless Mrs Gull Senior was called during office hours her first assumption was that someone had died unexpectedly during the night.

Liz took a closer look at the alarm clock. Her parents would already be up. She'd call them just as soon as her mind and her mouth could form the necessary words, which, from years of experience, she knew wouldn't be until after she had had at least one mug of tea and a couple of medicinal digestives.

And so it was that at just after eight o'clock, showered, dressed and feeling a shade more human, Liz stood in the kitchen and packed her things for college. Her mother was busy in the sitting room pretending to fluff the cushions and tidy up so that she could watch children's TV. Liz worked on stringing random thoughts together while she shuffled through her students' books and the course notes, her wallet, keys, turning the ideas over like the beads of a rosary, while ticking off the things that needed to be done:

First she really ought to call Maria Ludlow at *Ciao* magazine as soon as she got in from work. Hang out Joe's sheets. Liz looked round to check what else there was to do. The breakfast dishes were already neatly stacked to drain on the sink unit, bin emptied, milk bottles out – sometimes it was a real treat to have her mum about the place. Across the kitchen Tom was slumped miserably up against the door frame trying very hard to look pale and interesting.

'This had really better be good, love,' Liz said, buckling her bag. 'I've got to be off to catch my train in about ten minutes.'

He sniffed. 'I just don't feel very well.' He mugged closer, craning forward so that she could inspect him.

Liz lifted an eyebrow and then cupped her palm over his forehead. It was cool and dry. 'Nice try,' she said with a grin, 'but no cigar.'

Tom sniffed again, louder this time. 'Oh, come on, mum. Be a sport. Do I have to go to school today? Granny said that Joe can come downstairs later and lie on the settee with his duvet and watch a video if he's feeling any better.'

Liz waved him away. 'Please Tom, don't do this to me, not now, not this morning. I am totally and utterly shattered. Just go back upstairs and make sure that you've got all your sports kit, will you. Now. Oh and Claire is coming over tonight to baby sit you while I'm at work.'

Claire and Liz's parents took turns minding the boys on Wednesday evenings so that Liz could do her stint at the tech', and she was immeasurably grateful that they did. Although Tom was beginning to resent the idea of being minded by anyone.

He hunched his shoulders and pulled a face, struggling to look hard done by. Liz, hands on hips, made a show of staring him down. With a theatrical sigh Tom acknowledged defeat and slunk off upstairs. Liz glanced at the portable TV to check the time and to her complete surprise caught a fleeting glimpse of one of the photos from Jack Sandfi's catalogue, intercut with a still photograph of one of his latest pieces of sculpture. She grabbed the remote and upped the volume.

'. . . And on Art-Around tonight we will be talking to local sculptor Jack Sandfi, who'll be telling us all about his latest exhibition.' There was a little flurry of music, and then, 'And now it's back over to Lucy for the weather around the regions. So, Lucy, how's it looking after last night's storm?'

That was all there was. Frustrated, Liz picked up the TV guide from the kitchen dresser and flicked through the pages. 'Art-Around, 8.00. Arts magazine for the Anglia Region.' Nothing, no details, no write up. Damn. She'd have to get Claire or the boys to record it while she was at work; if it was possible to set hands on a video that had still got some space on it. It might be easier to pick a new one up while she was out.

'Liz, it's getting on for twenty past, love,' her mother's voice broke into her thoughts.

'Right, okay, I'm going now, and thanks, mum.'

Her mother laughed. 'I'm putting it all on your bill. And don't worry about Joe, he'll be just fine.'

Out in the hall Liz picked up her jacket. 'Tom, are you completely ready? Have you got everything? I just want to nip upstairs and say bye-bye to my baby –'

There was a squeal of indignation from the bedroom. Liz laughed and then jogged upstairs to see Joe. He was snuggled up under the duvet, with a bucket on the floor beside the bed which smelt of Dettol, but at least he was smiling now, despite looking heavy eyed and pale.

'Be really good for granny,' she said, pressing a kiss to

her fingertips and then touching his mop of soft curly hair. 'I'll be home around lunch time.' She leant closer and whispered, 'And I'm warning you now, Joe, don't think you can play Gran up. I've already told her what a little sod you can be when you're poorly. And don't you dare get her running up and downstairs after you. That's an order.'

Joe giggled. As if he would.

Liz caught sight of herself in the mirror; maybe the run down to the station would put some of the colour back into her cheeks. At the foot of Joe's bed, camouflaged amongst the last vestiges of little boyhood in a huddle of battered loved-to-death teddies and furry rabbits, Winston was keeping a weather eye on the patient.

* * *

Nick had written Liz Chapman's telephone number and address down in his address book. He looked at it and then turned it over and over in his mind and fingers. The plan was simple. He would drive over to Balmoral Terrace, turn up, pop in, tell her he was passing by. Invite her out to lunch, invite himself in for coffee. What would it take? A lot of bottle and an hour's drive, maybe a bit more but there was nothing to keep him in the flat if you discarded the latest gothic monstrosity in gilt and rococo for Newlens. What had he got to lose?

So he'd go, he would definitely go. Nick pulled on his jacket and slipped the address book into the pocket; then again what if Liz wasn't there or if she really didn't want to see him again, what if – a whole armada of doubts broke the surface like ice floes. What if . . . for Christ's sake what was he a man or a mouse?

Nick took a deep breath, struggling to still the small nervous voice that pointed out that driving over to see Liz was probably the daftest idea he had had since that time he decided to pretend to be Jack Sandfi, and picked up his car keys. There would be all the time in the world for every shade of self-doubt and every sort of fantasy good, bad and indifferent on the drive over to Liz's house.

*　　*　　*

'The thing is that I can't find my hat,' Jack Sandfi said to no one in particular. He sounded petulant and whiny. 'And the laundry doesn't appear to have sent any of my shirts back except for that terrible embroidered pale pink thing that Buffy bought me while he was in New York. And I'm certainly not wearing that, not on TV. And I can't find my hat.'

He was standing all alone in the dressing room that adjoined the master bedroom. In theory it was part wardrobe, part retreat. Panelled in antique oak, with a small bathroom off to one side, it contained a couple of battered easy chairs, a nineteen fifties style cocktail cabinet and a rather nice Edwardian rosewood dressing table and stool. It should be everything a gentleman might require to complete his toilette.

The problem was that over the years the dressing room had become the Rectory's clearing house, a poste restante for all things domestic, so that anything that had no place took up temporary residence there until a more suitable home could be found.

At the very back of the little room, arranged on the broad expanse of open shelving and in the cupboards, some of the temporary items had been there for the best part of fifteen years, since he and Morwenna moved in, while others closer to the door, stacked on the floor under the hanging rails or laid out on the tiles and the oriental rugs, had been there for less than a week.

Jack, still damp from the shower with a pale green bath

sheet wrapped around his waist, thin red-gold hair combed back into a fetching little quiff, stood back and stared helplessly into the maw of the souk. He looked at the great piles and the boxes and the bags, an entire herd of white elephants, just in case he was missing something obvious like a clothes rail of clean, freshly laundered shirts.

His progress round the room was marked by a set of foot prints picked out in water and talcum powder. Jack was very lean with milky white skin that had reddened around his throat and he had rounded shoulders which framed a narrow concave chest. A sprinkling of mouse coloured hairs across his back and belly added a little texture and light and shade, although his nakedness and vulnerability seemed an odd contrast to the rich brightly coloured jumble sale that otherwise filled the room.

Too nervous of the consequences of touching the piles of household trivia Jack finally stood very still and willed his clothes to appear. He would do almost anything rather than find Morwenna and ask for help, but time was getting on. The car from the television studio was due soon. He was fast running out of options.

And then all of a sudden Jack smelt something. Like a tiny flash of prescience the smell of cigarette smoke gave Morwenna's impending arrival away. All his wishing had summoned her up from the fetid bowels of the Rectory after all. Over the years he had begun to wonder if the two of them had some psychic link and then hastily retreated from the same thought just in case it might be true.

Morwenna didn't even bother to ask Jack what it was he wanted or what he was looking for, but swept around the room like an imperious wraith, smoke curling out from and around her like a vapour trail. Black silk socks, soft white cotton underpants, a freshly laundered terracotta coloured shirt, a rather nice pair of cream chinos that he had quite forgotten about, and a linen jacket, she dropped them all one by one onto the back of one of the arm-chairs.

'Do I have to do everything for you?' Morwenna asked rhetorically from behind the swelling clouds of cigarette smoke. Like a magician producing dark doves as a climax to the performance, she pulled his fedora from thin air and set it on top of the other things, and then she was gone.

Jack sighed, opened the drinks cabinet and poured himself a tot of brandy. Not too much, what the Australian girl might call a little heart starter, just enough to thaw out the ice crystals in his sluggish circulation. The liquid nestled in his empty stomach for an instant like warm oiled silk and then diffused out into his bloodstream as a rich amber fog.

He sniffed, relishing the sensation, and then turned to absorb his reflection in the dressing table mirror. Not in bad shape for his age, he thought; a man and artist about to be reborn, rejuvenated by the sweet breath of popular opinion.

What more could he want? What more indeed. Jack picked up the Courvoisier and poured a second glass, the new measure a little more robust than the first. He lifted the glass to toast his reflection and Liz Chapman. Liz Chapman. The name surfaced unbidden along with an identity parade of faces and bodies. His mind picked something almost at random from the line of sexual suspects, and while he dressed and drank his imagination wove the fabricated Ms Chapman into his own rich tapestry of carnal delight. Her presence and the brandy finally smoothed away the wrinkles left on his psyche by Morwenna's arrival.

*   *   *

Wednesday seemed to be proving very difficult for everyone, the day turning out to be as long and oppressively humid as the night.

'I'm afraid that you can't go over there this morning, Ms Chapman,' said the gate keeper as Liz arrived at the front gates of the tech'. 'It's all been red taped off.' He was carrying a walkie talkie and a lot of responsibility and this morning, for once, thankfully, he didn't wink at her.

Liz stared at him. 'Sorry? Can't go where? I've got a class in ten minutes.'

He gave her the look. 'The whole of the EFL block's off limits until we've had a man from the council in to take a look.'

'Take a look at what? What are we talking about here, Eddie? Core meltdown?'

'Worse'n that. Wasps' nest. Right under your mobile. Very nasty things wasps.'

Which in a nutshell meant all of Liz's tutorials that morning were held across the roadway in another mobile and as a result everyone else seemed almost as unsettled and fractious as the wasps.

When Liz left college at lunch time the train was delayed by a signal failure, and when she finally arrived home Joe had been sick again and then the high school had rung to say that Tom had been sick during Geography, and could she come and collect him, and in amongst that and about a hundred and twelve other things, Liz hadn't quite got around to phoning *Ciao* magazine but they, according to her mother, had rung twice even though she had already told them Liz was working at the college all morning. The whole house smelt of disinfectant and Winston had regurgitated something furry on Liz's bedroom rug out of pure spite.

'Oh yes, and before I forget, there was a man came round to see you this morning while you were out at work. Hang

183

on,' her mum said, pulling on her cardigan, as Liz finally dropped onto the sofa for half an hour's well deserved rest. 'He said he was really sorry he missed you, and he brought you this. I thought it was a lovely thing to do.' Mystified Liz got to her feet and followed her mother back out into the kitchen. Standing on the windowsill in a milk bottle was a single sunflower, with a big brown paper parcel label for a card. 'Sorry' was all it said.

Liz smiled and at the same time felt her stomach tighten. It just had to be Jack Sandfi. 'What did he look like?'

'Very nice, quite tall, sort of blondie grey hair; he said you would know exactly who it was.' Her mother grinned. 'He said he was planning to come round and take you out to lunch.' There was a little weighty pause. 'So, are you going to tell me who he is then and what it is he's sorry for?'

Liz sighed. 'No. I'm not sure really. He was just someone I met. Did he come in? What else did he say?'

'Nothing much at all. He said he was in the area and thought he'd call in on the off chance.' Her mother paused again. 'I did offer him a cup of coffee but he said he'd come over again when you were home. I thought maybe your luck had changed at long last.'

'You sound just like Claire.'

But before her mum could ask any more questions her father arrived to pick her up, and then Joe appeared at the top of the stairs and announced he felt really, really hungry. There was no time to daydream or to speculate.

As soon as her parents were gone Liz picked up the phone and rang Jack, just to say thanks, and maybe accept the lunch date, after all. She needed to ring quickly before the moment passed, and although Liz was surprised to get an answer machine in some ways that almost made it easier.

'I just wanted to say that I'm sorry I missed you today.

I'm out teaching this evening as well, but I should be back at around ten.' Liz hesitated. Should she say she would ring him then, or maybe invite him to ring back? In the end Liz said nothing other than, 'And thank you for the sunflower too. It's beautiful.'

So, at around half past four when Liz was making everyone toast and a plate full of nice little picky things that invalids always fancy when they have someone at their beck and call (particularly a someone who said they were trying to pull a fast one and sent them to school), and the phone rang, her heart missed a beat; which was silly but true.

The day seemed to have galloped away with her and looking up at the clock Liz realised that if she didn't want to be late for class she'd have to leave soon, but not before answering the phone.

It was Maria Ludlow. Liz groaned; calling *Ciao* magazine back had been the number one priority on her to-do list before real life had intervened.

'What we'd really like is a little bit more background if at all possible,' said Maria as soon as the niceties were tidied away.

Maria Ludlow polished her bright glassy PR voice. 'We'd prefer to have more story than we need and then cut it to suit. Far rather do it that way than pad out bare bones. Our magazine is human interest straight down the line, Liz, may I call you Liz? That's what our readership are looking for, what they have come to expect and that is exactly what we give them. They want the sensation that they are right there when the famous person – whoever that may be; royalty, pop star, sporting icon, Carol Vorderman – opens up and tells them their own very special story. And I really think it's time that *Ciao* readers knew absolutely everything there is to know about the *real* Jack Sandfi.'

Liz smiled thinly and looked at the sunflower, resplendent in its milk bottle, sitting next to the bouquet Jack had sent earlier in the week. She wouldn't mind knowing more about the real Jack Sandfi either.

Maria Ludlow took a breath. Liz was beginning to wonder whether the magazine editor had got gills or was perhaps breathing through her skin.

'Fine, the thing is –' Liz began but Maria was off again.

'So, I've already talked to Hermione Benn this morning. The gallery owner over at Norwich? I mean, she's such a real wealth of Jack Sandfi stories. They go back years. You've met her, presumably?'

Liz made a little non-committal sound but Maria had already rolled on by.

'She was the one who really instigated Jack's recent Norwich exhibition and set up the transfer to London. She sees it as a come-back, a revival. I just wonder if that is where the story is? I mean she is very very keen on him. I think she was married to an honourable someone somewhere back down the line, the name rings a bell, but perhaps you already know the details and where the bodies are buried?'

Maria managed to laugh at her own joke and still carry on without any apparent pause. 'Whatever, I think it's probably worth a look, I'm sure. At least a phone call. We'd like you to interview Jack at home, in situ, if at all possible, he sounds like a very territorial chap if you ask me. Do you know him very well?'

Liz was surprised to be asked anything. Up until that moment Maria Ludlow had been doing very well all on her own.

'The interview was the first time we'd met,' Liz began. Not adding that she had narrowly missed meeting him again that very morning.

'Right, well that is truly amazing. Jack's agent promised that he is going to contact me later this week with a list of possible dates. As soon as I've got those we can set up something mutually agreeable. Okay? You are happy about this, aren't you? I don't want you to feel you are being railroaded into anything.'

Liz took a deep breath while she framed a reply, but Maria was still well ahead of her.

'Wonderful. Well, in that case it's settled then. Now, money wise; we would obviously prefer to buy all rights but we do offer a very good fee, if I say so myself.'

Liz glanced up at the clock with a growing sense of unease. She could hardly have put the garrulous Ms Ludlow off or ask her to ring back and so now she was running late and Claire ought to have arrived by now, and while Ms Ludlow ran on and on about terms and conditions and world rights and tasteful presentation, the door bell rang furiously and to Liz's total consternation it was Mike not Claire who meandered into the hall.

He smiled as their eyes met and then lifted a hand in salute.

Liz groaned and slapped a palm over the receiver. 'Mike, what the hell are you doing here?' she hissed, with Maria Ludlow still burbling away in one ear. Just a few seconds behind Claire followed him in and shrugged apologetically.

'Sorry I'm late,' she mouthed, and then continued in a stage whisper. 'I couldn't really leave him at home on his own. He's been up in my office for the best part of the afternoon. This stalker thing is really getting to him.'

Liz pulled a face, while on the phone Maria Ludlow finally sounded as if she might be running out of steam.

The phone rang again while Liz was running upstairs to pick up her books and bag and get changed.

'Will one of you get that for me, p-l-e-a-a-s-e?' she shouted frantically from the bedroom doorway. 'Just tell whoever it is that I'll ring back later, when I get in from work' As she spoke, Liz tugged a blouse out of the linen basket, ignoring the landslide of clean clothes that came with it, and shook off the light sprinkling of cat hair, pulling it on over her head, finding the other sandal with her toes, hopping to slip them on and do them up. 'Can you just take a message?'

The ringing stopped abruptly mid-warble.

There was a new packet of video cassettes on the top of her college bag that she had picked up from the corner shop on her sprint from the station. The plan was to capture the soul of Jack Sandfi on tape, although it seemed that maybe there was a faint chance she might be able to lay hands on the real thing after all. The thought made her grin.

On the way downstairs Liz scratched at the pull tag on the shrink wrap and when that failed resorted to using her teeth to rip the cellophane away. It finally gave up the fight and clung on to her hair in desperation.

'Just went dead on me,' Claire said, waving the receiver as Liz stepped down into the hall. 'I rang 1471 but whoever it was had withheld their number.'

Liz hesitated for a millisecond and stubbed out the little flicker of paranoia. Dead line, happens all the time. Nothing too unusual about that.

'Don't worry. Probably someone selling double glazing, or a wrong number, and if it isn't they'll ring back later,' Liz said lightly. 'Do you mind recording a programme for me while I'm out?' She slapped the blank video cassette into Claire's open hand. 'It's called Art-Around and it's on at 8.00 on Anglia. Channel 3, for about half an hour, I think. It's in the paper.'

Claire turned the tape over in her fingers looking at it as if it was a land mine. 'No problem. You've already set the machine up, have you?'

Liz shook her head. 'No, I haven't had time but the boys

will show you how to do it, it's all on the remote control thing. Tom knows, and if all else fails the instructions are in the dresser drawer in the kitchen. Big A4 manila envelope marked, "You have nothing to lose". You can't miss it.' Liz paused for a second and glanced past Claire towards the sitting room. Through the open door came the sounds of an endless loop of frantic adrenaline pumping music, interspersed with stylised ricochets, zap and splattering noises. Mike and the boys were already busy on the Playstation.

Claire turned to follow Liz's gaze and lowered her voice. 'I'm really sorry about bringing Mike here with me. I just didn't know what to do with him. He's acting like some lost little puppy.'

Liz shrugged. 'It's no good worrying about it now. The only thing is that Jack Sandfi is going to be on this Art-Around programme, that's why I want you to record it for me, and you know how anti Mike has been about the whole idea. Not Jack Sandfi specifically but Jack as an example of men in general, I think.'

'Right,' Claire grinned. 'In that case, I'll make sure that we watch one side while I record the other.'

Liz frowned. 'Do you reckon you can do that? Five seconds ago you were saying you couldn't work the machine.'

Claire bristled. 'I did not, that is not what I said at all. It's just obviously much easier if it's all set up already. I didn't want to screw anything up if you'd already got it programmed in –' She paused, tapping the cassette against her open palm. 'Although I should warn you now that I'm only doing this on the condition that you let me watch Jack Sandfi later.'

Liz reddened. 'For God's sake, Claire. He's a middle aged sculptor not one of the bloody Chippendales, but okay, it's a deal.' She paused, smile broadening. 'You sound just like my mother; he came round today while I was out at work. Told her he had come to take me out to lunch as he was in the area.'

Claire's jaw dropped. 'No? Are you serious. Oh shit, fancy missing him.'

'He brought me a sunflower, I've left it in the kitchen.' She glanced at the clock. 'God, look, I've really got to go now or I'm going to miss my train. Thanks, Claire, see you later.'

Claire waved the words away. 'Don't mention it. I'm planning to raid the fridge the instant your bum is out of the door.'

Liz called her farewells to the boys and then hared off down Balmoral Terrace, bag hitched up over one shoulder, hurrying on past the newsagents and the hairdressers and the bakery and then down towards the railway station. The gates were just coming down as she galloped, breathless, up onto the platform.

So, it wasn't until the train was pulling out of the station that Liz realised that she hadn't had a chance to shop so the fridge was empty, or to tell either Claire or Mike that both boys had been off sick all day from school. Ah well. They'd find out soon enough.

Chapter Fourteen

At around the same time in the television studios in Norwich, in the green room, Jack Sandfi waited while a pubescent male minion in a misshapen white cotton tee-shirt and camouflage trousers went off to find him a little something to soothe his aching nerves; and it was a little something too.

The TV company's hospitality, like its hospitality suite, struck Jack as very sparse indeed. He peered at a tray on the side table; all very Californian; cranberry juice spritzer, a jug of freshly squeezed orange juice and something with prunes. Alongside the drinks tray was a bowl containing a pitiful handful of salted peanuts cut with Chinese crackers in pastel water-colours with that peculiar varnished look that made you suspect someone had already licked them and put them back.

Jack settled himself down on the sofa with a copy of the *Eastern Daily Press* and a slightly piqued expression. There was not a sign of Arturo, Hermione, no one, and no booze. It was just like the Marie-fucking-Celeste with designer lighting.

Jack shook the paper out. It wasn't at all what he had expected. The car had arrived on time; a nice navy blue Mercedes driven by a taciturn chap with a peaked cap and a dodgy porn star moustache. Jack had really quite enjoyed sitting in the back, barely able to suppress the childlike urge to wave regally at passers by. And then in the reception area he had been greeted by a very pleasant young woman who smelt wonderful and who had Pied-Pipered him away down through the bowels of the TV building, murmuring how very pleased she was to finally meet him, how wonderful his latest exhibition had been, how very much she had enjoyed it all. It truly was the most exciting thing she had seen at the Review Gallery for, well, for ever. And Jack had preened and fluffed and felt terribly important and well loved.

The girl smiled constantly, revealing two rows of perfect white teeth, her little breasts jiggling attractively under a very sheer cream silk blouse. While she laughed shamelessly at his wit and warmth and his sparkling repartee they had headed ever deeper into the building. It occurred to Jack as they turned yet another corner that he would never be able to find his way out again.

Although of course, now that he was in the hospitality suite, it was quite obvious that Ms Conviviality had been nothing more than bait, a delicious fragrant decoy, because the very instant that they reached the double doors, the perfumed girl had handed Jack over to Norwich's answer to GI Joe. He was a mere boy with lank shoulder length hair, a plastic clipboard, and a disproportionate notion of his own importance.

The production assistant, who was apparently also in charge of shepherding and refreshments, cracked the little metal cap on a miniature of brandy he had tracked down from God knows where, and poured it into Jack's glass. At least they used proper glasses.

'So, there we are, then.' The boy's tone was unbearably patronising. 'Would you like anything in that, Jack, a dash of soda, a splash of water maybe?'

A little more brandy wouldn't have gone amiss.

Jack had imagined that the green room would be cosier, shabbier maybe, but distinctly more womb-like and welcoming, when in fact the place in which he now found himself was verging on minimalistic, like some sort of East

Anglian interpretation of a Swedish airline departure lounge.

Two cut glass ashtrays, one each end of the coffee table glittered so hard it would be pure sacrilege to defile them. For once in his life Jack wished he had a predilection for cheap cigars. It was not at all as he had imagined, no not at all.

'Another ten minutes or so, Jack, shouldn't be too long now,' said the assistant, waving towards a mute wide screen TV. Jack didn't like the way the boy used his first name as if they had known each other for years.

'They're just finishing off the technical run through and then you're on; it's very good of you to do this at such short notice. Would you like me to get you anything else?'

Jack shook his head; one miniature of brandy had already constituted an heroic feat of getting. Instead he took a scattering of peanuts from the dish that the boy was offering and peered malevolently at the TV screen. He had barely given it a second glance since his arrival, assuming that it was showing normal programmes. Instead, as his attention focused Jack realised that it was an eye out onto the raw studio. As he watched a camera man glided silently into shot, grinned and lifted a thumb, while across the bottom of the screen a long strip of numbers and random words slowly processed.

'What about make-up?' said Jack, sipping the shamefully inadequate glass. 'Isn't someone supposed to come in and make me up; stuff, powder, hair? You know.'

The boy smiled indulgently. 'Sure. The make-up girl will be waiting for you when you get downstairs. But don't worry, for this kind of programme it's nothing much, it's really just so that you don't shine on camera.'

'Are we speaking metaphorically or literally?'

The boy shook his head, but before he could try to find a reply that didn't reveal his total non-comprehension, the

door to the room flew open to expose a statuesque bru-
nette. Her ample frame was wrapped up in a long brown
and black batiked ethnic confection, her claret coloured
hair swept up into a gravity defying beehive.

'Jack, darling, how absolutely wonderful to see you
again. How are you?' She lunged towards him like a scrum
half, ornate earrings clanking like windchimes.

Bemused Jack struggled to his feet, where icy cold hands
caught him in a firm presidential two handed handshake
and carmine lips air-kissed him up and down until he was
dizzy with the blur of lipstick and the scent of sweat and
patchouli oil.

'And you are?' he began hesitantly, trying to claw back
the ground that was fast rolling out from under him.

'Oh Jack,' the woman brayed while dragging in great
breaths to fuel her growing mirth. 'You don't change one
iota do you? Always the jester king. I told young Randolph
here to keep you off the sauce until we had had a chance
to get the recording over and done with. Keep you frosty,
sharp, yum yum.' She laughed and wriggled her shoulders
as if she was confronted by a bizarre but sumptuous pud-
ding. 'Good boy. *Good boy.*'

Jack peered malevolently at Randolph, who resplendent
in his combat trousers, blushed a little, and wondered if
perhaps he was dreaming after all.

The woman was smiling still. 'So, no more ado, Jackie
darling, let's just get this little bugger sewn up and in the
can and then we turn you loose and you can hit the town.
Paint it every shade of scarlet. You know, I'm almost sorry
that I'm not coming with you tonight. But no rest for the
wicked, you know how it is. So, just a quick run down on
where we're going with this.' She extended a hand like a
surgeon waiting for a scalpel and Randolph, a name which
Jack realised meant that someone, somewhere called this
idiot boy Randy, handed her his clipboard.

She jiggled her head from side to side as she read through the line up. 'Blah-de-blah-de-blah, new exhibition, blah-de-blah, critically acclaimed, great reviews. London opening next week. Blah-de-blah-de-blah. Not a problem, eh Jack? All seems very straight forward to me.'

She looked up, feigning weariness. 'To be perfectly honest it makes me wonder what the world is coming to. It was very good of you to step into the breach.' She ran a fingertip down the sheet of paper on the board. 'Nothing new here. Same ole, same ole. Ah well. If we get the whole enchilada later on in the season and do a special on you, I'll make sure we break a little new ground, like your friend Liz Chapman in the *News*. Nice piece by the way.'

At last the woman had his complete attention.

Jack stared at her. 'Are you telling me that you know Liz Chapman?'

The woman waved her hand in a non-committal maybe, maybe not gesture that completely infuriated him, tipping the balance from his being slightly piqued to totally pissed off, and then she just smoothed on by.

'So, are we all ready then? In that case it's time to rock and roll, darling. I know you'll be just fine, Jackie-boy; you have such a wonderfully natural presence. I'll lead, you follow. Simple questions, in and out, two minutes, three at the most. We'll need to do a little nodding and looking into space at the end to cut in at appropriate moments, but it won't take very long, I promise. Sorry we've had to schedule the recording so late on but perhaps Arturo told you about all the trouble we had with the bloody Bolivian?'

She slipped her arm through his, totally unaware that she was now leading a bull by the horns. 'Come on, let me show you the way, sweetie.' She patted his forearm. 'Gosh, Jack, you're trembling, you feel so tense. Relax. Oh how terribly sweet, don't tell me that you're nervous. I won't bite. Well, not unless you want me to, that is.'

Jack growled miserably and downed the remains of the brandy in one.

* * *

Nick, who, after visiting Liz, had driven over to Newlens' factory to deliver the latest drawings, had two messages on his machine when he got back to the flat. He'd picked up the Newlens thirty pieces of silver too, had a beer on the way home at the bar he planned to take Liz to, and generally thought a lot about Liz Chapman, and, strangely enough Jeanna O'Hanlon, and as if by magic it seemed that he'd managed to conjure the pair of them up.

Jeanna's message was curt but still managed to sound unsavoury: what she *really* wanted to know was how Nick felt about her proposal, now that he had had time to consider exactly what was on offer. Scary thought.

And Liz? Well, to his genuine surprise she sounded sad that she'd missed him, which had to be a step in the right direction.

* * *

At the college the wasps had been moved on, so back in her own mobile classroom Liz was planning a little celebratory role-play. One of the desks was set up with empty cartons, cans and plastic bottles, all carefully and realistically priced, with carrier bags and a till she had rescued from a skip behind the canteen. There were just a couple more things to get out of the store cupboard. She'd finally started to settle after a day of dashing and running and worrying. Wednesday evening classes were almost always the best of the week. Liz wedged the doors to the classroom open so that the sounds of the rooks, and the babble of voices and, now the canteen had stopped frying, the smell of summer trickled in to keep her company.

After the previous day's storm the evening was turning into something wonderful, soft green shade and old-gold faded sunlight dappled everything into something botanic by Monet. It was the kind of evening when it would be really nice to have someone to meet up with after class, someone to have a drink with or maybe cook supper for, someone to ease off your shoes with and then walk through the park arm in arm. Someone not unlike Jack Sandfi.

Liz shuffled the make-believe shop into some sort of order, while her mind ran around unhindered, dabbling its toes in a whole series of romantic possibilities.

Around her the students drifted and rambled and hurried in, until the whole group was arranged around the impromptu mini-market.

'Good evening, Mees Chapman.' Each one greeted her in turn, Liz replying in kind until Louis, the agricultural engineer, arrived.

'Hello,' he said, picking up an empty cereal carton that had been overlooked on one of the tables behind her. 'There was a woman looking for you. Did she see you here, maybe?'

Liz felt the tension, which she had been so glad to leave behind at Balmoral Terrace, slither up over her like icy mist. 'I'm sorry? What did you say, Louis?'

The boy, who had quite obviously not expected to be asked to repeat what he'd said, pulled a pained face, and then fumbled around for a few more words. He looked nervous.

'Here. You did not see her? She was coming here. She was here a very small while ago. A little time ago. She says she is asking for you.'

'She asked for me? Are you sure?'

'Oh yes, Mees Chapman. She asked for you and then she asked if this here was your classroom.'

'Did she say what her name was?'

Louis shook his head in a blanket gesture of non-comprehension.

Liz cursed quietly under her breath, wondering if whoever it was that Louis had seen looked as if she might be obsessed with a middle-aged ex-husband, a man who couldn't recognise a psychopath when he saw one? Liz needed to know what time the woman had been there, what she looked like, and where she was now, and a lot of other things besides, but if she pressed Louis it was obvious he would panic.

'Was she blonde?' Liz asked in a moment of inspiration, pointing towards one of the girls in the front row.

Louis shook his head and pointed to a red-head in the row behind. 'No, not like that, like this,' he said triumphantly. 'And old, like you.'

Liz nodded ruefully, side-stepping the accidental insult, and wondering instead if perhaps Mike's little psychopath had a mother.

* * *

With one eye screwed up to shut out the smoke from her cigarette, Morwenna divided the remains of the indian tonic between the two glasses of gin on the pub table. Through the grimy leadlights of the snug bar she could see across the road into the neatly manicured grounds of Bishopston College of Art and Technology.

It seemed to be a pretty quiet night. Propping up the bar across from the table where she and Lily Howard were sitting was a sprinkling of long haired individuals, staff, students, male and female, although without shifting her concentration to look more closely Morwenna found it hard to work out exactly what or who they were.

On the far side of the table Lily Howard sniffed. 'So what are we going to do now then? Only I said I wouldn't be late home.' She looked at her watch. 'Are we going to go and have another look round? She must be there by now, it's nearly eight. That girl in reception said they have a tea break about now. We could maybe clock her on the way across to the canteen.'

Morwenna sucked her teeth. 'Just give it another minute or two, we'll finish these first. And there's no need to rush anyway, the receptionist said the class doesn't finish until nine and we know exactly where she is.'

Morwenna took another nip of the gin, relishing the florid perfumed hit. After all Jack and Arturo's impotent fretting about Liz Chapman's whereabouts, as Morwenna had predicted all it had taken were a couple of phone calls to track her down. Just a few phone calls and a few white lies about working for *Ciao* to whoever it was who was staying at Liz's house, probably her cleaner. Morwenna lit a cigarette off the butt of the one she had just sucked down to the filter.

She didn't want to admit to Lily Howard of all people that she was nervous about meeting Liz Chapman, and not for the first time, Morwenna wondered why she was reduced to bringing the hired help along for moral support.

Lily lifted her glass. 'Bottoms up then, I'd better make the most of this as I'm driving, hadn't I? Just have the one. What do you think of the new Montego then? Runs nice, don't it? My eldest, Colin, bought it for me out of the car auction up at the dog track. Not bad for two hundred quid.'

Morwenna nodded dumbly, grateful for the babble. She took another long pull on her drink, trying to ignore the very slight tremor in her hands. Odd to think that her rival was probably no more than a hundred yards away and completely oblivious to her presence. Morwenna smiled. It gave her a peculiar sense of pleasure.

Lily was still talking. 'He's going to spray 'at green as soon as we can borrow the compressor over a weekend. Got a job lot of top coat.'

Morwenna wondered if her uncharacteristic state of uncertainty was because she hadn't expected that Jack would pick a college lecturer. It seemed out of character and this change of habit disturbed her far more than she cared to admit.

Women with brains, women with bodies; until Liz Chapman Jack had always pursued a very clear vision. Once she got over the initial shock of serial infidelity, Morwenna had learnt not to fear the string of nubile heavy-breasted bovine creatures that habitually crossed Jack's path.

In fact, as the years had gone on she had almost welcomed them. They were disposable, like lighters, almost interchangeable and their presence in her life saved Morwenna from the increasingly onerous task of servicing Jack's sexual needs; not to mention the emotional leverage they gave her. It was true that sex was power. Up until this latest incident with Liz Chapman Morwenna had been a co-conspirator in Jack's adultery, only too pleased to turn a blind eye to his string of uncomplicated liaisons.

Morwenna leant forward to disguise the slight tic that was worrying away under her left eye, fished the slice of lemon out of the gin and sucked at the plump fleshy little citrus droplets. Of course, she really ought to have realised that at some stage or other Jack was almost bound to meet someone special, someone who broke the mould.

Viciously Morwenna bit down into the pith allowing the sour taste to fill her mouth. Bastard. She'd soon see about that, she certainly wasn't going to lose all the things she had suffered for all these years without a determined fight.

'Come on,' Morwenna said, downing the rest of the gin in one. 'I think it's time that we went over and paid Ms Chapman a little visit.'

'Oh right-o,' said Lily, who had been talking about the new tailgate her Colin had fitted to the Montego. 'We're going now, are we?'

Morwenna tugged her dress straight. 'We most certainly are although I'd be grateful if you kept out of the way. You know, stay back.'

Lily nodded. 'Tell you what, why don't you go on your own. I could stay here and have another drink and a bag of crisps. You can come and find me when you're done.'

Morwenna considered the suggestion. In some ways it would be a relief to track Liz Chapman alone.

* * *

Back at Liz's house Claire was on her hands and knees in front of the video, clutching the remote control in one hand, while Mike crouched alongside her peering at the glittering galaxy of little buttons behind the drop down display panel on the front of the machine. Two were glowing red already.

'So, okay what did you say you wanted to do?' said Mike. He already sounded long suffering. 'Record three, and then watch which one? One? The film? That's right isn't it? It's three, and then press play and record. Just give me the flicker over here.'

On the sofa Tom groaned as both adults reared up to face each other in a mute battle of wills; it was just like the good old days when dad lived with them all the time.

'Is the video tuned in to eight? It is eight, isn't it?'

Claire held her hands up in surrender. 'Please don't ask me. I really haven't got a clue, Mike. Liz just asked me to record the arts programme that's on three for her, that's all.'

Right on cue, on the screen between them the announcer said, 'And next on Anglia, the magazine programme Art-Around will be taking a close-up look at events, performers and artists all around the region. Amongst tonight's highlights we'll be going out to the North Norfolk Coast with Libby Roberts to look at an exhibition of naturally dyed fabrics and wall hangings, and bad boy sculptor Jack Sandfi will be talking to our very own Delia Hargreaves in our Norwich studios. That's Art-Around next here on Anglia.'

Mike made an odd, angry little sound as if he might be about to choke; Claire looked up and reddened furiously before belatedly flicking over to channel 4. There was an odd icy silence.

'You might as well turn it back,' said Mike, eyes fixed on Claire's. 'We need to sort this recording thing out. Are you sure you really want to watch the film on one? I would have thought you would have been much more interested in having a gander at Liz's new fancy man.'

Claire's colour deepened; she couldn't have put it better herself.

Chapter Fifteen

'Okay, so I'd like everyone back here in about fifteen minutes,' said Liz, indicating her watch. 'Fifteen minutes. And then after the break we'll talk about what happens if you want to take something back to a shop, and how to make a complaint. Okay?'

There was a murmur of assent from the class and a scraping of chairs as everyone got up and filtered out into the still night air. The first half of the evening had gone well. The guy from the kebab house had finally come into his own. A natural born shopkeeper in any language Liz grinned, he had relished the spotlight.

She took another quick glance at her watch. There was time enough to nip over to the canteen and ring Claire to see how things were going at home, make sure she had remembered to record Art-Around, and then maybe there would still be a few minutes to grab a coffee as well. Perfect.

It was a beautiful evening. Once outside the students settled around her, asking questions, eager to know more. It felt a little like being mobbed by a flock of brightly coloured busy birds. In the free-for-all Liz did her best to answer the students in turn. On Wednesday evenings the classes always seemed more intense, more animated, the students laying claim to her in a way that the day-time students never did.

'Mees Chapman,' said one particularly ardent young man. 'My boss, he has told me that if I can pass the company's test this summer at work, then I can have a counter job, serving, so then no more washing up for me.'

Liz smiled. 'You should be fine, Mustafah, honestly.' They were moving as a fluid group, spreading out across the roadway, over towards the main buildings, under covered walk ways, down through the double sets of fire doors towards the refectory, when all of a sudden Liz had the most uncanny feeling that she was being watched. 'If you want to bring in some old papers we can –'

The sensation grew until it was so intense that the words dried in her throat and the hairs lifted on the back of her neck. Instinctively Liz turned around, despite still being carried forward by the great phalanx of students on their way to tea break.

She coughed to cover the break in concentration, struggling to gather some sense of composure, although the peculiar feeling persisted.

'I'm so sorry, excuse me,' Liz murmured. 'Your work is fine in class, I can't see that you'll have any real problems. I could write a reference if that would help.'

Almost instantly another conversation sprung up between the boy and one of the girls on Liz's right. They talked across her; were there any more jobs at the restaurant, who would wash up once he was promoted? The class had almost reached the canteen doorway and Liz stepped back, ready to slip out from between the students and head off towards the phones.

As she turned, Liz knew that she wasn't imagining the feeling, and looked around to see if she could spot Louis. Maybe he would be able to point out the woman who had asked for her earlier, but he was way over on the far side of the pack, far too engrossed in his own conversation with another of the girls to notice that Liz was frantically trying to make eye contact.

And then, all of a sudden, Liz knew exactly who was watching her. Across the bustle of the noisy foyer a small slim red-headed woman looked Liz up and down with a pretence of complete indifference. Liz shivered and for the briefest of instants it was as if there was just the two of them in the vestibule linked by a corridor of complete all-engulfing silence.

The woman appeared to be absorbing every detail of Liz's clothes, her stance, her face and figure, every last shred of who and what she was. Liz stared straight back, skinned raw by indignation and anger and then as their eyes met she instinctively looked away; in that tiny fraction of time Liz recognised that she was staring straight into the cool hard gaze of one of nature's natural predators.

Although her eyes were as hard as glass marbles, the woman's facial expression was completely neutral, hiding the details of her thoughts away as effectively as a bank of freezing fog. Liz shivered. The whole exchange was over and done with in a matter of seconds and when Liz looked back again the woman had vanished in amongst the milling crowds; if this woman was anything to do with Mike's psycho they were all in big trouble.

*   *   *

At Liz's house, Art-Around was already well underway. Delia Hargreaves, the resident host, was maybe thirty seconds or so into the studio interview with Jack Sandfi, and both Claire and Mike were staring at the screen.

'Sweet Jesus,' Mike hissed, in complete disbelief. 'Please, just tell me that that is not Jack Sandfi. That can't be him, can it?' His voice held an element of appeal. There was a long second's pause; most of the silence seemed to be filled by a close-up head and shoulders shot of the man in question.

A back-lit halo of thinning hair framed Jack Sandfi's face, he looked puffy and pale, his eyes narrowed down to reptilian slits. As the camera moved closer still he pursed his lips and pressed his finger tips together, apparently considering his reply to the programme's presenter, the colourful Ms Hargreaves. She was smiling in his direction, obviously expecting some thought, some articulate erudite comment on the latest exhibition. The camera conspired instead to record the arrival of a small moist belch.

Mike turned towards Claire. 'We're not on the wrong station, are we? That can't be *the* Jack Sandfi, surely? Can it? The guy is a complete and utter arsehole.'

Tom had already gone up to his bedroom to play on his computer, Joe was listening to a story tape, which left Claire and Mike sitting a discreet distance apart on the sofa. Winston the cat was curled up between them, as vigilant a chaperone as any maiden aunt, although at that precise moment Mike had his mind firmly fixed on something other than seduction. He was hunched forward, remote control folded tight into his palm in an effort to get a clearer picture of the man who was supposedly taking his wife out to lunch and was most definitely sending her flowers.

And then Claire took another long hard look at the TV screen, and had to agree with Mike. Jack Sandfi and Delia Hargreaves were sitting in crimson armchairs, face to face across an arty driftwood table. Photographs of the sculptures in question were being projected onto the screen behind them, and appeared to be slightly out of focus. A little like Jack Sandfi.

There was something slightly roguish, piratical and care-worn about the man that Delia Hargreaves was struggling to interview, but even so Jack Sandfi was nothing like the kind of man Claire had been expecting.

Sandfi must be fifty if he was a day, with a great tangled but thinning mop of faded red-gold hair. He was dressed in expensive but well-worn clothes that hung untidily on his narrow frame. And he most certainly didn't strike her as sexy or good looking in any conventional sense of the word.

Claire might have given Liz the benefit of the doubt and taken a wild stab at the sculptor having a great personality if only it wasn't so painfully obvious that Jack Sandfi was totally and utterly obnoxious. Completely self-absorbed, bored now and horribly petulant. It was quite embarrassing.

On screen, Jack drank deep from the dimpled tumbler he was cradling and leered across at the interviewer; Ms Hargreaves was wearing the slightly unfocused expression of someone gamely working her way through the stock questions on the autocue.

'So, Jack,' she said, with the same rigid smile. 'Everyone is terribly excited about the exhibition transferring up to London. How do you feel that your latest work measures up against the so-called new wave, the bad boys, Hirst et al?'

Sandfi hardly seemed able to acknowledge her presence, instead he lifted an eyebrow as if that might be answer enough.

Ms Hargreaves smiled wearily; as popular entertainment it was about as excruciating as watching teeth being pulled.

'Actually I think we have some stills from the Review Gallery. Would you like to talk us through? Right, well, this is the . . .'

Gamely she launched herself into the void, gabbling out a bright, over-blown description of the hunched wooden shape on a plinth that now filled the screen.

Mike looked at Claire. 'Do we really have to watch this bloody drivel?'

The little red light was glowing above the record button. Claire shook her head. 'No, I don't think so. Liz can watch it later when she gets home, what about the film instead or there's a documentary on four about orphaned orang-utan –'

Mike hadn't quite finished with Jack Sandfi yet. 'I just cannot believe that Liz is interested in *that*.' He waved the flicker towards the screen. 'I mean, what on earth does she see in someone like him?'

Claire shrugged. For the first time since she had known Liz, Claire really had no idea either, but certainly intended to find out.

* * *

Usually, after the Wednesday evening classes finished Liz loved walking back up into town to catch the train home. There was something deeply satisfying about wandering past the little terraced houses with their pocket handkerchief sized front gardens, the window boxes, and tubs and the occasional rogue garden full of gnomes, plastic flowers and concrete swans. It was a real pleasure to watch the seasons change in the windows, and something wonderful about being able to look in through the curtains at night, catching a glimpse of other lives unfolding.

Normally Liz could feel herself unwinding, knowing that her teaching week was over, but not tonight, tonight she felt exposed and vulnerable. The insulating cover of students peeled away within a few hundred yards of the main gates, and although it wasn't really dark, there didn't seem to be any consolation in the fact that the roads were well lit and that there were people about. All the better to see you with; Liz shivered and pulled her jacket tight around her shoulders.

She was annoyed with herself too. It had taken a few minutes to recover from the brief encounter with the redhead in the foyer, but once everyone had settled down in the refectory her thoughts had moved on, although she had cancelled the idea of the phone call home and concentrated on the coffee and conversation instead. Everything had seemed fine when Liz was surrounded by the bright babble of students, and the same was true when they had gone back to the classroom, but to Liz's surprise a great wave of anxiety hit her the moment she set off for home.

It seemed to have tightened something high in her chest, and ignited a peculiar nameless nagging fear that had bubbled up from somewhere low in her belly. Whatever it was, it made her walk quickly, head down, pulse racing, all her senses stripped raw, worrying away at her heels like an angry terrier. As the feeling tightened its grip it was all Liz could do to stop herself from breaking into a run. And yet, despite the fear she was angry with herself too. Was this all it took to upset her equilibrium, a stray look from some unknown woman?

The train was already standing at the platform when Liz got to the station. The ticket office was closed and so even though the buildings seemed cheery and brightly lit any sense of reaching sanctuary was very short lived. The place appeared to be deserted except for two teenagers locked in an embrace, and two boys smoking over by the drinks machine. Part of her mind couldn't help itself and nervously scanned along the station platform, scuttling backwards and forwards taking in every detail of every shadowy corner, every face, still on the look out for any signs of the red-headed woman.

Liz climbed aboard the waiting train, her heart still kicking out a dance rhythm, unable to shake the feeling of being hunted. The trepidation and the anxiety were in full swing, all switched on and alert and it was a terribly hard thing to shift. What if she had completely imagined the redhead's interest in her? And where had this great abstract well of fear come from anyway, did it lurk there inside her all the time, just waiting to be summoned up? Liz looked up and down the train. The carriage appeared to be empty. So much for the mental image she had been working on of the grown-up confident single mother making her way in the world. If she wasn't so bloody scared it would be funny. God, what an imagination.

Liz pressed the button to close the carriage doors, dropped her bag onto the seat nearest and then forced herself to shut her eyes, trying to breathe the anxiety away. Because she had hurried to catch the train there were another ten minutes or so before it was due to leave. It was almost more than she could bear.

*   *   *

Morwenna was very quiet during the drive home. She stared without seeing through the smeared windscreen of Lily's ageing Montego, her gaze fixed on the dark landscape while her mind sifted through all the things it knew about Liz Chapman, and Jack Sandfi, and her life at the Rectory and life in general and one by one lifted the things up to examine the details in the last of the fading light.

Beside her, Lily Howard drove and talked; it seemed that having her employer in the car made the charlady nervous and when she was nervous she talked far too much. So, while Lily babbled on about Colin, her eldest son, and the rest of her extended family, Kevin and Andrew and her Gwennie and the new baby granddaughter, Kyra-May, and all things filial and familial, Morwenna lit another cigarette and thought.

It had been very odd finally seeing her rival in the flesh, face to face. And odd too that Liz Chapman's whole demeanour and appearance were so against type; slim, dark, with those bright intelligent eyes, this was a development that Morwenna realised she had feared most and that she hadn't allowed for.

Meanwhile, as she ruminated over the possibilities, Lily's running commentary ensured that not one single modicum of brain power was consumed by the need for light social chit chat, nor even to listen. It was an almost perfect arrangement. And so by the time the car puttered and spluttered and zigzagged between the pot holes in the Rectory drive Morwenna knew without a shadow of a doubt that she had to pursue Ms Chapman to her lair and find out exactly what she was up to.

* * *

In Norwich, Jack Sandfi was laying claim to his dinner.

'So,' said Jack, refilling his wine glass to the very brim, 'just tell me again, who was that bloody woman?' He pulled his face into an exaggerated impression of the TV presenter. 'Jackie-this and Jackie-that. What the fuck was all that about anyway? Nobody but nobody has ever called me Jackie. Not in living memory.'

He didn't feel that the recording had gone too badly at all, although the programme's host had been somewhat cooler towards him when he had finally bid her farewell than when they first met in the green room.

'Delia Hargreaves,' Arturo snapped in a disapproving undertone. 'And to be honest I find it hard to believe that you don't remember her. We met at some fund-raiser for a youth theatre project at the Guildhall. She was extremely keen to get to know you, she thought you would be a good connection to make; someone to give a little gravitas to the project.' He shook out his napkin, glancing around at the other early evening diners in the restaurant.

That would certainly explain why she had been so effusive in her greeting. Jack thought Arturo looked a little tense, although to be fair Jack was a few glasses ahead of his dapper little agent and he had already sensed that

Arturo planned to ride shotgun on the evening's proceedings; it would be such a terrible shame to disappoint him.

Jack ran his finger through the wisp of sour cream that encircled the quails' eggs on his plate. He wasn't really hungry. Adrenaline and all that. On the table next to them were a family party of six, two little girls out for their mother's birthday celebration dinner, together with rather elegant granny and miserable florid granddad and a fat little father sporting an unruly moustache. They were all keeping a very close eye on Jack. He winked at the youngest child, a plump little pink thing with a cruel haircut, who blushed furiously and then giggled into her clenched fist.

Jack toasted them all. He had finally just about managed to rinse the dust from his mouth after the long television studio drought, and the aperitif or two he had had in the bar while deciding on what to order had helped restore him to better humour.

To be fair he really didn't see himself as having a natural TV personality, which he thought made tonight's performance all the more impressive. Arturo and Hermione Benn had met him straight from the recording of Art-Around, taken an arm each and guided him out to a waiting taxi.

They both said that they'd been delayed in the traffic but Jack suspected Arturo had stopped off at Hermione's tidy little town house for a light pre-supper entertainment. He also suspected that Arturo had been a little nervous at the prospect of arriving too soon at the studios. He was too malleable by half, Jack would have had Arturo down to the nearest off-licence the moment that idiot boy from production had offered them all a cranberry juice spritzer.

Jack unfastened the buttons on his jacket and stretched back in his chair. The surroundings were really quite convivial, a wealth of mushroom coloured brocade and well polished mahogany gave an air of faded gentility, an effect not altogether substantiated by their waitress having a nose ring, but one couldn't have everything. Then again the claret that the restaurant had produced from its cellar was damned good, as full and spicy as Christmas, as wonderful a bouquet as man could wish for. Jack had already managed to put away one bottle and was well into his second; not that he was drinking alone, Good God no, Arturo and the lovely Hermione were right along there with him, glass for glass, toast for toast, well almost.

Beside him, Hermione spread a curl of mackerel and dill pâté onto crisp brown toast. 'I had a call from *Ciao* magazine today at the gallery.'

Jack grinned and then tapped the side of his nose. 'Oh good, we like *Ciao*, don't we, Arturo? Not one iota of fucking profile raising involved, just the rich perfume of cold hard cash.'

Hermione pressed on ignoring the profanity. 'Research for their article apparently, the editor said that Liz Chapman might ring and have a chat. I wondered if perhaps I ought to invite her over for lunch or something so that we can talk properly. What do you think, Jack?'

Now she had Jack's complete attention 'Liz? We are talking about Liz Chapman here?'

Hermione broke off a shard of toast and popped it into her beautifully painted mouth. 'Uh-huh, the woman at *Ciao* is terribly keen to get the interview and everything done asap, but I thought you already knew this?'

Jack waved her remarks away. 'No, no that's what I employ Arturo for.' He swung round to face his agent. 'So when can Liz do it then? Can we ring her up now? Have you got the number? Tell her that I'm free on Friday or over the weekend if they're that desperate to get the interview fixed up.'

Arturo frowned. 'This is not like you at all, Jack. Are you suggesting that we ring *Ciao* now? Or Liz Chapman?'

Jack grinned triumphantly. 'Whichever, both, asap. I

really don't mind, either, both would suit me just fine. Invite Liz over, tell her to come to supper, there is a spare place after all,' he indicated the extra seat at their table. 'Tell her that the claret here is quite superb –'

Hermione had already gone back to nibbling away at the toast.

Arturo blocked Jack's enthusiasm with a disapproving look. 'Hang on a minute, Jack. I haven't got Liz Chapman's number, and there's not going to be anybody at the magazine at this time of night. We'll probably just get a machine if we get anything at all. What about if I ring them first thing tomorrow morning?'

Jack waved Arturo to his feet and away. 'No, no, no. Try now, do it now. I've got a really good feeling about this,' Jack said jubilantly, flapping his hands in Arturo's direction. 'Just ring now. Now.'

Hermione dropped the toast back onto the little platter and watched Arturo make his way out into the foyer and the phones, and then turned her attention back to Jack.

'You run that poor man ragged.'

Jack laughed. 'Rubbish, he absolutely loves it. And you do too.'

Hermione reddened a shade or two. 'One thing I wanted to ask you, Jack, now that we are alone. When I talk to Liz Chapman, I wondered if there was anything you would prefer me to keep under wraps?'

Jack pulled a face. Where to begin exactly?

* * *

Even though she was the only one to get off at her stop, Liz couldn't help but look behind her, ears straining to pick up strange sounds and the echo of following feet, all the way through the familiar streets. It was proving impossible to shift the unpleasant feeling in her gut and it was making her increasingly angry. Those last hundred yards into Balmoral Terrace just about finished her off. Anymore adrenaline in her bloodstream and Liz suspected she would explode.

Everything would be fine as soon as she got home. The street light outside her front door had never looked more welcoming. She'd had the door key cradled in her fingers inside her jacket pocket since getting off the train. It had been a kind of insurance policy. Liz prayed that it would now just slip into the yale and give in without a fight. When the door swung open with not so much as a whisper of protest she could have cried with relief.

Once inside with the door shut tight, Liz leant back against the wood, heart racing, the sense of having reached safe ground washing over her in great cool tingling waves. The little house was still and calm and lamp-lit, and smelt of potpourri, Dettol, cats and pre-pubescent boys. She took a deep breath, hunting round for a normal tone and normal thoughts before finally speaking aloud.

'Hiya folks. It's only me.'

Almost instantly Claire appeared in the sitting room doorway, as if she had sprung to her feet. She was wearing an expression that implied Liz had caught her out.

'Oh, hi there,' she said, just a shade too quickly and much, much too brightly. 'How did the class go tonight? Are you okay? You look really odd.'

Liz sighed and swung her bag up onto the hall stand. All her senses were switched on, something was wrong, and whatever it was Claire hadn't got a hope in hell of hiding it. 'It looks like I'm not the only one. What have you two been up to?'

Claire blushed crimson. 'Oh God, I should have known you'd know, the thing is Mike and me –'

Liz felt her heart drop down through her diaphragm and braced herself for whatever was to follow.

'I'm really sorry, Liz,' Claire continued, 'but . . .'

Liz winced. What had they been up to? Had they got engaged? Got laid? Got pregnant. Got God? She pretended to shift her interest to the contents of her shoulder bag.

'. . . the thing is we screwed up the recording for that Art-Around thing. I don't know what happened, honestly. I was positive that we'd got it right – Anyway we've ended up with the thing about the orphan orang-utans in Borneo. I'm really sorry.'

Liz shook her head, relishing the mixture of delight and relief and amusement and every shade of every emotion in between. 'It doesn't matter,' she said, finally throwing the tension away. 'Honestly. It's not that important. I'll just go and put the kettle on. Do you want a cup of tea, coffee, only I'm parched.'

Claire hadn't moved. 'But we did watch part of it. The art thing.'

'We?'

Claire didn't bite. 'Do you really fancy Jack Sandfi, I mean it isn't some kind of wind-up is it? I thought Mike was going to spontaneously combust.'

'You and Mike watched Jack Sandfi?' Liz said slowly.

Claire nodded. 'Uh-huh that's right.'

'And?'

Claire pulled a face. 'I'm not sure you want to hear this. Tact has never really been my strong point.'

'Just say it. You didn't like him?'

At that point Mike appeared alongside Claire, he was slightly flushed and looked angry. It was an expression Liz knew only too well. One of the reasons she finally left Mike was that she couldn't stand the idea of spending the rest of her life looking at that disapproving face.

'About this Jack Sandfi thing –' he began.

Liz lifted a hand to silence them both. 'Look, I am completely and utterly knackered, it's been a really long day and I don't need either of you to okay my choice in men, right? Or to be my moral compass.' She glanced at Mike who looked as if he had been punched in the mouth. 'And while we're on the subject of morals I think there is a chance that your little psycho chum may have turned up at tech' tonight.'

Liz wasn't sure if that was true or not, and had no idea how the little redhead fitted into the bigger picture, but she knew that whoever the woman was her interest in Liz was most certainly not benign.

Mike flushed crimson. 'Oh, here we go again, for Christ's sake. That's right, Liz, just turn it around, why don't you? Trust you,' he growled, and then as if suddenly aware that Claire was watching his every move, smiled maniacally.

Chapter Sixteen

'I was really surprised that you didn't ring back straight away and snatch the job right out of my hand,' said Jeanna O'Hanlon, first thing on Thursday morning. 'But then again I like a man who can surprise me. Or is it just that you're playing hard to get, Nick? I wouldn't put it past you.' She laughed. 'Maybe you've already worked out that I just can't resist a challenge, eh?'

Something dark and icy shivered up Nick's spine and made his scalp prickle. He was having real problems moving his thoughts away from Jeanna O'Hanlon and Liz Chapman. Their fates appeared to be linked like some kind of celestial twins. In fact, it was the complex pattern of thoughts and relationships that had woken Nick up in the first place, and why although it was only half past nine on another very bright sunny morning, he felt as if he had already done a full day's work. It was a nice day for a drive. Did Liz work on Thursday? Before he could work the thought over Jeanna continued.

'I've already checked out your references with Teddy Newlen, not that you need to worry on that score, Teddy and I've known each other for years, it was just a friendly call. They're most impressed with the work you've turned out for them. Good on deadlines, excellent at bringing projects in on a tight budget. It seems that you were much, much too modest on your résumé –'

Nick Hastings slipped off the stool beside the drawing board and flexed, straightening up, all the better to fend

Jeanna off and make his excuses. But apparently Miss O'Hanlon could read minds.

'I've been having a bit of a rethink, Nick. Just follow me through on this one. I'm not altogether certain that we're ready to take on someone full time at the moment, you know, cottage on the estate and all that. It's a little bit of a re-shuffle of my original plan, I know, but I wonder if you might consider freelancing for us for a little while, just to see how we all get along. I'm extremely anxious to get the right man for this job and of course, it goes without saying that I'll make it well worth your while.'

Nick wondered if this was a gentle brush off because he hadn't found her totally irresistible. Maybe this way they could retreat without any blood being drawn or any loss of face on either side.

'We could certainly better the arrangement that you have with Newlens,' Jeanna continued. 'So what do you think? You strike me as a free spirit, Nick. This way you could do work for both of us if you wanted, and then, once we've seen how we work together maybe you and I can reconsider the full-time position. It'll still probably be much more hands-on than you're used to –' She left the words hanging in mid-air, ripening under a breathy sigh with all manner of possibilities.

'It sounds interesting,' said Nick, cautiously feeling his way forward. 'I was a bit concerned about giving up Newlens, after all they've put the bread on the table for quite a while now.' The words sounded clipped and horribly disjointed. He was lying on his toes; Nick had spent years waiting for the magic moment when he could cheerfully tell Teddy Newlen, and his range of neo-gothic monstrosities to go stuff themselves. If the job at O'Hanlons had been half what it promised Nick would have been delighted to move on with not so much as a backward glance and no regrets whatsoever.

'And doing it this way means that you won't have to uproot Liz what's-her-name and her family,' Jeanna continued casually, and as she spoke a lot of little pieces fell neatly into place.

Nick suddenly saw everything with blinding clarity. Jeanna thought that he saw the managerial position at the O'Hanlon factory as a stepping stone in his relationship with Liz, having presumably guessed that they weren't living together yet. Nick suppressed a wry smile, what was he saying, yet? They'd only met once and at the moment Liz Chapman still thought he was someone else and possibly clinically insane.

'So, there we are,' Jeanna O'Hanlon's voice nosed its way through into his thoughts. 'Would you be prepared to consider my revised offer? Not offended by the change of plans, are you?'

'No, not at all,' hedged Nick.

Jeanna's reply was a disturbingly hearty laugh. 'Well, that's good. Flexibility, that's what I need. I knew right from the start that you were the man for the job. If you could let me have your decision by the beginning of next week. I don't think I'm giving anything away when I tell you that you're head and shoulders above the competition. I've already come up with some very interesting possibilities. Maybe I could drop by and we could talk them over? I'm planning a trip down to London early next week, I could call in on the way to the station if you like.'

'Business?' Nick asked conversationally, still playing for time and a little space to think.

'Oh Good God, no, pure unadulterated pleasure,' Jeanna purred. 'I'm going down to see the Sandfi exhibition again, in London. Did I tell you that I've bought one of his new pieces?'

Nick felt a funny little flutter in his gut. It seemed that there was just no way he could break free of his alter ego.

Like Siamese twins his fate and Jack Sandfi's were joined at the hip. Liz Chapman and Jeanna O'Hanlon, Jack and Nick. Gridlock. Nick sniffed. 'Really? That's nice. Which one did you buy?' He knew the catalogue inside out.

Jeanna laughed again, although this time the tone was lower and more conspiratorial. ' "Passion Rising", you must have seen it. It is absolutely wonderful. Big and gloriously powerful, charged with the most amazing raw energy; it really was love at first sight, Nick, I can tell you. I'm like that, you know, when I see something I really want I'll move heaven and earth to get my hands on it.'

'So, when do you think you'll be popping in?' Nick said hastily, swallowing hard. 'Only I've got quite a hectic schedule lined up for next week.'

Her voice dropped even lower to an earthy, guttural purr. 'Do I make you nervous, Nicky?'

Defeated Nick slumped back onto his stool. 'No, not at all, Jeanna, it was just that I've, I'm . . .' the silence opened up in front of him like an elephant trap and he knew that he just hadn't got the strength to vault over it.

'How about Tuesday around ten-thirty, will that be okay?' said Jeanna in a completely normal voice.

'That sounds just fine by me.'

'Good, see you soon then, lover boy,' she murmured.

Nick was about to let it pass and then knew that if he couldn't stop her now he was lost forever. Time to break the pattern.

'Actually Jeanna, before you go –'

'Uh-huh?' Her voice rolled down the line towards him, warm, sensual and lazy.

'I don't want to string you along. I'd like to withdraw my application for the job. I had planned to ring you later today but you pre-empted me. Actually I'm planning to set up on my own.'

'On your own?' She sounded incredulous.

'That's right, although I'm not going to give Newlens up until I'm up and running. It's something I've wanted to do for a long time. Seeing your place helped me make my decision. I've just been waiting for the right moment.'

'I suppose Liz Chapman put you up to this, didn't she?' snapped Jeanna.

It was such an unexpected thing for her to say that Nick was stunned for a few seconds and then he grinned. 'Yes, you're right. I suppose in a way she did, yes. You probably think I'm completely mad –' but before he had a chance to say anything else, Jeanna O'Hanlon had hung up.

Nick's smile broadened and then he stretched. Somewhere deep inside he could sense that some celestial tide had just turned

*   *   *

In Balmoral Terrace, it was coming up to ten o'clock, and as far as Liz was concerned the morning was already proving to be difficult. Maria Ludlow, editor of *Ciao* had been on the phone for what felt like forever. Liz hadn't had a single opportunity to lever a word into the conversation.

'The thing is,' said Maria, her tone harrying and insistent, 'Jack Sandfi is awfully keen to get this interview organised. I had a message waiting for me on my machine when I got in first thing this morning. Basically he wants to know if you can schedule it for either Friday or Saturday. I do realise that this is all terribly rushed, Liz, but we really ought to strike while the iron is hot with this one. Jack Sandfi is notoriously fickle; though on the bright side he did suggest that you might like to talk to him over a nice lunch.'

Liz would have shaken her head in disbelief if she hadn't got the phone nipped between neck and shoulder and wasn't very quietly trying to peel off a pair of rubber gloves. It seemed that Jack was determined to see her again, one way or another, and as an added bonus *Ciao* were prepared to pay her a lot of money for the privilege. What had she got to lose. The guy was nothing if not persistent. 'Okay,' she murmured acknowledging defeat.

The events of the evening still lingered like dark fog in her mind, the redhead in the foyer and Claire and Mike. Her plan was to spend the day close to home, doing something cave-ish, and domestic, something that would re-establish some sense of order and control.

She'd been on her hands and knees scraping something furry out of the back of the fridge when the phone rang. Some nasty sausages, a limp little gem lettuce, two fading sunset peppers and a rind of mousetrap cheddar stood sentinel on the drip tray by the open fridge door. It was wedged ajar to give the ice floe that was clinging to the freezer box a sporting chance to give in and drop off before Liz set to with the steak tenderiser. Glacier-like the ice had grown over night so that the fridge door wouldn't shut properly; Ms Ludlow couldn't have timed the call better.

As Liz listened, a small portion of her brain watched Winston moving silently across the kitchen, feline SAS, up on tippy-toe to avoid the growing puddle of icy water, craning forward to investigate something in the bowels of the fridge. Resisting all Liz's wavings and silent encouragement to leave well alone he leant forward and an instant later re-appeared with a white polythene bag stapled between pin-point teeth. He glanced up at her for the briefest instant, and froze, his sulphurous eyes reduced to pinpricks, appeared to note her annoyance and then made a speedy get away through the cat flap an instant before the balled-up rubber gloves ricocheted off the door frame an inch or two above his retreating rear end.

And all this while Ms Ludlow talked on and on, filling

the still hot air with sound. Liz pulled a notebook closer and settled herself comfortably at the kitchen table before finally leaping into the great flood tide of words.

'That sounds fine. Really, I don't mind it being short notice. What time did Jack say it would be convenient for me to have lunch with him?'

Maria sounded startled. 'Around twelve-ish on either day. Do you know where the Rectory is exactly?'

'The Rectory?' The address sounded the first little alarm bell.

'Uh-huh, that's right. Here we are: The Old Hallgate Rectory, Church Lane, Elverstone.' She was reading. 'His agent gave me the directions this morning if you'd like them. Have you got a pen handy. It's quite near to Swaffham apparently. Do you know where that is? I mean, is it close to you?'

'Jack lives in Norwich I think. I've got an address for him in the city.'

Maria laughed. 'What can I tell you? A *pied-à-terre* maybe or his office, or perhaps it's a little love nest, who knows? We are talking about Jack Sandfi after all. No, whatever he told you last time you met, this time he wants you to interview him over at the Old Hallgate Rectory, Elverstone. Did you see him on the TV last night? My God, wasn't that a performance? The man was like a caged tiger. All that brooding passion, posing, the unco-operative tainted genius, glorious glorious stuff. I can't wait until they do a whole programme about him. His agent said it's on the cards. And I'm sure this interview will be pure dynamite. You must ring and let me know how it goes.'

Liz decided not to mention that she had missed Art-Around. 'I'll need to sort out transport to get myself over to Elverstone. Can I ring you back?'

'Of course, now if you've got that pen I'll give you the address and the directions. And I've got Hermione Benn's number at the Review Gallery as well if you'd like to contact her – the one in Norwich.'

Gamely Liz wrote it all down, her mind still chewing over the mystery of Jack's two addresses.

*   *   *

Meanwhile at the Rectory, Jack Sandfi took a long hard look around the interior of the apple loft above the studio. It didn't look too bad at all now. He had been clearing it out in anticipation of Liz Chapman's arrival, whenever that might be. Morwenna had gone off into town shopping with the cleaning woman and so he had had the chance to smuggle some clean sheets out of the airing cupboard in the students' dormitory, along with two plump new pillows and a rather nice heavy cotton bedspread.

The little blonde Australian had swept the floor and cleared away the rook's nest of wine bottles and fag ends that had accumulated in the corners. From beside him on the bare board floor a double helix of smoke from a joss stick headed up into the rafters joining the plump cumulus of perfume already released. No, not bad at all.

On an upturned apple box in one corner was a vase of over-blown scarlet roses, a bright focal point in the dusty white washed room. It looked fine, just fine. Jack sighed, wondering whether it would be too forward just to bring Liz straight up here as soon as she arrived; he would have to play it by ear. What he really needed after all the work they had done was a little drink to lay the dust.

Jack tweaked the fringed edge of the smoky blue counterpane so that it hung straight. He was uncharacteristically nervous. There were so many things that he seemed to have forgotten, the idea unsettled him; what else might be missing from his memory besides the encounter with Ms Chapman? But then, when he and Liz met again surely he

225

would be able to tell whether he had slept with her or not. He would remember, wouldn't he? And if he couldn't Liz would give him some hint, some deep meaningful look. He would know then, wouldn't he? Jack would decide what to do next when he knew for certain what it was he had done before.

He tied up a black bag half full of rubbish and dragged it over to the stairs. It was most definitely time for a drink, a long cool revitalising drink, and after that Jack intended to make a start on cleaning the summer house, which was where he planned that he and Liz should hold their interview, unless of course he had persuaded her up to the apple loft in the meantime; it was definitely time for a drink.

As if by magic the blonde girl appeared at the top of the stairwell cradling two cans of lager, their smooth sides still glistening with condensation. She threw him one and popped the ring pull on hers, lifting it to toast their surroundings.

'Very Thomas Hardy,' she said, taking a long pull on the beer, leaving a creamy moustache on her sun-tanned top lip. 'It looks great. I'll get the lads to give the studio a quick going over too while we're at it. You know, make it look like something deep and meaningful is going on down there. Is she gonna bring a photographer as well?'

Jack shrugged. It hadn't occurred to him that Liz would be bringing anyone with her. 'To be perfectly honest I've got no idea who's coming. I just wanted to be ready, tidy, prepared.' But in his imagination Liz arrived alone, anxious to spend a few more hours with him; her expression hunted and hungry. Jack smiled, he was both impassioned and eager to recapture whatever it was that had made him trust her with all his secrets that first time.

Liz Chapman came to Jack in all sorts of shapes, sizes and situations. Gratifying though that was, it would be a great relief to finally see her again in the flesh. He shivered at the prospect and hastily made a start on the ice cold lager.

The blonde girl was still crouched on the top step, watching him with those large feline eyes. 'So, are you going to tell us all about her, then? All that crap with Arturo. What is she? Some old flame of yours or something? I've never seen you get so arsy about anything before. This meeting is real important to y', ay?'

Jack settled himself on the end of the bed. She was absolutely right, and for the first time in his life Jack was very anxious not to squander that feeling of specialness that was tormenting him; he didn't intend to fight his instincts. He wanted to make a good impression on Liz Chapman for lots of reasons, not least of which was because it felt that in some strange way she held his future in her hands.

*   *   *

When Liz rang the *Bishopston News and Advertiser* Claire was in her office. It was coming up for lunch time and it sounded as if Claire was having hers at her desk – Liz could hear her chewing the cud between words. It didn't take very long to explain that Jack Sandfi and *Ciao* were pushing to get the interview done.

Claire's initial enthusiasm turned to hesitance. 'Of course you can borrow the car, that's not a problem, but are you sure you really want to go and see this guy again?'

Liz took a breath to speak but Claire was ahead of her. 'Okay, okay, I'm sorry I even bothered to ask. Of course you do, and you'll be getting paid for it, so what's to talk about? Just be careful that's all. Saturday would be better for me if that's okay, I'm out all day on Friday covering an agricultural show near Norwich.'

'Thanks, that would be just great. I've got to organise

something for the boys. I was going to ask Mike, but under the circumstance –'

'I could stay with them when I drop the car off if you like.'

'Are you sure? That wasn't meant as a sneaky backdoor hint.'

Claire laughed. 'Oh really? Anyway, you know what I'm like. I've got a real nose for gossip. I want the exclusive on how it went with Sandfi and what the hell it is you see in him. The guy came across as an utter bastard on that arts programme.'

'Whatever you do, Claire, please don't try and sugar-coat the pill.' She spoke with jokey indignation that masked the genuine prickle of hurt. 'I'd hate to think you were holding back on my account. It's weird, I thought he was really nice when we first met in Norwich. I'm beginning to think that the guy is some sort of schizophrenic. What do you think?'

'C'mon, give me a break, I'm not paid enough to think,' Claire mumbled, through a mouthful of something thick and doughy. 'I'm just here to record it all for posterity. But whatever else happens I want to know all the ins and outs of whatever it is you and the ghastly Mr Sandfi get up to. Oh and are we still on for tomorrow night?'

Liz grinned. 'Do you really need to ask? Video, vino, I'll get the snackie stuff tomorrow. You could stay over if you wanted to save you a drive Saturday morning?'

'Uh-huh, thanks but no thanks, things to do. You know how it is. Anyway I've got to go and get some work done. Off to right wrongs and leap tall buildings at a single bound. What are you up to today?'

'Actually I was cleaning out the fridge just before *Ciao* rang.'

Claire giggled. 'In that case may the force be with you,

kid. Was there anything else you wanted or can I go and finish this tuna baguette in peace?'

Liz was very tempted to try to turn the conversation around to Mike and his stalker and the appearance of the strange red-headed woman at college. The night before she'd been so busy trying to defend Jack Sandfi against Mike and Claire, and then Mike had been so bloody defensive about the blonde girl that she'd had no real chance to talk about how threatened she had felt. Somewhere down the line her sense of vulnerability had been side-stepped by Mike's raw angry indignation. And anyway her sense of fear had seemed too big and foolish when it was out in the light and she was safely back at home. But now was not the right time either; Claire was already heading towards a round of goodbyes.

Liz stretched. On the far side of the kitchen the fridge appeared to have defrosted completely without resorting to any hammering or hot water. There were just two more phone calls to make, one to confirm that the meeting was now on with Jack for Saturday and the other to Hermione Benn over at the gallery to get some background information. Which seemed like the polite thing to do given that *Ciao* had set it up, and besides Miss Benn might be able to answer a lot of the questions that refused to go away, like the two addresses. After that Liz planned to mop up the tidal pool of glacial water that was slowly seeping towards her across the quarry tiles and then spend an hour or so outside in the sunshine before picking Joe up from school.

She made a coffee and settled down with the phone; *Ciao* first. Fortunately she got Maria Ludlow's machine, which was a blessing, and then she rang Hermione Benn.

'Oh hi there, I was hoping that you would call,' said the gallery owner pleasantly. Liz immediately recognised the voice as belonging to the woman she'd met when she and Claire had gone to see the Sandfi's on the last day of the Norwich exhibition.

The voice was cultured, with a finest patina of something transatlantic.

'Funnily enough I was talking to Jack about you last night,' Hermione said, 'and you know he is really, really excited about you two meeting up again. I'd hoped that you and I could maybe get together before you did this next interview. I've never seen Jack like this about anything, you must have made quite an impression, Ms Chapman, and I'm really quite curious about that.'

Liz felt the colour in her face rising. She wanted to say something casual and clever but no words floated to the surface although Hermione Benn appeared only too pleased to fill in the gaps.

'Jack and I go back years, you know.' The woman laughed, though Liz felt that like the clever curling gloved hand of a magician the gallery owner's amusement was meant to deflect Liz's attention away from other, older things, real things that still hurt.

'It all seems rather crazy now on reflection,' Hermione said, with the same contrived lightness and sleightness, 'I used to have such a terrible crush on Jack. We were at college together, and we've always stayed in touch down the years. Nice really –' There was a fraction of a second's pause, Hermione's tone cooling a little by the time she moved on. 'Although of course, it never went anywhere, you know, didn't come to anything very much; nothing to talk about. We were both terribly young back in those days, barely more than children, neither of us keen to get tied down. And as I'm sure you're well aware Jack is a very complex and rather self absorbed man. The nature of the beast, I suppose, and then of course his drinking has always been a problem. Maybe I had a lucky escape, after all –' She stopped again, paying her respects with a moment's silence to mourn the might-have-beens and then continued, 'I know that I'm supposed to be filling in some background material but to be perfectly frank Jack seems to have opened up to you in a way that he has never done with any of the rest of us. You've seen a part of him denied to we lesser mortals – even Morwenna. It really was quite astonishing to read all those things in your article.'

There was an odd and very deep silence and then Liz heard a small voice say, 'Morwenna?' apparently lightly, almost casually, although it took her a few seconds to realise that the voice was her own.

'Morwenna Pearce, the watercolourist? You must know her. We had some of her work in here, it was before Christmas, I think. Jack's wife, have you two not met? I'd assumed that you would have. Actually though I'm not sure that they are married but they've lived together for years and y –'

Hermione's voice died back and if anything the silence intensified and then she whispered, 'Oh my God, I'm so sorry. You didn't know about Morwenna, did you? Didn't Jack tell you? Jesus, that bastard.'

Liz nipped frantically on a tight breath, strangling the life out of a tiny gasp of shock and pain, fighting to suppress the great sense of betrayal and outrage that seeped up through her body like bloody fog.

At the far end of the line she was aware of Hermione Benn scrambling around for something to say, a suitable thing, a thing that the gallery owner could later commend herself on as being the right thing under the circumstances, and at the same time Liz's scalp prickled with the most horrible sense of foreboding.

A long slow second passed, after which Hermione tried filling the hiatus with abstract placating noises. It was almost more than Liz could bear and she was about to try to heave the conversation back on to the rails, say something hearty and self-depreciating, when she looked up and across the kitchen saw the red-headed woman from the college foyer standing by her back door.

It seemed so bizarre and yet on the other hand it was almost as if some part of her had expected to see the woman there, even though the rational portion was stunned into open-mouthed silence.

The woman did not knock, instead she peered in through the windowpane, small hands cupped around her face to cut out the light, and as their eyes met Liz knew without a shadow of a doubt that the woman staring in at her was Jack Sandfi's woman, Morwenna Pearce.

Chapter Seventeen

Liz sat very still, as if there was some strange possibility that she might blend into the background and vanish, chameleon-like. Meanwhile she was aware that the red-headed woman's focus had tightened on the table, and then, knowing that there was no escape, without really thinking about the consequences, Liz got to her feet, circumnavigating the great flood plain of fridge water and unfastened the back door.

There were a few seconds of total silence in which both women stood and looked at each other, one inside, one out. Liz's unexpected guest was extremely pale and dressed in an elegant sage green trouser suit that emphasised her delicate creamy white skin. She had quite obviously dressed with considerable care, the whole outfit, her handsome brown leather brogues and bag, whispered elegance and old money. She took a step back from the doorway and then held her ground.

'Hello,' said Liz, after what seemed like an eternity. 'Can I help you?' She made every effort to keep her expression impassive. Her anxiety, in fact all her emotions, cowering behind a great solid wall of anonymous civility.

The woman looked her up and down but said nothing, so Liz pressed on, 'Is there something I can do for –'

'Oh, for God's sake, do we really have to go through this ridiculous little charade?' the woman snapped, taking a long pull on her cigarette – oddly enough she was wearing gloves that matched her shoes and bag – and then she sighed heavily. 'We both know exactly who I am and why I'm here.' Although the tone was icy, her voice was surprisingly high-pitched, almost girl-ish. 'I want to know what your relationship is with Jack Sandfi and I want to know now.'

Liz stepped away from the door and fighting all her instincts, seeking to find some way to dis-arm the small red-headed woman, waved her interrogator inside.

'Look, this is complete and utter madness. There's nothing to know, really. Why don't you just come in and take a seat and I'll put the kettle on. Oh and please be careful, there's water all over the floor. I'd hate you to slip –'

It sounded ridiculous.

Morwenna hesitated for an instant; it was quite obvious that whatever else she had been expecting, she hadn't imagined that their encounter would go in this direction. The redhead lifted an eyebrow and took a deep breath as if to speak, thought better of it and finally picked her way across the kitchen, stepping deftly between the little things that had been carried along on the edge of the flood tide: a fine wet slick of cat hairs, a couple of wizened tomato stalks, a milk bottle top and one of those long curled security strips that hold plastic lids on. Along the water margins were the flotsam and jetsam of the fridge's interior, like ice floes against the dark slippery tiles.

'Have you been flooded?' Morwenna asked, settling herself at the cluttered kitchen table.

'Defrosting.'

Morwenna nodded, and as she did peeled off the very thin brown leather gloves she was wearing and dropped them onto the table beside her amongst the debris. Something about the way the woman moved and the gloves themselves really disturbed Liz. First of all it was the height of summer, who wore leather gloves in the summer? And secondly, curled up on the battered pine they looked uncannily like something that had died and was now very slowly decomposing.

Morwenna was speaking; Liz forced her attention away from the two little heaps of sloughed skin.

'Mine does that on its own sometimes,' she was saying. Liz was surprised, the very last thing she had expected was small talk. 'It has some sort of auto-defrost feature the assistant in the shop told me, although I really do think that there ought to be a red light or something to tell you when it's going to happen, some sort of warning device. I came home from Norwich one afternoon and the whole of the pantry was totally flooded. It ruined the flour, and it makes everything smell so ghastly. I said to . . .'

Morwenna stopped and then reddened slightly, both women aware that in her nervousness she had inadvertently crossed a bridge too far. 'So,' she gathered herself back up, squaring her shoulders, returning the game pieces back to the start. 'Jack Sandfi.'

Liz took a deep breath. 'Jack Sandfi.'

'Let's just get straight to the point, shall we, Ms Chapman? I'm here to talk about what went on between you and my husband. Would you care to tell me about the nature of your relationship with him?'

While she was speaking Liz lifted the coffee by the kettle and Morwenna's head nodded a fraction, although very little of either woman's attention was really on the jar. The gesture and acceptance had a ritual significance that was not lost on either of them and it also gave Liz something to do with her hands while her brain ran frantically from room to room looking for the appropriate things to say.

She took another deep breath, trying to tidy the landslide of ideas back into order, while all the time a great deal of her concentration and her eyes were fixed on Morwenna's pale and very beautiful heart-shaped face, just in case – and the thought had crossed her mind the moment she spotted the strangler's gloves – Jack's wife had cooked up a more violent and permanent solution to all her problems.

Liz shivered. What if Morwenna had already murdered Jack and then driven over to finish the job off? The more Liz dwelt on the notion the more sense it made. She glanced down at the other woman's handbag, which was standing on the floor next to her chair rather than within cleaver grabbing distance, and then fought very hard to close down the flickering slide show of guns and knives and other bloody images that threatened to engulf her. Something on her scalp tingled, forcing Liz to suppress another more violent shudder. What made it all the more difficult was that Morwenna Pearce looked more than capable of murder.

How could Jack Sandfi be married to this woman, and how could he lie so convincingly, so seamlessly? Liz felt a great surge of pain and anger bubble up inside her. What was it with men, first Mike and now Jack.

Liz took yet another breath – she was aware of every single one – this one the kind of long launching breath normally taken before embarking on a poem or a song.

'I really don't know why I'm making this so difficult. The bottom line is that I had absolutely no idea that Jack was in a relationship when we met for the interview in Norwich. Not a clue. He didn't mention it, he certainly didn't bring it up during our conversation, and when we were done I said my goodbyes and chalked our meeting down to experience. I enjoyed interviewing him, he wasn't at all what I had expected.' She paused and bit down on her lip, running the events through one more time; married or not that *was* what she had done. Jack had been nice, attractive, sexy but realistically she had had no real expectations of seeing him again after their interview. She must tell Morwenna that.

'It was Jack who contacted me after the second article appeared in the *Sunday News*.'

Morwenna nodded, her hypnotic dark eyes snake-bright. She waved Liz to continue.

'I'm not sure that there is that much more really. To be fair, when I thought about it, I did realise that Jack was trying to hide something from me, but I wasn't sure what it was. It didn't cross my mind for a moment that it was a marriage, a wife, you.'

Liz paused, trying to gauge Morwenna's reaction but there was nothing, not a flicker, not a twitch, not the slightest hint on that perfect little face to betray whatever emotion was playing itself out inside Morwenna's head, just those great glittering eyes focused on her, as if Morwenna could make out her words and read them as they were being formed, weighing them up, gauging their veracity.

Watching Morwenna so intently, Liz realised that Jack Sandfi hadn't struck her as being a married man at all. There had been a rangy, rather endearing disconnected quality to him, unearthed, un-settled, certainly there was no sense of Jack being a part of something bigger, none of the veneer of care and polish that usually comes from being part of a couple. He was so convincing it was dangerous, perhaps Jack and Morwenna were better suited than Liz first thought.

'I do realise that under the circumstances you may find this hard to believe but I'm not the stuff of which other women are made,' Liz paused and slid the mug of coffee and the sugar jar towards Morwenna. 'If anything, up until now I've been in your shoes.' Liz winced; that wasn't quite what she had meant to say.

Morwenna looked around for somewhere to flick her cigarette ash. Liz took a saucer off the windowsill and handed it to her.

This was like pulling teeth. 'My ex-husband had a roving

eye during the last couple of years we were together, but I didn't so much as kiss Jack, not once, not ever, not so much as a peck on the cheek. I think we may have shaken hands when we said goodbye after the interview but that was it –'

Liz paused and looked heavenwards trying to marshal her thoughts. What was it exactly that Morwenna wanted to know or hear? Liz knew that she was giving away far too much of herself but didn't seem able to stop the flow.

'And I certainly haven't chased him. We've only met once, for the interview in Norwich and I've spoken to him on the phone a few times since then, maybe two or three, four at the most. And that is about the long and the short of it.' Liz stopped; what else was there left to say?

But those were only the bare facts, not the emotions whispered a small subversive voice in her head. Liz lifted her hands to imply surrender and completion and as she did an unpleasant, triumphant little smile skittered across Morwenna's face.

'So are you telling me that you haven't slept with him?'

Liz shook her head emphatically. 'No.'

Morwenna tidied the answer away into whatever dark place she was using to store their encounter and then said, 'But you were attracted to Jack, weren't you? You're not trying to tell me that all this, this desire, this sense of expectation on his part is part of some misguided fantasy cooked up by his over heated imagination?'

Liz reddened, aware that confronted by Morwenna she felt almost as guilty as if she had slept with him – and that some crazed part of her was excited by the knowledge that Jack had been as attracted to her as she had to him. Madness, that was the only answer. It was pointless to lie, she might have got away with it if she was talking to a man but Morwenna would have been onto her in an instant. In the sharp pointed silence, the eerie little smile surfaced again to haunt them both. Morwenna lit another cigarette and ground the old one into a mess of fluff and fragments. 'I'm right, aren't I? You are attracted to him, aren't you?'

Liz nodded.

'But you definitely haven't slept with him?' There was something prurient and deeply unpleasant about the way she said it, and a flare of indignation rose up from low in Liz's gut.

She knew then that Morwenna Pearce hadn't come to fight for Jack or even to warn Liz off her turf, but to gloat, exacting some measure of revenge or retribution that Liz really didn't understand. Whatever it was, it made her feel sick.

And then, before Liz could find another sort of answer, the phone rang, once, twice and she knew without a shadow of doubt somewhere deep in her soul that it would be Jack Sandfi, and that if she left the machine to get it he would say something sweet and soulful and maybe, just maybe, Morwenna Pearce would reach down into that expensive brown leather handbag and pull out a meat cleaver after all. Liz got to her feet well aware that Morwenna was watching her every move and hastily picked up the receiver.

'Hello? Can I help you?'

* * *

Nick Hastings, who had settled himself down on one of the chairs in his kitchen, grinned from ear to ear; bingo. The magic was holding. Wriggling free of Jeanna O'Hanlon had altered the balance of everything. Now *was* the time to make things right. Now was the moment to move on, make good and insist that he and Liz sorted this thing out face to face. Right.

'Hello, who is this?' asked Liz, breaking into his sense of euphoria.

After talking to Ms O'Hanlon, her voice sounded as clear and warm and as unambiguous as sunlight.

'Hi, how are you? I'm sorry that I missed you yesterday. Nice to meet your mum though. I had planned to ring you first but to be honest I chickened out. I thought there was a good chance that you'd just tell me to sod off. Anyway, how are things going with you?'

At the far end of the line Liz made a peculiar kind of squeaking sound somewhere high up in the back of her throat. Nick wondered if she was feeling ill, maybe she had caught her sons' stomach bug, maybe he had got her out of bed, maybe; a whole flock of doubts flew down to mob him.

'Are you feeling okay?'

He heard Liz cough and then she said in an odd brittle voice. 'Thank you so much for ringing, but actually we've already had double glazing fitted, thank you.'

'Sorry?'

'We had it installed just before we moved in. And to be perfectly honest I'm not that interested in a quote for a conservatory either, but thank you for ringing anyway.'

'Is this a bad time to talk?'

'Well, actually yes it is.' She sounded almost angry.

'Would you like me to call you back later?'

'No, not really. In fact to be perfectly honest I can't imagine that we'll be wanting any of your products for the foreseeable future, so there's really not a lot of point calling me again. I'd be obliged if you would take my number off your list. Thank you.'

And then Liz hung up. Just like that. Nick stared at the receiver. Sometimes life was messy and complicated and then other times it was just plain peculiar.

*   *   *

'And what the fuck do you think you're looking at, exactly? You told me you were going to go over and clean out the summer house when you'd finished the loft.' The blonde girl was defiant, hands on hips, legs akimbo, everything about her as prickly and sharp as a feral kitten.

Jack Sandfi grinned and stood a can of lager down on one of the tables beside an unoccupied drawing board in the studio. 'I thought I'd start on it later, maybe you and the boys could give me a hand. Have you got a pencil I can borrow?' he said, still struggling to control a lopsided grin. 'Only I thought I might do a sketch or two. While I'm in the mood.' The grin widened. 'You know you look lovely standing there in the sunshine. All hot and busy and cross.' He took another mouthful of beer and then waggled the can in her direction. 'I thought I could show you where you're going wrong.'

Since helping to clear up the apple loft the little Australian had gone back downstairs to work in the studio. When Jack came downstairs with the last of the rubbish bags, he couldn't help but notice her from the shadow of the stairwell. She was standing at her bench, one leg bent at the knee resting on a stool, pencil between her full lips, leaning forward a little, all of her thoughts fixed on a new set of drawings that she was working on for some part of the great metal sculpture. He hadn't realised that she knew he was watching her.

Pinned to the cork boards around her work space, were snips and snaps and clippings and cuttings and postcards and poems and bits of bent wire and oddments of fabric and paper of every sort and colour, all of which framed her spikey white-gold hair. It was like her bower. A tangled magpie's nest of ideas and inspiration. Against the random brightness she seemed as pure and uncomplicated as a bolt of white silk in a bazaar.

And for one blissful all engulfing revelatory moment

Jack had also seen the magic of the sketches on the board in front of her, born witness to that act of creation. The sensation had reached in through his ribs and grabbed hold of his heart. In some dusty cobwebbed part of himself, he remembered exactly how it felt to make the journey she was engaged on; he could see what she was doing, and why and how and for the first time in more years than he cared to remember Jack wanted to do it too.

The idea kick started his pulse and made him feel heady and breathless. 'So, have you got a pencil then or should I just open a vein and use my life's blood?'

The girl curled her lip and then pulled a well-chewed stub from behind her ear. 'You can be so fucking melodramatic, Jack. Here.'

'I've been thinking,' he said, opening the plan chest in search of paper. 'Perhaps I might experiment with something similar to the kind of thing you've been doing. It's terribly interesting, the whole area of art from found objects. When I was at college, there was this friend of m –'

Jack stopped. The girl was glaring at him now, her face set, those workish warm capable hands back on hips, her thoughts torn reluctantly away from her own idea and then, when she had his full attention, through a row of perfect pearly white teeth she growled, 'If you copy any of my stuff you thieving little bastard I'll stick your balls in a blender. And I don't give a tin-shit whether you're famous or not. Do y'follow me?'

Jack grinned. 'Would I?' he said, turning back to rootle in the plan chest.

Just above his stomach, in the odd and infinite space that lay somewhere between his heart and gut and head, was a sacred spot that until that moment Jack truly believed had atrophied and died some time back in the seventies.

It was like a stirring movement, a quickening, this need to draw and make that had been denied him since God knows when. Very nonchalantly he slid a sheet of A2 cartridge paper out from the drawer and clipped it to a board, moving very casually in case the feeling sensed his excitement, took fright and scurried to ground in terror.

Jack wanted to make something; it was a most basic need, although what it was exactly that he wanted to make was still an abstract unformed thought. Even so, Jack could already sense some of the lines and the curves growing organically somewhere deep in the eternal cauldron that was part thought and part instinct. He wanted to make something for Liz Chapman or maybe about Liz Chapman, he wanted to make something special and mysterious and powerful and hidden and yet burgeoning with all manner of wonderful sensual possibilities.

'Fucking hell,' said his blonde companion. 'Exactly how long have you got?'

Until that moment Jack hadn't realised he had been thinking aloud.

*   *   *

In the still seconds after she had hung up from talking to Jack Sandfi, aka Nick Hastings, Liz tidied the phone back onto the dresser, scooping up notebooks and pens in an effort to re-establish a sense of order and some sense of control. She couldn't quite bring herself to meet Morwenna's eyes.

When Liz finally looked up the redhead had lit yet another cigarette which was nipped tight between elegant fingers, while she sipped her coffee, apparently completely absorbed in admiring the dimensions, detail and content of the kitchen.

Liz picked up her own mug. There was a part of her

which was beginning to feel angry now, angry and put upon. It was obvious that this kind of thing must have happened before. Jack and this unnerving woman were squeezing her into a role in a play that she had no part in, acting out some drama for their own personal amusement. And it did cross her mind that perhaps Jack had called knowing full well that Morwenna was already sitting there in the kitchen, listening to what was being said.

Liz straightened up; it was time to put an end to their nasty little game. 'So, is there anything else you wanted to know before you leave?' Her tone was cooler and far less conciliatory.

Morwenna turned her head and smiled; it was not altogether pleasant.

'No, not really, I don't think so, things seem clear enough now,' she paused, 'though of course there is still the matter of the interview for *Ciao*, but I am assuming that after that there will be no more of this nonsense.' She took another mouthful of coffee and then set the mug down with an air of finality. 'I considered suggesting that Jack cancel it, but I'm sure we could all use the money.' She began to gather her things together. It seemed that their audience was at an end. 'I won't keep you, Ms Chapman, I'm sure that you have plenty to do and I have someone waiting to drive me home.'

Morwenna's eyes appeared to darken a little. 'It's odd. Jack can't wait to see you again, Ms Chapman. All this subterfuge and excitement. At his age.' She laughed a tight, dry little laugh. 'I really do think he is quite smitten with you, you know. Sad really. Under the circumstances.' She stopped and got to her feet, picking up the strangler's gloves as she did so. She pulled them on, easing them down finger by finger. 'And of course, although we all try not to make too much of it, his memory isn't what it was. I'm never sure quite what he does remember these days. You see, he seems to think that you are something very special, but he can't quite remember whether he slept with you or not, a rather pathetic state of affairs, wouldn't you say? It's the drink you know. Don't look so surprised, Ms Chapman, Jack can make an effort to hide it if he thinks it's to his advantage. These days my role in his life is part wife, part nurse, part minder.'

Liz felt her colour rising under Morwenna's unflinching gaze. And then very slowly the small red-headed witch bent down, picked up her handbag and headed towards the door. A few seconds later she was gone, out across the water's edge back into the sunshine, leaving behind just a trail of footprints across the stone floor and a sulphurous whiff of tobacco smoke.

The moment the door closed behind her Liz let out a long strangled breath that she didn't know she had been holding. At around the same time Winston poured himself in through the cat flap carrying a plump baby rat. It was an appalling act of transubstantiation.

They looked at each other and Winston growled.

Liz stared him down – it took a while – and then finally with an angry flick of his tail the cat retreated.

Liz took another deep breath and closed her eyes tight, struggling to hold back the great bow waves of tears that threatened to break. She clenched her fists, stomach knotted tight, full of spite and fury and pity for herself and for Jack Sandfi.

*   *   *

Morwenna didn't look back once she was out of Liz's garden and on the pavement. Lily Howard was waiting for her in the Montego, which was parked two streets away from Balmoral Terrace, in a wedge of shade close to a little post office store and an old-fashioned ladies hairdressers where a huddle of beehive dryers were arranged in one dusty window.

As Morwenna approached the car she could see that Lily was sound asleep in the driver's seat, snoring softly, her head thrown back, mouth open, a little slick of spittle glittering like hoar frost on her pock marked chin.

Morwenna was relieved to have some advantage, however small. It would have been uncomfortable to know that her retreat was being observed by her charlady, and somewhere deep inside Morwenna conceded that it was a retreat. Any success, any concession that might come of the meeting with Liz Chapman was dependent not on what Morwenna had done or said but on the honourable nature of her opponent. It was a sensation that did not sit at all well with Morwenna.

Against all the odds, Liz Chapman had turned out to be kind and honourable and clever and far, far, far too good for the likes of Jack. Morwenna also knew, without a shadow of a doubt, that for all Jack's love and lust and all his red hot desires and good intentions, if he took a step closer and Liz Chapman was in the least bit tempted to reciprocate, and get more involved with him, then Jack wouldn't be able to help himself. The self-seeking, uncertain, self-destructive, hungry demonic part of Jack's nature would slowly ruin Liz and drain her dry as surely and certainly as it had Morwenna.

Morwenna brushed something wet and unlikely away from her eye. Her one real hope was that Liz Chapman would also have good sense amongst her arsenal and, once she saw Jack in his natural habitat, drunk and flawed and selfish, would recognise him for what he truly was and run away back to her comfortable little house and her tidy little life, as fast as those long slim sun-tanned legs would take her.

Morwenna took a few deep breaths to settle herself.

Something, perhaps a shadow or the sound of her footsteps, disturbed Lily Howard, who snuffled and stretched and snorted and blinked her way back into consciousness, her stubby fingers searching out the ignition key before she had barely had time to focus.

Morwenna pulled open the car door and slid in beside her.

Lily looked across expectantly, mouth working to clear away the remnants of sleep. 'So, how did it go then? Did you get to talk to her? What was she like?'

Morwenna made a great show of fiddling with the seat belt, pulling it across her lap and snapping it into place. 'Nothing to worry about. A one night stand that got a little out of hand, that's all. You know what Jack's like, promising so much, delivering so little,' Morwenna said, picking up her handbag so that she wouldn't have to look into Lily's sharp little eyes; what she really needed now was another cigarette.

Chapter Eighteen

Under the circumstances the rest of Thursday and most of Friday were remarkably uneventful for everyone, as if the eye of the storm was passing slowly over them. The sun shone, the sky was a powder-blue cloudless cliché and both days were long and hot with the promise of many more to follow. Summer was most definitely on its way.

In the little house in Balmoral Terrace Liz Chapman eventually finished sorting out the contents of the fridge, although it took a lot longer than she had intended. She worked with one eye on the door. The encounter with Morwenna had left her feeling fragile and hurt, not to mention vulnerable and deep down to the core angry. In the afternoon she walked up into town to meet the boys from school, she shopped and cleaned, marked some of her students' work, passed a long slow evening working on a new lesson plan for the autumn term, and spent a lot of time soothing and settling herself, which mostly involved sitting outside on the sun lounger with a book, under a big umbrella, with a large pot of tea and Winston curled up on her lap.

The pocket-sized garden at the back of the house was shady until mid-afternoon when the sun rose slowly above the roof tops and cut the air with the scent of melted tar and hot dusty flagstones; it felt really good to be outside. When she had sat for long enough, Liz knelt on the low retaining walls that held back a tumble of summer flowers, velvety night scented stocks and fragrant climbers and weeded and pruned and tidied, all the while striving to regain some sense of connection and possession and calm.

Until Morwenna's arrival the house had seemed like a sanctuary against the world, a new, emotionally clean place where Liz was learning to live without Mike, learning to stand alone with all the things that haunted and delighted her. Learning to be alone after years of being part of something bigger had taken more strength than she would ever have guessed. Now Liz needed to find something to make the house feel that way again.

Until she and the little house felt healed and Liz could put some distance between herself and the raw urgency of the wound, she planned to let the machine answer the phone. It was plugged in, under the hallstand with the volume turned down low, where it couldn't cause any trouble and where, with all the doors closed, the people leaving messages were almost impossible to hear.

*   *   *

Meanwhile, over in Norwich after his peculiar cryptic conversation with Liz, Nick Hastings headed off into the sunshine for a couple of bottles of ice cold beer and a tomato and pastrami sandwich at the wine bar on the corner of Kingsmead Terrace. It was siesta; the whole of the street appeared dusty and faded, sun-bleached, the lines of the buildings softened and fuzzed by the all-pervading heat.

Even inside the cafe, where in theory it was dark and cool and cave-like there was still a sensation of airless sleepiness. Nick picked up his beer and carried it out to a table under an umbrella. If he had wanted to be alone he could have stayed in the flat. He settled back in the shade to watch other people walk by arm in arm. Apparently the whole of the rest of creation had finally divided itself up into cosy, comfortable twosomes, with only one left over. Him. Nick wiped the neck of the bottle and took a swig of the icy liquid. The sharpness electrified his taste buds and then slid, still glacier cold, down into his belly. A man hurried past carrying a bouquet of roses – even those who looked as if they were alone were just heading off to meet their other half.

Maudlin, Nick drained his second beer to the suds and ambled home. He spent the rest of Thursday afternoon and all of Friday at the drawing board, and would have got an amazing amount of work done, if only he hadn't spent so much of the time staring unfocused into the sunlit, dust spinning space above his desk, re-running the events of the last two weeks, and wondering what the hell to do next. Indecision was as itchy as nettle rash.

Early on Thursday evening Nick began to doodle aimlessly. From amongst the doodles a logo was slowly beginning to emerge; a stylised bird rising up from the ashes.

The things Nick had said to Jeanna O'Hanlon about wanting to set up his own workshop to design and make furniture had been the truth. What he hadn't expected, once the words were spoken aloud, was just how quickly they would begin to gain their own momentum; maybe this was the right time for something to change after all. His mistake had been in thinking it was Liz. He sat back; it was odd that there was this great aching need still buried deep inside him, that he had ignored so well for so long that he had almost forgotten it was there. Nick had dreamt of starting his own company since college. But things had always got in the way, real life, a real job and then a real house and a real wife, an ex-wife.

The Jack Sandfi interview was still pinned to the cork board above his desk. One of the first things Liz Chapman had asked him was why it had taken so long to make a come back. She had been closer to the truth than she knew. Nick stared down at the doodle of the bird; perhaps it was time to come out of the wilderness and start over.

He grinned and coloured the bird's eye in with a red felt-tip, maybe Phoenix Furniture was a bit corny but even so the name felt about right. Having a name unleashed all sorts of desires and dreams that he had been suppressing for years. Just how long ago had he decided to weigh his hopes down with excuses and leave them to drown?

He pulled another sheet off a pad, slapped the doodle onto the light box and redrew the design, this time with cleaner, clearer, crisper lines. Red eyes, gold plumage, the bird spread its wings and drew breath for the first time.

'There we are,' murmured Nick. 'Time to fly.'

By lunch time on Friday Nick had had an awful lot of ideas; he'd written a list of people to ring, things he'd need, suppliers, shops and people who might be prepared to stock his work. While the idea took flight, twisting and turning in the bright lights of his imagination, Nick hurried back into the street, bought a local paper from the newsagents and spent the rest of the afternoon scouring the classifieds for potential premises. Something had most definitely changed.

*   *   *

'I'd like to stop over there,' said Morwenna on her way home from tracking down Liz Chapman. 'Next left.'

Lily Howard pulled into a garden centre that had attracted Morwenna's attention on the drive to Liz's house. It was set back from the main road, surrounded by high green nets to break the sharp easterly wind, and row after row of mature trees grown in containers.

It looked for all the world like an untamed desert island, a wild and magical oasis floating amongst acres of subdued farm land: it might offer a safe harbour after the rigours of the storm. Morwenna was out of the car the very instant

251

the engine died. She slipped on her sunglasses, hoisted her bag up onto her shoulder and set off towards the entrance, with Lily Howard just a second or two behind her.

Across the empty car park a slight breeze, barely more than a breath, rippled the tops of the trees, making leaves flash from green to silver, red to amber and back. Morwenna dragged a trolley out from amongst the stack and made her way into the main nursery, hunched, head down, incognito beneath a whispering arch of dappled greenery.

She had an almost overwhelming urge to buy plants, plants for tubs, great rich luxuriant plants and huge verdant shrubs to help her heal the horrible chilling ache that lingered inside her. She wanted to buy tubs too. Robust tubs, half barrels and vast honey-glazed Chinese pots with hand-painted characters around the sides, that promised peace and harmony and all things spiritual and wholesome and new. While Morwenna embraced the epic, Lily picked up two trays of salvias that had been reduced, and a tub of slug pellets.

It took three students to unload the Montego when the two women finally arrived back at the Rectory.

Over in the studio, Jack Sandfi, who was oblivious to everything except the totally unexpected return of his inspiration, worked away at the drawing board. He was amazed at what there was inside him, still waiting to be tapped after all these years. He drew for all of what remained of Thursday using the Australian girl's pencils, sketching random imaginings onto snowy white cartridge paper, and then later worked with charcoal and chalks on terracotta coloured ingres paper, filling page after page, sheet after sheet with something approaching manic compulsion – though this was only because Jack knew that if he once stopped drawing he would have to start making, and the way he felt now, so rusty and ill prepared and out of shape, the making might consume him whole.

It was exhilarating and terrifying and Jack realised that he had quite forgotten how wonderful it felt to be standing on the very edge of this sensation, looking down into the swirling depths of the abyss.

The only time Jack stopped to catch his breath was when the Australian girl brought in a plate full of cheese and onion rolls, a packet of exceedingly good apple pies and a six-pack of lager, and even then, though they talked and bickered and did all the things that they always did, Jack's centre, the busy spinning white hot part of his mind, was still firmly fixed on the drawing board.

She came back again at dusk dressed in a short summer dress, carrying plates of pasta and a bottle of red wine. By that time, the daylight had begun to fade to cinnamon, gold and navy blue, and Jack had finally worked through the frustration of discovering he could no longer render his thoughts clearly and accurately straight onto the page. But he was getting closer. His arms ached from the effort. And even though some part of him was aware that for a while the blonde watched his progress with a kind of sensual hungry curiosity, it no longer seemed to matter so very much. They ate together, side by side at one of the desks safe under the shade of a comfortable silence.

When darkness finally fell Jack flicked on the cold dead fluorescent studio lights and began a scavenger hunt through the workshops. Bobbing up and down like a demented bird he scoured under and on the benches, up on the shelves, and in the store cupboards, eyeing out lengths of light steel bars and different weights of wire to make an armature for his sculpture, tracking down a new bag of fine modelling plaster, chicken wire and a great sack of wood straw that he would need to cover the bare bones of his thoughts.

Jack worked with a quiet intent sense of purpose, clearing a good space to work in, finding his tools, a plastic bowl, a rasp, rags, a great unfinished lump of wood to make a temporary working plinth, a plaster knife, hammer and nails, his hands comfortably busy while all the time he turned another sort of energy inwards, nurturing the once familiar sensations inside his head, encouraging his mind to play with the ideas that were still even now refining and redefining themselves. The thoughts rolled around inside his brain like a wine connoisseur would work with a mouthful of something smooth and expensive and wildly exciting.

It made Jack smile. It was not so much a process of creation as one of discovery, and when Jack knew that he had finally found the thing he wanted that brief, joyful sense of arrival and relief and deep recognition shifted the process, altering his focus, making his imagination move in closer to work on the details, editing and re-editing, adjusting and considering every angle and facet.

Finally when the artificial light began to hurt his eyes and had bleached the colour from the ragged bunting of sketches pinned along the boards around the work bench, drunk with pleasure and power and anticipation, Jack headed upstairs into the newly cleaned apple loft. After working in the hollow span of the studio it seemed very cosy up there under the roof timbers. The skylight, like a pane of grey fabric stapled to the ceiling, broke the shadows up into soft-edged shades of dark.

Jack finished off the can of lager that had lit him to bed and then rolled back onto the virginal blue bedspread. The soft mattress rose up around him and drew him closer like warm arms, it felt wonderful. Jack eased off his shoes with his toes and closed his eyes. There in his head the idea, the possibility, hung like a burning star against a midnight black sky, a comet come to guide him home.

He was asleep in a matter of moments. For the first time in years Jack's sleep was awash with dreams, deep and clean and clear, his head full of exquisite sweeping lines, and light, and the sound and feel of charcoal biting into rough paper and the soft wet, warm sensual delight of plaster being moulded over wire and rag and wood straw.

First thing on Friday morning Jack began to work.

* * *

'So, Jack Sandfi is most definitely married then?'

It was late Friday evening; Claire poured two glasses of wine and slid one across the coffee table towards Liz Chapman.

Liz shovelled a handful of cashew nuts into her mouth and then nodded, 'Uhuhm, and then some – very, most definitely married, and to be honest I'm not sure that I want to talk about it. She was ghastly. So, my current plan is that I'm going to drive over to Swaffham tomorrow, have lunch with Jack, try to keep my distance and my cool, do the interview, keep my head down, cash the cheque and move on. The end. Chalk it up to experience.'

Claire considered the possibilities while she picked out a few whole, choice crisps from a bowl in front of the TV. 'Right, and so you can do that, can you?'

Liz frowned and made a disapproving noise.

'Okay, okay,' said Claire in defence, 'it's just that you –' she stopped. Liz grinned as Claire struggled to shuffle her thoughts into something more tactful than whatever it was she had right there on the tip of her tongue

'What I'm trying to say is that speaking from experience, it's always much much harder to write an objective piece when you've got an emotional interest in somebody. Something,' she corrected herself hastily. 'And you said yourself, you do fancy Jack Sandfi.'

'*Did* – please note the past tense – *did* fancy Jack Sandfi,' snapped Liz, 'which is what got me into this mess in the first place. And Morwenna is totally terrifying. I really thought there was a good chance she might knife me. God only knows what's going on there between those two.' Liz paused to suck a nugget of cashew nut out of her tooth. '*Ciao* said that they are looking for emotional interest. It's going to be tricky but I'm sure I can do it. I did wonder whether to forget the whole idea but if I don't do it the pair of them have won.'

Claire pulled a face. 'If you ask me I think you've had a very lucky escape. The woman sounds like a nutter.'

'Uh-huh – but she doesn't worry me as much as Jack; how the hell could I have been so wrong about him in the first place? I'm normally really good at sussing people out.'

'Don't be so hard on yourself,' said Claire, through another mouthful of crisps. 'We can all have an off day. Besides, it's probably some sort of game that he plays with all his women; he's got to have done this kind of thing before, honing his act over the years, and no doubt he'll do it again. Trust me, it's a pattern.' Claire nodded towards the TV screen, where a non-stop slipstream of trailers and warnings and phone-in competitions were rolling by on fast forward. 'So what did you say this film was about?'

Liz picked up the video cassette case and flipped it over to read the blurb on the back. 'Blah-de-blah-de-blah, an exciting action packed thriller. *Time Out* said it was one of the best action adventure films of the year.'

'Fair enough.' Claire stretched luxuriously. 'So here we are again, Friday night, Keanu Reeves on the video, bottle of wine, lots of munchies and a great big bar of –'

The doorbell rang.

Both women turned to look at each other. It was several seconds before Liz got to her feet. Whoever it was rang the bell again. And again. Jack Sandfi? Morwenna Pearce?

It just didn't bear thinking about. When she got into the hall Liz peeked reluctantly out through the bull's-eye glass.

Mike was standing on the doorstep. He was ashen. He had his hands stuffed in his pockets. As she watched Mike looked over his shoulder out into the street lights where they cut silver trails through the twilight, nervously he shifted his weight from foot to foot.

'Thank God, you're in,' he said, pushing his way past Liz the very second she opened the door. 'I was going to go round the back but the bloody gate's locked. Is Claire here?'

The sound of his voice catapulted the boys out of their bedroom and onto the landing.

'Dad? Is that you?' called Joe.

'Dad?' said Tom, blinking and rubbing tired eyes. 'Are we going with you for the weekend, mum didn't say anything about –'

Mike waved them both away and into silence.

Liz glared at him. 'At the very least you could say hello,' she hissed in a furious undertone.

'Sorry, I didn't think they'd still be up. Look, I really need to talk to Claire. If you don't mind that is,' Mike grunted.

Claire was already up and out in the hall. 'What on earth are you doing here? I thought you said you were going to go home tonight.'

Liz reddened and set about gently shooing the boys back to their rooms. It was uncomfortable to be privy to a conversation that wasn't really hers and yet was between two people who played such a huge part in her life. It chafed and rubbed and eventually she scurried into the sitting room to wait for it to end.

In the far corner of the room, under a halo of lamp light the video was on pause, straining and desperate to be off and running. After she had paced a little, trying to block out the sound of their voices, Liz picked up the bar of chocolate. She snapped off a row of squares and then let a single piece melt slowly on her tongue while she waited. It was three squares later that Claire came in wearing a tense expression and picked up her jacket from the sofa.

'Are you all right? What is it?'

'Oh come on, Liz. I don't have to tell you what Mike is like,' Claire said crossly and then let the tension drop from her shoulders and waved the words away, apologetically. 'I'm sorry, I didn't mean to snap at you of all people. I just think it would probably be better if we go over and get this thing sorted out once and for all. It's gone on far too long already. I'm not sure how long it's going to take. I'm sorry.'

Liz flinched. Did Claire mean *we* in the collective warm humanitarian sense or *we* in a cosy two's company sort of way?

'Sort what out?' she said in a small strangled voice.

Claire was hurriedly collecting together the bits and pieces that she'd brought with her. 'Apparently Mike's cheery little blonde stalker is sitting outside his flat in her car even as we speak and he's too bloody scared to go inside.'

'Too scared? Oh shit. And you're going to go over and sort it out?'

Claire looked up and sighed. 'What choice do I have? Someone's got to do something and it sure as hell isn't going to be Mike, now is it?'

Liz made a little noise of agreement, followed by feeling a great upsurge of disconnected guilt, while behind them the video clicked, burred miserably and then switched itself off. 'What about Keanu Reeves?'

'I've got no idea how long this is going to take. I might not get back.'

'That sounds a bit melodramatic.'

'C'mon. It's Mike we're dealing with here, what do you expect? What I meant to say is that it may be too late to come back here tonight and do the video any sort of justice.'

'On your own head be it, just don't give me a hard time if there's no chocolate left by the time you get back here tomorrow.' Liz made a real effort to sound cheerful and unconcerned.

Claire turned to leave. Just beyond the open door Mike was prowling up and down the hallway, anxious to be off. It was an image that Liz found deeply disturbing.

* * *

The apple loft was illuminated by a crown of slim wax tapers stuck into a tray full of silver sand. It looked exquisite.

The flames threw a golden halo up into the rafters, the light moving slowly to and fro like leaves rippling in the evening breeze. It was late on Friday evening and Jack was filled with a tremendous sense of well-being and a pleasant tingle of anticipation; taking shape in the studio below, and still glowing white hot in his consciousness, was the comet that was guiding him back towards his goal, closer and closer to Liz Chapman.

Far too tender and much too vulnerable to go across to the Rectory to eat, he and the Australian girl had had a steak down at the Old Grey Hound accompanied by a very nice bottle of merlot. They had wandered back to the Rectory together, arm in arm under a star-spangled sky at around half past ten with a couple of bottles from the offie in carrier bags. All in all it had been a cracking good day. For the first time since he had been a child Jack had a real sense of Christmas Eve. And now there was this –

'Christ, that was totally amazing,' said the little

Australian, the words propelled on a gutsy sigh of pleasure as he finally rolled off her. 'Totally and utterly fucking amazing.'

Her short blonde hair was darkened and slicked down by sweat and exertion. Jack brushed a stray curl back off her forehead and planted a kiss on the little vortex of lines directly above her eyebrows; art it seemed was the ultimate aphrodisiac. He rolled over onto his back to catch hold of his breath and his thoughts, and as he did the girl reached out and teased a crisp gobbet of plaster from his hair.

Jack grinned and grabbing tight hold of her wrist drew her hand towards him. 'Seems that there is life in the old dog after all, eh?' he said, drawing one of her fingers into his mouth and running his tongue over it.

She giggled; it was the most girlish sound Jack had heard from her since they first met, unguarded, warm and totally pure. 'Yeh, you could say that,' she said.

Jack eased over onto his side so that he could look down into her tired and stormy eyes. 'You weren't so shabby yourself.'

She snorted. 'I thought I'd better have a little taste of what your Ms Chapman was so keen to hurry back for.'

Jack's smile held, just. 'Did you persuade the lads to clean out the summer house for me?' he said, gently moving the subject on.

'For you and the lovely Ms Chapman?' The girl drew a roll-up out from behind her ear and lit it. 'Nah, but don't worry.' The brief intense moment of tenderness had already turned over into something more sparky and confrontational. It was a type of intimacy that delighted him. 'When we got over there the lovely Morwenna and Lily were already hard at it. They'd got all sorts of plants and stuff, rubbish bags, rubber gloves, Hoovers, shovels, mops and buckets and Christ knows what.' She ran the long damp finger down over his chest. 'So I reckoned that it would be okay if we left them to it. They were making a real good job.'

Jack was about to say something, maybe to protest, maybe to express a few words of regret, or anger, or indignation that Morwenna had invaded his territory, and then realised he had no idea what he really wanted to say and swallowed the flurry back down. When it came to it, it really didn't matter what happened to the summer house any more. Let Morwenna have it, let her clean it, let her do just what the bloody hell she liked with it. Things had changed.

The blonde girl arched up and kissed him on the end of the nose. 'You're really a good guy, Jack, fuckin' weird but good.'

What could he say? He smiled and gently kissed her on top of the head. Sleep was already pulling him down into its arms, and before the blonde had a chance to finish her cigarette he was snoring softly. So he didn't hear her padding across the rough board floor to blow out the candles, although he did sense the cool silkiness of her body on the periphery of his consciousness as she slipped back under the sheets, and the icy sensation of her pert little nipples brushing over him as he curled up, sliding her arm over his waist. She warmed quickly, her skin melting into his. Contented and safe in her embrace Jack slept like a baby.

Chapter Nineteen

The following morning Liz stood in her bedroom looking down at the things laid out on her dressing table. There was Claire's spare tape recorder and two new cassettes, a new spiral bound notepad, three pens – she swallowed hard trying to shift the unnerving and very unsettling sense of *déjà vu* that had been haunting her ever since she got up. Although of course, in this particular case Liz thought, she really had done this all before.

Liz was hoping that like surgeon's instruments the tools of her trade would help her excise Jack Sandfi from her life once and for all. It might take a little while for the wound to heal over but at least the patient would survive. In the dressing table mirror her reflection paused for a few seconds to brush an imaginary stray hair off her shoulder. It was just such a terrible shame that the first man she had really fancied since leaving Mike had turned out to be married and mad and – Liz stopped the thought dead in its tracks and turned her attention back to implements that would help to remove him. This was not a time for compassion or empathy. If she tried to see any of this from Jack Sandfi's point of view there was a very good chance that she would crumble.

No, today, unlike at their first meeting at the Flag, Liz would be less inclined to follow her instincts, her intuition or anything else that couldn't be weighed out in a set of scales and bagged up. She would do this thing with Jack Sandfi just one more time and then no more. Today would be the end, no more Jack, no more Morwenna Pearce, no more crazy phone calls, no more invitations to lunch or dinner, no more juvenile fluttering in her stomach every time she heard his voice on the phone, and certainly no more weird stray sexual fantasies about things that might have been. Oh no, today would see an end to all of that if she played it right.

Liz stood very still while her mind huffed and puffed and tidied her thoughts away like an ageing aunt, and then she grinned; despite all the aggravation it had been quite intriguing while it lasted. It was exciting to add a little spice into the equation occasionally, even if it hadn't amounted to that much when you weighed it all up. Liz slid her tools into a shoulder bag alongside her purse, mints, and make-up.

Perhaps it was just that she was too old to believe in fairy tales after all, too old to believe in the potency of magic and impossible glorious romances. The idea hatched cool, dark and cynical and was ultimately far too uncomfortable for Liz to look at straight on. Despite the disastrous marriage to Mike and now this fiasco with Jack Sandfi, there was still some part of Liz that liked to believe in the existence of handsome princes, white chargers and the possibility of happy ever after.

Fortunately the sound of Tom thundering up the stairs broke her chain of thoughts.

'Mum, Claire's just arrived. I saw her pull up outside in the car, do you want me to let her in?'

Liz sniffed back a surprised tear. 'Sure, oh and while you're at it, love, can you stick the kettle on and make some tea, please, just while I finish getting ready?' Her voice sounded more brittle and unnaturally cheery than she intended.

Tom hesitated for the briefest instant of time and then added, 'Oh and by the way, I think dad is with her.'

Liz felt a little white hot flare of regret and resentment.

Now there would be no chance to earth out the nervous tension in her belly with giggles and gossip and plans for the week, no chance to find out what had happened the night before with Mike's stalker – at least not in any unguarded way – and most definitely no chance to speculate about what would happen when she met Jack Sandfi again, what he might say, what he might do. And then there was this thing with Mike and Claire.

Liz couldn't help wondering whether things had already shifted between the two of them. Liz realised – and this was an icy little pinch – that she was even beginning to think of them in a loosely linked, twosome kind of way. She let the thought bob around in her head. Had some invisible line already been crossed that she was unaware of, had she and Claire already moved past intimate gossip now? And if Mike was sleeping with Claire just how long would it be before those two saw themselves as a couple and saw Liz as an outsider, on the edge, the enemy?

Liz shivered. It was a ghastly uncomfortable thought which amongst a lot of other things made her angry; how dare Mike try to muscle in on her best friend, and how dare Claire want to be with Mike after all the years they had known each other, and the things she had seen them go through. Liz sniffed again and tucked her tee shirt into her trousers; like it or not this was real injun country.

If Claire ever planned to have a deeper relationship with Mike then somewhere down the line she would slowly but surely have to shift her loyalties. Liz kept her eyes fixed on the mirror and then, after a second or two stuck out her tongue and pulled a devil's face; surely it was way too early in the morning for out and out paranoia.

There were voices in the hall and a few seconds later the familiar sounds of Claire loping on the stairs. Liz turned just as Claire popped her head around the door.

'Wow, you look great. Love that shirt. Are you all set? I filled the car up this morning and checked the oil and water, oh, and the tyres.'

Liz smiled half-heartedly.

Claire stepped into the bedroom and then peered left and right onto the landing before pushing the door to. 'I asked Mike to go and check on the spare before you go; Christ, how the hell did you ever put up with him? He is driving me totally and utterly nuts. And last night was completely bloody crazy. I wanted to come back here but Mike insisted that we went out and had a meal.'

Liz sat down on the bed, any lingering anxiety burning away like fog under a warming sun. 'What happened?'

Claire looked heavenwards. 'For Christ sake, what didn't happen. There is just no way I am ever going to have any kind of meaningful relationship with your husband. I'd like to make that perfectly clear now, the man is a complete arse-hole.'

'That's my ex-husband.'

'Okay, ex-husband. I'm counting on you to remind me when I get desperate.'

'So what happened?'

'All the way over there Mike was wittering on about how this girl was ruining his life, how she followed him everywhere. He painted a really good picture. How she was making him ill, how threatened he felt, how he had done nothing to encourage her, on and on and –'

'And?'

'When we got to his place Mike scurried upstairs into the flat like the devil himself had hold of his shirt tails and left me standing there in the middle of the bloody road. Anyway this girl saw him, and just as she was getting out of her car I went over and asked her what the hell she thought she was playing at.'

Liz leant forward in anticipation.

Claire grinned. 'Oh don't worry it gets better. She was a bit defensive at first and then I offered to buy her a drink so we could talk about it. I told her I was a reporter and then the flood gates opened. She is, apparently, trying to teach Mike a lesson about walking away from his promises and obligations.'

Liz laughed. 'Bloody good luck to her.'

'My thoughts entirely. She can't be any more than about twenty. But anyway, it seems that over the last few months Mike's borrowed about four thousand pounds off her. He said he would pay her back when some loan which never materialised, came through. He used her car all the time, got her to wash and iron all his clothes and then persuaded her to work in his office without paying her, and when she complained that he was using her, Mike was, and I quote, "totally amazed" that she was so upset. She's told Mike that if he doesn't pay up by the end of the month, her father, who is furious, is going to set the law on him; this is his last chance to do the right thing. Far from stalking him she has been trying to get Mike to see reason before it goes any further.'

Liz sighed. 'And what did Mike say?'

Claire grimaced. 'Do you really want to hear?'

After a few seconds Liz shook her head. 'No, no I don't, it's none of my business any more, but go on,' and then she added, 'and I'm really glad that you're back in my gang.'

Claire laughed. 'Oh, trust me, I never left it. After I talked to her I went back to his flat for a coffee, where he tried very hard to convince me that this girl was totally crazy, and a liar. And then after we'd eaten he seemed to be under the misapprehension that I'd like to round the evening off by going to bed with him, and he was a bit put out when I turned him down. I think he's only over here with me today because he sees me as some sort of challenge. Did you know that Mike thinks that he's basically irresistible, told me himself.' Claire launched herself onto the bed with a maniacal cackle. 'What I want to know is how the hell you managed to live with him for so long without killing him?'

*   *   *

In the cool, shady kitchen at the Old Rectory there was a superficial air of calm. Truce. Jack accepted the mug of tea that Morwenna offered him with a murmured word or two of thanks and then followed her, as bidden, out of the kitchen door, through the garden and across the still dewy lawn towards the summer house. *The* summer house, no longer *his* summer house; the times they were a-changing.

Morwenna had dressed with some care in a very beautiful long flowing sea-green dress that clung to her creamy white flesh like wet kelp. It made Jack's heart ache; it was such a terrible shame that he no longer wanted her. Morwenna was his nemesis, his siren, an exquisite but dangerous creature who had drawn him across the oceans to destroy him on the great craggy rocks that lurked just beneath her smooth glassy surface.

As he trailed along in her wake, cradling the mug of lukewarm tea, Morwenna looked back over her shoulder at him, those great demon-dark eyes glittering out from under her straw sun hat and Jack knew then, without a shadow of doubt, that Morwenna could destroy him whenever the whim took her. That he had survived this long was quite miraculous.

As the thoughts formed and reformed and shifted in his head, her smooth sinuous alabaster body tried very hard to re-enchant him, but he held fast to the things that he knew; until the moment she opened her mouth and her mind Morwenna could very easily appear to be everything a man might want.

Jack was so busy decoding the bright flares of revelation that, when he looked up, the state of the summer house came as a complete surprise to him. It looked beautiful, a colourist's dream.

'Sweet Jesus,' he murmured in astonishment. Arranged around the slatted deck was a vast array of plants; interesting plants, plants in pots, trailing plants and variegated plants, spiky succulent plants that almost defied description, and two little trees that had been clipped into a pyramid of spheres which flanked the steps up to the open doors. A little further back in the cool shadows of the overhanging roof stood two white cane chairs, cosied up by plump burnt orange cushions and a matching table, none of which Jack recognised. The table was topped off with a generous bowl of fruit and a vase of summer flowers; the whole picture looked shady, serene and extremely inviting. Jack sighed. If only he could paint.

Morwenna lifted her hand to introduce him to his old friend. 'I thought it might be in everybody's interest if we gave Miss Chapman the right impression.' She spoke in a very clipped, measured tone.

Jack didn't ask how Morwenna knew about Liz Chapman, or why she assumed that he would want to meet her in the summer house, aware that Morwenna's uncanny knowing was just one more weapon in her vast arcane arsenal.

'I thought that you could eat lunch out here, unless of course you would prefer to take her down to the pub.' A pace or two ahead of him Morwenna climbed the steps and turned to beckon Jack inside. Even though he felt an icy chill teasing up his spine Jack knew that he was powerless to resist her invitation. For an instant their eyes locked and he shivered; it was like looking into the pit.

Inside the summer house, if anything the transformation was even more startling than the exterior. Someone had colour-washed the walls with some sort of a warm crumbling off white emulsion. The battered red moquette three piece was still there, draped now with Indian throws and soft cushions and arranged around a war-weary rug, whose colours emphasised the faded beauty of the old board floors.

Under one window stood another battered, time-stained table and a mismatch of chairs which contrived to make it all look like something out of a double-page spread in an expensive life style magazine. It was certainly a most masterly transformation.

Morwenna lifted one arched feline eyebrow. 'So Jack, what do you think of all our efforts, then? Not one word of thanks? I suppose that's what I've come to expect after all these years. Will it do for your little tryst?'

Jack nodded. He found it very hard to take his eyes off her elfin face. Despite a growing sense of dread he desperately wanted to be able to read whatever else it was that Morwenna knew and exactly what she planned to do about it. The smile that his attention ignited made him shiver. What on earth had he been thinking of inviting his muse into this terrible, terrible place?

Jack was suddenly caught up by a great tumbling rush of apprehension; it was far too late now to suggest that he and Liz met somewhere else, somewhere neutral and unsullied.

Morwenna was still holding his gaze and he wondered if his passion could ever be selfless enough. If it came to it would he throw himself under the wheels to stop Liz being crushed by the great Moloch of Morwenna's loathing.

* * *

In Norwich Nick Hastings had finally made up his mind that enough really was enough; he had paid through the nose for his one, albeit very stupid, error of judgement. He could hardly begin a new life until he had resolved the tangled ends of the old. Time to sort out this celestial debt once and for all. Today, now. This very instant.

First off he was going to ring Liz, tell her all about his plans for Phoenix, tell her about his life, ask her about hers, tell her about the things he had done, the things he wanted to do, the things he loved, and the things he wanted to love. It wouldn't matter at that point who the hell she thought he was. Then he'd drive over and see her and take her kids and the cat and whoever or whatever else it was that shared her life out to lunch. A big lunch, a generous lunch, in a gesture that would finally clear the air, make everything all right, and then they could begin again properly.

Nick wanted to do something warm and strong and wholesome and had a feeling that at last this was exactly the right time to do it. He made himself a mug of coffee, pulled up a chair, and dialled Liz's number. Now was the moment.

'Hi, how are . . .' he began, the sense of certainty draining away almost before his quest had begun, 'that isn't Liz, is it?'

The woman who had said hello didn't sound at all familiar and he knew, even in just that one word, that whoever she was she was already on her guard. Even so Nick pressed on. 'Sorry. I think I've got the wrong number. I'm trying to contact Liz Chapman?'

There was a small but very meaningful pause at the far end of the line. 'You've got the right number but I'm afraid Liz is out at the moment, can I take a message for you?'

Nick hesitated; he had been so very certain that now

was the right moment. 'Right, okay, well I'm . . .' Who exactly was he? While Nick considered the possibilities his mouth cheerfully hurried on. 'The thing is, I was hoping to meet up with Liz today; I thought that we could have lunch together.' After a few more seconds he admitted defeat. 'Could you tell Liz Jack called –' He stopped for an instant to consider the implications of what he had said, and as he did the woman seized the opportunity with both hands.

'Jack Sandfi?' she snapped. 'Are you Jack Sandfi?'

'No, well not exactly, you see the thing is,' Nick began unsteadily, running his fingers back through his hair. 'God, how did it get this complicated?' The last few words were spoken so softly that they were almost thoughts.

But whoever the woman was she really had no time for his guilt or his ruminations.

'You have got a bloody nerve ringing up here after the other day's little fiasco,' she continued. 'Liz was incredibly upset.' Her tone was as sharp and invasive as a rapier thrust.

Nick flinched, although as the words settled he felt even more confused than before. 'I'm sorry, I'm not with you. What fiasco?'

The woman was quite obviously having a real struggle to stay civil. 'What fiasco? You think you can operate on a totally different set of moral values to the rest of us, don't you? Do you get some sort of warped pleasure out of all this? Or are you just checking up to see where she is; is that what this is about? There's no need, Liz is already on her way over to Hallgate for your precious bloody interview.' She paused and drew in a long breath. When she spoke again each word was crisp and nasty and stung like icy cold water. 'Or were you ringing up just to let her know that you're married after all, before she runs into your wife today, that is –'

Nick felt as if someone had just jumped on his chest, all he could manage by way of reply was a faint, breathless grunt.

'– because if that is the case, Mr Sandfi, there is no need to bother. You're a couple of days too late. Your wife turned up here on Thursday to warn Liz off.'

Somewhere in the background Nick could hear an angry male voice growling, 'Is that right, is that him? Is that him on the phone now? Just let me talk to him, will you? Give me the phone here.' But thankfully the woman stood her ground.

Nick cleared his throat, behind it the truth was all ready and waiting to pour out. He took a breath. He made a real effort to sound calm.

'There has been the most terrible mistake here. The thing is that I'm not Jack Sandfi at all, but Liz thinks that I am, and that's my fault. I rang up today to try and sort all this out once and for all and find some way to make it right. My name is Nick Hastings. I suppose you could say that there has been a misunderstanding, not really a mistake, more an error of judgement and that was my fault too. I'd really like to explain what's happened, if you've got the time to listen, that is.'

The woman didn't say a word, and so Nick continued to speak very slowly and he told her the truth because he had to start it somewhere, and maybe she could find a good way to explain it to Liz, and that might mean that against all the odds there would be something for them out on the far side. Maybe.

Oddly enough, once Nick got started it didn't take very long at all to explain, and once he had made his confession it was followed by such an overwhelming sense of relief that he felt almost dizzy.

Afterwards there was a small, quite intense pause and

then the woman said, 'I didn't think you sounded very much like the guy who was on the telly the other night, but there is one problem that you haven't taken into account. Liz really is on her way over to interview you, no, sorry, not you, the real Jack Sandfi. She's arranged to meet him at his house near Swaffham. And his wife really did come over here to warn Liz off.'

It seemed that telling the truth wasn't enough. 'Have you got Jack Sandfi's address there by any chance?'

The woman laughed. 'You really are a glutton for punishment, aren't you? No wonder Liz thought that you were one of the good guys. Hang on I think I saw it written down on a pad somewhere.'

* * *

Liz looked up at her reflection in the rear view mirror. Sharp grey eyes ringed with a smoky haze of brown kohl and thick dark lashes looked steadily back at her, and then winked mischievously. The drive over to Hallgate had been totally uneventful and the traffic thankfully light. Despite the flutter of nervous energy she looked good, felt fine, the only problem was that Liz had arrived early, far too early and didn't really need any extra time to think or weigh and turn the circumstances and possibilities over and over in her mind.

A hundred yards away at the end of the lane where the car was parked stood the Old Rectory, framed by a generous stand of mature trees. The road was potholed and weedy. The intimate details of the house were cut off from prying eyes by a thick tangle of unkempt hedges. The only thing Liz could make out clearly from where she was sitting was the roof line and an impressive gothic tower, picked out by a shaft of sunlight, set against a backdrop of horsechestnut and brooding copper beech. The single visible window appeared to be looking down at her, its glass as bright as a crow's eye.

Liz cursed her overdeveloped sense of imagination and then pulled the very dog-eared copy of Jack Sandfi's exhibition catalogue out of her handbag – a lucky talisman that she had kept since the first interview. Re-reading the biographical notes Liz wondered briefly why she hadn't asked Jack to autograph it. Was it because it would have seemed presumptuous, even slightly crass? Or was it perhaps because she had hoped that they would meet again some time? Find some way out of a chance meeting to be friends, lovers even? Liz began a search for the packet of mints in her handbag trying to distract her mind; it was a real mistake to have arrived so early.

In front of her the Rectory and its gardens gave off an air of genteel but slightly sinister decay, an almost fairy tale quality. It was very easy to imagine Morwenna wandering around inside it, a wraith confined by a powerful dark enchantment, but much harder to visualise Jack living there. In her imagination Liz saw the sculptor as having an altogether sunnier disposition than the one suggested by his wife and his surroundings. Perhaps that was why he kept the flat in Norwich, not as a love nest, but somewhere that was lighter and more generous and more hospitable.

Liz glanced at the clock on the dashboard, there were still a good twenty-five minutes before her appointment with Jack. Was there enough time to find a pub and have a coffee? Maybe it would be better if she drove around the block, found a quiet out of the way spot to read the catalogue again or buy a newspaper and – the thought froze over and died as Liz realised that she was being watched. It re-enforced the earlier sense of *déjà vu* and made her whole body flutter with an intense wave of apprehension.

Morwenna Pearce stepped out from a gap in the hedge, from under the shadows where she had been lying in wait or in hiding, Liz wasn't keen to contemplate which. The slim redhead was wearing a straw sun hat and was smiling, although it did nothing to warm her expression or to quell Liz's nerves.

'Good morning, Ms Chapman, you are terribly keen, aren't you? Can't wait to see him again? How touching. I do hope he won't disappoint you second time around.'

Liz opened the car window just a fraction wider. 'Hello, Morwenna. I misjudged how long it would take me to drive over here. But please, don't mind me.' There was a forced cheeriness in her voice. 'Now that I've found out exactly where the house is I thought I'd go and find a cafe, kill a little time until lunch.'

Morwenna was not impressed. 'You won't find anywhere here in Hallgate, the nearest place to get a cup of tea is a transport cafe out on the Norwich Road.' Morwenna paused for a fraction of a second. 'Or do you have a penchant for lorry drivers?'

Liz felt herself redden with a volatile mix of discomfort and frustration.

Morwenna continued. 'I'm sure you'll be delighted to know that Jack is a bag of nerves.'

Liz's colour intensified.

'So perhaps it might be better for all concerned if you just came in now and got this damned interview over and done with, put us all out of our misery. We just want to get on with our lives, Ms Chapman.'

There was a horrible sense of finality about everything Morwenna said.

Liz clenched her hands tight around the steering wheel, making a real effort to quieten her adrenaline fuelled pulse. 'Of course. Can you just give me a few minutes to get myself organised?'

Morwenna nodded and then turned to indicate a rusting pair of wrought iron gates at the far end of the lane. Although they were open, the scrolls and bars of the gates were threaded through with tendrils of morning glory, dried dead grass and brambles, all of which added to the impression of malign decay.

'Just drive in through there and park up under the conifers by the main house. And then I'll take you out to meet Jack. He's already waiting for you in the summer house; perhaps your arriving early was fate.'

Liz shivered and looked away first, breaking eye contact. When she looked back again it seemed that her audience with the lady of the house was over. Morwenna had already turned to leave, silently melting back into the dappled shade beneath the overhanging trees. An instant later she had vanished through the gap in the hedge.

Liz felt slightly sick, and took a long deep breath to try and quieten her nerves. Her first and strongest inclination was to fire up the engine of Claire's nippy little GTI and leave them all to it, get away from the Old Rectory, Jack Sandfi, and Morwenna Pearce as fast as she could. Instead, with great care, Liz made a show of brushing her hair, re-applying her lipstick, and collecting together the things that she needed for the interview.

If Morwenna Pearce was still watching, Liz needed her to believe that she was calm and totally unrattled by the woman's unexpected appearance. She tidied away the mints and the catalogue, and with them all the stray dark thoughts that begged for attention, tucking them back into her handbag, and then Liz turned the key in the ignition. After all, Jack Sandfi was waiting for her over in the summer house and there were one or two things that she really wanted to say to him.

Chapter Twenty

Jack was nervous, more than nervous. He paced out another circuit around the inside of the summer house, while all the time like a prayer wheel his mind spun on through the morning's plan of events. On one rotation he concentrated on the purest and most simplistic form that his encounter with Liz might take, before another turn moved him on very swiftly to consider every possible opportunity for divergence, digression and sweating, heaving, delicious deviation. Fantasy could be such a rewarding pastime. Even so, the erotic wall art inside his own skull couldn't quite quell the little gaseous fizz of apprehension.

Outside in the sunshine, hunkered down on the slatted wooden deck surrounded by Morwenna's newly arrived rainforest, the Australian girl took a long hard draw on her roll-up and then stopped to pick a stray thread of tobacco out from between her teeth. Jack was very conscious that she had been watching his ruminations for some time. As their eyes met the little blonde grinned and then blew a smoke ring.

'Okay?'

Jack nodded and then set off once more around his self imposed circuit. It would probably have made better sense to spend the morning working. He could have found something to occupy his mind in the studio, the time would certainly have passed more quickly there. But the possibility that he might have been sucked down into the creative vortex which he had been so delighted to have finally rediscovered, and to be so absorbed in working on the new sculpture that he would see the arrival of his muse as a distraction and inconvenience, horrified Jack. Liz Chapman deserved much better.

Another equally alarming possibility was that while working on the new piece, but unable to concentrate on anything except Liz Chapman's impending arrival, still trying to dissipate the growing sense of anxiety, Jack might very easily ruin that portion of work he had already completed. In the process he could very easily snuff out the warm sensual fuel of confidence and anticipation that he had so recently found.

So instead of working, Jack had spent the whole morning wandering around the ruins of the Rectory gardens, trying to find something to distract his attention. He had ambled in and out of the orchard between the rows of unpruned fruit trees and overgrown hedges. He had admired the way they were plaited through with periwinkle and glossy ivy, and then walked down past the herb garden and wild asparagus beds, and then up around the ornamental pond. It looked like a great torn cushion discarded amongst the ragged grass, with its huge fluffy gobbets of moss bursting out at the side seams. In one of the few remaining puddles of dark silky brown water a sherbet lemon water lily tried hard to keep up appearances.

Jack had ended up, very prematurely, in the summer house. Since his arrival he had paced and thought and thought and paced and time had passed so slowly that he could almost feel the passage of every second, turgid and flat, moving through his bloodstream.

'So, have you finalised the details of your master plan yet?' said the little blonde from amongst a rolling boil of tobacco smoke. She was stretched backwards now, taking her weight on long strong arms, uncurling under the sun's heated insistence like another of Morwenna's exotic plants. 'How far have y'got? Coffee and buns first and then over to the studio to admire the masterpiece, after which she'll be so knocked back by y'genius that you can head straight up to the apple loft for a leg over.' She grinned, those even white teeth accentuating a golden syrup tan. Jack knew that she meant it to be funny but the humour was absorbed and deadened by his anxiety.

Thoughtfully he chewed down on his bottom lip. 'I don't know about that. So far Liz arrives. We get re-acquainted, talk and we sit here,' as he spoke Jack pointed out the sofa and arm chairs, seeing himself there with Liz already alongside him, although her face, even her shape were still totally nebulous, 'and then unless things take a very sharp left turn towards the apple loft, we'll have lunch in here too. Here.' He indicated the shabby chic kitchen table under the window. 'Or maybe if she wants to we might sit outside, admire the view, that kind of thing. That should be at around one. Poached salmon, butter sauce, new potatoes, green salad, a decent bottle of vino, and so on. Oh and before that, when she arrives, we'll have the coffee, a tray of coffee and some of those fancy biscuits.'

The girl lifted her hands to settle him. 'I've already told you that I'll make the coffee and do the honours. No sweat, just relax. It's all taken care of.'

Relieved Jack pressed on. 'Right. And then at some point, I take her across to the studio, introduce her to all the students,' he lifted an arm to encapsulate the gesture of welcome, 'which will be followed by the guided tour and then I take her to see the new work, my new work. Oh, and can you make sure that you get someone to sort the lights out. I want two spots, soft, indirect and I would very much prefer if you didn't move it.' He grinned, warm with the sensation of what had been accomplished so far, and then the words dried in his throat as sticky as new varnish and Jack stopped.

He was afraid to push the words much beyond the image

of standing side by side with Liz in the sunlit studio, both looking at his new piece, both admiring the strong sensual lines and the perfume of raw potential. They would be so close that he could smell her perfume too and the soft inviting scent of her warm skin. Jack swallowed, unable to tell the girl how he had imagined the long steep climb up the open tread steps that led into the cool shade of the apple loft. He would take Liz's hand, she would be a little nervous, afraid of the intensity of what she was feeling, and guide her towards heaven. He could see her looking up at him. Hastily Jack looked away as Liz's face began to melt and change into the familiar features of the Australian girl. A great jumble of intense abstract erotic thoughts simultaneously bubbled up in his head like champagne; Jack laughed. 'So there we have it, what do you think of it so far?'

The blonde rubbed the back of her hand across her forehead to disperse the day's heat.

'You want my honest opinion?'

Jack nodded.

'I reckon too much planning can bugger everything up, Jack, you ought'a lighten up a bit, mate, play it by ear. Trust your instincts. If she is after shagging yer senseless over here in the summer house, here, there, anywhere, then I should just go with it. Take it as it comes. Straight up, no messing. Life's too short.'

Jack stared at her and then at the rows of artfully arranged planters. 'No, I couldn't, not in here, not now, not with Morwenna on the prowl –'

Something made him stop speaking, some sixth sense which warned Jack that by saying her name aloud he had already managed to summon her up. The hairs on the back of his neck tingled; the magic still worked after all this time. He knew that she was close by.

Jack stepped out onto the veranda and like a captain on

the bridge of his ship stared out across the great ragged rolling expanse of lawn into the late morning sun.

In the near distance, through the trees and great bowed branches of heavy green, Morwenna was moving slowly towards him, any expression hidden by the brim of her sun hat. Beside her, her face obscured by a heady combination of wind dealt light and shade was another woman, a small slim woman dressed in cream trousers and a gold coloured tee-shirt with a scoop neck, a jacket casually draped over one arm, and some sort of straw bag over her shoulder.

Jack absorbed every detail by osmosis, sucking the woman dry as he tried hard to match what he could see with the images inside his head; there was no exact match. As she moved her body formed enticing shapes against the variegated back drop of summer greenery; it could only be Liz Chapman. Jack's pulse quickened.

He squinted to tease out even more details; she had jaw length dark hair which moved like a black flag in the breeze and although quite small, maybe five feet five or six at most, she appeared to have a wonderful selection of soft womanly curves. Jack tried very hard to focus in on her face, eagerly waiting for that warm glow of recognition that he had been anticipating all morning. With every step she took he pre-empted its arrival, the tension in his belly and chest winding itself tighter and tighter until he could barely breathe.

Liz was more than halfway across the lawn now. She walked with an easy grace, not too fast, not too eager, as if she was savouring this moment of arrival, processing slowly towards him deep into the very heart of his very own kingdom. Jack swallowed hard. God, this was the sweetest torture.

And of course they all knew that he was watching her progress, the blonde girl, Liz, Morwenna. And then, just when Jack thought that he couldn't bear it any more, Liz Chapman looked up and their eyes finally met.

Jack shivered and took a step closer, desperate to shorten the distance between them. A whole maelstrom of emotions passed over Liz Chapman's face – like a time lapse film of cloud and sunshine – although the whole show was over and done in a matter of seconds, so quickly and so acutely that as the two women approached the steps, Jack wondered if perhaps he had imagined it. When he looked again Liz's expression was neutral, impassive, fixed in a pleasant but not wildly exciting or excited smile and he was left with no idea whether what he had seen was a good or bad omen.

It occurred to him a fraction of a second later that Liz was in the presence of Morwenna. She could hardly afford to be spontaneous, rushing forward to embrace him or – He stopped as Morwenna caught hold of the rail alongside the steps and slowly climbed up towards him, there was a good chance that she might be able to read his mind.

'Ah Jack, there you are,' Morwenna said, happy with the obvious. 'Ms Chapman arrived a little earlier than we had expected but I didn't think you'd mind if I brought her over.' Her manner was stiff and unnatural and it occurred to Jack that Morwenna was just as nervous as he was, but the idea did not take root and within seconds it was lost and unrecognisable.

On the periphery of his vision, Jack saw the Australian girl lift a hand in salute and then, dropping down over the edge of the raised deck, lope off across the grass towards the studio. The heavy Timberland boots she was wearing made her look like a giraffe. He only hoped that she wouldn't forget to make the coffee.

Liz was climbing the steps a pace or two behind Morwenna. Beneath the calm exterior Jack could sense the shorting out of nervous energy, earthing and crackling beneath her lightly tanned skin. Deep inside those interesting blue-grey eyes something flashed with a heady mixture of pain and panic. God, she was so very lovely, so why was it that he hadn't got the faintest recollection who she was? He didn't remember her face or her body although she was hardly the kind of woman one ought to forget so completely.

Much as he regretted it, Jack couldn't deny the truth any longer. He had got absolutely no idea who Liz Chapman was or where it was they had met before, or worse still what had gone on during their momentous if brief encounter.

Jack extended a hand and warmed up his smile; he was going to have to wing it, and not let on that he couldn't remember her, although he had quite obviously made a lasting impression; the last thing he wanted to do was hurt her or to spoil his chances of repeating whatever it was that had been so momentous about their previous encounter.

His smile broadened a degree or two as he found his form, protective and tender, while some other more venal part of him still clung to the hope that, as their hands touched, there would be a moment of divine revelation, the scales would fall away and he would remember Liz Chapman in all her glorious sensual splendour.

'How very nice to see you again,' he said. His fingers closed tight around hers. Her handshake was warm and firm but regretfully lit no fuses. 'I thought it would be rather nice if we talked out here in the summer house. It's one of my most favourite places.' He lifted a hand. 'Over there the formality of the main house, over there the anarchic industry of the studio; this is middle earth. I do hope you don't mind.' He indicated the shadowy interior behind him.

Liz shook her head. 'No, that will be absolutely fine. It's a lovely spot you've got here.' There was a very slight tremor on the edge of her voice, which made Jack quiver with pure delight; strong but vulnerable. God, this was perfect. And he'd also noticed that she hadn't stopped looking at him since the first time their eyes met. He smiled and as their gaze met again she blushed. It was so unexpected, so totally delightful that he had to stifle a nervous giggle.

There was curiosity, surprise, shock even on her small even features. He must seem very very different to Liz Chapman now that he was so close to sober; but not too different he hoped. He had just had a little something to calm his nerves first thing. God, if there was ever a good reason to cut back on the juice forgetting a woman like Liz Chapman had to be it.

'Shall we?' He indicated the door to the summer house and with an abbreviated bow guided Liz inside.

* * *

As Liz stepped over the threshold she took a very deep breath, trying to settle her nerves in those dark, unfocused, abstracted seconds before her eyes adjusted to the gloom inside the room. A great bottomless sense of panic was busy heading up through her spinal cord and stomach, the sensation so potent and so awesome that she didn't dare contemplate it too hard.

Jack Sandfi. The name glowed in the front of her head like night-time neon. This was meant to be an interview with Jack Sandfi, the Jack Sandfi she had written about for the *Bishopston News and Advertiser*, the Jack Sandfi whose secrets she had sold to *Sunday News*. The man she had had coffee with, not this man. It had all seemed relatively simple when she left Balmoral Terrace, Morwenna Pearce and a nervous sense of emotional vulnerability not with-standing.

She and Jack had got on so well when they met in Nor-wich the first and last time round, except of course that this couldn't be Jack Sandfi, or at least this wasn't the Jack Sandfi she had met then. Which all sounded too much like madness; there couldn't be two Sandfi's, could there? And if there weren't two of them, then what the hell was going on? Who was it exactly that she had interviewed in Nor-wich? That was a little fire that would have to rage, unattended, in a quiet corner of her mind, because at the moment there were other more pressing matters. The man was still watching her with considerable interest. Liz tacked on a smile.

This man, this other Jack Sandfi was being so solicitous, so gentlemanly, showing her to a chair, smiling warmly, this rambling shambling obviously tortured, slightly drunk, troubled, clever very damaged man was most definitely not the man she had met at the Flag. As the implications or at least the thin end of the implications wedged into her mind, the ground felt as if it was rapidly moving out from beneath her feet.

'Thank you,' she said, sitting down, aware that her ner-vousness made her sound breathy and girlish.

He waved her thanks away and perched on the edge of the sofa as close to her as he could, his long fingers steepled together, his expression expectant and eager.

'It's so nice to see you again. How have you been?' he asked.

Liz struggled to suppress a groan. Everything about Jack Sandfi's manner – for surely, logically, this must be the real Jack Sandfi – implied that they had already met and that he knew her well enough to consider her, if not a friend then certainly a very close acquaintance.

She nodded slowly. 'Fine, I've been fine, thank you, and

how about you?' And as she spoke, Liz noticed that on the wall by the sofa, hanging in pride of place, was a framed copy of her article in the *Sunday News*.

Liz closed her eyes for a split second and there in that dark safe place, made up her mind that there really was no choice. She had no idea what was going on here or why, but whatever the answer was, whatever had really happened that day in the hotel in Norwich, whoever she had really met, she'd just have to wing it, and not let on that she didn't know this Jack Sandfi.

He believed they really had met before and as she looked into his warm spaniel brown eyes, Liz knew that the last thing she wanted to do was hurt him any more than he was hurting already or to spoil whatever it was that she quite obviously believed had been so memorable about their first encounter.

Her smile broadened a degree or two as she found her form – protective and tender.

Nervously Jack glanced out through the doors into the sunlight. Morwenna was already scuttling across the lawn back towards the main house.

'I've been incredibly well, in fact better than I've been for years,' said Jack enthusiastically. 'I've been working on a new piece actually. Oh and I've organised for some coffee to be brought over for us. You didn't have too much trouble finding us, did you, only it is a little bit out of the way here.'

There was a very slight tremor on the edge of his voice, which made Liz shiver. God this was so awful. Liz had also noticed that he had barely taken his eyes off her since Morwenna had introduced them. She smiled and as their gaze met again Jack blushed. It was so unexpected, so totally unnerving that Liz had to suppress a groan.

'I thought,' Jack continued just a fraction too quickly, 'that you might like to take a look round the studios while you're here. It will give you a real sense of place, the inner man, what goes on here – tortured artist and all that malarkey. But later, that is, in a little while, after we've had coffee. Or tea.'

Liz nodded and began to unpack the contents of her shoulder bag onto the low table that stood next to the sofa, her notepad and the pen, the tattered battered catalogue. It was an attempt to establish some sort of perimeter fence around her discomfort, something that would help defend her from her own confusion. She could feel Jack Sandfi watching her every move.

'Rather awful isn't it, under the circumstances, to be this nervous?' he said after a second or two, as she fumbled the new tape out of its cellophane and into the little recorder. Liz didn't look up, afraid to meet his eyes, and uncertain whether he was talking about her or himself.

'Here, why don't you let me help you with that,' he continued, leaning closer still and extending his hand.

Wordlessly Liz passed the machine over; this was going to be difficult.

Jack smiled, his breath smelt of alcohol and poor digestion, but nevertheless as he pressed the cassette into place, for some horrible and inexplicable reason, with both pairs of eyes fixed firmly on it, the gesture and its symbolism seemed uncompromisingly and uncomfortably erotic. Liz blushed furiously.

'There we are, all done and ready for the off,' he purred, his smile sly and knowing now. He stood the recorder between them on the arm of the sofa. 'I wondered how this would go, you know, what we'd talk about, where

287

we'd begin, how we would feel about each other. How things would go *this time*.'

The emphasis was unnerving.

Liz knew she had to take control before Jack's libido wrestled it from her.

'Well, exactly,' she blustered. 'I thought that perhaps it might be interesting if we just talked informally for a while and see what comes up. *Ciao* are particularly interested in the human angle.' She made an effort to sound bright and brisk and competent. 'So maybe a little bit of background if you like. Is there anything in particular that you'd like to talk about. I wondered if there is anything you would like to be remembered for?'

It was one of the questions she had prepared for the other Jack Sandfi, the Jack Sandfi who had made her feel special and sexy and flirtatious, but what the hell. One thing was for certain, this Jack Sandfi couldn't claim that he hadn't noticed her tape recorder.

Jack laughed nervously. 'Remembered for? Right. I was rather expecting the questions to be a little smaller to begin with. You know, the easy stuff, bite-sized.'

As he spoke a handsome blonde girl appeared at the door bearing a large wooden tray. She was grinning in an unfocused good humoured way that suggested the greater portion of her concentration was being used to balance the load.

'Here y'go. I told you I wouldn't forget, Jack, you really ought'a have a little more faith in human nature,' she said, settling the tray on the side table, and then she stuck out her hand in Liz's direction. 'You must be the famous Liz Chapman. Christ, I'm real glad you've finally shown up, it's been bloody murder around here for the last few days.'

The girl's grip was rough and capable; Liz warmed to her instantly.

She waved towards the tray. 'So there y'are. Fresh made, fresh perked and poured the Aussie way. Enjoy.' The girl turned her attention back to Jack. 'Would you like me to stay and play mother, or just bugger off and leave the pair of you to it?'

Jack waved her away, seemingly unsettled by the heavy-handed good humour. 'Liz and I can manage, thank you very much, and we want none of your damned hammering today. All right?'

The girl grinned. 'Sure thing. See you later.'

As soon as she was gone Jack picked up the coffee pot, two fingers holding down the lid while he filled two large cups. It was impossible not to notice the tremor in his hands. He poured, and then in the few seconds afterwards when it would be normal to offer cream or black, milk or sugar, Jack slid a bottle of brandy out of his jacket pocket with all the skill of a night club magician.

'Would you care for a little nip?' he asked lightly. 'A little something to help kick start the old grey cells?'

Liz shook her head.

'You don't mind if I do, do you? Only I find it helps me concentrate my energies.' It was a rhetorical question. As he spoke Jack poured a very healthy slug into the top of his coffee, magicked the bottle back into his pocket and then lifted the cup to his lips in what seemed like a completely seamless movement. As if suddenly remembering his role as host Jack then waved a hand briefly over the tray and added, 'Please Liz, do help yourself, coffee, milk, sugar, and do have a biscuit. They came in a Red Cross parcel that my agent had sent down from Harrods.'

Liz picked up the milk jug.

'You know,' he said, glancing up towards the framed article. 'I couldn't wait to see you again. I do realise that that must make me sound like a foolish love-sick teenager with a crush.' He paused as if carefully working through whatever it was he wanted to say next. 'The thing is that I truly feel that you reached in and found the very heart of me, Ms Chapman. I've waited so long for someone like you to come along and see what is truly here inside.' He touched the centre of his narrow concave chest. 'You really have no idea how very long I've waited for you.' He sounded distant and wistful. 'There is just so much I want to talk about, that I need to tell you, so much that I would like to share after all these years. Perhaps you are that special voice that every artist seeks to accompany him on his journey.'

Liz felt an icy track of apprehension moving down her spine. Very deliberately she moved the tape recorder closer; it was an act of definition, a gesture to announce that what they were doing was not about romance or seduction – or any of the things that Jack Sandfi might have fantasised about – but about a public encounter with a wider audience. The little whirring, hissing beast that recorded Jack's words without compassion or condemnation was Liz's sword and shield.

'I'd be very happy to listen to anything you would like to say,' she said in a low, very even voice. It was the voice of a counsellor and confidante, the confessor, not a lover or even as a might-have-been.

Jack sighed. Liz wasn't certain that he understood the inflection but instinctively he had already moved back a little.

'It's a job to know exactly where to begin,' he said, taking another mouthful of coffee. 'Are you certain that you wouldn't like to join me in a little nip of brandy, I'm sure that I can find a glass if you'd like one.' He pulled out the bottle to re-enforce the point and then, as if suddenly seeing it in his hand for the first time, added another measure into the top of the cup.

Liz picked up a pencil and pad to emphasise that this was the beginning of the interview.

'Well,' Jack began, taking another mouthful, 'where exactly would you like me to start?'

Chapter Twenty-one

Morwenna could feel a great wave of loss and grief rising up inside her, so large and so painful that it threatened to sweep away all her defences. She was sitting at the kitchen table, slowly turning the pages of a cuttings book; a triumph it said. Summer 1976. Her first major one-woman exhibition. A total triumph.

Lily Howard stood a cup of coffee down by her elbow. 'I've got them lunch trays all done for the two of them, just gotta wait for the 'taters to do now.' She paused, obviously struggling to hold back her thoughts. Finally it proved too much for her. 'I don't know how you can be so calm about it. I wouldn't have it, not inviting her here. I don't care whether he's slept with her or not, it ain't right. It ain't proper. And I wouldn't stand for the way he treats you. You want to stand up for yourself more not creep around thinking that he will just guess and then change his ways, 'cause he won't. No one really respects a martyr, not deep down, they just take you for another mug they can walk all over. If it was me I'd leave him, you know. While you still can.'

Morwenna looked up in surprise, not certain that she had heard the woman correctly. 'Leave Jack?'

Lily pointed to the photos and the yellowing reviews clipped from the *Sunday Times*. 'You ought to have been painting all these years not looking after that ungrateful sod. You've got no family to worry about, only him out there, and what comfort is he going to be in your old age, none as I can see, he's only here when it suits him. You aren't bad looking; you want to get yourself fixed up with some bloke who knows quality when he sees it. That's what I think. Not be stuck in here crying over spilt milk. You should be up in London somewhere getting on with life.' She paused and then pointed to one of the glossy eight by tens of one of Morwenna's paintings. 'I saw some of them ones you put in that gallery in Norwich last Christmas. Very nice that was an' all.' Lily paused again and then said very quietly, 'He'll just use you all up, you know, his sort always do.'

Morwenna looked up into the woman's great wise florid face, wondering where all the words were coming from. Were they really coming from Lily or was it a voice inside her own head? A plump tear rolled down her cheek.

'Do you really think so?' she said in a small broken voice.

Lily nodded and then prised open the lid of the biscuit tin. 'What is it that's keeping yer here?'

Morwenna thought for a few seconds, looking at the view out beyond the battlements. She had hidden for so long behind Jack, blaming him for her lack of success and opportunity, when it was suddenly very clear that she had done it to herself. The view was quite frightening. Looking after Jack, his needs and his self-obsession had not only fuelled her resentment but had also provided her with a perfect excuse for not getting on with her own life. Morwenna stared wordlessly up at Lily, seeing herself reflected in the woman's big compassionate far-seeing eyes.

Minding Jack had been Morwenna's cross and at the same time her answer to everything, their fates tied tight together. From where she was standing on the desolate windswept reaches of high ground Morwenna could see all the years she had spent convincing herself that it was Jack who was holding her back, laid out before her like felled trees.

In that little moment Morwenna saw it all, a rich rolling verdant landscape of excuses and self-delusion and deep deep dependency. It made her feel sick. After a few seconds Morwenna picked up the cup of coffee and took a digestive out of the tin that Lily was holding. Perhaps this was the perfect moment to take her first steps towards another kind of life.

'How long do you think the potatoes will be?' she said.

* * *

Jack Sandfi didn't notice Liz turning over the tape cassette in the machine, although from time to time during the interview he did look up at her as if to seek reassurance that it was going well. There was an element of appeal in his voice and no doubt in her mind that Jack was totally besotted by his own version of the Liz Chapman fantasy. What Liz found hard to understand was where all of this breathy expectation, longing and desire had come from. It was a complete mystery to her; surely Jack Sandfi hadn't managed to spin all this from one short article written about someone else?

It was warm in the summer house, warm and dark, the unmoving air heavy with the scent of dried grass and warm wood. If she had been meeting the other Jack Sandfi this would have been the perfect setting. Rogue imagination. Liz made an effort to drag her attention back to the man sitting on the sofa. It was a real uphill struggle; he was speaking in a flat hypnotic monotone. Thank God the tape recorder was on.

Letting the pen rest on the spiral bound notepad Liz struggled to keep focused on the interview, while another part of her mind turned over the sequence of events since she had met the other Jack Sandfi at the Flag. It was rich and very fertile soil but far too dark and too muddy to find any kind of logical explanation for what had happened since then.

'Perhaps,' said Jack, suddenly sitting up straight, interrupting his own lava flow of thought, remembrance, pain, pleasure and random unconnected ramblings, 'we should go over and take a look at the studio. Did I tell you that I'm finally working again? I mean, really working, new work, new ideas. It's quite exciting to be back in the fray, creating, making, and after so long too. You really have no idea just how much that means to me, and the thing is,' he reddened, furiously trying to claw hold of the rush of emotion, 'I want you to know that it is you, Liz, your compassion, your mystery and your veiled magic that has fuelled my –' He held up his hands palms up to stem the tide, an act both of contrition and surrender. 'No, I'm sorry. I promised myself that I wouldn't do this to you, please accept my abject apologies, dear lady. I'm taking all this much too quickly, aren't I? Do please forgive me.'

He nodded towards the open doors to divert her away from his discomfort. 'I thought that they might have brought our lunch over by now. They said it would be ready at around one. What is the time? What do you think? Shall we take a little stroll over to my studio, do the whole Cook's tour, look at the work in progress? Would you like to see it now or later? We could have a look around the garden too if you like, it is quite beautiful. What do you think?' His lack of surety was uncomfortable and horribly poignant.

Avoiding eye contact, Liz set her pen and pad down on the little side table, trying hard to mask her eagerness to be away from the increasingly tense atmosphere inside the little cabin. 'That sounds like a wonderful idea. I'd really like to see where you work –' she began.

Jack grinned. 'Excellent. Well, in that case . . .' He pushed himself up onto his feet with some difficulty. The brandy was long gone, as was whatever it was that he had retrieved from down the back of the sofa. Although upright there appeared to be a real element of luck to his performance.

'. . . we'll be off then,' he continued almost to himself. 'After all it's only some sort of salad so even if she does come over and . . .' Jack Sandfi stopped and flapped something unseen, or perhaps more precisely something only he could see away from his face, as if he was swatting a wasp. 'What I'm really trying to say is that our lunch won't spoil even if it is delivered in our absence. So away then –' He took a step forward and offered Liz his arm, '– into my lair, my holy of holies, my sweet sanctuary.'

Liz was deeply reluctant to accept, but what excuse could she possibly use to decline such chivalry? Would he see her touch as further encouragement? Just as she got to her feet Liz heard a voice and then another, carried towards the summer house on the light breeze. It came as a relief to know that they weren't alone. Liz could pick out the Australian girl and a man, a strangely familiar sounding man. One voice overlaid the other mixing with birdsong and the breeze in the trees, twisting a skein of bright and cheerful summer sounds; they were laughing and getting closer.

Liz hurried across to the door, using the opportunity to side step Jack, and emerged blinking into the bright sunlight. Jack, encouraged by her sudden break for freedom was no more than half a pace behind and gaining fast.

Liz stared out into the garden. Striding across the lawn with the blonde girl hurrying, half running, half walking alongside him was, was . . . Who the hell was he this other Jack Sandfi, who was most definitely the man she had interviewed at the Flag.

He was taller and had broader shoulders than she remembered. He was wearing a white cotton shirt, open at the neck, sleeves rolled back to reveal a light tan, the shirt tucked into faded Levis, and he had a nervous grin that extended from one ear to the other. He looked up at her and as their eyes met he ran his fingers back through his hair. Liz felt her pulse quicken. He was beautiful. Alongside a totally misplaced sense of relief, seeing him standing there made something deep inside her stomach go taut and then flutter excitedly.

Fortunately the Australian girl came to the rescue. 'Hi Jack, I found this guy wandering about round the back of the studio, he was looking for Liz.' She grinned and then waved in his direction. 'Jack Sandfi, I'd like you to meet Mr Nick Hastings. He said he'd arranged to drive over and meet up with Liz here.' She looked pointedly at Liz, as if daring her to deny it. Liz said nothing.

'I was just on my way over to the house to help out with lunch,' the girl continued, smoothing over anything that might have sounded like over-emphasis. 'And there he was skulking about in the shrubbery.'

Nick meanwhile was busy climbing the steps in two big strides. Liz watched his progress closely and then he looked at her again, and although the flutter in her stomach was still there, she knew that she had to say something to call a halt to this farce. Liz took a breath, but in the instant before she started to speak Nick, who was now alongside her, caught hold of her by the elbows and pulled her towards him. She gasped and then he kissed her hard, so hard that the last remnants of the breath evaporated along with a few words and an awful lot of thoughts.

Liz pulled away, struggling with a mixture of shock, indignation and complete astonishment. For the first time in a lot of years she couldn't think of a single thing to say.

'I've been wanting to do that for ages,' he said smiling. 'I'm really sorry about this whole mess.' He lifted his hands to encompass the garden, Jack, the blonde girl. His eyes were alight with delight and amusement. 'But not about that.'

God, he was good looking. Maybe she ought to slap him.

'I've been trying to explain the situation to you on the phone. I'd got no idea that things would go as far as this before we managed to get it sorted out. I should have said something when we first met, but it was so hard to find the right words to tell you the truth. I knew the interview was incredibly important to you, and we both made all sorts of assumptions. The wrong assumptions as it turns out, but the thing is when I discovered it wasn't me you wanted to talk to, or had been looking for, I couldn't find a way to back pedal, because I really wanted it to be me. I'm sorry.' He paused, grin finally fading to a mellow smile. 'So, that's it. Do you think there is any chance at all that we could find some way to try and make it right? Start over. Will you give me another chance?'

Before she could frame any sort of reply Nick kissed her again, as if it might help seal all her questions into some sort of explanation.

This time Liz's hand settled unself-consciously in the small of his back. It felt good to touch him. He was strong and warm and smelt of sunshine and soap and a tantalising male musk that made Liz's head spin. Outrage and desire were a desperately volatile cocktail.

'You're sorry?' she stammered. Pulling away again Liz struggled to regain her composure and with it her sense of indignation resurfaced. 'What sort of excuse is that? Is it supposed to make things better. *You're sorry?* I can't believe you said that. Are you totally and utterly mad? There is just no way that sorry gets anywhere near covering any of the things that you've done. The mayhem, the total – do you know – I just can't believe that you let me –' the words tumbled over themselves in a ferocious effort to get said. Liz fought to find some way to try to express her confusion, not to mention all the other things in her head that were clamouring for attention, including an intense and very unsettling hope that Nick would kiss her again. 'I don't think anyone has ever made me this angry or this, this . . .'

And then Liz stopped short, suddenly aware that standing under a wing of shadow, just inside the summer house Jack Sandfi was watching their exchange with a mixture of immeasurable hurt and disbelief. The pain on his face made her flinch. As he became aware of her gaze settling on him and their eyes met, Jack pulled himself up to his full height and proffered a hand to Nick.

'Hello, I'm very pleased to meet you. I'm afraid that I didn't quite catch your name?'

He was not alone in that.

'Nick Hastings, I design furniture, mostly for a company over in Norwich at the moment, although I've just decided to start my own.' He turned to glance at Liz again and then choked on his CV. 'The thing is, Mr Sandfi, Jack, there's been a misunderstanding. I suppose I ought to try and explain what's been going on here. I owe you and Liz an apology.'

Jack looked totally bemused. 'An apology, I'm not with you. We've never met before, have we? I'm not sure that I entirely follow.'

Without thinking Liz stepped forward and caught hold of Nick's arm, desperate to pre-empt his planned confession; she had seen the look of desperation and despair on Jack Sandfi's face. Her fingers tightened, pulling Nick back from the edge.

'What Nick is trying to say, Jack, is that he didn't want me to come here at all. Not today, or any other day come to that. He doesn't realise just how important this interview is to me, to both of us,' she said quickly, launching herself feet first into the void. She turned to put herself physically between Jack and Nick, hoping that he would see the desperation in her eyes. 'You can think exactly what you like, Nick, I'm not really sure that I understand what happened, but that is no excuse.' She daren't look directly at him, afraid that what she saw might make her lose the thread.

She turned back towards Jack who was watching them both with exaggerated interest. 'The thing is, Jack, Nick is terribly terribly jealous. To be honest we've done nothing but argue about this whole episode since you and I first met at the hotel. It's been so terrible, I can't begin to tell you. He's certainly nothing like the man he pretended to be.'

Liz stopped, reddening furiously, praying that Nick would be sensitive enough to follow her lead even if he didn't know why – after all, he certainly hadn't had any problems lying before.

There was a long and very sticky silence and then Nick coughed uncomfortably as if he was having trouble gathering his thoughts. 'I, I really don't know what to say, Liz. I just wanted to find a way to put it right. Er . . .'

But Liz, who was up on her toes, thoughts fuelled by undiluted adrenaline was already way ahead of him. 'I don't think there is anything you can say, Nick, nothing at all. I want you to know that I'm prepared to give this relationship – you and me – another chance, but not if you ever behave like this again. Do you understand what I'm saying?'

Nick, not altogether sure whether this was real or part of the make-believe stared at Liz in astonishment. 'Are you serious? You and me?' His smile broadened. 'You are serious, aren't you?'

Liz nodded. 'I think you probably deserve one more chance, but don't push it too far.'

At that moment Morwenna, flanked by Lily Howard

appeared on the horizon, both carrying covered trays set out with lunch.

Jack looked from face to face as if unsure exactly what it was that had happened, but good form finally got the better of him.

'Right-io, well in that case, now that that's sorted out, would you care to join us for lunch, Nick? I'm sure there is plenty enough to go around.'

Nick lifted his hand and made as if to decline but Jack waved his refusal away. 'Rubbish man, please, do join us. I think that Liz and I are almost finished here, aren't we, my dear? Not a lot more to be said really, is there, under the circumstances.'

Liz flinched.

'We've just got to go over to the studio and take a look around but that shouldn't take too long. I was telling Liz that I've just started a new piece, perhaps you would like to come and take a look too. I'm rather pleased with the way it's going.'

Morwenna and her lackey mounted the steps to the summer house shoulder to shoulder like the foot soldiers of an invading army.

Containing the sense of loss, Jack Sandfi looked up into the woman's pale familiar face, wondering exactly what it was that kept him there.

In those few seconds Jack saw the view out beyond the battlements. He had hidden for so long behind Morwenna, relied on her to be the self-sacrificing energy behind his success and his scold and succour in times of failure. It was suddenly horribly clear that he couldn't have got this far without her. The view was quite frightening. Looking after Jack, his needs and his self-obsession had consumed Morwenna whole; she had offered everything and he had taken it. And trampled over it. Jack stared wordlessly up at Morwenna, seeing himself reflected in the woman's enormous far-seeing eyes.

He had been Morwenna's cross, and at the same time she was his answer to everything, their fates tied tight together. From where he was standing on the desolate windswept reaches of high ground Jack could see all the years he had spent using Morwenna, convincing himself that she was happy, laid out before him like felled trees.

In that little moment Jack saw it all, a rich rolling verdant landscape of excuses and self-delusion and deep deep dependency. It made him feel sick.

Perhaps today was the perfect moment to take his first steps towards another kind of life. He looked squarely at Liz Chapman and knew without a shadow of doubt that while she had been a perfect fantasy she was not looking to be anyone's martyr.

After a few seconds Jack spoke. 'My dear Morwenna,' he began expansively, 'this is Ms Chapman's er ... her partner, Mr Nick Hastings. I was wondering if we could perhaps stretch to accommodate another person for lunch? It wouldn't be too much trouble, would it?'

The sound of relief in Jack's voice was almost palpable and took Liz by complete surprise; she turned to stare at him in astonishment. Jack Sandfi looked almost beatific, perfectly at peace now that he had been denied the very thing he so obviously wanted, the source of his fantasy. Liz shook her head, perhaps imaginary love, unrequited and totally impossible, was the easiest to live with after all.

Morwenna rolled her lips back over a row of little sharky teeth, pulling her mouth into something that vaguely resembled a smile.

'How very nice to meet you, Nick,' she said, setting the tray down on the table under the shadow of the veranda roof before proffering a limp pale hand. She really did sound as if she was pleased to see him. Liz noticed a fold of crushed and broken lettuce peeking half heartedly out from under the cover on one of the plates.

'And of course, you really must stay to lunch,' she continued. 'We insist, don't we, Jack? Liz should have told us that you were coming.'

Jack, moving cheerfully into the role of host, nodded. 'Do take a seat, Liz, Nick. And then after we have eaten we can all go over to the studio. Maybe we could have our coffee over there.'

* * *

It was the middle of the afternoon when Liz and Nick finally walked back across the unkempt lawn towards the main house. Behind them the sun picked out silver highlights in the trees. They were accompanied by the Australian girl.

When they got back to where the cars were parked, the little blonde turned to shake Liz's hand. 'It was really great to meet you at last, Liz. It was a good thing that you did back there for Jack.'

Liz flushed scarlet. 'I'm sorry?'

The girl grinned. 'You might have fooled Jack and Morwenna but you didn't fool me. I thought there was something dodgy going on right from the start. Seemed so bloody weird that no one had ever met you or knew who you were. One of them, Jack or Morwenna, Arturo or one of the other hangers on ought to have remembered something about you. But, don't worry, I don't plan to let on. This way you'll become another one of the great Jack Sandfi's infamous legends, the great white might have been. The love of his life, snatched back by her jealous lover.' The girl laughed warmly. 'Jees', I can practically hear him going on about it now.'

'You knew that I'd never met Jack before?'

The girl nodded towards Nick. 'He told me as soon as he arrived, said he'd come over here to rescue you from Jack. But it was really kind of you letting the pair of them off the hook like that, good thing too that it was me that Nick met and not Morwenna. Christ, she would've really loved that.'

The girl was right; Liz had no doubt that Morwenna would have tormented Jack forever.

'So what's going to happen now. With Jack and Morwenna?'

The blonde shrugged but it was not a dismissive gesture of resignation so much as one of hope and prescience. 'I reckon they'll be just fine. He's working again; real passionate Sandfi originals for the first time in years, not that stuff that he'd been churning for the tourists. You saw for yourself how powerful the new work is, and all those sketches he's doing make yer think that there is more where that came from. And I'm planning to be around for a while yet to keep him off the straight an' narrow. And the Morwenna's of this world always make it through. So thanks again.' She shook Liz's hand firmly, Nick's too and then turned back towards the studio, trotting across the weed strewn gravel until finally she vanished back into the shadows under the trees.

For a moment Liz imagined that Jack Sandfi was waiting for her there, and then Liz was aware that Nick Hastings was standing no more than a breath away from her.

'So,' Nick said in an undertone, looking back towards the two cars parked side by side under the conifers. 'Now that you know that I'm really not Jack Sandfi, where do we go from here?' He sounded uneasy and uncertain and looked deeply uncomfortable.

Liz, expression forced into neutral, pulled the car keys out of her bag. 'I'm surprised you've got the nerve to ask really, after today's fiasco. Morwenna tracked me down, you know. I thought she'd come to murder me. I'm lucky that Jack didn't find out the whole story and sue me over the article in the *Sunday News*. You've got absolutely no idea how much chaos you've caused in my life, have you, Nick?' Her tone was deliberately cool.

Nick reddened and shook his head. 'I'm sorry. Look, maybe it would be better if I just leave now. This isn't how I meant things to turn out. I don't know what to say to make it right or even where to begin.'

Liz couldn't keep up the pretence any longer even though Nick undoubtedly deserved to suffer a whole lot more. A smile thawed her expression.

'Well, under the circumstances I thought that perhaps we could start over at my place. You can meet my kids and my cat and my best friend.'

'Are you serious?'

'Totally. Although I'll probably live to regret it. I'd better ring first to warn them we're on our way.'

She could sense the mixture of delight and relief in him. Nick sighed and then smiled. 'Do you know that you're totally amazing?'

Liz nodded. 'Oh yes,' and then she caught hold of his arm. 'Mind you before you go, Nick, there are three things I want you to know. First of all if you ever lie to me again then there are no more second chances. No ifs, no buts and definitely no pseudonyms. Secondly when we get back to my house I would really appreciate if we could go through this whole thing, one step at a time, so that I can try and work out what exactly happened.'

The birds sang and the sun shone and a second or two passed by when both of them were silent and looked deep into the other's eyes.

'And the third thing?' asked Nick in a low sensuous voice.

Liz looked into his face. He was so close now that she could pick out the tiny lines that framed his eyes, so close that she could breathe in the soft inviting scent of his body. Her mouth began to water.

'Well?' he asked again, taking her into his arms.

Liz slid her hands round his waist and up over his broad muscular back. 'Would you mind kissing me again?'

Just Desserts

Sue Welfare

Katherine Bourne has been a member of that endangered species, the full-time housewife, for over twenty years, but things have finally turned sour. When she disembowels her delicious home-grown tomatoes, she dreams of murdering her husband. Why can't Harry have an affair with a younger woman and just leave, like normal men?

But Harry has no intention of giving up his home comforts; he's been sampling forbidden fruit for a long while. Glamorous banker Carol accompanies him on weekend trips and business beanos, but she too is beginning to find that the pleasure's growing stale.

So who's fooling who? Harry, happy in his illusion that he's a sex god and that all his women love him really? Katherine and Carol, unlikely partners in Harry's parallel lives?

Against a background of succulent suppers, cosy Cambridge cafés and the unexpected joys of unexplored freedom, the women decide that revenge is a dish best eaten cold. And discover the perfect recipe . . .

ISBN 0 00 649993 7

Divorcing Jack

Colin Bateman

'Richly paranoid and very funny' *Sunday Times*

Dan Starkey is a young journalist in Belfast, who shares with his wife Patricia a prodigious appetite for drinking and partying. Then Dan meets Margaret, a beautiful student, and things begin to get out of hand.

Terrifyingly, Margaret is murdered and Patricia kidnapped. Dan has no idea why, but before long he too is a target, running as fast as he can in a race against time to solve the mystery and to save his marriage.

'A joy from start to finish . . . Witty, fast-paced and throbbing with menace, *Divorcing Jack* reads like *The Thirty-Nine Steps* rewritten for the '90s by Roddy Doyle'
Time Out

'Grabs you by the throat . . . a magnificent debut. Unlike any thriller you have ever read before . . . like *The Day of the Jackal* out of the Marx Brothers' *Sunday Press*

'Fresh, funny . . . an Ulster Carl Hiaasen' *Mail on Sunday*

ISBN 0 00 647903 0

The Last Place You Look

Norma Curtis

'Sharp, funny and observant'   KATE ATKINSON

Faye Reading has given second place to her career as a lighting designer in order to be a good wife and mother – to her husband Nick, their adopted son Samuel and their daughter Isobel. If her lifestyle has been on the reckless side, Nick's conscience, sense and good nature have always compensated, giving her the security she has craved since childhood. At least until now.

For a message on the answerphone, a visit to the doctor and the return of Samuel's natural mother – Nick's wayward young sister – are about to upset the balance of their lives, casting shadows where there was light, and doubt where there was certainty. As they each confront their own personal demons, Faye and Nick must find a way forward, but first they must learn where to look . . .

Theirs is a story of courage, tenderness, fear and faith, which Norma Curtis deftly recounts with her unique blend of dry humour, warmth, wisdom and originality.

0 00 651021 3

Tell Me No Secrets

Maggie Hudson

A fast-moving, hair-raising novel about a notorious criminal gang, and the women who run it

The Sweeting family are well known in south-east London, and not for their honesty. Jock is a professional armed robber and proud of it, and Kelly, his daughter, takes after him. By the time she's 20, she is running with the family gang.

Her sister Jackie, yearning for a life of respectability, marries high-flying policeman Raymond. But his middle-class background has its own kind of hypocritical dishonesty.

And Rosamund, Raymond's unsuspecting sister, meets via the Sweetings the devious and irresistible Kevin Rice – but how long will she last as the wife of a criminal on the run?

When the men in their lives lie, cheat and betray them, Kelly, Jackie and Ros decide that it will be for the last time. Their revenge is both outrageous and apt as they plan the biggest heist of the decade. And after the adventure of a lifetime is over, there will be no more secrets, and no more lies . . .

0 00 651153 8